ADVANCE PRAISE

"Claypole White's gift is her ability to put us into the troubled minds of her characters in a way that helps us not only understand them but fall in love with them as well. We discover that while their minds may be different from ours, their hearts are the same."

—Diane Chamberlain, *USA Today* bestselling author of
Pretending to Dance

"*Echoes of Family* is a masterfully written novel that is both difficult to put down, and difficult to forget after the final page. In this powerful novel, Claypole White weaves that narrative that draws the reader into a personal relationship with the characters and has you rooting for them, in spite of their many flaws. This book kept my attention until all secrets were revealed in its dramatic conclusion. I look forward to many more from Claypole White."

—Sally Hepworth, bestselling author of
The Things We Keep

"Barbara Claypole White has done it again—created a quirky cast of characters and then taken us along as they go on a journey through madness and out the other side. Music, England, love, loss, and nature all collide in this beautiful exploration of how the echoes of our past can sometimes drown out the present. Matthew Quick fans will feel right at home."

—Catherine McKenzie, bestselling author of
Spin and *Hidden*

"*Echoes of Family* is emotional storytelling at its best, crafted, as always, with Barbara Claypole White's signature wit and charm. Filled with riveting characters and the poignant unraveling of long-buried secrets, White's latest is both lovely and gritty, heartrending and heartwarming; a story about tragedy, resilience, and the one thing that ultimately holds us all together—family."

—Barbara Davis, author of *Summer at Hideaway Key* and *Love, Alice*

ECHOES
of
FAMILY

ECHOES
of
FAMILY

BARBARA CLAYPOLE WHITE

Text copyright © 2016 by Barbara Claypole White
All rights reserved.

Published by Lake Union Publishing, Seattle

www.apub.com

Amazon, the Amazon logo, and Lake Union Publishing are trademarks of Amazon.com, Inc., or its affiliates

ISBN-13: 9781503938137
ISBN-10: 1503938131

Cover design by Shasti O'Leary Soudant

Printed in the United States of America

*For my aunt Elizabeth Claypole White, who lived and died
in an era devoid of understanding
For my old pal Carolyn Wilson, for a thousand reasons only
she and I know
For my childhood vicar Rev. Peter N. Jeffery, because I'm
still learning the lessons he taught me*

My malady doesn't belong to me: it weighs on all those who love and depend on me.

—Melody Moezzi, *Haldol and Hyacinths: A Bipolar Life*

We are all differently organized.

—Lord Byron

She came home
clutching the ghost
of autumn melodies
to her chest
and all the trees are gone
the highway sings on
and the cars never stop
for a hitchhiking song
memories pour down
lost in the holy sound
of mortality and moonless nights
no one
no one
could ever rewrite the summertime
no one
no one
we're just lost in the b-side.
—"Summertime" by the Arcadian Project

UNC MEDICAL CENTER, NORTH CAROLINA

MARCH

If purgatory exists, it comes without sound. Nothing to deaden thoughts.

Marianne had long believed that to be true, and the handful of compliant crazies in the waiting room proved her right. No one spoke; no one moved; no one exchanged glances.

No one reacted when ice pellets began to fall on the skylights like beans tinkling inside a rain stick. Nature could be so deceptive, conning you into believing that the start of severe weather was a harmony meant to soothe. And passive insanity must be contagious. What would happen if she yelled, "Let's make noise and be heard. Who wants to sing?"

She turned to Jade, who was frowning at the workbook on dialectical behavior therapy. DBT to insiders. A wonderful gesture from her baby girl—who was neither a baby nor hers—but Jade didn't need to learn emotion regulation so she could help Marianne. What Jade needed was a gloriously messy life of her own.

The door to the offices clicked open and Dr. White jerked his chin in greeting. He'd nicked himself shaving again—but he didn't trust her with a razor?

Jade looked up. "Need me to come in with you, Mama Bird?"

"As if, sweetheart. The shenanigans you've witnessed, when you felt as if you were watching my moods explode on a 3-D IMAX screen?" Marianne stood. "Nothing compared to the way I used to be. No way I'm handing you or Darius VIP tickets to the extravaganza of my past."

"Yeah? Let's get real. What could I possibly not know about you after thirteen years?"

"Has it been that long?" Marianne raised her eyebrows. She knew exactly how much time had passed since she'd taken in the teen runaway with the secondhand fiddle. Every string broken.

"Marianne?" Dr. White's voice rattled with the goopy phlegm of year-round allergies.

Another psychiatrist appeared. This one didn't have to call for his patient.

"Gotta go before Dr. White starts the stopwatch. Love you, baby girl."

"Can we ditch the *baby* part on my thirtieth birthday?" Jade said.

"Nope. Not happening."

Without a backward glance, Marianne followed Dr. White down the pale corridor that stank of new construction. He shuffled more than usual. Either the weather or his patients were taking a toll.

He eased his door shut, sealing them inside. On the other side of the window, gray nothingness swallowed the white blossoms of the Bradford pears.

"Nasty weather brewing. If this keeps up you'll be my last patient of the day." He settled in his favorite chair. "How's the head?"

Marianne sat on the edge of the scuffed-up, marked-up two-seater—to avoid the indentations of strangers' backsides, not their stains—and touched her scalp, still sore from the impact of skull on metal. "Not bad as head injuries go. Guess I'll live."

"And your moods? Has anything shifted since we last met?"

As if the prospect wasn't terrifying enough—better the mood devil you know—he kept warning her that a bonk on the head could annihilate an established pattern: the tendency to mania in the spring and darkness in October. No major incidents for five years, and she'd been asymptomatic for the last two. Until Valentine's Day.

February 14. Why did the cosmos have to pitch that echo forward through time?

"I feel pancake flat, just the way I like, Doc. Bring on the kickass drugs, I say."

He smiled, clearly mistaking truth for irony. But then she'd never been honest with him, had never confessed that she wanted all those supernova emotions smothered in Bubble Wrap—no sharp edges. No edges, period. Anesthetize her with mind-numbing benzos; forget the hand trembling and give her the highest dose of lithium that wasn't toxic. If she'd shared that information, Dr. White might have put her back on his addicts watch list.

Full disclosure had never been her thing. Except thirty years earlier with Gabriel. Before she'd participated in a whopper of a lie and broken his heart. Before she'd won the Olympic gold for teen drama. Before the bipolar monster had claimed her as his. Before.

"I'm doing fine for a recovering nutjob responsible for the deaths of her former lover and two unborn babies." She paused. "One of them my own."

Dr. White shifted but failed to take the bait. It was too early in the session for the big guns. He would, no doubt, proceed with the warm-up questions. "I see Jade drove you here again."

"She insisted, once the weatherman mentioned the possibility of trace amounts of ice. We're hitting up the supermarket on the way back.

Doing our bit to contribute to panic food shopping. Want us to buy you some bread and milk?"

He glanced at his watch as if to calculate how long before he could kick her out and rush to the stripped shelves of the nearest Harris Teeter. And then he straightened the eclectic mix of pens in his penholder. "Last week we talked about driving that new Miata. Have you taken it out for a spin?"

"No."

"Then I suggest a trip to the Maple View Farm Country Store, with Jade. After the weather warms up. I'm quite partial to their Carolina Crunch."

"I have a childhood aversion to ice cream. Zero tolerance for the brain freeze."

He smiled again. Smiley Dr. White, who didn't see a contradiction in a conversation about ice cream while a late winter storm swirled. She knew what was coming next. The most robotic question of all when dealing with the deranged: cover your bases by establishing if they're about to off themselves.

"How're the suicidal thoughts?"

Yup. There it was, like stinky kitchen garbage you forgot to dump the night before. "You think I have the energy for suicide with the drug regime you've got me on, Doc?"

"Is that yes, you're thinking about suicide, or no, you're not?"

"No. I'm not suicidal."

That last attempt when she'd welcomed the millennium by swallowing enough lithium and Prozac to fell T. rex—the dinosaur, not the British band her mom used to crank up on the radio—should have taken Marianne Stokes out of the game for all eternity. According to the ER doc, her recovery—as opposed to death—was miraculous. But the true miracle had been surviving the previous decade as a medical dartboard: "Let's throw everything we've got at the wackadoodle and see what sticks." Madness was such a waste of life.

"And how's Darius? Things between you are still good?" He broke eye contact to scratch the back of his neck, and Marianne smiled. She may have overshared last time.

"Bringing me coffee in bed, massaging my feet, folding the laundry. Running my recording studio." She looked at her lap. "Being the devoted husband."

"And this is a problem because . . . ?"

"I'm scared." *See? I can be honest, Dr. White.*

"That Darius loves you?"

"No." Her head whipped up. "The last five years together have been like *Love Story* meets *The Sound of Music* but without all the kids." *Without any kids.* Jade was right, it was time to drop *baby girl.* She should have dropped it when Jade turned eighteen.

"So what is scaring you, Marianne?"

Ice pinged against the window. Was it getting worse? Should they not have left the house? Had she put Jade at risk?

"Me." Marianne stared at her huge engagement ring. "I'm terrified of me."

"You're manic-depressive, not a monster."

"That homeless guy everyone avoids, the one who wanders up and down Weaver Street in his socks yelling? Take away the meds, forget the psychotherapy and enough mindfulness to turn Jack the Ripper into a world-famous orchid collector, and that could be me. I've seen what happens when I'm full-blown Marianne, and I have crap impulse control, even on the meds. What if I become violent?"

"I would like to point out that Eric, the homeless guy, is not violent. And neither are you. Have you ever been violent? No. Have you ever hurt anyone except yourself? No."

Tugging down her sweater sleeves to cover the scars, Marianne curled her fingers around red cashmere.

"You're back on your meds, stabilized, and what happened last month with that stomach virus was unfortunate, but—"

"Unfortunate?" She slid back into the dip in the seat cushion. "I haven't messed with my meds in over a decade, and after thirty-six hours of hugging the toilet, they're out of my system, I'm high on mania and a freakishly warm day, and an unborn baby is dead. Let's agree that's a little more than unfortunate."

"I understand that last month's accident is a painful reminder of all that happened when you were sixteen, but you were not behind the wheel of the car when your teen lover died. And as for last month's incident, the other driver slammed into you after a herd of deer ran into the road. Sadly, a common hazard around here."

"For a shrink with a wall of accolades, you're one poor listener. I told you last time, the deer bolted because I screamed at them through the open window. I should never have been behind the wheel of a car that day. And thanks to my behavior, a baby was stillborn at seven months. Don't you think the parents had already redecorated the nursery and ordered I'm-a-big-brother T-shirts for their little boy? I was five months along when I lost my baby, and it sent me into intergalactic lunacy for at least a decade. Seven? That poor family."

"Marianne, the mother made a tragic error by swerving."

"She wouldn't have needed to swerve if I'd slowed down, flashed my lights to warn her. Been someone other than Ms. Manic Road Warrior."

In the corridor outside the office, a photocopier whirred. *Error—* she imagined the word printed over and over on a piece of paper. When she screwed up—made an *error*—she got restrained and stuck with a sedative. Once or twice handcuffs had been involved.

"I was manic for the first crash, too. When Simon died—"

"Yes, Simon. Sorry. I blanked on your lover's name."

Sometimes she wished she could, too. "And Gabriel was practically roadkill, and I lost my baby. Two fatal car wrecks thirty years apart, and manic Marianne is the common denominator." She paused. "What do you know about mockingbirds?"

"Are your thoughts racing?" His voice tightened. Now she'd gotten his attention, but for the wrong reasons.

"No. My thoughts are jumbled because I'm tired, not hypomanic. I know the difference."

"Of course you do. I can give you something to help with the sleep."

She waved him off. "Mockingbirds are nature's imitators. They steal songs and sing them again and again. Over the weekend a mockingbird flew into the deck door and died in my hand. And I couldn't help but wonder: What if I'm stuck repeating the same song? Because if those two car crashes don't scream repetition, what does?"

"Tragedy often repeats for no reason. You're trying to find logic where there is none."

"Shit happens, that's your theory, Doc? Here's mine: I have an unpredictable disease. What if it's evolving? If I can't trust my own mind, how can I protect Jade and Darius? And no, that's not grandiose thinking. That's a mother and a wife saying, 'I love my family; I would die before putting them in danger.'"

"So you *are* thinking about death?"

Marianne slammed her hands against the side of her head. *Round and round it goes. Where it stops nobody knows.*

ONE
JADE

"Jade!" Darius screamed. "Where the fuck is my wife?"

She held her phone at arm's length and counted: *One Mississippi, two Mississippi, three Mississippi, four.* Jade put the cell phone back to her ear. Nope, he was still swearing at full volume, his venting pitched higher than usual.

She flicked a kamikaze no-see-um from her right eye and eased the driver's door closed. Poor Ernie. Her duct-taped 1989 VW Bug, the love of her life, was overdue for an oil change and a tire rotation, a state inspection and a fluids flush. She never messed with Ernie's maintenance, but this latest Marianne crisis was siphoning off her ability to function in the real world. That damn car wreck five months earlier. Of all the body parts Marianne had to bash, why her head? Wasn't it damaged enough?

Jade sucked in Carolina humidity—thick as grits—and waded into Darius's monologue. "You done losing your shit, boss?"

"Sorry. I'm putting a dollar in the I'm-the-studio-douche jar."

"Whoa, time-out." Jade fanned her black gauze top against her turquoise bra. What she wouldn't give for a good tropical storm. "I stopped counting at four Mississippi. You owe me five bucks minimum."

"I'll make it ten. Happy?"

No, not really. That was way too easy. "Did I miss something?"

"You tell me. I did *ex-act-ly* what you suggested."

If he didn't cut the sarcasm he'd owe her a bottle of tequila, too. A good one.

"Against every instinct of my being, I took your advice and left Marianne alone since yesterday afternoon. I even slept on the control room sofa."

"That thing is seriously comfortable. I've spent many nights there, and—"

"She's not answering her cell. Where is she, Jade? Where the hell is my wife? Is she at the house?"

He hadn't run over to check?

"What was I thinking leaving her alone?" The slapping noise at the other end of the line suggested he'd walloped his forehead.

She waited for the sound of a projectile chair. If he trashed her control room on the morning they were expecting megastars at the studio, swear to the music gods she would lock him in the closet with the spiders, the old analog tapes, and the lingering smell of pee left over from some guitarist's incontinent pit bull.

"Jade?" He sniffed.

Holy crap. Was he crying? "Hey, you did the right thing. There's no manual for loving someone with faulty brain wiring, and bottom line: *our* mental health matters, too." Jade crossed the parking lot and walked through the opening in the living wall of bamboo that concealed their world. Instead of turning right to the front door of Nightjar Recording Studios, she turned left and followed the stone path lined with solar lights that led to the deck of Marianne's funky little house. Correction:

Marianne and Darius's house. Although if Darius had taken to sleeping in the studio, how much longer was that true?

"I was fried every which way when I left here yesterday," she said. "Turned off my phone and implemented full radio silence."

He didn't need to know about the trip to orthopedic urgent care to get her finger splinted. Admittedly Marianne had been a hot mess of remorse, but still: master bedroom door slammed on index finger; index finger now broken and throbbing; index finger nonfunctional, which would mean developing contortionist skills to work the console. Washing her hair this morning had been more challenging than a course on *American Ninja Warrior*.

"Please tell me I didn't screw up, Jade. Suppose something . . . bad has happened?"

None of them talked about *the bad*. Hadn't even hinted at it since Marianne and Darius's tailor-made wedding vows when Darius promised to tell the truth in AA—that he wasn't an addict; he was drawn to the comfort of the group after flunking out of anger management classes—and Marianne promised to take suicide off the table because she loved him enough to live. True love, the last great hope. If you believed your tarot deck had been stacked with that baloney.

"Stop right there, boss. You're burning out and not listening to Aunty Jade. We need rested minds to be the bipolar police. Have you slept?"

"I catnapped. If anything has happened to M—"

"Darius, I've got this. Hang tight while I rattle her cage." Dealing with Darius was no different than troubleshooting in front of clients. It was all about faking her engineer om. "And if you've been in the studio for the last twenty-four hours, might I suggest following me over to the house for a shower? I hear deodorant's the bomb."

Jade paused under Marianne's arbor. A poison ivy vine had begun to weave into the passionflower. Poison ivy creeping back onto the property was not a good sign; neither was the empty base of the hummingbird feeder, black with mold and filling up with dead bees. And the elephant ears in the huge ceramic pot definitely had the dehydrated droop. As did all Marianne's prehistoric-looking plants, their heads hanging in the July heat. Even the metal garden art and Junkanoo-colored birdhouses looked wilted. Nature didn't do much for a Bronx girl, but every summer this garden was a tropical sanctuary. Not today. Today Marianne's pride and joy looked neglected. Possibly abandoned.

"Jade? You still there?"

"Yup. Watching some cute little frog hippity-hopping into the pond."

"Can you *please* hippity-hop your ass over to the house and find my beloved?"

"On it. My guess? She's still asleep. Probably snoring like an old truck without a muffler."

Darius failed to clock her faux pas: Marianne never slept this late. She called it maintaining a quasi-normal persona. And Darius never missed a trick. What the hell was going on with those two?

He paused. "How were things last time you saw her?"

"Intensely Marianne-ish." Jade glanced down at her bandaged index finger. "Listen, I don't mean to pull the I-know-her-better-than-you-do card, but I've been with Marianne since I was sixteen. Do the math, Darius, that's nearly half my life. We're not the only ones who need to withdraw when her illness explodes. Trust me, if she's in bad shape, she doesn't want us hanging around looking all bummed out." She took a breath and waited. Darius didn't reply.

"Maybe she's been up all night reorganizing her shoe closet and had to run to Home Depot for more shoe trees." Plausible enough for a woman obsessed with shoes. Except that Marianne's new red Miata was still parked under the carport.

"And her phone?" Darius said.

"She forgot to charge it." *On purpose.* Marianne's manic-depression danced to a tune only she could hear. Dig deep enough, however, and there was always an explanation that made sense in Marianne's fractured mind. And an uncharged phone screamed, *Let there be no contact.* For a crazy person, Marianne was anal about charging her phone.

"Did you guys mic the drum kit after I left?" Jade stepped up onto the wooden deck and stuck a nonbandaged finger into a plant pot. Bone dry.

"Yes. The drummer plays with balance and feel. Has great groove." Darius's voice was flat; his mind was not where it should be—on setup day. And not with any old band but Media Rage minus their drummer who, following a highly publicized police chase, was back in rehab with a broken arm (given the CNN footage of the car he'd rolled, he was lucky not to be a paraplegic). The nonrehab members plus the ghost drummer would be on Nightjar's doorstep within the hour to lay down basic tracks for their new album in a weeklong block-out session that would lead to two more sessions. And serious money. The label was paying for Darius's expertise, but he'd insisted they were a package: he was going to produce; she was going to record and mix. Had he only agreed to the gig for her, or was he ready to return to his glory days? A legendary LA engineer in the nineties, Darius went off the reservation in some born-again walkabout to "rediscover raw music that came from the soul." What he'd discovered was Marianne. And Nightjar.

The former music legend gave a long sigh. "The drummer also helped me move the baffles. You'll be happy to hear we've created multiple musician-friendly spaces—if that's what our stars demand."

"You go, boss." The huge partitions used to isolate sound were way too cumbersome for her to manage, even with casters. "And the amps?"

"Arrived this morning." He paused. "Did you check on the band's flight?"

"Yup. Landing in five and Sasha's already at the airport. I told her to be Princess Charming or else I'd kidnap her pet turtle and force-feed him non-organic lettuce. I'm hanging up now. See you in a few."

She slid open the deck door. "Hey, it's me. Anyone home?"

Her phone made the ticker tape ring tone reserved for Darius's texts. For so long it had been just her and Marianne in the studio plus a string of misfits from Girls In Motion, Marianne's brainchild. The nonprofit group had become a safe haven for teens in crisis, giving countless girls a second chance at life and a first chance at being around music. Now Girls In Motion was Jade's baby until the new executive director was trained, and in the studio she answered increasingly to Darius. Most people mislabeled him a dickish genius, but most people hadn't seen him sitting on the floor with Marianne after that car crash, cradling her while she'd cried herself inside out.

Double shot of espresso? Darius had texted.

On it.

Total lie. No way was he getting a double, which would make him twitchy as hell. He needed focus so that he could read the band and figure out everyone's hang-ups. Then discern whether the band wanted to perform together or record separately. It was all about creating comfort zones, keeping clients relaxed and on their game. Recording was as much about psychology as science or art, which was why Darius and Marianne made a killer team. They understood the personalities that were drawn to the drug of music; they knew how to manipulate the emotion of sound.

Holy shit, she loved her job.

Another text came through from Darius. You're a doll.

Remember that when I'm due for a pay raise.

She closed the door behind her and walked from one room to the next, calling. The house that pulsed with Marianne's moods 24/7 responded with silence. There was no Marianne echo.

"Dammit," Jade said, scratching a fresh mosquito bite under the hem of her black miniskirt. "Where the hell are you this time?"

Take out the bipolar brain chemistry, and she and Marianne were as alike as two people without shared DNA could be. Marianne was also a survivor. That was the invisible umbilical cord that connected them. When the going got tough, self-preservation kicked in and they ran. Although in Marianne's case that usually meant camping out in her shoe closet.

"Marianne?" Jade swallowed hard. "Mama Bird?"

No answer except for the squelch of her rubber-soled canvas boots on the white oak kitchen floor. A clutterless environment, the kitchen was devoid of personality and tchotchkes, and the countertops were clear but for Darius's high-tech coffee machines and gizmos. Give her a mess any day: piles of thrift store bric-a-brac and secondhand books that screamed, *I have a space called home, and I don't have to share.*

Jade opened the fridge. It was empty but for a row of bottled water and the birthday cake with three slices missing. Although she was the only one who'd eaten her portion. Darius merely speared his repeatedly with a fork, and Marianne claimed she wasn't hungry. In addition to not watering her garden, Marianne had stopped eating.

The fridge was supernaturally clean. *Shit.* Hadn't she specifically told Darius that forcing the interns to clean the house smacked of intern abuse? Or—she chewed that spot inside her mouth—was this mania at work? Despite the new drug combo, Marianne had entered some weird, unstable cycle Jade had never seen before: crying one moment, laughing the next. It was like mania and depression squished together into one big vortex.

Holding her breath, Jade opened the cupboard door that hid the garbage can and peered inside. *Phew.* Empty except for two take-out containers. No evidence of a Marianne cleaning frenzy.

The air-conditioning whooshed on, and Jade jumped. Yesterday she and Marianne had been as pissy as a pair of beauty pageant contestants slugging it out over a tiara. Truth be told, she'd been feeling a little PMS-y. What if Marianne, the emotional dowsing rod, was simply feeding off *her* mood? This, whatever this was, could be her fault.

"Marianne?" Jade called up the free-floating staircase that hung like an accident waiting to happen.

Nothing. Marianne was not upstairs in the huge open-plan office she shared with Darius. Jade turned down the hall and knocked on their bedroom door, her smudged handprint still visible on the frame. "Honey?"

Swallowing, she reached for the doorknob. *Locked.* She pulled out her phone.

"You've found her?" Darius said.

"No, and you need to come over."

He hung up.

Jade scrolled through her texts. Nothing since she'd muted her phone to spend what remained of her Thursday reading Daphne du Maurier's *Rebecca* in peace. The word *library*, scrawled on the back of her hand with a black Sharpie, stared at her like an accusation.

The front door slammed open and Darius catapulted down the hall, his black hair streaked with gray flying in all directions. He shoved his face up close to hers, and yes, he needed a shower.

"What's going on?" he said.

"It's locked."

He rattled the doorknob. "What happened to your finger?"

"Slammed it in the car door." Jade rolled her eyes. "Such a klutz."

"Babe?" Darius bashed on the door. "You going to let us in? The band's due in an hour and I need you to work your magic with what's-her-face. Their manager thinks she might be a high-functioning sociopath like Benedict Cumberbatch's Sherlock Holmes."

He fell silent as he bashed in his bedroom door with two Rockettes-on-steroids kicks. Had he done this before with his first wife—an alcoholic—after she'd gone on a bender?

Jade raced into the room and stopped at the foot of the king-sized bed, neatly made with the six-hundred-thread-count linens Marianne ordered annually from England. She insisted anything less made her want to scratch off her skin. Marianne never made the bed. If she was manic, she couldn't slow down long enough to do it; if she was depressed, she lacked the energy. When she was neither, she didn't care.

While Darius blew hair from his face, Jade moved quickly to block his view of the nightstand where Marianne's medical alert bracelet lay. Reaching behind her back, Jade eased the bracelet to the floor with her fingers and then nudged it under the bed with her foot. No need to fuel the situation with more Darius drama.

He shot toward Marianne's shoe closet, and Jade ran into the master bathroom. One solitary pill container sat between the two sinks: Xanax for Darius. Marianne always left her meds out—lined up as a constant reminder. Jade opened every drawer in the cabinet under the sink. Nothing. *Nothing!* Marianne's meds were gone.

Jade's mind tore through a hundred explanations crashing into one realization: a three-time suicide survivor was alone with a stash of pills. Six months ago there would have been a logical explanation; but six months ago Marianne would have said she thought about suicide the same way she dreamed about the taste of alcohol and that thinking didn't equal action. And now?

What was the yoga breathing Marianne had tried to teach her? Breathe and count, or count and breathe? Or give up and scream obscenities like Darius? Which would so not help because if Darius suspected she was freaking out, he would join in.

"Our wedding picture's gone from my nightstand. The one with the three of us." Darius appeared in the doorway, hands clawing at his hair. "And I can't see her travel bag, which was out on the floor yesterday. You okay?"

"Yup. A-OK. That's a great sign—I mean about the picture. She loves that picture." And Marianne loved her Queen Bee weekender travel bag. Maybe she'd skipped town for the weekend—with the mood stabilizers and that new antipsychotic she needed the way a car with the oil light on needed oil. Maybe they were overreacting.

Darius frowned at her. "Nothing makes sense. She never goes out through the deck door. And why, for Chrissake, would she lock the bedroom door?"

That question was easy: to stop other fingers from getting smushed.

"I guess I should log on to my support group and ask for advice. They totally nailed it last time she did something a little out of left field." Lame, but it was the best she could offer.

"You're in a support group?"

"Aren't you?" Jade pulled out Marianne's makeup bag and rifled through its contents. Overnight bag and meds missing. Couldn't-live-without eyeliner not. Maybe they weren't overreacting.

"You've been my support group since they kicked me out of AA. She's left me, hasn't she? Tell me what's going on, because I'm drowning in quicksand and . . . What are you doing?"

"Speaking of running away, don't panic, but her meds are gone."

"Are you fucking kidding me?" He slapped the wall and then cradled his hand, his face creased in pain.

"I told you not to panic." She nodded at his hand. "Need some ice for that?"

"No." Darius collapsed onto his knees and hung over the side of the bath. "I think I'm going to puke."

"Not in front of me, you're not. I don't do other people's vomit."

He made a choking noise, which was totally fake.

"Come on, hurling up last night's dinner isn't going to help."

"I didn't eat last night." He twisted himself around to sit on the side of the tub.

"Well, that wasn't very smart. You're not making good decisions for yourself."

"Really. I hadn't noticed."

"You did get Marianne's permission to talk with Dr. White, to tell him what we were seeing at home, right?" Jade said.

"I tried and she threw a suede boot at me. Thankfully she missed, which is the reason I skipped dinner. I wasn't coming back over here so she could practice her aim. Or did you forget my first wife was a psycho?"

"Marianne isn't a psycho." Jade spoke as slowly as she could.

"I know. I don't mean that, but it's like she's ripped up the rulebook. I don't know what to do, think, feel. All I want is to help. To understand, to be there for her. But I'm the enemy, and it's killing me, Jade. Loving Marianne is killing me."

"I know, honey. Which is why you have to try and get Dr. White to talk with us." Jade walked back into the bedroom, yanked the portable phone off his nightstand, and returned.

"Psychiatrists must be used to family members calling in a crisis. Here—" She scrolled through to the first number she'd programmed in when the phone was new and handed it to Darius. He grabbed the phone without bothering to look up.

"This is Darius Montgomery, Marianne Stokes's husband." He stood. "I need to speak with Dr. White."

Jade made the keep-it-going hand signal they used in the studio; Darius scowled and turned his back to her. "I don't care if he's hiking on Mars with Mick-fucking-Jagger. My wife has vanished with three months' worth of meds, which I know because I refilled her prescription on Monday. This is an emergency. Emergency with a capital *E*. Get ahold of him. Now."

He thrust the phone at Jade, who thanked the receptionist profusely, and hung up.

"Listen, I've been through all kinds of crap with Marianne over the years, and she always bounces back. Plus, you and I are smart enough to figure this out. Tell me the last thing Marianne said to you."

"It was nonsense. Like she was speaking in tongues." Darius rubbed his scruffy stubble.

"You mean full-blown mania?"

"No. Her speech wasn't racing, it just didn't make sense. She'd trashed her shoe closet, pulled out everything to create a mountain of shoes—"

Or to create extra hiding space.

"—and then she spat out a disjointed sentence about the English village where she grew up and sleeping with this guy Simon, some teen stud who excelled at . . . you know, sex." Darius blushed. In any other circumstances it would have been cute. "And when I asked if she was trying to make me jealous, she yelled at me to get out. And then I asked about Dr. White, and that's when the boots started flying."

"I thought you said a boot. Singular."

"Does it matter at this point?"

Jade tried and failed to connect the dots. "What happened to the pile of shoes?"

"Dumped back in her closet. I should have listened harder to what she was saying. Why didn't I listen harder, Jade?"

"Interesting. I've never heard her mention anyone named Simon before. There was this kid, Gabriel. She used to talk about him. Nothing concrete, but I'd always assumed he was her first love."

"And why would you assume that?" Darius gave her the look that had sent more than one intern scurrying into the control room in tears.

"From the change in her voice when she talked about him."

Darius's eyes turned from brown to black.

"But, you know, he could just have been her playmate." *Shit. Seriously bad word choice.*

"Tell me more about this *Gabriel*," Darius said.

Despite all the huffing and puffing, Darius was a little boy lost, thanks to his overprotective mama. You could blame everything on the mother. Jade did. Her mom had been an inadequate excuse for a woman who should never have had one kid, let alone two more with different men. Jade left her behind on the day she blasted out pleas for help to the police and social services. And then she ran, stopping only when she reached Carrboro and heard about this place where street kids could crash, no questions asked. The sign above the doorway had said "Girls In Motion."

"It was years ago, Darius. And she didn't tell me that much. They used to hang out in the local cemetery and smoke weed. He was Robin to her Batman—the person she had heavy philosophical discussions with, her compadre-in-arms for the crazy shit like . . ."

"Like what?" His voice turned hard.

"Why don't I go check the passports? On the off chance she's gone to England."

"No."

Darius taking charge was far more problematic than Darius freaking out. Like Marianne, he didn't think small.

"Start packing a bag for me. Enough clothes for a few days. I'm heading to the airport."

"Whoa." Jade raised her hands. "First, we don't know where she is, which means no way am I letting you dash off to parts unknown. Second, you don't pay me enough to handle your boxers. And third, have you lost your friggin' mind? We have superstars due any minute, and they'll be expecting you to meet them with smiles and all that catered shit Sasha ordered last week."

"Fine." Darius threw his hands up. "I'll pack my own bag."

"Darius"—she pointed to the side of the tub—"sit."

He did, and she glanced at her watch. Where were the interns? After she'd implemented the no-cell-phones rule in the studio, they'd started coming to the house to dump their bags. Should she have given them wake-up calls when she'd buzzed Sasha? Maybe it was time to quit recording and mixing and become the studio nanny.

Darius twisted his platinum wedding ring. "We're wasting time."

"No, we're not." She sat next to him and draped an arm around his shoulders. "You're a hothead, and I have a working theory, which means you need to listen to the voice of reason. That would be me. Sasha's going to take over as head engineer, because she's more than capable of keeping the mojo flowing, and you're going to deal with the band."

"Bullshit. You're not flying to England without me." He jumped up.

"No one's flying to England." She used her inside voice. "I'm going to search for Marianne while waiting for Dr. White's call. If we need to, we can contact the cops. But let me find her. I've done it before, and I focus better when you're not scrambling my thoughts. And while I do that, boss, you're taking a shower." She made an overly dramatic gesture of wafting away his strong male odor in case he hadn't gotten her original message. "Go, do the thing that generates our paychecks and let me do what I do best—deal with Marianne. I've got this." How many times did she have to say that to Marianne and Darius: "I've got this?"

"I know, doll. You're a star." He grabbed her hand and held on too tight.

"Hard to believe, but this episode will burn itself out. I'm guessing she needs another meds shift; and we haven't considered this, but the change in her pattern could be hormonal. We've been blaming everything on the head injury, but perimenopause could be the culprit."

Discussing Marianne's menstrual cycle with a fifty-year-old guy had become Jade's new normal. Bipolar illness had ripped away their privacy bumpers, thrown her and Darius together like castaways.

Hormones, head injury. The words flitted around her brain but refused to settle. They were too easy, and nothing about understanding

Marianne was easy. Something was driving Marianne hard—something locked deep within her. Something that meant the shoe closet was no longer cutting it as a hiding place. And who was this Simon dude?

Darius loosened his grip and planted a smacker of a kiss on her knuckle. "Do me a favor while I get ready for the band? Run a Google search on a village called Newton Rushford. That's where she lived until she was sixteen. Names, we need names. Someone we can call."

"Gabriel's not a common name. Could be we'll get lucky and he's still there."

"Hack into her laptop, password crazylady-asterisk-one. No! Better plan. Call the English cops, and—"

"Shower," she said.

Closing the door, Jade retreated into the bedroom and placed her hand on Marianne's pillow.

Where are you, Mama Bird?

The universe answered. Peeking out from under the pillow on Darius's side of the bed was the corner of a white envelope.

TWO

MARIANNE

Marianne hadn't visited the village cemetery since the first time she died. In a spectacular display of melodrama, even for a sixteen-year-old mental patient, she hacked at her wrists with a dull penknife until blood had seeped into the black soil of the freshest grave.

Facts would suggest a time lag between important events: losing her sanity at Simon's memorial service, being shipped off to the nuthouse, her release and subsequent failed suicide. The details, however, were MIM—missing in madness. She'd learned decades ago to not trust her own thoughts, but the villain here was electroconvulsive therapy. ECT zapped those memories right out of her brain. Along with the identity of the person who'd saved her sorry ass that night in the cemetery.

Marianne grabbed the handrail as the black cab screeched around a sharp bend on the winding country lane. Maybe she should suggest the cabbie stick to London-only fares, but that would involve talking, and she hadn't talked to anyone since slamming the door on Jade's hand. Not in whole sentences that mattered. If you were running away you had to travel light—with language as well as baggage.

Cool midafternoon air rushed through the open window. Her right leg jiggled, and her fingers tapped a frantic beat. After thirty years she was back.

Honey, I'm home.

"Good kip?" the cabbie said.

"Hmm." Faking sleep for the last hour had been a necessary tactic against his incessant questions: "On your holidays? No, what brings you all the way out 'ere, then? Bit off the beaten track for a tourist. Can't say anyone's ever asked me to drive them from Heathrow to a village in Bedfordshire before. You sound like a Yank. Been 'ere before, 'ave you?"

Too many questions, and she was clean out of answers.

She'd done everything right for years: stopped messing with her meds, quit guzzling handfuls of nonprescription drugs as if they were jelly beans, dumped all her liquor, and joined AA. Implemented a strict eleven p.m. lights-out and learned to meditate. Mindfulness? She could write the manual. And where had all the self-discipline, psychobabble, and mood stabilizers taken her? Back to being a volatile girl with blood on her hands.

A red haze of grief hovered over the road as the countryside sprawled into the sheep-riddled fields of her childhood. She quashed the impulse that said, *Jump. Jump out of the cab and watch your flesh rip, watch yourself bleed on the road. It's what you deserve.*

She had killed her own baby; she had killed someone else's baby. And then she saw Jade's hand on the door frame and slammed the door anyway. Hurt her with intent. Once could have been an accident; twice was a pattern; and maiming Jade should belong in the realm of the unimaginable. Where did you run to when you had nowhere left to hide? "Go to your safe place," one of her meditation tapes said. Apparently hers was a cemetery. In rural England. She had abandoned her family for a plot of land full of dead people. What happened next would be anyone's guess. Manic-depressive illness should come with an ejector button. *Hit that sucker, let me bail because this isn't funny anymore.*

Visions of bloody corpses danced in her head like perverted sugar plum fairies. She scratched the scars on her wrist, and watched white claw marks form and disappear.

A black mass of jackdaws rose as one, cawing and flapping into the sky, and the buzz of unharnessed thoughts became a deafening riff, a melting pot of craziness twenty-four hours a day. No furlough for good behavior. Grabbing the side of her head, Marianne tried to focus on the scent of wild hedgerows and something slightly rank. Probably sheep shit.

The road dipped down a small incline, and the sun pushed through the clouds scudding across the sky. There, up ahead: the yew trees, those majestic guardians of decomposing bodies, ashes in urns, and bone-filled coffins. The endless mental chatter dimmed, and her pulse slowed. *Imagine that.* Her lying, cheating brain had not tricked her: the cemetery of Newton Rushford, isolated on the edge of the village, could still offer peace.

"You can stop here," she said loudly.

The cabbie glanced over his shoulder. "You sure, luv?"

Marianne reached for the door handle and paused. A graffiti-covered van blocked the gate, and voices came from inside the cemetery. Real ones, for once. She'd had no plan—who had time to slow down and plan?—but she'd had expectations of solitude. Did people have nothing better to do on a Friday afternoon than hang out at a cemetery?

"Lady?"

A weed whacker roared, then made a kickback sound as if hitting something large and solid, and a girl laughed. High, giggly, a teenage laugh. A teenage girl was in the village cemetery. *No, that's not possible.* The only girly laughter that had ever belonged in the cemetery was hers. This was where she and Gabriel came for existential debate, where they picked apart the mysteries of life and death. Most adolescents hung out in parks and basements. Not them. They had a one a.m. rendezvous every Sunday in the cemetery and dared the village ghosts to join them. And then, one night, Simon had gate-crashed. And altered history forever.

The girl laughed again.

Marianne swallowed a primal scream of *Mine*. "Did you hear that?"

"Hear what?" The cabbie swiveled round and stared at her as if she'd sprouted horns.

Right, a hallucination. Good to know, hadn't had one in a while.

She foraged in her bag for sunglasses and slipped them on. "I've changed my mind. Go straight, then turn right, and drop me by the pub. Please. Thank you." That sounded confident and reasonable. Certainly not the voice of a woman who had, the day before, boarded a transatlantic flight with the attitude of someone running out to pick up Carolina pulled pork for lunch.

The cab started moving again, each jolt bouncing her thoughts between Simon and Gabriel: her lover and her love. How was that for a contradiction? During her first inpatient psychiatric stay, she'd written both of them rambling letters filled with the horrors of restraints and sedation—unfazed by the fact that one of her addressees was dead. But back then she was labeled schizophrenic, and no one expected rational behavior. She'd kept those letters. Knew exactly where they were: in the back of her shoe closet. Best hiding spot until it was no longer big enough.

Old stone houses closed in on both sides as the driver inched past the line of cars squashed bumper to bumper. They circled the village green and parked by the church, in an open area that surrounded the war memorial. The poppy wreath, left over from last year's Remembrance Sunday, was propped against the base. Poppies, the color of blood, the symbol of death. On July 17, her birthday, they'd planted the first ceramic poppy at the Tower of London to commemorate the outbreak of World War I. That should have been her sign, a personal message from the Grim Reaper. A warning that death never lets go.

Images swarmed: a sea of ceramic poppies bleeding out of the Tower of London. Heads on spikes. Traitors' Gate. Anne Boleyn on the block. Anne Boleyn, a mother who had miscarried months before her execution.

A small gasp escaped and Marianne disguised it with a cough. The cabbie didn't ask if she was okay. He merely stopped the meter and turned, hand extended. She counted out enough bills to keep a small country afloat. As always, she listened to the inner voice that whispered, *Yes, I'm insane. But please like me,* and overtipped.

Her stomach gurgled. She'd eaten nothing on the plane except for a bag of pretzels and the Twizzlers purchased at the Raleigh airport. The Twizzlers might have been a mistake. The pretzels too. She meant to eat at Heathrow, but there were so many people she couldn't breathe, couldn't swallow, couldn't do anything as panic turned her heart into a conga drum. And then she'd retreated to the business class lounge, curled up, and slept.

"Hungry, are we?" the cabbie said.

"I guess."

Adrenaline hit, sideswiping her as she reached for her Queen Bee bag. Her limbs ached with exhaustion and yet her mind crackled with the need for a quick spin of the lunatic-in-the-attic routine. Random thoughts marched like ants on the move. She needed to lie down and listen to music. Music would bring relief. Something classical, a little melancholic. Yes, music was always the cure. She took a shallow breath.

"Wanna receipt?" This time the cabbie didn't bother to turn around. She was already old news.

"No, thanks."

Marianne clambered out and frowned. Nostalgia wasn't everything it was cracked up to be. The leaded windows of the pub, an old coaching inn, had been boarded over. Two hanging baskets, dangling plant skeletons, swayed and creaked in the wind. And the stone building opposite that should have been a post office was some type of café. The iron rings once used to shackle prisoners during coach changes remained, but the striped awning had been replaced with a hot-pink banner that screamed "Puddings Galore: Best Homemade Desserts in the County!" She might be a certified crackpot, but she would never announce her business in pink. *Pink.*

Alone on the uneven cobbles, Marianne stared up at the Victorian spire of the church. An anachronistic monstrosity, her mom used to call it. The flag on the top of the bell tower whipped back and forth hypnotically. *Come inside. Stay a while,* it seemed to say. *Relive your public disgrace.* Although technically she'd discovered psychosis in the churchyard, not inside the church. When volts of electricity had blasted shotgun holes into your memory, details mattered.

The air filled with muffled organ music, and like a rat following the Pied Piper, she wobbled toward the church in her high-heeled boots. Her mother always said that if you grew up in the village it was your home for life, that the villagers would welcome you back. Although in her case a lynching might be more appropriate. After all, she was the reason one of their own had met a grisly death on the A428, where traffic now droned. A constant stream of people in transit, traveling over the site of the crash. The first crash, one of two, a matching pair. A repeating pattern.

Adjusting her sunglasses, Marianne walked up the stone steps and entered the churchyard through the lych-gate. On her right was the family mausoleum of the lords of the manor; on her left, yew trees planted over mass graves of victims of the Black Death. Someone had created perfect lines of cut grass around the ancient lichen-covered headstones. How long since they'd stopped burying villagers here and opened the cemetery?

As she inhaled the smell of fresh grass clippings and gasoline, a memory flashed of ranting and raving to a crowd of spectators. She glanced up at the gargoyles, the grotesque stone faces—part beast, part man—that had played silent witness to her naked downfall. Yes, she had removed every piece of clothing before going oh-so-publicly psycho. If only you could choose which memories to lose.

The music stopped, and her thumping heart filled the void with a steady, deafening rhythm.

Positive thoughts, positive thoughts.

Hadn't she and Gabriel discovered a pair of swans nesting down by the old bridge on the night of their first teenage kiss—a messy tongue job that took her by surprise? And what about stealing candy from the village shop and daring him to do the same? But the good memories were shoved aside by flashbacks of roaring out of control.

Spots danced before her eyes, and she scratched at her wrist—her fingernails moving faster and faster. *High heels on cobbles be damned.* She ran to the ancient porch of the church. The smell of rotting funeral lilies hugged her tight; panic, bitter and metallic, filled her mouth. The decorative iron and oak door, unchanged since the thirteenth century, barred her way. Seizing the cold metal ring of the handle, she threw her weight against the door.

Let me in, let me in.

The latch on the other side clicked up, and a muscle in her shoulder screamed. She half fell into the church, a place she hadn't visited since Simon's memorial service. The last church she'd been inside. Her parents abandoned organized religion after they left the village; Darius was a self-professed agnostic; and her commitment to this church, as a choir member and a bell ringer, had only ever been about music.

A flash of sunlight blasted through the clerestory windows, briefly illuminating the wheeled bier, a wooden wagon once used to transport the dead. Now it gathered dust motes in the corner of the north aisle. North aisle, south aisle, the Lady Chapel, nave, chancel . . . The building was ridiculously grand for a village church. Something to do with the lords of the manor having too much money in the nineteenth century.

The sun disappeared and the Saxon nave became dark like the inside of a womb. As the heating system thumped a soothing heartbeat, a blurred memory returned of the choir singing the Lord's Prayer while Simon's mother wept. Marianne removed her sunglasses and walked past the Norman font where she had been baptized. Tucked behind it, a freestanding cardboard display board labeled "The Great War" was covered in kids' research projects and what appeared to be posters for the women's land army. In England you could never escape the sweeping strokes of history.

The brass plate, the one they used to pass around for the collection, had been replaced by a locked wooden box with a sign asking for donations to save the organ. Yes, she would donate! Whatever she had left of her sterling! She unsnapped her wallet to remove a fifty-pound note, but her hand paused. Up by the altar, voices twittered. First the cemetery was full of people and now the church. What had happened to perennially quiet village life? This place was like a Black Friday mob scene. Now where should she go to find solitude—the deserted tables under the hot-pink Puddings Galore banner?

Staying in the shadow of a pillar, Marianne leaned forward to spy. A small group of women were working on freestanding floral arrangements, weaving greenery in and out of white and cream flowers. Wedding flowers.

Her left hand closed around the gold-and-diamond locket hanging at her neck—a wedding gift from Darius. He wouldn't care about the cost of the plane ticket—well, he might scream and stomp and look sexy as hell when the credit card statement arrived and he realized she'd flown business class. Okay, so that was not a normal thought. Normal people weren't turned on by anger. Not that Darius did rev-up-the-chain-saw rage, but his moods were as mercurial as hers. Although these days he didn't hurl anger. He lugged around a feeble sadness that said,

Aren't I enough, Marianne? as if love could magically, inexplicably cure mental illness. Or obliterate her taunts, weighted with enough hostility for two: "Leave me alone. I don't care what you think." Except that she did care. A conscience was a terrible thing to waste on a mad person. And running away armed with the knowledge that her absence would gut him positioned her squarely between the Tin Man and a killing machine. Heartless, brutal . . . *Wait!*

A burst of arpeggios soared through the church, pumping through her bloodstream like cocaine. Widor's Toccata! *How perfect, how absolutely perfect.* And the organist wasn't rushing, was playing the piece exactly the way it should be played. The chords separated into individual notes that danced around her like butterflies and then exploded into fireworks. A rhapsodic mimicry of mania—her favorite state of being before it tossed her into the fireball of damnation.

Warm memories trickled out: playing hide-and-seek around the gravestones with Gabriel, laughing when the churchwarden yelled at them; singing carols by candlelight at midnight mass, imagining her future as a rock diva; stumbling through the darkness of a winter's evening, groping along a flying buttress until she saw the light from the open belfry door; running up the spiral stone steps of the bell tower, vowing to be the best bell ringer in the parish.

This vast space, filled with sound shadows, reverberated with her *before* history. The pure joy of a life lived without the knowledge of all that would follow. She had run back to the village like a hunted animal needing to burrow, but what if here, in her past, there was a chance at rebirth?

Moving with the stealth of a ghost, not wanting to cause a single vibration in the air, Marianne lowered herself into the back pew, slipped her sunglasses back on, and positioned her bag on a needlepoint kneeler. As the wooden foot pedals of the organ clacked, she cut Darius loose and lost herself in the past. A place where he didn't belong.

The first wave of mania had been intoxicating. Never-ending spring nights of beautiful thoughts cantering through her mind, too fast to capture. Gabriel had already withdrawn, but Simon was a moth to her flame—or maybe he was addicted to the glut of casual sex no eighteen-year-old guy could reject. And how could any girl have refused attention from Simon—charming, gorgeous, and hero-worshipped at the private school where he was head boy?

Nothing but harmless fun until they both discovered she was pregnant. Until her mind spun so fast she could no longer speak in complete sentences. Until her world blew up along with her sanity at Simon's memorial service, delayed because Mrs. Bonham insisted on waiting until she and Gabriel were released from the hospital. That took a while since they both had fractured pelvises. Gabriel, who'd been in the backseat, also fractured his skull and broke his collarbone along with several ribs. Mrs. Bonham told Marianne she was the lucky one, as if losing a baby she'd felt moving inside her womb and the subsequent infection that meant no other baby would ever grow there were gifts. The doctors should have moved her to the loony bin right then, after condemning her to a life of infertility. But no, they released her into the world with her frayed mental fuse already lit.

After the psychotic break, the medical profession screwed up again, labeled her psychosis understandable, and sent her home to a black depression. Everyone said she should return to school. In the end she agreed, but only because she'd begun to plot her death. And she would have succeeded had someone not held her wounds closed.

Surviving suicide was not for wimps.

Deciding a fresh start was best, her parents—gentle beings who'd adopted her as a newborn and knew nothing about the roots of insanity—sold the house, packed up twenty years of English life, and returned to the faculty at their alma mater, Duke University. An ocean away from everything Marianne had ever known. Maybe they hoped she would reboot like a malfunctioning computer. Sedated and past caring, she never bothered to ask for explanations. Gabriel refused to say good-bye. In North Carolina, her family began the long journey of denial, treatment, remission, and two more suicide attempts. With each episode, her mind unraveled further. By the time she could make sense of her permanently medicated existence, Gabriel was part of something she had long discarded.

And now she'd discarded Darius.

The organist ran through the toccata several times, practiced a few hymns and Mendelssohn's "Wedding March," and then slipped out the side door by the altar. Marianne's buttocks were numb. Shouldn't honoring God come with more padding than a paper-thin cushion on English oak?

The flower arrangers migrated down into the aisle to twist ivy up the brass candleholders on the pew ends, and Marianne turned her head away. She should leave, but go where? The music had zapped her energy. Rendered her officially useless. Marianne stared at the ornate raised tomb in the Lady Chapel. So English to have centuries-old remains buried inside a church. What lay beneath the alabaster baron and his two wives, their eyes closed and their hands folded in prayer? A sweet deal of never-ending rest.

No, Dr. White. I'm not suicidal. But I think about death all the time. I want to be nothing. To hear nothing. To see nothing. To feel nothing. I want my mind to stop.

A woman stomped down the aisle carrying a huge tin pitcher. "Good afternoon," she said. Her voice commanded; the knotted scarf at her neck covered in pictures of bridles and saddles suggested she was the horsey type. Horsey types were almost as bad as café owners who chose eyesore banners of pink. Her footsteps receded and water ran. They must have added either a kitchen or restroom in the choir vestry. How very progressive.

Horsey Woman came back, walking slowly, holding the pitcher with both hands. She was wearing a green quilted vest over a taupe sweater, a knee-length tweedy skirt that looked unbearably itchy, and flesh-colored pantyhose. Someone who understood the English summer. Marianne shivered. The day before, it had been ninety-eight degrees in Carrboro.

And the woman was wearing brown brogues. The only time Marianne wore sensible shoes was for working out. Not that she'd exercised for months, since she could no longer do it alone. Darius had never understood that exercise—shared or solitary—was not about pleasure. It was merely a means to exorcise her mind and exhaust her body.

She could no longer do anything alone, not even retreat into her shoe closet. In his concern, Darius had become a stalled-out storm cloud that hung with suffocating heaviness.

Horsey Woman reached the altar and talked with an older woman, who glanced back at Marianne with a shrug. Time passed, and the women began to gather their tools and leave. No one spoke to her. The door clanged shut, but two women remained, whispering by the font.

"Don't you think one of us should ask if she needs help?" The voice was high, anxious.

"I can't stay another five minutes," voice B answered. "I've got the ferret man coming to deal with my rabbit warren."

"I'll go fetch the reverend." Voice A again. "He'll know what to do." The door opened and shut; silence swallowed her whole.

✳

Marianne shot awake to the smell of the outdoors and a hand shaking her.

"Hello there," a man's voice said.

Where was she? She inhaled the stale scent of ten centuries of religious ritual with a hint of furniture wax. *Newton Rushford, the church.* She glanced over her shoulder at the thousand-year-old stone pillar blocking her in and then back at the man crouched down on his haunches at the entrance to the pew. No exits and only skeletons to hear her scream.

Good job, Marianne.

"Welcome to Newton Rushford. The flower ladies came to find me. They were somewhat concerned about this elegant and rather sad woman who's been sitting in the church for the last few hours by herself. I was wondering if I might offer some assistance?"

"No." Marianne sat up but kept her eyes down. Where were her sunglasses? "Sorry. I'll be on my way."

"Right, then." He sounded casual, friendly. Like they'd had this conversation a hundred times before. "Can I give you a lift somewhere? All the cars parked by the war memorial belong to parishioners, and my keen eye tells me you're far too well-dressed to have arrived on the bus from Bedford or Milton Keynes. I'm the vicar, by the way. Perfectly harmless. Worst thing I ever do is nod off in the Swan after a pint or two with the bell ringers. The barmaid insists I snore."

She glanced at the U2 T-shirt strained across his chest. "You don't look very vicar-ish." What he looked like was an obstacle.

He stood, letting out an *ooff* when one of his knees cracked. "I've been volunteering with the youth group, so thought a T-shirt would be more appropriate than a dog collar. And who doesn't love U2?"

Marianne nearly said, *My husband.*

"We've been attacking weeds in the cemetery," he said. "The nettles love all this rain."

Bracing her hands on the back of the pew, she wobbled up to her feet. He was tall, this middle-aged guy who claimed to be a man of God but was wearing ripped black jeans and a band tee. Give him a few tats and he could have been Zeke, their freelance sound engineer. Zeke was also big with dirty-blond hair. Although not as big as this guy, who had to be at least six two. Trying to push past him would be pointless. He towered over her, and he had that wide, solid chest. Why couldn't they have left her alone, those twittering women? For once she hadn't been causing harm.

More sleep, her body said. *No.* Her fingers scurried through air. *Go to the cemetery.* She patted down her pockets—where were her sunglasses?—and glanced up.

He was smiling at her, a smile that seemed to reach into his eyes. Pale blue rimmed with navy. A memory flashed: she was trapped inside the body of a raving lunatic, flailing against leather restraints and screaming at those same pale eyes, "Why couldn't you have let me die?" So. He was the one who had saved her that night. How could she not have guessed, and how could she not have suspected he'd stayed in the village? That had been part of his plan, and unlike her, Gabriel had always stuck with his plans.

His smile slipped away, his eyes widened, and his face drained of color. "Marianne?" he whispered. "Is it you?"

"In the flesh."

"This is . . ." Gabriel ran his hands through his hair, still thick but horribly short. What a sacrilege to hack off those locks. Bits of leaves drifted out like snowflakes. He lowered his arms and shoved his hands into the pockets of his jeans, then tugged them free. His chest began moving rapidly.

"Sit," she said, backing up. "You've gone horribly pale."

"This is"—he gave a feeble laugh—"most unexpected."

With the filled-out biceps, darker hair, and what must have been a serious growth spurt, he resembled his big brother more than ever. Simon and Gabriel had always been a stunning pair—physically similar and only a year apart but with personalities that contradicted each other at every turn. Simon was charm, danger, and raw sex appeal. The classic bad boy that teen girls and little old ladies couldn't resist. Gabriel was easygoing, sweet, and predictable. The kind of guy mothers loved because he always cleared the dishes. One of them was safe; one of them wasn't. And one had never been a good number for Marianne Stokes.

Gabriel collapsed into the pew and wiped his forehead, spreading a smudge of dirt. "Gracious. This is . . . I don't know what else to say . . . unexpected."

"Sorry about that. It's a bit unexpected for me, too." If she'd passed him on the street, he would have been a stranger, this man who had once been her coconspirator, her conscience when she didn't have one, her best friend, her childhood sweetheart, her first love. The guy who represented childish pranks and first gropes. The person who had every reason, plus a few extra, to hate her. Or had they grown to hate each other? Another memory tumbled out, of him screaming at her, calling her a whore. Except that Gabriel never screamed. He wasn't wired for strong emotions. Surely that was the reason she'd strayed to his tempestuous older brother.

She'd dreamed big, of escape. Gabriel dreamed small, of putting down roots in the village. And she laughed when he talked about ordination. Yes, he loved visiting old churches and prattling away about the architecture, the music, the sensory experience—the bells and smells—but she never took him seriously. Seemed he'd known his heart all along.

Gabriel sat up and placed his hands in his lap. "You look good, Marianne. A little thin, but good." He'd always been a pitiful liar. His hands were shaking, and the tone of his voice had changed. The camaraderie had gone. "What's brought you back after all this time?"

She could make something up. Deceit always came easily, but the entire scene took on a dreamlike quality, and for months she'd had nothing but nightmares. Standing here in this church that had witnessed centuries of history, with this stranger who had known her better than anyone, it was almost a relief to be honest, to not have to pretend to make sense.

She sat next to him and laid her hand on top of his, pushing down lightly until he stopped shaking. "Damned if I know. Best guess? This is my endgame. But I need to visit the cemetery, and you have to come with me."

THREE
GABRIEL

He would never quibble with God over his job description, certainly not the part about helping a suicide survivor in distress. But surely there should be an exemption clause for the woman who had destroyed his life. Gabriel looked up at the angel ceiling of the nave and prayed, briefly, for the strength to be a compassionate Christian, not a small-minded weasel. Although he was definitely leaning toward the latter.

After thirty years of silence, Marianne had returned. And in true Marianne fashion, she was embarking on a grand adventure and eager to drag him along for the ride. Admittedly the cemetery was only a five-minute walk from the church—ten in those heels—but she might as well have said, "Follow me into the maw of hell. It'll be fun."

She looked rather poorly. Was this some last hurrah to cross off her bucket list? He spent enough time visiting deathbeds to recognize the signs: the sunken cheeks and unhealthy pallor. Cancer, it was probably cancer. He'd never wanted to see her again, but never hadn't included a terminal disease. This must be a test, God booming, "Don't be an arse,

Gabriel. Get over yourself and offer comfort." Except he couldn't find his voice, let alone words.

Gabriel dragged his hand across his mouth and glanced at her sideways. Looking at Marianne for too long had always been ill-advised. Within microseconds she could convince the strongest-willed boy to sell his soul or steal sherbet lemons from the local shop. Yes, under her tutelage he had enjoyed a brief career as a thief.

"Are you ill?" he said quietly.

"Yes, but not in the way most people think." She jumped up, her hands fluttering through the air like dandelion clocks.

He'd forgotten how small she was—a waif powered by a high-voltage battery. In his memories she'd been taller.

"I'm sorry. I should have called, sent a carrier pigeon, something." Her mouth twitched as if trying to remember how to smile. "My problem is that I don't think before I leap. Never have, never will." Had she always talked so quickly? "You know that better than anyone."

"Do I?" he said.

She pulled down the cuffs of her jacket, covering up her wrists. Her hands continued to shake. Why would she hide the scars from him, when he'd held the gashes closed? Gabriel's eyes moved to the wedding band and a huge diamond. A little garish for his taste.

"Is your husband with you?" He turned his attention to the thirteenth-century fresco of the Crucifixion, rediscovered during nineteenth-century renovations.

"No, he's back in North Carolina. He doesn't know I'm here."

The painting was such a wonderful treasure for the village. Craning his neck for a better view, Gabriel stared at Christ on the cross. "You don't think your husband has a right to know where you are?"

"None of your business," she snapped. "Sorry. Sorry. I don't mean to be . . . I'm a little adrift right now, and it's so much work, Gabriel. So much work."

"What is?"

"Being me. Sometimes, I don't feel strong enough."

"I'm a little confused. Would you mind if we started at the beginning?" Turning back, he held her gaze and understood. He'd seen that look before—in his mother, in his father, in his own haunted reflection. She was in pain, but not the physical kind.

"It's complicated, Gabriel."

Gabriel tugged on his lips. "It always is with you."

"I can't explain." She backed up into the pew and began rubbing her arms. "And by the way, this country is still freezing. It's July, for goodness' sake."

Her flare of anger caught him by surprise, which it shouldn't have. Her temper had always been quick to spark. Apparently his memory was selective where Marianne was concerned. But he was also bombarding her when he should take his time, let her come to him. This was not his usual way, but then again, the rules had never applied to Marianne. Until this moment, he'd never realized how empty the space around him had become, the space that she'd once filled.

"Please, can we go to the cemetery?" she said.

"The youth group's an eager bunch, which means if you were hoping for a peaceful"—he stumbled over his words—"visit, now might not be a good time."

"I—I can't cope with groups of people. The noise—" She hunched her shoulders.

"Marianne, you look exhausted. Why don't you come back to the rectory, have a nap and something to eat, and we'll go to the cemetery tonight, when it's quiet?"

"I've missed you," she blurted out. "I spent years missing you."

An interesting comment from someone who'd never once got in touch. And yet how could he trust anything she said? Despite planning four children with him, she'd happily done the deed with his brother.

The Madonna and Child in the large oil painting by the door locked eyes on him. "If you're looking for a partner in crime, I gave up shoplifting and smoking pot after you left." *I gave up everything except my faith.*

She sat down on her hands and rocked back and forth as if gathering momentum for a sprint.

"You really did it." She nodded at the pulpit. "I never believed you when you rambled on about ordination."

"It was a calling." She didn't need to know his real decision had come as he prayed over her wounds. That was the night he'd started believing in angels. What else could have explained her survival in the pre–mobile phone era?

"I assume you followed your passion for music?" Judging from the expensive-looking leather jacket and gaudy jewelry, she'd been successful.

"I own a recording studio . . ." Her voice trailed off. "It's called Nightjar."

Nightjar. His nickname for her because she used to sing for him in the dark—just him—until she'd settled on a bigger audience. He inhaled deeply, held on for a moment, and released the breath. If only she'd stayed away. Was she going to unpack his life, force him to reexperience events he'd wrestled with himself to forget?

"What's your specialty?" he said.

"Whatever pays the bills. Local artists, audiobooks, a few out-of-state bands. I'm a little disappointed my nefarious plot to turn you into a petty criminal failed." She nudged an embroidered kneeler with her foot. "I'm guessing you went to college and majored in religious studies or theology? Bristol was your top choice, right?"

"Indeed." The game of catch-up was inevitable, but please, God, let it stay within the time period after she left and not stray into the before. The name *Nightjar* whirled like mental fog. "Then Cuddesdon for theological college and Sandhurst, the Royal Military Academy, for the professionally qualified officers' course. I was a chaplain in the British army for five years."

Marianne sat still. "That part wasn't in your script."

"No. It wasn't." He paused. "But this is what I always wanted—to come back and preach the gospel here, in the village. I blame those deep, meaningful conversations we had in the cemetery about life, death, and the hereafter. Or maybe I wanted to prove to everyone that I wasn't a shoplifter."

"Or was it how you moved on after Simon died?"

He balled his right hand into a fist. "Let's not go there, Marianne." The warning should be obvious, even to her. "I put the past behind me for my parents' sake. I trust you did the same."

"I never meant to hurt you." Her green eyes, sharp and fierce, darted as if anticipating danger from all angles. "I didn't mean to hurt anyone. I didn't understand at the time, but I was manic back then. It was another ten years before I was diagnosed. The psychotic episode at Simon's memorial service and the suicide attempts threw the doctors for a loop."

"There was more than one?" His voice came out hoarse.

"What do you think? Have you ever known me do anything in moderation? After a series of false starts, I was branded bipolar. Bipolar I if you're interested. The real deal—no wimpy affective disorder for me. And I'm an alcoholic."

Gabriel unclenched his fist. What a relief to have a reason for her slightly odd behavior and the hand tremors. For a moment he'd been thinking junkie.

"Should I hide the communion wine?" He smiled.

She smiled back. "I see you've learned to be sympathetic."

"A divine gift that comes with wearing a cassock every Sunday. The benefits of my job are mind-blowing."

She laughed. "I've forgotten what that sounds like."

"What?" he said.

"My laugh."

"You have a great laugh, it's—"

"Deranged?"

"No. I was going to say infectious."

"I sincerely hope nothing about me is contagious. It's not something I normally tell people, that I'm, you know . . . But I guess normal doesn't exist between us. Besides, aren't you bound by priestly confidentiality?"

They had slipped back so easily. It had always been this way between them—lots of banter. Or rather it was until she and Simon fell into lust, or love, or teenage angst. Mania made perfect sense, given her wildly impetuous behavior in the months leading up to the accident. If he was being completely honest, he would have to admit that she had terrified him.

"Are you going to ask for the gory details of my diagnosis?" she said. "Do you want to know if I'm a danger to myself, society? You?"

"Want to tell me?"

"No." Her prickles were back up, like hedgehog spines.

"Then I won't ask."

For a brief moment he had sensed the old Marianne. The one who was full of passion, laughter, and creative curiosity. Before Simon's death she was a fighter, but what started as a combustible mix of teenage hormones and exam stress exploded into despair, disgust, and malice. It nearly destroyed both of them. It had destroyed his brother.

In the bell tower behind them, the hour struck. A harsh intrusion that faded into ripples of aftershock. A dying melody. This time tomorrow all the bells would peal out, announcing the start of matrimony. The village loved weddings, but he preferred christenings. They gave him hope and took the sting out of the endless, small-minded bureaucracy of the Church of England. He'd offered himself for ordination with such idealism. Now he struggled to not be argumentative with the rural dean and to find time for daily prayer around his parishioners' needs plus the demands of running a benefice of three parishes, each with a crumbling Grade I listed building. Unlike Marianne, he never wanted to change the world; he'd merely wanted to slow it down for prayer and contemplation.

"When did you get here?" he said.

"I landed around eight, I think. We had to circle for ages. Then I hung out at Heathrow for a while and picked up a cab."

She'd just arrived from America and paid for a taxi from Heathrow? What an extravagance when public transport was perfectly adequate.

"Do you have somewhere to stay?" He didn't want to know the answer, but he had to ask.

"I thought the Tinker might have rooms, but it's closed. I don't remember where the other pub is. I don't know. I hadn't thought it through." She trembled as if cold or frightened, or both, and his decision was made.

He bent down and picked up the ridiculously light bag that looked like something Mary Poppins would use. "Then you'll stay with me." He rose to his feet and took a deep breath. The village gossip brigade, with Bill Collins leading the charge, was going to love this one.

"Is the rectory still haunted?"

Something tangible passed between them—a shared memory of ghost hunts. Why had they devoted their teens to searching for signs of life from the dead?

"Highly doubtful it ever was. But the church sold off the old rectory years ago. It's a private house filled with children, as it should be. I live in the new rectory—a modern shoebox off Nell's Lane. It's fine for a bachelor."

"You never married?"

"Married to the job. I'll have you know that I take the spiritual lives of my flock very seriously. Except for that miserable old cowpat, Bill Collins." Gabriel raised his eyes heavenward. "Sorry, God. Still trying with that one. And you—children?"

Gabriel swallowed. He should have deflected that thought. Had he made the mistake of pretending they'd both moved on?

She crossed her arms over her chest and huddled into herself. "Bill Collins is still here?"

"Unfortunately, yes. And he's no more even-tempered." Gabriel paused. "I'm sorry. I shouldn't have asked about . . ."

"To answer your question, no. It wasn't possible after everything that happened." Her hands started agitating.

"I know," he said. "But I thought you might have adopted."

"Yeah. Like you can see me at a PTA meeting." She waved some unseen shadow from her face. "Bottom line, my monster's not always chained. And a mother has to be in control."

"A mother has to be human."

"I guess God forgot that bit when He said, 'Let there be bipolar disease.'" She pointed at the brass cross on the altar. "Besides. I've been married three times. Husband number one, I met on a locked psych ward. I met the other two in AA. And let's not forget three serious suicide attempts plus a few near misses that don't count. Who wants to dump kids into that much instability?"

Again, something had shifted, forcing him to lag two beats behind in the conversation. It was as if he kept slipping back into thirty years of unshared secrets. Life had pried them apart for a reason. Reconnecting might not have been in anyone's best interests.

"Listen—" She kneaded her right eye. "That was kind of you, to offer a bed. But I should give you an out. I'm not sure anyone can be around me at the moment."

"Didn't you ask for my help?" An odd sensation grew in his chest: an unexpected and unwanted tightening in his lungs. A creeping specter that whispered, *Please don't go.*

"Yes. No. I don't know. I thought, but—"

He slung her bag over his shoulder, out of her reach. "Rest, sleep, and then I'll cook supper and we can talk."

"I don't want to talk." She sprang up and glowered at him.

"Righty-ho. I'll chunter on and let off steam about the bishop while you fake an interest."

"I don't owe you anything, Gabriel. And your life certainly turned out peachy, despite me. Was I even a ripple in your space-time continuum?"

He managed to not sigh. Whatever currents were bubbling under the surface, he was simply trying to be a decent bloke. "I'm merely offering a bed and a meal to someone who's short on options."

"Sorry," she said. "I don't mean to be a snarky bitch. But I have this anger, all the time, and it's growing like some sort of tumor."

"Apology accepted. If you prefer, I can talk to the nuns. They have a few private guest rooms at the Abbey, and I could explain that you're an old friend in need of shelter. The mother superior will take you in, no explanation necessary." The mother superior might be in a motorized wheelchair, but she'd outwitted Nazis as a girl in rural France. She was more than capable of handling Marianne. But if Marianne had come back because of all that had happened thirty years ago, she was his responsibility. He'd known that the moment she'd looked into his eyes.

"No." She shook her head. "No strangers. Only you. At least you know I'm a killer. No explanations required."

"Stop. You are not responsible for Simon's death." He didn't mean to boom at her. Less than twenty minutes in her presence, and he was cracking apart at the seams.

"Gabriel, there was another crash. A second one. This time I was driving. My husband was in the passenger seat and we were arguing, and he told me to turn down the music, but I was too busy screaming at this herd of deer on the roadside. I spooked them and they ran out into another car, and the other driver she—she was pregnant, and she—she lost her baby. Another unborn baby died because of me, Gabriel." She sucked in a sob.

We were arguing, and he told me to turn down the music. A strange whooshing filled his ears, the distant hum of unwanted memories. Gabriel focused on the Crucifixion scene in the stained-glass window behind the altar.

"Two fatal car wrecks. Two babies dead before they've had a chance at life, and I'm the link, the connector. Me. And I'm scared, so scared. Where does it stop, Gabriel? Where?"

He opened his left arm to her: an instinct, a reflex. Learned behavior he couldn't control any better than the crashing of his heart against his ribs.

FOUR

JADE

Darius flung himself across the breakfast island, a balled-up nonsensical love letter from his wife in one hand and his passport in the other. Both of Marianne's passports were missing, including her red UK one. A large water stain had spread down the shoulders of his black T-shirt, and his mop of hair dripped onto the granite. He was creating his own mini water feature in the middle of his state-of-the-art kitchen.

The doorbell rang and Jade glanced at her watch. The food delivery, right on time. She headed to the front door, texting Sasha:

```
MC. Start playing head engineer honcho
because I'm out of the picture.
```

She and Sasha, another Girls In Motion alum, had developed their own shorthand. MC equaled Marianne crisis; DD equaled Darius drama. Both contained the same hidden message: tread carefully.

Jade paused and added: `Don't text and drive.`

Sasha replied with a thumbs-up emoticon.

Jade helped the delivery guy carry in deviled eggs, fried-green-tomato sliders served on mini brioche rolls, Beaufort shrimp salad (her favorite), mini crab cakes, a huge tray of beautifully rolled cold cuts decorated with olives, a basket of crusty bread, a large plate of grilled vegetables with fresh mozzarella, a display of individually labeled cheeses, and assorted mini tarts that belonged, surely, in the window of a Parisian patisserie. If she were a dog, she would drool. Breakfast had been at least two hours ago.

They lined up the platters next to Darius, who remained prostrate on the counter.

He okay? the delivery guy mouthed.

"Don't worry about him," Jade said loudly. "He's fine."

"I. Am. Not." Darius's voice rumbled like something from *The Exorcist*. Not for the first time, Jade wondered why he'd abandoned his potential career as a musician to go behind the scenes. He could do public theatrics way better than Rob Zombie.

The delivery guy scurried out before Jade could find her wallet for a tip.

"Nice way to scare the locals," she said as she loaded lunch into the empty fridge and then popped a mini pecan-bourbon pie into her mouth. "Hmm, delish." She brushed piecrust crumbs from her bottom lip.

Darius pushed himself up. "She's run away and I'm not to follow? How can she say that? Doesn't she know she's tearing out my heart?" He punched his chest.

His red eyes screamed, *Deranged on devotion.* Thank God for the standing order of benzos or she would be dragging him off to Dr. White's office pronto. Should she suggest he pop a Xanax before the band arrived?

Jade swallowed her mouthful and resisted diving back into the fridge for a deviled egg. Once you eliminated grits, southern food wasn't half bad. "This has got nothing to do with her feelings for you."

"Bullshit." He smashed a chrome stool into the breakfast island.

"Come on. She rambles on about how much she loves you." Jade pointed at the letter. "This is a plea for time. I think we should give it to her. And FYI, having a temper tantrum won't change a thing."

He stood still, chest heaving, and she had a weird image of a trapped bull about to charge.

"Look. The band should be here in half an hour. We're going to stick with plan A. Okay, honey?"

"No, far from okay." He paced in a circle. "I'm going to do whatever it takes to find her. Hire a private eye, report her as missing to the cops. Call out the National Guard. I don't care, but I have to find her. Have you tried her cell?"

"What do you think? I've sent enough texts to overload AT&T central. But I'll keep trying if you'll haul ass over to the studio and starting behaving like you're worth every cent the label's paying us. Enough money to fund Marianne's shoe habit until you guys move into assisted living."

He didn't smile.

"Come on. That was funny."

"Christ, how can I do this? My wife ran away, she may or may not be suicidal . . ."

"No, we're not going there, because that's you being melodramatic. Marianne isn't suicidal. Hasn't been for years. Do I have to remind you that she took suicide off the table on your wedding day? That's how much she loves you. I know her current actions seem a bit screwy, but our Marianne's more Iron Lady–ish than that dead British leader who was Reagan's best buddy. She assures you she's got plenty of meds and will use them responsibly. I believe her and so should you. We have to trust her."

He opened his mouth to speak, but she kept going.

"This makes sense to me. A controlled fall or something. As if she knows, in some corner of her mind, what she's doing." Or close enough. "Marianne and I are survivors. We recognized that in each other from the beginning. When the chips are down, we protect ourselves. I think that's what she's doing."

"Why?" He started pacing again, this time going counterclockwise.

"Could you please stop moving and park your butt on a stool? Try flipping your thoughts to find a different approach. When you have a migraine you don't want anyone around, and—"

"My wife has more than a headache, Jade." He didn't sit, but at least he stood still.

"Fair enough. Crap analogy, but it's like being really sick and not wanting others in your business fussing, and—"

"I don't fuss."

"Stop interrupting." She wagged a finger at him. "I know you're scared—"

"Are you scared?"

"No, because my gut's telling me it will all work out. She'll come back to us when she's ready." God, she was good at making up shit. "But trying to force ourselves into whatever's going on isn't going to achieve anything other than turn a bad situation into a total shitstorm. We have to sit this one out, boss."

"Give me more, more to hang on to."

A hawk screeched as it flew over the garden, and Jade shivered. There were far too many birds in the backyard thanks to Marianne's obsession with feeding the damn things. It was like being on the set of a Hitchcock movie.

"Let's use logic," Jade said. "Marianne's at her best when she's focused on others, but that car crash has pushed her inward—to a place she doesn't want us to follow. Isn't her teenage wasteland the reason she banned us from her therapy sessions? What if there's something in her past she's never dealt with, something related to this Simon?"

"Then I need to go after her. I'm sorry, but I can't do this." Darius shook back his hair and sprayed droplets of water in every direction. "Book the first flight to England. You deal with the band."

"Darius, listen to me. If you corner her this will end badly for you."

"You're telling me you've seen this before. With my predecessor?"

Yes, but no need to elaborate. "No, I'm telling you that the best thing you can do for Marianne is keep her business safe. Nightjar is her passion, her lifeblood, her reason for getting out of bed every morning."

"I thought I was," he said quietly.

"Unfair comparison. The studio has been her baby for twenty years. By keeping it safe, we're showing her that we understand. We have to stay here. For Marianne. And whatever's going on, I'm thinking Dr. White's in the loop. That's why she wouldn't give permission for you to talk to him. Which means we're not taking any action until he's called."

Darius stared out the kitchen window, silent. Finally he was listening.

"And here's another thought: What if she's in the village and you arrive and spook her? She could run again, and we might never find her."

"England's smaller than Illinois," he said. "We'd find her."

"With bloodhounds?"

Two squirrels started a squawking match in the black walnut tree by the deck, and Darius tensed.

"Compromise time," she said. "Give me this afternoon to figure this out. I'll talk to Dr. White when he calls, get his take, and then dig up proof that she's in the village. If we know where she is and we know she's safe, we can figure out our next play. Fair enough?"

"Anything could be happening to her, and doing nothing is—"

"You're not doing nothing. You're protecting Marianne's reputation in a reputation-based business."

He stood up straight. At last she was talking his language. For all his amateur dramatics, Darius was a professional.

"There's only one direct flight a day from Raleigh to Heathrow. I checked while you were in the shower. It leaves at eight tonight, so I still have time to get you on that plane. But right now you need to meet with the band and I need to find Marianne."

He took a breath. "Deal. But you better be right about all this."

"Always am, boss."

The moment Darius slammed the sliding patio door shut, she slumped into the spot he had vacated on the breakfast island. Pain jabbed the back of her skull and radiated around to her eye. If she waited, the headache flare would burn out. Unlike the masquerade of being a studio manager with her shit together.

She had also run away on an escape route for one. And hers left behind a casualty. Two if she counted the baby asleep in the upstairs crib. Jesse, however, was wide awake and whimpering on the hall floor when she bolted out the front door. The sirens were getting close, and she had only minutes to get away. But minutes could give a grown man plenty of time to beat the crap out of a skinny kid he detested. She knew that and had left her brother anyway. What if Marianne was doing the same thing—abandoning her family to save herself?

FIVE
MARIANNE

Shake her hard, and *Edward Scissorhands* meets *A Nightmare on Elm Street* would tumble out. She saw herself grabbing a carving knife from the butcher's block in the kitchen; she saw herself hacking off her fingers.

A carousel of depraved images spun as Marianne paced in the cell of Gabriel's guest bedroom. Her mind snapped back and forth with as much energy as a saggy piece of elastic, marshaling every part of her body, even her eyelids, to never-ending movement. To do the fandango, as Freddie Mercury had sung. Clearly the singer knew a thing or two about dysfunction when he wrote "Bohemian Rhapsody."

Rest, the sane part of her brain said, the part that knew bipolar illness and international travel were mortal enemies. *Visit your baby!* the crazy part countered. Meanwhile the grains of time filtered through the hourglass. One day ended, another began. Sleep eluded her.

The twin beds, squished into opposing corners, were reminiscent of beds in a mental ward. Who had twin beds for adults? Someone who didn't approve of sex, someone who had run away on an Easter pilgrimage to Saint Albans after she made the moves on him with a box of condoms. A ludicrous overreaction given their years of fooling around. Or maybe leaving her alone was a test. Sixteen-year-old Marianne with no social plans never ended happily, and only an idiot could have failed to notice her flirting with Simon. And Gabriel was far from stupid. Gabriel, her alternative future. Missing him had been her penance for years, and now they were back under the same roof.

Chasing Simon had started as a game. He was everything Gabriel wasn't, and she'd grown restless. She wanted more—more danger, more of the unknown. More sex. Under all that charm, Simon had a temper. Gabriel was stable, sunny, and ridiculously optimistic. And she held such power over both of them. The art of manipulation—a talent she'd never wanted.

She flopped down on the rumpled bed, sinking into the old-fashioned eiderdown.

Once again, Gabriel had made everything easy—bundled up the mess of her like dirty laundry he would wash and press. No harsh words, no demands, nothing but acceptance and the offer of a place to rest. Was he acting out of duty as an upstanding vicar, or was he also haunted by the tiniest seed of doubt that had whispered through the years, *What if?*

He had led her upstairs to this tiny bedroom and suggested she take a nap. And she tried to do the sensible thing, huddling into the slightly damp bedding that smelled faintly musty. But then she needed to pee and couldn't remember where the bathroom was. Only three other doors off the landing and all closed. The first one revealed a pack rat's dumping ground, with an old exercise bike, a record player, piles of books and magazines, a broken chair, and a stack of sealed cardboard boxes. The bottom two were labeled: one said "Simon," the other "Marianne." He had packed up their memories and hidden them away. And she was bringing the ghoul out of storage. That was when she decided to run again. Gabriel was logic and reason tied up with a big red bow; the best of her and the worst of her. And she couldn't unpack all those feelings stored in a box. The knowledge of what she'd done to Gabriel was the one part of the past she didn't want back. She had all but flayed him alive.

Around seven p.m. he'd knocked quietly to announce supper: bangers and mash. When she didn't answer, he returned five minutes later and said, "There's a plate of food and a glass of water outside your door." She drank the water, left the food, and snuck out to brush her teeth. The rest of the evening she plotted her escape and listened for Gabriel. He came up to bed after midnight and was moving around the hall until at least two a.m. Insomnia had always been the only glitch in his otherwise perfectly tempered personality.

She tiptoed to her bedroom door and leaned against it. Finally he was quiet. Going back to the window, she tugged open the faded floral curtains. Hand-me-downs from Gabriel's mother, no doubt. Or white elephants from the church bazaar. Nothing belonged or complemented in his long, narrow house. The walls were mostly bare but for a few framed prints of tormented angels.

She pried up the stiff latches on the window and filled her lungs with night air. What time did it get light: four a.m.? She needed to get to the cemetery before sunrise. Before the village woke up. Before anyone could recognize her and say, "Look, it's that batshit insane girl who killed her boyfriend and got buck naked in the churchyard." Did they use *batshit* in England? Probably not. *Quite mad* would likely be the phrase. And not *quite mad* in a romantic Ophelia way. Paranoid, delusional, dangerous. That kind of mad.

Gabriel had offered to drive her over to the cemetery after breakfast, but she planned to be gone before then. She'd head north, hitchhike to Scotland. She and Simon had once planned a trip to Glencoe, drawn to the idea of camping on the site of a historic massacre.

Marianne glanced down at the clothes she'd been wearing for two days. Showering took energy she needed to conserve for flight. Except first she had to pee again. Damn the weak bladder, the curse that leveled the playing field between all middle-aged women: sane and insane.

She creaked the door open and paused while her eyes adjusted to the gloom. Clearly Gabriel didn't believe in night-lights. Inching forward her foot found something large, warm, and alive. Instinctively, her hand stifled a scream.

Gabriel.

What the hell was he doing curled up asleep outside her door? She backed into the wall and squinted hard. He was oddly cocoonlike in a sleeping bag. Surely it was not *their* sleeping bag, the one they had used for ghost hunting? Sliding down the wall, she hugged her knees to her chest. Nothing rumbled his breathing; nothing clouded his sleep.

What do you dream of, Gabriel? Rainbows and puppies? She smiled. *Sherbet lemons?*

Simon had called Gabriel her loyal Labrador because whatever lunacy she concocted, Gabriel followed obediently. And when things went wrong, he took the blame. And here he was—guarding her as if she'd never left his life, as if she hadn't broken his heart. As if he hadn't relegated her to a cardboard box.

Shivering, she rested her cheek on her knees and listened to Gabriel breathe. Unlike Darius, he didn't snore. Darius did nothing quietly; he was not someone you could ignore. When he arrived on the local music scene pretending to be a nobody, his subterfuge didn't last a week. Wild and sexy, almost as impetuous as she was, he wasn't wired to blend in. She rubbed her chest, but it didn't ease the longing.

I love you, Darius. Please forgive me.

A lifetime of hurting others may have been her greatest achievement to date. She'd run from Gabriel before reaching adulthood; she'd run from two husbands; she'd run from Darius and Jade. She was still running from herself. And now that she was back at the beginning, it was time to stop. For decades she said, "Drug me. Let me forget who I am," and allowed meds to become her crutch. Before that, alcohol and broken memories did the job. Not anymore. It was time to face herself here, where it had all begun, with the person who understood her darkness better than anyone.

All those discussions she and Gabriel used to have about life and death had only one point of intersection: they both believed hell existed within the hearts of men and women. And they'd been right, because she was the proof. And if hell was a person, not a place, maybe the same was true of home.

Marianne raised her head and stared into blackness. Forgiveness—from God, from herself, from her ghosts—had never been part of the equation, but she had been searching for something in the last few months. A reason to keep living for Darius and Jade. And here was her answer, asleep outside her door.

She flopped forward onto all fours, clarity lighting up her brain with halogen spotlights. She was making a stand here, in Newton Rushford; she was turning inward to stare down the monster. Face the devil within. And Gabriel's protection would be the string that would lead her back out of the maze. No matter what he saw, even if she transformed into her full fiend persona, he would keep her safe, as she had done for all those kids with Girls In Motion.

Girls In Motion started as a summer band camp. But she wanted to expand, to keep the music going. Which led to a physical space for girls to hang out year-round and a recording studio so campers could take their songs with them when they left. Her summer ended long ago, but Gabriel was the keeper of the memories she needed back. And he was going to be her savior one last time. Had she suspected, the moment she'd opened the fireproof box to find her passports, that Gabriel could be the key?

Crawling back into the bedroom, she retrieved her pills from her bag. Then she stepped around Gabriel, walked into the bathroom, and slid the bolt across the door.

Hell, here I come in all my unmedicated glory.

She lifted the toilet seat, dumped her pills, and flushed. As they swirled around the toilet bowl and disappeared, she started humming Leonard Cohen's "Hallelujah."

SIX

JADE

In the larger of the two tracking rooms, Sasha perched on the drum throne talking with her hands. The long, skinny legs that had once earned her a decent living as a pole dancer were crossed demurely. Even the sociopathic singer, whose body was splashed across the current issue of *Vanity Fair*, was transfixed. The studio was full of ridiculously famous people, and Sasha was impressing the heck out of them.

Hell yeah.

The interns scurried around collecting trashed sushi containers from the Japanese restaurant and dumping beer bottles in the recycling crate. Occasionally they exchanged smug looks that said, *Can you believe we're in the same breathing space as Media Rage?* Fame was overrated—seen one musician's meltdown, you'd seen them all—but these guys were in a different league for Nightjar. Although no one would have figured that out from watching Darius. He might have worked with music deities, but couldn't he at least feign interest? Instead he stood slightly apart from the group, scowling at the row of guitars hanging on the wall.

"Don't you agree, Darius?" Sasha said.

Darius didn't react.

"Boss!" Jade cleared her throat loudly, and five famous faces turned from staring at Darius to staring at her. Her heartbeat bounced all over the place. Okay, so she was kinda starstruck. "A word?"

Darius shot forward and pulled her into the narrow corridor lined with Nightjar's history: floor-to-ceiling shelves of CDs, hard drives, and old two-inch reels. The corridor, lit only with recessed lights, even smelled like the past. Or that could have been lingering mold from the last time the studio had flooded.

Jade glanced around Darius to make sure no one was listening. "I talked with Dr. White."

"You tracked him down in the remotest corner of Appalachia?"

"His receptionist wasn't joking about him being out of cell range. And you were right—he won't discuss her treatment, but Marianne's talked enough about me over the years that he was willing to listen. He said if she contacts either one of us, we need to establish she's taking her meds and encourage her to seek treatment on an outpatient basis." She withheld the final piece of advice—that if the situation worsened, she or Darius should fly to England and offer support on the ground. Darius would translate *if* into *must do this right now*, which would amount to tossing a dozen matches into a tanker of gasoline.

"That's it?"

"He did ask for her cell phone number."

"Oh, that makes me feel so much better." Darius narrowed his eyes.

"In other news, I've found Gabriel." Jade held up a scrap of paper. Darius tried to snatch it from her, but she hid it behind her back. "I'll go call him from the house." The lack of a landline in the studio had never annoyed her before today.

"No. Use my cell."

"Why? So you can call later and interrogate him about their past relationship?"

"No," Darius said slowly. "Because I want you to call him right now and then interrupt me again. And since the call's going to be expensive, I don't want you using your cell."

"Fine, where's your phone?"

"In the control room."

"Seriously, boss?" Did he think none of the studio rules applied to him?

He gave her a wolfish grin. "Thank you, doll. I owe you big-time. Come get me the moment you hang up."

Then he returned to tracking room A. Jade walked in the opposite direction, back through the tiny office with all the hard drives of projects she was working on and into the control room. She closed the door, sealing herself in a space designed to tame and deaden sound. The control room was more than command central: it was the chamber of a heart. With the wooden diffusers on the wall and ten inches of insulation above the cloud—the ceiling panel angled low over the console—it pumped silence.

The studio had no exterior windows, but in here two huge sections of plate glass looked into the tracking rooms. On the other side of the larger pane, the singer talked to Darius while the bassist watched Sasha with greedy eyes. No surprise there. For a stick-thin white girl Sasha was one hot chick, but the last thing they needed this weekend was a megastar who couldn't keep it in his pants. Darius glared at the bassist. Good, he'd picked up the vibe.

The control room glowed with warm light from the old standing lamp, her lava lamps, and the red holiday lights looped over invisible command hooks. Smiling at her collection of rock-and-roll bobble heads, Jade bobbed Iggy Pop. Then she flopped onto the leather sofa Marianne had found on Craigslist—Nightjar was filled with rescued junk or rediscovered treasures, depending on your outlook—and picked up Darius's phone. Many guys had drifted through Marianne's life pre-Darius. All of them totally off their rockers. Marianne wasn't drawn to straightforward guys, which meant that if Reverend Gabriel Bonham had been Marianne's first love, chances were high he was fucked up. Fucked up and religious? This could get super weird super quick. Across the Atlantic, a phone rang once.

"Newton Rushford rectory," a male voice whispered.

"Is this Gabriel? Like *the* Gabriel?" On her mixing desk little boxes of light framed her white computer screen. She should ask Marianne's dad for the scoop on this dude, assuming he could even remember his daughter's first sweetheart. *So many guys, so little time* had been Marianne's motto until she turned forty.

"The Gabriel? Interesting, I'd always assumed there were many Gabriels. Including the archangel." He yawned.

"I'm looking for *the* Gabriel who was Marianne Stokes's sidekick way back yonder."

"It's been a while since I've been given that label, but yes, this is he. Gabriel Bonham." His voice wavered as if he was walking, and then a door closed. "How can I help?"

"My name is Jade Jones, and I'm trying to track down Marianne." Jade curled her legs underneath her. The pain in her temple returned, pounding like the crack of a snare drum. "Is she with you?"

"Ah," he said, as if it all made sense. "I'm not at liberty to answer that."

Jade sat up and gave the leather cushion a victory punch. She'd found her. She'd found Marianne! "Are you Catholic?"

"No. I'm an Anglican priest."

Her mind flashed to the sleazebag on the streets with the clerical collar and the wandering right hand she'd broken. "No idea what that means. Do you have sanctuary, the confessional, all that jazz?"

"Not per se, but I do hear confessions and have a code of professional confidentiality that—"

"How's her mood?"

"Excuse me?"

"Her mood." Good grief. Did the guy need a PowerPoint? "Marianne's manic-depressive. A person with a mood disorder. Have you seen her take her meds? Has she slept, eaten? How does she seem to you? Agitated? Overly happy? Frantic? Depressed? Is she talking too fast?"

"I wondered when you'd pause for breath," Gabriel said.

"Is she with you and is she safe?"

"Do you know what time it is over here?"

"No clue."

"Hang on a sec, let me—" Birds tweeted down the phone line. "That's the dawn chorus. It's four in the morning."

"Yeah, whatever. Listen, let's cut the crap. I have a dilemma. I know she wants space, and I intend to respect that, but her psychiatrist won't speak to me or her husband, and I need proof that she's safe and on her meds. Do you have any idea what she's like unmedicated?"

"Can I ask what your relationship is with Marianne?"

Interesting. She hadn't expected a display of male protectiveness. He'd better not be planning on rekindling teenage love lost. And he'd better not be part of some secret plan. The moment they were off the phone, she was Dumpster diving through Marianne's email and Facebook messages. If these guys had stayed in contact, she wanted to know before Darius.

"Okay, buddy. Let me back up." Jade shifted position and the leather sofa creaked. "You want a credible detail so you know I'm not bullshitting you? You guys used to lift candy from the village store and smoke weed in the cemetery. How do I know this? When I was the same age, I was living on the streets and Marianne rescued me. She's my best friend, my mom, my employer, and the one person on the planet I would die for. So I need to know she's safe, and you will give me a straight answer or my next call will be to the cops over there in the English boonies."

"Boonies?"

"The boondocks."

"We appear to be speaking a different language." His voice was jovial, right up until he sighed. "Please don't call the police. I think that would be most unwise." He paused. "People have the right to disappear."

"Not if they're a danger to themselves."

"What evidence do you have that—"

"She's been in a good place for years, but there was this car accident in February and something shifted. I think she might be in a mixed state, which is the worst of the worst."

"I'm sorry to hear that."

"Marianne blames herself for the accident, although the other driver was at fault. And I'm worried she's up to something with her meds. And without treatment and properly used medication, bipolar is a fatal disease that comes with a one-in-five chance of suicide." She may have shouted that last bit. "Do you know her mania can morph into hallucinations and psychosis? Do you know she's been hospitalized five times, three of those for attempting suicide? Do you know how to handle that shit?"

"Yes, I believe I have both witnessed it firsthand and handled it. And I can assure you that I have saved her life once and would do so again if need be."

"That's not enough, Gabe."

"Gabriel."

"If I can't get confirmation that she's okay and taking her meds, her husband's going to be on the next flight to London, and that's not a situation you want to provoke. He's the jealous type and won't take kindly to someone pissing in his paddling pool."

"Delightful image. Thank you."

"Come on, Padre."

"I'm not a—"

"Give me something I can work with or I'll make your life hell."

"Are you threatening me?" His voice lightened. "Because if so, it seems only fair to warn you that I'm six two and a former rugby player."

"Yeah? I'm five feet, four inches of New York attitude with a black belt in tae kwon do. Rock-paper-scissors, I win. Plus I can hang up and call the cops."

"Truce," he said. "How about I inform you that my drinking buddy is a semiretired psychiatrist who lives two villages over?"

"You drink?"

"Isn't that rather a personal question?"

"Aren't you all saintly and abstaining?"

"Again. Isn't that rather a personal question?"

"Let's get back to your shrink."

"My friend."

"The shrink."

"Why does this conversation feel like a chess match?"

"Because I outmaneuvered you?"

Gabriel laughed. "I believe you did."

"Look. I don't care what went down between you guys in the past. And I'm not asking you to betray a confidence. I just need to know that someone I love is safe. That's all I'm asking. Please."

"If Marianne were here," Gabriel said, his voice slow and hushed, "I'd give you my word that I would ask my friend Hugh, *the shrink*, to come for a visit. But not tomorrow, since I have a wedding to officiate. I believe something could be arranged after services on Sunday. Possibly a picnic. I have neglected my afternoon walks of late."

Just when she was beginning to like the guy, he turned all pompous.

"Not till Sunday?"

"I do have a job, you know, quite a demanding one."

"Here's my final offer: you get your psychiatrist buddy to meet with her on Sunday, but you have to check in with me at this time tomorrow—"

"At four in the morning?"

"How about six p.m. my time. That's what over there?"

"Eleven at night."

"You're still up then?"

"Yes. I'm something of a night owl."

"Me too." She paused. "And if anything happens that you're not comfortable with before then, you call 911."

"911?"

"The emergency services. Men in white coats with big syringes of happy meds."

"Ah. 999."

"And I'll need evidence she's taking her meds. I'm going to give you some phone numbers. Grab a pen."

She recited her cell phone number and the landline at the house. "If you text me tomorrow and assure me that Marianne's okay, I'll prevent her husband from calling the cops or issuing a hit on you. You do know how to text, right?"

"I'm a clergyman, not a dinosaur. Yes, I know how to text. I even own an iPod Classic."

"Dude, you know you can't text on that, right?"

"Yes, I do. I was merely trying to make a point. But if I were to agree to this hypothetical situation"—Gabriel's tone turned serious—"you would need to assure me that her husband is not abusive."

As Jade watched through the glass, Darius turned his back on the band members and covered his eyes with his right hand. "What has she told you about him?"

Sasha tapped Darius on the shoulder. He swiped at both eyes and, turning with a fake smile, mouthed, *Headache.* Good recovery, but the poor bastard needed a hug so bad. If not for the megastars, she would hang up and go give him one. And take him out for espresso gelato. How could Marianne treat him this way?

"Correct me if I'm wrong," Gabriel said, "but a few seconds ago you mentioned a hired assassin. That leads me to believe this man might be dangerous."

"He's a pussycat who likes to flash his claws. Darius can spend an entire afternoon trying to capture a skink trapped inside the house so he can release it back into the wild without physical or psychological trauma."

"What's a skink?"

"A small lizard. They shoot in from the deck when one of the girls leaves the door open."

"Girls?"

"In addition to the recording studio, Marianne runs a nonprofit group to empower teen girls through music. Well, I do, these days. Some of the girls end up working in the studio. The high-risk ones end up sleeping at the house. Look." Jade stared into a speaker cone. "Despite the messed-up brain chemistry, Marianne's found some kind of equilibrium with her illness, especially in the last ten years. But this thing with the car accident—I've never seen her like this. You should know she sustained a head injury, which means we've entered the vast unknown. And Darius is about to snap. Worry for Marianne is ripping him in two, and I'm hoping that's part of the reason she left—to protect us. I'm also hoping she'll come back, because God only knows what'll happen to Darius if she doesn't."

"And you—what will happen to you?"

"That's not a place I can go." One of her red lightbulbs had blown. The fat, old-fashioned Christmas bulbs that were getting harder to find. "There's something else you should know. A piece of information that stays between us, whether you do confessionals or not. She made Darius a promise, when they got married, that she wouldn't try to kill herself again. I think she might be struggling to keep that promise."

"You said part of the reason she left. What do you think the other part is?"

"Something to do with a teen stud called Simon. Do you know him?"

"He was my brother. He died." Gabriel's breathing changed. "The first time she tried to kill herself, it was on his grave. I'm the one who found her."

"Wait. You two had a thing and then she moved on to your brother? Man, that's harsh."

"Thank you for explaining that to me."

"Out of curiosity, how did he die?'

"Car crash. He was driving, but Marianne and I were in the car."

"That's it. That's the link. Omi-fucking-god. That's it!"

He coughed.

"Sorry. Didn't mean to swear, Father." She paused. "One last thing. Marianne left Darius a letter, asking for space to figure out whatever it is she needs to figure out. If she knows we're talking, she could run again—and I don't want to think about what could happen if she's in crisis and alone. Clearly she trusts you. You need to keep that trust, and we need to pull together to watch over her. Even if that means acting in secret."

"I can't lie, Jade."

"Is it lying if you omit to tell the truth? Isn't that what you've been doing with me for the last fifteen minutes?"

"She's safe," he said.

"Thank you." She rested her head on the back of the sofa. "Thank you."

"And you, are you alright?"

She sat up. "Me?"

"Yes, you. You sound weary."

"Killer headache." Unlike Darius's, her headache was real. "And a famous band just arrived for a week of recording. Marianne's timing's a little off."

"Or maybe she did this so you and Darius could focus on work and not on her?"

"Nice idea, but the bipolar part of her brain has poor impulse control. I think it has more to do with a broken finger. That can be tomorrow's bedtime story."

"If Marianne is here—"

"Which you can't confirm or deny, but we've established she's safe."

"Precisely. If she is here, how about I try to persuade her to stay while you deal with your band. When do they leave?"

"Next Friday."

"I could probably handle an imaginary houseguest till then."

"You would do that? Omigod, I could kiss you. Or not. Sorry. That was completely inappropriate." Jade stood up. "But she has to stay with you. And you must check in with me every day at the same time. You miss one message and the cops will be pounding on your door. And I—Oh shit! You moron!" Jade screamed through the double-plated, soundproof glass.

"Excuse me?" Gabriel said.

The bassist, eyes still on Sasha, had leaped up—straight into the boom arm over the drum kit. He appeared to be out cold, while the singer, frowning as attention in the room shifted to the body on the floor, raised her arm dramatically to her forehead and collapsed next to him.

"One of the band members knocked himself out on an overhead mic. Another appears to have fainted. Welcome to my life."

"Gracious. I hope no one needs a doctor. Call if I can be of assistance."

Was this dude for real?

"Marianne's family, *capisce?*" Jade said as she flew out of the control room door. "You screw this up and I'll have your balls for breakfast."

"Jade!" Darius screamed. "Get your ass in here."

"Go." Gabriel laughed. "I've got this."

Jade stopped. People never said that to her, and if they did, she didn't believe it, certainly not if it came from a man.

SEVEN
MARIANNE

Still wearing her clothes from the flight, Marianne woke to the scraping of a chair across a noncarpeted floor, a phone ringing, and a bizarre picture of an angel bent double in anguish. A celestial being with issues was an odd choice, especially for Gabriel, the guy who only knew how to proceed on a steady line of normalcy. She'd done everything a girl could do to provoke his anger, his jealousy, his passion, and gotten nowhere.

Do you have a breaking point, Gabriel?

Brr, the room was freezing. As she stretched over to relatch the window, her diamond engagement ring flashed. Unless he was a masochist, Gabriel couldn't still be in love with her, but how did you waltz back into someone's life after thirty years and not let in a gust of past emotions? Or was she, once again, measuring him by her standards? She might never have outgrown her mom's nickname of *my emotional mess,* but Gabriel had matured into a staid-looking adult.

Below, a pair of blue tits splashed in a concrete birdbath centered in the neatly trimmed rectangle of lawn. On one side a thin flower border rioted with color. Not the hot tones of the American South, but tall spikes of crimson hollyhocks, blues of Canterbury bells, and a mass of lavender. How her mom had loved that plant. Marianne crossed her hands over her chest. She would buy Jade the biggest basket of lavender when she got home: pass the love forward a generation.

Hopefully Darius and Jade would see that she'd made the right decision, that she'd run away to protect their future as a family. Her mom would've understood, and Gabriel would too, once she'd extracted an open-ended promise from him. Easy-peasy, provided she could find the boy thief inside the man.

Marianne grabbed a hair claw from her unpacked bag. After securing her hair in a haphazard french roll, she opened the bedroom door. No evidence of Gabriel or a sleeping bag. Maybe she'd imagined the whole thing. Wouldn't be the first time.

When she reached the bottom step, she smelled fresh coffee. Gabriel's voice called through the open kitchen door. "Morning."

She walked in, rubbing her arms. Gabriel was sitting at the kitchen table in a T-shirt and sweatpants, one leg resting loosely across his knee, his feet bare. He rustled the *Church Times* and peered over his turquoise reading glasses. They amplified the blue of his eyes, like a visual version of Fender reverb—the effect Darius loved to use to expand bass tracks.

"Cold?" Gabriel said, as if they had breakfast together every morning.

"This"—Marianne pointed at her mouth and mimicked teeth chattering—"is a big clue."

"Right. I'll find you a sweater." He pushed back his chair and nodded at the half-full french press on the kitchen table. "The coffee's fresh. Or I have tea if you'd rather." He threw out an easy smile. "Back in a jiffy."

The table was set for two with a small cut-glass vase of lavender in the middle. She leaned forward to inhale before looking around.

Everything was laid out by the cooktop with military precision: plates, frying pan, wooden spoon, whisk, a Pyrex dish lined with paper towels, eggs, and a small stack of Tupperware. A loaf of whole wheat bread sat on the wooden breadboard, already sliced by the large steel knife. She touched the scars on her left wrist and focused on the cluster of jars: two different jams, marmalade, and Marmite. Gabriel wasn't taking chances with her choice of condiments.

He returned with a sweater that matched his eyes. "Cashmere, I believe. A Christmas present from Mum and a casualty of my lack of expertise with the washing. Mrs. Tandy, you might remember her—?" Marianne shook her head. "These days she's my cleaner. Anyway, she told me off for putting it in the dryer, but what do I want with an expensive sweater that needs a gentle spin cycle and air-dry?"

"Thank you." Marianne pulled it on. "I love cashmere."

"Consider it yours. I was going to take it to the charity shop, but it never moved out of my pile of good intentions. Scrambled eggs and bacon before we head to the cemetery?"

Marianne forced back a scream of *Let's go now.* "Sure."

Traffic hummed in the distance, and down the lane a car backfired.

"I don't remember the constant buzz of traffic."

"Heavier than it used to be. The A428 has been de-trunked, but it makes no difference. Satnavs still send lorries through when the M1's closed. We've given up hope of a bypass."

"Satnavs?" And what the hell did de-trunked mean?

"A navigation device that still recognizes the road as a major one, even though it's been downgraded to a common or garden A-road. I think you call it a GPS?" Gabriel moved about the kitchen in a slow dance. One by one he cracked eggs into a white porcelain bowl and dropped the shells into a tin container labeled "Compost." Would he whistle while he worked?

"I thought a full English breakfast might be just the ticket. I've warmed up a few sausages from last night, too." He removed a plate from the microwave and put it on the table. "Chipolatas from the butcher's. Your mother used to love them, if memory serves. How is she?"

"She died of breast cancer ten years ago. I miss her every day." And that was the most honest statement she'd made in a long time.

"I'm sorry to hear that. I remember her Victoria sponge fondly. And her treacle tarts."

"I see your sweet tooth hasn't changed." She paused. "Len's still in the village?"

"Indeed. Although I suspect we may lose the butcher's shop when he retires. His son has no interest in keeping the family business going."

"That's a shame." What would Simon have made of this perfectly normal conversation? "Shouldn't you be out doing something meaning-ful like saving souls?" Might be an idea to establish how much time she had to talk him into what Baldrick on *Blackadder*, once her favorite TV show, would have called a cunning plan.

"I am doing something meaningful. Or I was." He pointed at the pile of *Church Times*. "Catching up on my reading." He separated out slices of bacon, laying them carefully on the paper towels, not slapping them down as she would have done.

"What about tending your flock?" she said.

He hit the timer on the microwave. "I need to lock myself away after breakfast for morning prayer, and then I have a wedding at two, but other than that, I'm at your disposal this weekend. I do have a meeting tomorrow night for the organ fund-raiser, but Donald, a retired non-stipendiary priest, has already agreed to cover tomorrow's service. Fortunately only the one, but since it's the monthly benefice service, I prefer not to hand it over to one of my lay band. I called earlier and explained a long-lost family member had turned up unexpectedly, and Donald was more than happy to oblige. His wife's visiting her family and I suspect he's bored silly. Eggs slightly runny?"

Marianne nodded, her mind caught on one thought: *After everything I've done to him, I'm family?*

"Did you sleep well?" He kept his back to her.

"Few hours. Sleep's not my thing." Once upon a time he'd known that. "And how about you? Find the floor comfy?"

"Ah." He turned with a grin. All dimples and coyness, as he'd been when he was the Artful Dodger. "You noticed."

"Hard not to. I nearly broke my neck tripping over you in the middle of the night. Gabriel, you don't need to guard my door."

The microwave bleeped while Gabriel put a plate of eggs in front of her. Lovely peppery eggs. She pulled the silver napkin ring off her blue linen napkin and twirled it around and around on the pine table.

"I like the lavender," she said.

"I picked it half an hour ago."

"You've been busy." Something else that hadn't changed. His energy levels never matched hers, but Gabriel hadn't been one to sit still.

The toaster popped, and he slotted toast into the silver toast rack in front of her. Then he put four strips of bacon on her plate, one by one, using a pair of tongs. A slow memory returned of what those hands used to do. She shook it away.

"And your father? How's he doing?" Gabriel said.

"In a retirement home with a caregiver. Some days I think he's fading, others I think he'll live to be a hundred. He still has a sharp mind, but he falls easily. I wanted him to come and live with us, but I would never have been able to cope, and then my husband"—easier to not speak his name—"would have tried to mother-hen both of us and failed. Jade and I take Dad to Sunday brunch every week. Eating out with him isn't a barrel of fun, but he loves his shrimp and grits. Jade laughs it off when he spits food or splatters his meal down his shirt; I want to cry. Tough watching a human body fail. I put them through hell, you know, my parents."

He appeared to be watching her plate, so she speared a sausage, cut a small bite-sized piece, and made appreciative noises. He smiled.

Marianne swallowed. "But they always stood by me." *As I'm hoping you will.*

Gabriel nodded. "Good people, your parents. I had the utmost respect for your father."

Food had tasted of nothing for so long. Rich and slightly spicy, the sausage was full of childhood memories—a happy time in her life despite the mood swings that caught everyone, including her, by surprise.

"Will someone check on your father while you're here?"

Such a Gabriel comment. "Are you going to insist I call home like E.T.?"

"It's not my place to tell you what to do, but I would like to extend an open invitation. Stay as long as you need."

"Thank you." Her objective, all shiny and new, simmered away. How long before the meds were flushed from her system? "That would be great." Another bite of sausage. "And yes, Jade will check on Dad. She's constantly plugging in the holes I create."

"She sounds special, this Jade. Who is she?"

"My baby girl. Well, she's about to turn thirty, so I guess I need a new nickname. She was living on the streets when I took her in, and now she's my chief sound engineer, but that doesn't begin to describe our relationship. Dad introduces her as his granddaughter—even paid for her college. She's my almost-daughter."

Gabriel grinned as if releasing something that had been causing him stress.

"When did you learn to cook?"

"At uni," Gabriel said. "You studied music?"

"Majored in music performance at Carolina. But it took a while. Kept dropping out for vacays in the psych ward."

"I'm sorry."

"Yeah, I guess we both are. And your parents?" His dad, the military guy, had been eccentric and funny; his mom had been distant. Had either of them forgiven her?

"On the cusp of a major life change, I suspect. I found them a small house outside Milton Keynes a few years back, new with all mod cons. Mum fakes it, but they can't really cope."

"Medical problems?"

"Dad, yes. Truthfully Mum's gone a bit barmy."

"Alzheimer's?"

"No, but some form of dementia. It's almost as if she's had a personality transplant. And not for the better."

"Have you considered calling in a geriatric psychologist?"

"Such things exist?"

"Welcome to the twenty-first century. Psychology has evolved since Freud's day."

He smiled his sweet smile again. Why had life—and death—not battered that out of him?

"Is there anything I should know about your illness?" He hesitated. "Stuff I can do to help while you're here? I'd like to be prepared if my houseguest is going to sharpen the kitchen knives at the stroke of midnight."

She noticed he'd hidden the bread knife in the sink before joining her with his loaded plate of eggs and bacon.

"I'm unpredictable, irrational, impulsive, and sometimes a tad psychotic." Might as well throw in that last point and see if he reached for his holy water.

"Right," he said, passing the test without knowing. "And how's your creative life? Do you still sing? Pen those beautiful poems?"

"No. The studio takes up all my energy and focus. I learned a long time ago I have to manage my time carefully, otherwise I get a bit too enthusiastic. I took up knitting, though."

"We have a popular yarn shop ten minutes away. Or so Mrs. Tandy tells me."

"I don't have the focus right now. Plus my doc upped the lithium and it makes my hand shake." She held out her hand, but it barely moved. Interesting. Soon the sharp edges would return.

"Gabriel. If I asked you to follow me into hell, would you?"

"Is this hypothetical?" he said.

"That depends on your answer."

He stared hard, his pale eyes unblinking, and she tried to remember why she'd strayed to Simon.

"I'll do whatever you ask," he said, "provided it's legal and doesn't include petty thievery. But I need a promise in return."

EIGHT

GABRIEL

Gabriel had questions, and despite a troubled night of tossing through different scenarios, he doubted Marianne could provide trustworthy answers. Embellishment had always hung from her like brightly colored costume jewelry.

"Would you mind if we said grace first?" It seemed utterly pointless, given that she'd eaten at least a bird's portion of her meal, but the talk of visiting hell with a suicide survivor had unnerved him. He tried to focus on the word *survivor*.

Slowly, she raised her pale face and nodded.

When he'd finished, he said, "Bon appétit," and turned his attention to his food. Chewing gave him time to think.

Marianne cut another small piece of sausage, then laid down her knife and transferred the fork to her right hand. He should have expected her to eat American style, but still, it struck him as alien. She never used to have an American accent, either. A jarring example of the different paths their lives had taken. And yet he had welcomed her back into his life, and promised what?

She scooped up a small portion of egg. Good, that was two mouthfuls in addition to several small bites of sausage. He would drop a hint to Mrs. Tandy about fattening up his houseguest. Hopefully this would lead to plenty of Mrs. Tandy's specialty: chocolate and caramel millionaires.

"How long ago was this second car crash?" he said.

"Coming up on six months."

"That's a hard anniversary."

"I suppose grief's a sideline for you."

He raised his eyebrows but said nothing.

"I can't do pleasantries right now. Sorry."

"Then don't. We can discuss the weather if you'd prefer." With Marianne there was always subtext. The trick, if he remembered correctly, was to keep her talking.

"And after that?"

"Entirely up to you." He cut into a sausage and kept eating. Testing him used to be her favorite game, and he'd fallen for it every time. "You're welcome to treat my house as a B and B while you find whatever you're looking for. Our paths have crossed again after thirty years. I have to believe there's a reason."

"You mean your boss"—she nodded heavenward—"has a grand plan?"

"Marianne. My brother cared deeply for you." Did she not remember Simon screaming *I love you*, using it as a weapon against him? "And throughout childhood and adolescence I . . . Our relationship mattered a great deal to me." *Maybe it still does.*

Marianne glanced up. "It mattered to me, too. More than you knew."

There was a knock at the door. Marianne's fork clattered to her plate.

"No cause for alarm." Gabriel patted his mouth with his blue napkin. "That'll be Colin, the local tramp. We have breakfast together when he's passing through on the weekends. Don't worry"—he stood and grabbed the meal-to-go he'd packed earlier, a ham sandwich and a bottle of ginger beer—"I won't invite him in."

Gabriel opened the front door and tried not to recoil from the smell. He kept one hand on the door and handed Colin the brown bag. "I'm afraid it's a bad time, my friend. I've got a bit of company. Same time next week?"

Colin nodded, mumbled his thanks, and shuffled off. Gabriel returned to the kitchen to find Marianne huddled in the corner.

"The rectory's a bit of a train station," Gabriel said. "But I'll do my best to keep people away while you're staying. And I won't push you to explain anything you're not comfortable with. I will only say that you're welcome to use the phone or computer if you need to contact your husband. Or Jade."

"No." Marianne shook her head repeatedly. "No. They can't know where I am."

He gestured for her to sit. Guiding Marianne through marital problems appeared to be another divine test. What if she'd been unfaithful to her husband? Monogamy hadn't been her strong suit. What if she set her sights on him again? Simple, he would resist. He was no longer a teenager guided by hormones . . . and he had his confessor, the mother superior, on speed dial.

"Let's enjoy our meal."

With another glance at the kitchen door, Marianne returned to picking at her food.

When she pushed her plate away, he decided to tiptoe back into the conversation. "Can we return to the one thing I need from you?" Would he fall at the first hurdle and have to text Jade before eleven p.m. to admit his failure?

"I don't do promises anymore," she said.

"Not even for old times' sake?"

"Is this going to be your standard knee-jerk response?"

"Possibly." A memory cartwheeled: singing "Auld Lang Syne" on the stroke of midnight, his arms around Marianne.

The phone rang.

"Don't you need to get that?" Marianne said.

He shook his head. "I've been getting prank calls this morning. Someone keeps dialing the rectory and hanging up." He brought his knife and fork together in the middle of his empty plate. "I need you to promise that you won't harm yourself. Because if anything happens on my watch, you'll doom me to eternal fire and brimstone."

"You don't believe in the devil."

She remembered? "I don't. But evil can prevail in man's inhumanity to man. And I believe we each have the power to create our own private hell"—he patted his heart—"in here. Which is where I'll be if you kill yourself." Was that too blunt?

"And heaven and the afterlife—do you still believe in them?"

Like Marianne, he preferred not to discuss certain things. "Modern scientific proof makes it hard to believe in life after death. I guess I would say my mind objects but my heart hopes."

"You always were far too hopeful."

"Is that possible?"

"Yes. Because false hope is as destructive as no hope."

He'd forgotten how he loved these cat-and-mouse conversations with Marianne: her pushing him to the edge of his beliefs, him pushing back.

"I see from your taste in artwork that you believe in angels," she said.

"I guess we all have a weakness."

"Even you, Gabriel?"

In the field opposite, a pheasant coughed.

"Especially me," he said quietly.

She stood. "What time can we go to the cemetery?"

"How about you shower first?" He stood too.

"That bad, huh? Do I smell?"

"I don't care if you wear the same clothes for a week, but a shower can work wonders for jet lag."

She turned to the sink. "I'm sorry, I seem to have forgotten my manners. Go do your prayer thing. Cleanup's on me."

"Absolutely not. I have a house rule that guests can't help." He followed her gaze to the bread knife.

"Let's drop the pretense, Gabriel." Her eyes stayed on the knife. "We both know I don't fit any of your neatly checked boxes."

And then she left the room. As her footsteps moved around above him, he piled the dishes in the sink—on top of the knife—and retreated to his study. Before anything else he would call Hugh and ask how to implement a suicide watch, because once again, Marianne had promised him nothing.

NINE
DARIUS

Darius tossed his phone to the floor and stared at the green goo sliding up and down the inside of Jade's lava lamp. Four in the morning, and he was acting worse than the Media Rage bass player who had faked his own concussion. Even a moron couldn't brain himself on a boom arm. And the moment Jade suggested calling 911, the bassist made a miraculous recovery. Still. On the off chance *SPIN*'s new darling wasn't faking it, Darius had typed his cell number into the guy's phone and told him to call if he felt a brain hemorrhage coming on.

The idiot had clearly been trying to cover up the fact that he was too much of a dumb fuck to watch where he was going. Something they might have in common. Dumb and Dumber. Calling Newton Rushford rectory and then hanging up—more than once—hardly smacked of sensible behavior. What it did smack of? Some really stupid shit he'd pulled in his first marriage. Yup, if the bassist was Dumb, Darius Montgomery was Dumber.

But whether the accident was real or not, it had raised an interesting point: the studio was overcrowded. Tomorrow he would give the interns the week off. And compensate them well for cleaning his house. The place he was currently avoiding.

He reached for Absalom, his Gibson, and lay back on the control room sofa. Eyes closed, he held his baby against his chest and strummed, letting his mind wander as the muscle memory in his fingers created music.

It seemed he was stuck in a repeating pattern of dysfunction, dating and marrying into crazy like a repeat offender who'd never heard of three strikes. Had he learned nothing from a string of failed relationships with batshit musicians and an ex-wife who was borderline? When Marianne told him she was manic-depressive, he actually smiled—yes, smiled—and thought, *Darlin', that's nothing. My ex has borderline personality disorder.*

A fucking loony tune, the ex had been as hypnotic offstage as on for their too-brief pre-tie-the-knot fling. He fell for her hook, line, and sinker, which proved how shallow he was back then. Famous, gorgeous, and experimental in the sack met his criteria in those days. Spoiled little rich kid who saw what he wanted and went for it.

His friends told him to leave her the first time she tried to kill him. (Admittedly, her attempt wasn't serious. Pretty pathetic, in fact.) But he stuck it out for another two years, and the only thing he learned during that time was how to dodge missiles. He didn't fight to get her help; he didn't attempt to understand. Why? Because her highly publicized antics were good for his career. In and out of rehab and catfights, she was weekly-gossip-column fodder. And when she announced her affair, he packed up, walked out, and filed for divorce. His mother, who never quit anything—even marriage to an arrogant drunk—told him Montgomerys didn't get divorced. His sisters were smart enough to work around that by never getting married. And that had been his amended life plan until he'd met Marianne.

His whole life he'd been surrounded by successful people behaving like self-absorbed jerks. Marianne was more temperamental than half of them put together, and yet manic-depression never held her back. She had strong radar for bullshit and terrific feel for people's potential. And from the beginning, she glimpsed something in him no one else had: what she called his humanity. For the first time in his life, he liked who he was—the person he'd become with Marianne. And he didn't want to go under again. Be just another asshole. Be Dumber.

Hmm. That was an interesting riff.

He sat up and played it a few more times. Tried to expand it by moving to different chords. His hands slid up and down the guitar neck, experimenting. Then he started humming to get a sense of a vocal melody. He smiled. A song was creeping out. Right here in the dark of an empty recording studio.

He laid Absalom down carefully on the sofa and walked into tracking room A, flicking on light switches. Touching the drum kit was a really bad idea. It was mic'd, it was in tune, and it was ready for recording. But for the first time in forty-eight hours he was thinking about music, not just the state of his marriage.

Drums were the backbone, the foundation of the sound. You could record guitars anywhere, but not drums, and this room was one of the best he'd ever worked in. It had become his cathedral. Marianne knew exactly what she was doing when she bought this old building with a nice decay—*the time sound takes to diminish to silence, like a fading echo.*

Darius sat on the drum throne. Jade had been trying to convince him to back off and give up the stage to some guy from Marianne's past, but there was only one way to do that—if he started thinking about the sweet spot in the studio for recording drums. If he thought about the decay of the natural room reverb.

He disliked acoustically dead spaces—hermetically sealed rooms. As did Marianne. And now that her previous history had started reverberating through their lives, maybe he should accept that he couldn't eliminate those pulses of the past. They might even be necessary. After all, recording drums was about considering the individual sources that together created one cohesive sound. Could be it was even time to come clean with Marianne about the true horror of his first marriage: his mismarriage. Tell her what a crap husband he used to be. Tell her he'd resolved to get it right with her.

Darius picked up the sticks and started to bash the newly tuned heads on the drums. Over and over, harder and louder, till his vision blurred. Then he peeled off his T-shirt, used it to mop sweat from his face and chest, tossed it down and started playing again. Playing like he hadn't played since his punk days. Stomping, hitting harder and harder. His arms flailed, his hands ached, fresh blisters throbbed . . . And then the hi-hat split. And a drumstick splintered and took out one of the carefully placed mics. *Fuck.*

Or maybe not. The roaring anger had stilled. Vanished. Sitting here, on the drum throne, he would make a pledge to do what Marianne and Jade were asking of him. He would back off and try to be the husband Marianne needed him to be, and if he wasn't going to lose his mind in the process, he had to concentrate on making music. If not his own, then that of Media Rage. He would push them to create fire. But first he needed to replace a broken cymbal, sleep for a few hours, and then get the drum tech out to tune the kit he'd wrecked.

TEN

GABRIEL

The air smelled of endless midsummer nights. Pigeons cooed and sheep bleated; in the adjacent allotments, someone sneezed. A microlight drifted across the pale, cloudless sky; above, a jet stenciled a white vapor trail. If you were struggling to make sense of death, then surely you could find answers in this place of solitude surrounded by the melody of the English countryside. He was particularly partial to the large stone angel over the grave of Miss Ursula Finch, beloved sister and aunt, who had died in her sleep in 1915, aged eighty-two.

Gabriel closed his eyes and gave quick thanks for the beauty of the day and the small miracle the youth group had achieved. The grass had been clipped to perfection around the graves, and the foot-high weeds along the stone wall were trimmed to ground level. If you hadn't been here in thirty years, it was a good day to visit.

As they passed through the gate, a magpie hopped in front of them. Marianne stopped and leaned against Gabriel. "Which one?" she whispered.

Of course, she hadn't seen the grave since it was freshly dug and she lay on top of it to die. When he found her she had black Bedfordshire soil under her fingernails and in her mouth. Before losing consciousness, she had tried to claw her way underground to join Simon.

"I'll show you and then leave you be," he said, but waited to follow her lead.

"Is it the one covered in roses?" She began moving, pulling him with her.

"Indeed. Mum chose them, but they're not quite as low maintenance as she led me to believe. They fight back." He pointed at a latticework of scratches on his free arm. From beyond the grave, Simon could still inflict pain.

"Do you think about him often?" she said.

"No." It was an honest answer, because everything to do with Simon was colored by that final conversation, the violence of those last minutes of his life. Truthfully, it was easier to not remember.

"Time doesn't erase the missing," Marianne said.

Was she talking about Simon or her baby?

"But our scars become the map to our present." He supposed that was true. Would he be married to his job if Simon had survived? He'd certainly planned for this future, but he'd also planned for Marianne to live it with him.

"Is that what I am, a scar?" she said.

A jackdaw laughed.

Yes, a bloody big one. "You're someone who left my life, and now you're back. And I'm grateful for that."

"I'm surrounded by death. I bring death. Simon's was the first, but I—"

"Marianne"—he stopped by his brother's grave—"you bear no responsibility for my brother's death."

She kissed her fingers and then placed her palm flat against the headstone, which was pitted with age and stained with mold. Porous

Italian marble might not have been the best choice for the English climate. Following his mother's wishes, there was no mention of the baby. At the time, Gabriel hadn't understood, but now it made sense. A year after the ground had settled enough for the headstone to be put in place, the inquest was concluded and his mother had been fighting to control what remained of Simon's legacy.

"Why then, Gabriel? Why did they die if not because of me?"

"I don't know why you lost your baby, but Simon died because he was angry and he'd been drinking. Because he made terrible decisions. We all did that summer."

"You didn't."

"Yes, I did. But none of it matters anymore." Or so he had told himself for the last thirty years. "This is our history and that's all it is: history. Over and done with. And we did what we were supposed to do. We moved on."

"Predestination?"

"No, life. Life trumps tragedy, Marianne."

She sank onto her knees in the wet grass. The dew had been heavy that morning, but Marianne seemed not to notice. "Don't you ever tire of being the optimist?"

"I have to find the good in the bad." *Otherwise I too would lose my mind.*

"And what good came out of Simon's death? None. It destroyed our lives."

"No, it changed their direction. We were all running too fast that July. You could feel the tension between us, gathering like a thunderstorm. But two of us survived."

"It wasn't my choice to survive." She looked up at him. "It was you, wasn't it, who saved me?"

He nodded. "All those skills I learned in lifesaving classes. You don't remember?"

"Sorry, no. Electroconvulsive therapy gave me little-old-lady brain overnight. Although I do have a fuzzy memory of screaming curses at you when you came to visit me in the hospital."

"Your mother was quite shocked by your language." He smiled. "Marianne, let's not punish each other. I refuse to regret saving your life. If I had to relive that night, I would do nothing differently."

She picked up a fallen rose petal and turned it over in her hand. "I always admired your certainty, your belief that you were doing the right thing. Never a hint of regret."

She had no idea, nor would he enlighten her. The details of that time were no longer relevant. To her, to him, to anyone. Besides, she hadn't come back for him; she'd come back for everything that was buried in the cemetery.

"I'll wait by the gate. Take as long as you need." He started walking away.

Hooves clattered on the road. Two girls on chestnut ponies passed the cemetery, falling and rising to an elegant trot. And thunderflies, those tiny pests that could drive a man to the brink, settled on his arms and began crawling over his skin.

"Gabriel?"

"Yes?" He stopped, and started scratching.

"Thank you. For taking me in; for not making this difficult."

He nodded. But as he positioned himself across from the entrance to the cemetery, the past he had just dismissed as irrelevant clobbered him in the gut. Marianne's mind might have erased chunks of their history, but he remembered every detail with sickening clarity, including Marianne lying unconscious and bleeding on Simon's grave. If Marianne had died that night, there would have been no way forward for him. He could not have survived. And he would have had no one to blame but himself, because his anger, which had spread around that car like anthrax, had been the catalyst for Simon's death. Marianne was not responsible for the crash—he was.

ELEVEN
MARIANNE

Sunday, and they had a scheduled activity! Not a nothing day like yesterday. *Yay!*

They were going on a picnic with cucumber sandwiches, fondant fancies—would Gabriel remember she liked the pink ones?—and an old tartan blanket. Add a thermos of orange squash and they could have been characters in an Enid Blyton novel. And it was warm, like a Carolina spring day.

Sun streamed through the frosted glass on either side of the front door. Perfect, everything was perfect. Except Gabriel was taking way too long to get his cute ass downstairs. She swung back and forth, one hand on each banister. For better or worse, she'd rewoven their lives together; and in forty-eight hours they'd reverted to childhood roles—him lagging behind, her urging him to move faster.

"Gabriel," she whined. "Aren't you ready yet?"

"I most certainly am." He appeared behind her. How had he gotten downstairs without her noticing? She grinned. Perpetually barefoot, he moved around the rectory like a ghost. He was carrying hiking boots, and in his jeans and T-shirt, with a sweatshirt knotted around his waist, he could have been a grad student.

"Excellent, I see the wellies fit," he said.

After breakfast he'd foraged in his garden shed to find the Wellington boots of some former girlfriend. Bizarre to think of Gabriel with a dating life. Was there a current girlfriend skulking around? He'd told her he was single, had been for years, but she'd caught him texting late the night before with that smile. Some things about Gabriel were impossible to forget.

She held up a leg. "Yup, but they were full of cobwebs. I'm super glad you don't have black widows in Bedfordshire. You still not a spider fan?"

"I call Phyllis next door when I find one in the bathtub." Gabriel gave a mock shiver.

Yup. They'd done the time warp. "So are we *finally* ready?"

"Not quite," he said.

The doorbell rang, which it did a lot. A constant stream of people dropped by to see Gabriel, and she'd become adept at hiding in the kitchen. Still, news had circulated that the vicar was shacked up with a wanton woman, or so Gabriel had told her after he'd donned his dog collar to walk down to the village shop earlier that day. Apparently Sunday late morning was prime time for gossip gathering. Although how anyone knew she was in the rectory was a mystery, since she hadn't left the house. She started to retreat, but he touched her arm.

"Stay." He edged around her in the narrow hall. "I'd like you to meet an old friend. He's joining us, but he's discreet."

"I don't care if he's royalty," Marianne said. "I'm not up to meeting new people. I'm the crazy woman who ran away on a jet plane, remember?"

"Hugh's different. You'll like him. And I'm afraid I need his advice on a delicate matter."

Gabriel opened the door wide and greeted a short man whose paunch was restrained by a too-small *Doctor Who* T-shirt and scarlet suspenders. The stranger looked part hobbit, part Albert Einstein, part stunted Santa. Plus he was wearing bifocals with the line. Hadn't progressive lenses made those things obsolete?

"Lovely day for a walk. Hope you don't mind but I brought Sybil. The old girl needs some exercise, and I thought she could rough up a few squirrels." Hugh gestured to a midsized mutt sniffing around the postage-stamp-sized square of grass.

Gabriel sat on the doorstep and started lacing his boots. "Hugh, this is my old partner in crime, Marianne. She taught me to steal sweets. Marianne, Hugh."

Sybil barked at a magpie, and Marianne flinched. It wasn't too late to change her mind and stay behind. Shame, she'd been looking forward to the fondant fancies.

"Not a dog lover, my dear?" Hugh said.

She couldn't help but smile. With his bulbous eyes and crazy hair, he could have been someone she'd met on a locked psych ward. "Not especially."

"Sybil's perfectly harmless. Deaf as a post and daft as a duck." Leaning around Gabriel, Hugh swung his right arm in a wide arc and then zoomed in for an enthusiastic handshake. He clasped both hands around hers and held tight.

"Bill Collins's dog chased us when we were children. We had to leap over a fence." Gabriel pulled up his pant leg to reveal the faded scar. "But not before the blasted thing bit me."

Because you pushed me over the fence, insisting I go first. Dear Gabriel. With him at her back, all things were possible.

"Did you really teach this honorable gentleman to steal sweets?" Hugh said.

"Not any old sweets," she said. "Sherbet lemons."

"And long before Dumbledore made them trendy." Hugh handed Gabriel a box of cookies. "Milk chocolate digestives, can't picnic without them. Who's got the basket?"

"More of a rucksack, I'm afraid." Gabriel squeezed past her to grab a backpack from the hall table.

"Standards *have* dropped. The thermos in there, too? None of that builders' tea, I trust."

Gabriel shut the door but didn't lock it. "Lady Grey."

"Good man." Hugh reached up to pat Gabriel's shoulder.

They walked toward the public bridle path at the end of Nell's Lane, and Sybil lollopped ahead, nose to the ground, tail gyrating. As they cut across the edge of the field called Dead Woman, the men strode out in companionable silence. Where did that name come from, Dead Woman? *Must remember to ask Gabriel.* Marianne skipped off to inspect a clump of wildflowers and skipped back. Clips of faded memories returned. Did they pass the stream on this route, and if so, might she see a kingfisher?

Hopping over squished rabbit remains—*gross*—she glanced up at Gabriel and Hugh. Such a mismatched pair. Not of the same generation, not of the same anything. Short and stumpy meets tall and strapping. She held back a giggle.

Gabriel probably had boatloads of friends. An entire network. Marianne slowed to a stroll. She had no one outside her studio family. What was Jade doing? Fingers and toes crossed she was impressing the band. Media Rage had been set to record in Nashville until Marianne made sure their manager, an old fan of Darius's, discovered his whereabouts. Media Rage was Jade's ticket to the future and a world beyond Nightjar. Marianne wiped her eyes but failed to erase the image of Jade's hand shoved under her armpit as she'd said quietly, "Ouch. That fucking hurt, Marianne."

Hugh turned. "Everything alright back there?"

"Allergies," she said.

"High pollen count this month. Bad time of the year for hay fever sufferers." Hugh beamed. "Are you enjoying your time in Newton Rushford? Such a special place. I expressed my doubts about Gabriel leaving the army to come back, but who can resist that magnificent church?"

"You guys met in the army?" Marianne said.

"Yes. I did some work with Gabriel's regiment."

How bizarre. Nothing about this guy said military. In the copse up ahead, a woodpecker tapped away. Gabriel asked Hugh something, and their chatter slipped back into a pattern. They seemed to be discussing a personality clash in the youth group. Marianne stopped listening and ran lyrics silently to keep her mind from Jade.

Skirting the unkempt hedgerow, they continued on an uneven, overgrown path. Marianne raised her arms to avoid brushing against stinging nettles, and watched her feet. Tripping and falling face down in rabbit droppings was not high on her agenda. The landscape, no longer pancake flat, rolled across the estate of Gabriel's patron, the modern-day lady of the manor. Apparently she had given her approval for them to enter private land. And yet Marianne had often dragged Gabriel across the estate to see the spring display of bluebells and primroses in the Old Wood. How odd that as an adult he sought permission for something they'd taken for granted as kids.

They clambered over the stile into the cool shade of the wood and followed the compacted dirt path. The air smelled of peat and fox, and a large bird swooped to their left.

"My, my," Hugh said. "I think that was a tawny owl. Wish I'd brought my binoculars."

The remnants of bluebell plants, their leaves yellowing and their flowers long gone, drooped on either side of the path. Birds sang to each other, and another woodpecker tapped.

"No bugs," Marianne said.

"I'm sorry, my dear?" Hugh turned.

"At this time of the year in the North Carolina forest you can't escape the stereo of frogs, crickets, katydids, and cicadas. Here it's just birdsong. I mean, we have birds. Tons. The hawks are my favorite. Oh and the hummingbirds! I love my little hummers."

"Feeling homesick?" Hugh beamed.

"No," she lied, and continued walking past gnarled trees, her head down.

They crested a gentle slope, and a small clearing opened up ahead, bathed in sunlight. The perfect setting for fairy circles. Or satanic rituals under a full moon.

"Right," Gabriel said, and pulled off his backpack. "Anyone for tea?"

Hugh shook out the tartan rug and gestured for Marianne to sit.

"Not joining me?" she said.

"Gummy knee, my dear. If I get down, the two of you will have to haul me back up." He leaned against a twisted tree trunk. Sybil plopped down next to him, her chin resting on his boot. "Gabriel mentioned you work in the music industry?"

"My husband and I own a recording studio."

"Record anyone big?"

"All the time," she said.

"Got it. Discretion and all that. Most admirable."

Sybil watched everything coming out of the backpack. When Gabriel reached in for the fondant fancies, she sat up, ears pricked. If Sybil weren't a dog, Marianne would have said, *Back off.* "What's your line of work?"

Hugh scratched behind Sybil's ears. "I'm a psychiatrist."

A setup, and she never saw it coming. Gabriel held out a plastic cup of milky tea, which she refused. Slowly, eyes fixed on him, she stood. "Wanted an opinion off the record, did you?"

"I'm semiretired and here as Gabriel's friend, nothing more," Hugh said.

"A friend who can give expert advice." Ignoring him, Marianne kept glaring at Gabriel. "I'm going back to the house."

"Please stay," Gabriel said.

"Why? So your friend can give you free advice about the resident freak? I don't appreciate being blindsided, Gabriel." She turned to Hugh. "No offense, I'm sure you're an A-plus psychiatrist, but I have a long history of being misdiagnosed, mistreated, and mismedicated. Not game for more of the same. I'm sure you understand."

"Only too well, my dear. Were you first diagnosed with schizophrenia or unipolar depression?"

Gabriel, the treacherous toad, had shared more than her work experience. "The former. And then followed, *ohhh*, a good twenty years when every word that came out of my mouth was second-guessed and reinterpreted. The last time I was admitted to residential treatment, I was told my career was a delusion." She turned back to Gabriel. "They took away my music, the only part of me that isn't defective."

At least he had the sense to stay quiet. Hugh, however, did not. That was the trouble with psychiatrists. They always assumed they knew best.

"I'm fully aware that my profession is not above reproach," Hugh boomed, his voice so much larger than his stature. "But my job doesn't define me any more than bipolar disorder defines you. I can only repeat that I'm off duty and not here to spy on you."

"I didn't accuse you of spying. Don't put words into my mouth, I'm not paranoid." *Not yet.* "I thought I could trust you, Gabriel. I thought you weren't going to box me in. That was some impressive crap you dropped on me."

Gabriel held her gaze with icy blue eyes that betrayed nothing: no drop of remorse, no twitch of anger. "I asked Hugh to join us because I needed help figuring out a possible problem with one of the girls in the youth group."

"And if he happens to observe the deranged woman at the same time, that's okay?"

"Quite frankly, yes."

"Oh." She sat back down and picked at the edge of the blanket. Honesty was the last thing she'd expected. In recent months she'd grown used to being discussed behind closed doors.

Something rustled through the ferns in the shade behind them, and Sybil bounded off to investigate, heading in the wrong direction.

"I asked you to promise me that you wouldn't hurt yourself," Gabriel said. "You declined. Hugh's my backup." He attempted once more to give her a cup of tea. This time she accepted. "You know how to manage your illness; I don't. I was hoping Hugh could advise me on my behavior, not yours, so I don't inadvertently makes things worse."

"Mood disorders are fascinating: schizophrenia, schizoaffective disorder, cyclothymia, bipolar I, and bipolar II," Hugh said, between slurps of tea.

"Not if you have one, I can assure you."

"Are you bipolar I or II?"

"You're the expert. What do you think?" Marianne tightened her grip on her plastic cup.

"It's not for me to guess, my dear. Are you taking your meds?"

"Yes." She looked him straight in the eye.

"Are you sleeping?"

"Not much. But I'm not used to these long days of never-ending light."

"Are you in touch with your psychiatrist?"

"Affirmative."

Gabriel glanced at her. That lie wasn't quite so believable. "I know what I'm doing, and no offense, but you know nothing about me or my version of the illness."

"Quite right." Hugh chomped on a chocolate digestive. "Pick one hundred people with bipolar disorder and no two would have the same pattern. But might I make a suggestion?"

Seemed he was going to.

"Since you're a long way from home, it would be wise to have some protocol in place here. Would you be willing to register with Gabriel's GP?"

Gabriel gave a hesitant smile. "That's not a bad idea. I'm still with the Pytle Surgery, Marianne. They might have your old medical records."

"I'll think about it. And for the record, *Doctor*, if you're concerned about suicidal ideation, no, I don't own a gun—oops, wrong country—and no, I'm not having suicidal thoughts. Although"—she narrowed her eyes at Gabriel—"I am thinking about throwing hot tea over an old friend."

"How about a fondant fancy?" Gabriel sat next to her. "Are the pink ones still your favorite?"

TWELVE
JADE

Jade sat on the shaded front steps of Nightjar. Despite the heat, a summer evening was in full swing in downtown Carrboro. A band played folksy music on the green space outside Weaver Street Market, and kids squealed. And now that she'd cleaned out and filled the feeders, the hummingbirds were back. Two red-throated males were fighting over the sugar water, their wings buzzing like souped-up bees, their chittering as soothing as wind chimes. Media Rage was still closeted in the studio with Darius and Sasha, and after only four days, this six p.m. ritual with the English vicar and the hummers was fast becoming an oasis of bliss. Not that she'd changed her opinions about birds or holy rollers, but those little feathered guys were so many levels of adorable, and what was not to love about a dude who was punctual to a fault, considerate as fuck, and funny?

If she was being flat-out honest, their text exchanges had become the highlight of her day and a much-needed escape from Darius, who had transformed into an aggressive perfectionist intent on making tracking room A explode with music day and night.

Her phone sounded the Sherwood Forest text alert she'd programmed in for Gabriel. Smiling, she read the screen.

```
Sorry I'm a little late. You're not
reporting me to the police, are you?
```

Jade glanced at her watch. He was two minutes behind schedule,
tops. `Let me consider that. How's our favorite
crazy person?`

The gray bubble came up. She loved this part, the anticipation of
what he'd say next.

```
I'd forgotten how she can suck all the
air out of a room.

Too much energy?

No, just intense, and I'm used to living
alone. It's hard to find quiet time for
my vicar-ish contemplation.

Contemplation?

Prayer.
```

That was a conversation killer. `I'll order you some
noise-canceling earplugs on Amazon UK.`

```
Gracious, no. Please don't!
```

```
Dude, I have the company credit card
number. Think of it as a thank-you gift
from your imaginary houseguest.
```

```
I'm serious. I'm not comfortable with
that.
```

Fine, she'd pay. She typed k and then went back and deleted it. He might text, but she doubted he used text shorthand. `OK. How's her mood?`

```
Lighter. Moments of happiness.
```

Was that because of Gabriel? And if so, was that regular happy or this-guy-still-floats-my-boat happy?

`Is she sleeping any better?` Trick question.

```
Can't say, but if that was an either/
or question, I'd pick no. I'm not the
world's best sleeper and she's often
moving around when I'm up.
```

No late-night romps in the vicar's bedroom, then. Hopefully Gabriel was fat and bald. He had to be Marianne's age, which meant a couple of years younger than Darius, but Darius had the good-hair genes and a decent body since he was a health freak. Despite his weakness for chocolate and espresso.

```
You still haven't reported back about
her meds.
```

I won't snoop, but she assured Hugh she
was taking them. I'm choosing to trust
her.

Not the smartest move, but she'd give him that one. Is she
eating?

Like a bird. But she did sing for me
tonight. Still has the voice of a
nightingale.

Or a nightjar? Jade chewed the corner of her lip. Marianne
had once told her the studio name was a random choice for a bird lover.
What else had she lied about?

It would appear you've rumbled me. Yes,
that was my nickname for her.

Darius must never know, OK? So, she's
still awake? Tell her it's lights-out
time.

Yes, ma'am.

Jade smiled. Marianne had never failed to choose good men. Even
husband number two was a stand-up guy. Insane, with an armful of
track marks, but he'd made Jade promise to take care of Marianne.
Would Darius, one day, demand the same promise?

We've never talked about music. Are you
musical?

Tone deaf. The choirmaster has forbidden me from singing hymns into the mic.

I meant real music, not churchy kumbaya.

Hymns aren't real music?

C'mon, Padre. Not in my world.

He didn't reply. *Way to end a cozy little chat, Jade.*

How about rock music? She typed quickly and hit "Send."

U2 is my sermon writing music. Does that improve my street cred? And I like Tears for Fears, the Style Council . . .

Great, he was trapped in the eighties with songs that reminded him of life circa Marianne. I'll work on a song list for you. Do you have an iTunes account?

Of course.

Praise the Lord. You do live in the modern age. Now that's a band for you, the Strokes.

The studio door opened behind her. "What's the news?" Darius said.

She turned. "Nothing much to report other than the fact she's messing with his prayer time."

"His prayer time?" Darius frowned.

"Man of God, remember? Let me sign off and I'll be right there."

```
Gotta get back to work. Nighty night,
Father.

Nighty night, Atheist.
```

She smiled but kept her head down so Darius couldn't see. "Gabriel's more than up for the challenge of Marianne-sitting."

"You think they're having sex?"

"Yuck, no. He's like Friar Tuck in that Robin Hood movie with Kevin Costner. Jolly and a bit spunky." She got up and stretched. "Hard as it is for you and me to believe, he takes all this religious shit seriously. Would probably poke out his eyes with one of Marianne's knitting needles before making the moves on a married woman."

Great, now she was making up more shit. Gabriel seemed decent enough, but if she were placing bets on whether one of them crossed the line while they were shacked up together, her money would be on Marianne. She was always the wild card. And Darius's glower suggested he'd taken her words for what they were: fake reassurance.

THIRTEEN
MARIANNE

Sleep? Who needed sleep? It was always light here. And God said, "Let there be light!" Light came with such energy, such creativity. Such power. Marianne spun around the kitchen and laughed. She could fly! Happiness beyond all reasoning. The world was hers for the taking! Girls In Motion needed to expand. Go global! Had the great minds of the world ever mapped out how productive you could be without sleep? No? Then she would!

Was this what happened to Gabriel when he found religion—the knowledge that he could move mountains? Had God seduced Gabriel the way mania had seduced her?

Hello, old friend, I've missed you.

Time to organize a fund-raiser for the organ. *Committee, schmittee. Blah, blah, blah.* Gabriel had far too many committee meetings and they led to nothing. Nothing! She could stage a gig, bring in rock stars. Snap her fingers and raise millions. Put Newton Rushford on the map.

She zipped around the kitchen. Only one cabinet left to clean out. Gabriel, Mr. Secondhand Guy, needed new everything.

She would cook tonight. A four-course meal! Now that the weather had warmed up, they ate dinner outside under Gabriel's pergola. She needed a pergola for her deck. Must hire a local carpenter to make one. Sometimes they talked, she and Gabriel, sometimes they didn't. They listened to music. It was always her iPod, not his, plugged into the dock. He let her choose the songs, but whenever she turned the music up, he turned it down. Party time! She would throw a party for the neighbors. Music. She needed music.

She swiped her iPod off the kitchen table and scrolled from one song to the next. Why could she not find the right music? She threw the iPod down and started fiddling with Gabriel's radio. Last night he'd asked her to sing. She didn't sing for an audience anymore, but she had for him. And she would for the organ fund-raiser. It would net millions. Millions! Her music would soar to the rafters. Inspire, move, transform.

Marianne ran through some warm-up vocal exercises. Then belted out the first verse of "Amazing Grace." Still had the best voice in the world!

What was Gabriel doing today? Like a watchdog, he never strayed far. Hugh, who wasn't so bad when he stopped acting the shrink, had popped in yesterday while Gabriel was out dealing with some dead guy's family. After Hugh left she watched the entire first season of *Downton Abbey* because Gabriel had a wedding couple over, followed by a meeting with his "lay band," the glorified group of helpers he talked about as if they were some kind of cult. Gabriel gave her the DVDs as a belated birthday present. He remembered her birthday was July 17. What a guy! Couldn't remember when his was. Around Thanksgiving? Enough to put him a year ahead all through school. In playgroup she used to tell everyone they were twins, until some snotty-nosed kid called her stupid, and Gabriel had defended her honor with a wooden sword.

She spread her arms wide. Julie-fucking-Andrews in *The Sound of Music*! Her mind whirred, spitting out ticker tape facts, plans, answers to the universe. Faster than a computer, faster than the speed of light.

What was she thinking, using meds to control this? She didn't need meds. Life was so clear, so sharp, so beautiful. She could see particles. Quanta!

She needed a new outfit for the fund-raiser. Something spectacular! Her first performance in twenty years. She danced into Gabriel's study, the one room in the house with personality: lots of lamps; a huge, black, messy desk—very contemporary, that was a shocker; a saggy black leather two-seater next to a small, round chrome table with a box of tissues—guess that was for the recently bereaved; rows and rows of books. Murder mysteries on the top shelf. Lots of memoirs about grief. And photos too. Him in graduation robes with his parents. A family photo of a beach vacay, the boys in shorts: Gabriel laughing; Simon frowning slightly with a forerunner of that sexy smirk. Total hunk, total fuck-up. Had Simon ever been truly happy? He put on a good show. World-class actor. But when people stopped applauding, Simon stopped pretending. Not with her, though. He didn't hide shit from her. God, the things he used to do to her . . . Where was it the family went on vacation every summer? Cornwall!

Her eyes ran along the small mantelpiece: a Palm Sunday cross, an angel Christmas tree ornament, a framed ticket stub for the U2 360° Tour. Ha! Darius would puke.

Swiveling Gabriel's desk chair back and forth, she squinted at his computer. A Dell? How quaint. She was an Apple girl. She hopped into the chair, her thighs making sucking noises against the plastic seat. Giggling, she tugged down the ends of Gabriel's old T-shirt, but it wasn't long enough to cover her lace panties.

Gabriel had been on her case to buy some clothes, and he was right. She was living in his old T-shirts—like she used to. Given his skill for shrinking clothes in the wash, she'd had no choice but to take over his laundry. And reorganize his kitchen cabinets so he could actually find stuff. Had he always been this disorganized?

Marianne cracked her knuckles and hit the "Return" key. He left his computer on sleep? How very trusting. Anyone could browse his web history, discover his dirty little secrets. Did he look at porn?

How do you feel about sex these days, Gabriel? Nothing like your brother on that score.

Sexy underwear—*a must!* And designer jeans that showed off her still-toned butt! And tight-fitting tops with cleavage. Tons of cleavage. She bounced her boobs with her hands. Yup, the girls were still looking good. And she definitely needed shoes. Wedges and flip-flops since summer had finally arrived in England. So cold when she'd landed, but now it must be close to eighty. Capris definitely. Could you buy shorts in England?

She checked all her favorite designer outlet sites and tried to place a few orders. None of them accepted her card. She called her credit card company, explained that she was in England—made up a return date since that seemed so important to the voice at the other end of the phone line—and started again. A few places had a problem with the UK shipping address, which she took from the unopened mail on Gabriel's desk. She should sort his mail for him. *Wait!* The Google gods be praised. Oxfordshire had a huge designer outlet mall. Marianne flattened her hand over her chest and squealed. All those stores only an hour's drive away. Gabriel would take her.

Her hands fluttered around as she searched Gabriel's desk for a pen.

"Gabriel?" she called out when the stairs creaked. "Take me shopping?"

He appeared in the doorway, barefoot, wearing a too-small T-shirt—another laundry mishap—and slouch pants. His hair was sticking up every which way. Beyond cute. Kinda hot actually. Like an older Simon. Marianne gave her most radiant smile.

"Marianne, can you turn down the music, please? It's seven in the morning, and I have neighbors, who—"

"You never used to be so boring!" She turned the music back up. "All work and no play makes Gab—" The guy needed slippers. Lots of slippers! She'd buy him a whole closet full of slippers.

Gabriel frowned, which wasn't the response she'd been going for.

"Your mood's changed," he said.

"Yeah, how about that? I feel great! And we need to go clothes shopping. Why didn't you tell me there was a designer outlet mall somewhere called Bicester?"

"That's in Oxfordshire." He scowled. "And it's Thursday."

"So?"

"I write my sermons on Thursday. And I have to meet with a family I'm preparing for baptism at six. And I need to . . ."

He droned on and on for all eternity. What drivel. She jumped up, and he stared bug-eyed at her legs. Seriously? He'd seen way more than her legs by the time she'd sprouted breast buds.

"Guess you don't go skinny dipping in the river anymore?" She flashed her eyes at him.

"No."

"Good golly, Miss Molly, don't be such an old fart. Let's fix breakfast and go shopping. Be a wild vicar and write your sermons on Friday. You need slippers and I need shoes. I have tons of money to spend. Darius is megarich. With family money! I can buy whatever I want. Darius will pay! And I want you to have slippers. My treat. Your feet must be so cold."

"I like going barefoot." Now he was plain old sulky. "I have a full day planned, Marianne. There's only so much I can palm off on Donald and my lay band."

"But it's so boring, and I thought you were taking a leave of absence to deal with this long-lost family member who needs to go shopping because she doesn't have a thing to wear." She put on the pout Darius could never resist. "Pretty please?"

"Marianne, I have to work."

"Be boring, then. I'm a grown woman. I'll go by myself." She waved her arms and laughed. "But you're missing out big-time. I'm a world-class shopper. Do you have a GPS? Can I borrow that little thing on wheels you call a car?"

"No." He turned and shuffled toward the kitchen.

When had Gabriel ever said no to her—except when she'd cornered him with those condoms? How had she ended up with the only seventeen-year-old guy who didn't believe in premarital sex? And why did that still piss her off?

He opened the pantry door. "Did you clean out my cupboards?"

"Couldn't sleep. Gorgeous day, all those birds tweeting away like they're extras in a Disney movie. And your house is a disaster, so I've reorganized your kitchen. I could paint it if you like. Put some color in here. Your walls are so fucking drab."

"Why are you swearing, Marianne?"

"Why the fuck not?"

He rubbed his forehead. "You don't normally use such colorful language."

"Fuckety-fuck-fuck. Hey. I can reorganize your study next."

"Don't even think about it. And please don't clean anywhere else. Mrs. Tandy will be here at nine, and she's very particular."

Borrring. "Cancel the cleaning lady. I've taken care of everything. Did the bathroom too. But you're the one who told me I needed clothes. Look what I'm wearing." She pulled up her T-shirt, his T-shirt, and a glorious breeze caressed her skin.

He held her gaze. "If you want to have a conversation with me, please go upstairs and put some clothes on."

"But that's the whole point! I don't have any clothes. Only brought one outfit with me. Now what's this about not borrowing your car?"

"Marianne"—he turned his back on her—"have you ever driven in England?"

"No but—"

"Can you drive a manual?"

"A what?"

"A nonautomatic car. One with a gear stick."

"A stick shift? God no. But how hard can it be?"

He sighed. "I'll take you this afternoon. But I need to be back for my meeting at six."

"Why wait that long?" She pirouetted.

"It's seven a.m. I'm pretty sure most shops don't open before ten."

"But that's hours to wait. I want to go shopping." She put her hands on her hips. "What d'you want for breakfast? Do you have English muffins? I'll go see if the village shop sells them."

She made a move toward the door, and he blocked her way.

"No," he said. "You're not."

"Not what?"

"Going down the village half naked."

"You're not my keeper, Gabriel Bonham. What's the matter? Been a while since you saw a girl in lacy panties?" She snapped the side of her Hanky Panky boy shorts.

"John's doesn't open for two hours. And if you wander down the High Street dressed as you are, someone will have you arrested for public nudity." He pulled a loaf from the bread box and hacked off a piece with the bread knife. "I'm going to have Marmite toast at my desk, but if you want bacon and eggs, please help yourself. Give me until one, and then I'll take you into Bedford. There's a decent Marks and Sparks there."

"Are you joking? Mom used to shop there for work clothes."

He jammed a thick slice of bread into the toaster and pulled out a plate and a knife.

"I want designer stuff. From the Bicester outlet place. And you need new jeans."

"New jeans are expensive."

What a grump. "That's what credit cards are for. God doesn't care about debt. Your jeans look as if—"

"As if what?" He opened a cabinet door. "What did you do with my Marmite?"

"You mean this?" She snatched it from the counter and held it above her head.

"Marianne." He sighed. "Please give me my Marmite."

"Not until you tell me where you get your jeans from," she sang.

"Oxfam," he said.

"A thrift store? Honey, no wonder they don't fit! Time for a make-over. Don't you care what you look like?"

Gabriel grabbed the Marmite out of her hand and backed away. "I'm a vicar on a vicar's salary. And no, I don't care."

"Would you stop saying no? Darius never says no to me."

"A husband's burden. I, being free of any such obligations, get to say no."

"Dearest *Gaaabriel*, please take me to the outlet mall. For old times' sake?"

Gabriel yanked his toast from the toaster, picked up the plate and knife, and shot from the room. Without bothering to zap a cup of coffee.

"Be ready to leave at one," he called from the hallway. "And do not go down the village wearing nothing but knickers and my old Elvis Costello T-shirt."

FOURTEEN
GABRIEL

Clutching the makings of breakfast to his chest like a talisman, Gabriel leaned back against his study door. *Mental note: take the car keys off the hook in the kitchen.* Although worrying about Marianne using his car without permission seemed the least of his problems.

Never before had he considered the need for bolts, chains, and heavy-duty locks. Heart racing like the clappers, he gave a quick apology to God for his brief lustful thought about a married woman. He also assured God he would not be venturing into the rest of the house until Mrs. Tandy had made her presence known. She would, no doubt, rap on his door the moment she arrived and then express her opinions on the clean kitchen cupboards. Since Mrs. Tandy was thorough in her venting, more sermon-writing time would be lost. He pushed off the door and put his breakfast things down on the desk. Great, he'd forgotten the butter.

Punishment for the lustful thought, God?

He accidentally nudged his computer, and it lit up with scantily clad young women advertising some shop called Agent Provocateur.

Did Marianne expect him to take her to a lingerie shop that sold—he leaned closer—something called Naughty Styles? Quickly, he turned off the Internet and opened a file on his desktop labeled "July27Sermon." It was blank.

Seductive Marianne, looking at him like a very randy, very married woman who wanted to eat him alive, was more disturbing than the busty mother of five who often licked her lips at him as he handed out the sacrament.

He closed his eyes. He had withstood temptation many times, and surely this was part of her illness. Yesterday Hugh had suggested she might be hypersexual, which could be a symptom of hypomania. But Gabriel assured him Marianne had been a sexual creature since the moment she hit puberty. Although, God help him, he worked hard not to notice for years. And all those months they were "taking a break" and he never suspected she was messing around with someone else, he'd found it impossible to ignore the way her body moved. He would never wish to be seventeen again and at the mercy of all those hormones. Life was much easier at forty-seven. Even if she did still scare the pants off him.

Good Lord. Bad colloquialism.

He spread a thin layer of Marmite on his cold, barely toasted bread and munched his butterless breakfast. If only he could text Jade, but it was still the middle of the night in North Carolina. And what would he report: *Marianne's coming on to me?* Besides, he'd insisted he could handle her for a week, and if he wanted to be nitpicky, his week wasn't up until tomorrow afternoon. How hard could it be to handle this for another twenty-four hours?

Piecing together what Marianne had told him and what he could remember of life before Simon's death, Marianne had been manic for months leading up to the crash, which meant this stage could go on for a while. Surely the dangerous part came when she hit depression.

He stared at his blank Word document. Temptation might be an appropriate sermon topic. Yesterday it hadn't bothered him that Marianne was wearing his old clothes. Passing on the cashmere sweater had merely ensured it went to a good home. But how could wearing his gardening T-shirts over her naked breasts be appropriate?

Something heavy landed on the floor above, and the bulb in his desk lamp flickered. He grabbed the noise-canceling headphones Jade had overnighted him earlier in the week. A generous gift that he'd insisted he couldn't keep, and she'd insisted he could because it would help him tune into nothing but U2. He plugged them into his iPod and started listening to "All That You Can't Leave Behind." And then he checked off a to-do list on his fingers: morning prayer, a call to Donald to ask him to visit Mrs. Perkins in the cardiology wing and take Sunday's services, and lastly, rearrange everything on the calendar until Monday. That would give him plenty of time to observe Marianne like a pro and make a full report to Hugh, which meant shopping was a brilliant idea since he would not be participating.

His pulse slowed and so did his thoughts. With minimal effort—and headphones—he had achieved what Marianne seemed incapable of doing in her present state: he had ordered his mind.

He picked up the framed photograph snapped during a family holiday in Cornwall and stared at his brother. A reel of memories played: Simon wandering into the cemetery, clutching a bottle of vodka stolen from their parents' drinks cabinet. Luck had been Simon's friend that night, because alcohol was the fastest way to Marianne's heart. No one noticed the vodka was missing until after the inquest. His mother went ballistic and screamed all sorts of accusations: *Had his brother's death meant nothing? Did he not understand the findings of the inquest? Was he trying to torture his own mother?* Standing by his belief that incriminating a dead person was morally reprehensible, Gabriel kept quiet. To this day, his mother assumed he, not Simon, had stolen the booze.

Would things have been different if he'd tattled on Simon that night? No. Because already it was too late. Even without the benefit of moonlight, he was aware of Marianne sidling up to his brother. As Gabriel walked her home later, he knew something had changed between them. All because Simon couldn't keep it in his pants; because Simon was weak and selfish; because Simon took whatever he wanted.

Gabriel threw the photograph against the wall, but it landed faceup on the sofa, refusing to smash. A taunt from a ghost.

Right, then. Not quite as calm as he'd thought.

FIFTEEN
JADE

The crepe myrtles thrashed back and forth, the water in the fountain blew sideways, and the green space that normally buzzed with kids and arty types was deserted. Jade looked up at the sky and ran. But not fast enough. Hail pelted her head and shoulders as the clouds dumped a motherfucker of a payload a block and a half from Sweet Winnie's Café.

She hurled herself inside the door, her stomach rumbling loudly as she eyed the seven-layer bars decorated with coconut flakes and stacked under the glass cake dome. Her personal record was three in one sitting.

"Gracious, girl," Winnie called from behind the counter. "Have you plumb lost your mind? There's a severe thunderstorm warning out."

Jade put her hands on her hips and panted. "Been . . . recording . . . didn't know . . ." She pointed at the sky.

"Sit yourself down and Winnie's going to bring you a warm carrot cake muffin on the house. I'm guessing five decaf chai lattes, one double espresso, one cappuccino, and a green tea?"

Jade held up her index finger.

"Only a single shot for Darius today?" Winnie put her hands on her hips and gave a dramatic tut. "He misbehavin' again?"

Jade gave her the thumbs-up. Being the studio flunky was a new experience, but since the band had settled on Sasha and Darius as their team, Jade had pulled back into the shadows. It wasn't so bad, since it meant she got daily samples of all the baked goods in Winnie's café. There was a reason this place displayed a wall of framed "Best Of" plaques.

"And can you add a seven-layer bar to the to-go order, please?" Jade sat down at a small table by the window. Something dug into her butt. *Shit.* She pulled her mercifully dry phone from her back pocket and turned it on, which she should have done the moment she'd left the studio.

A text from Gabriel: `Call me.`

Double shit.

`Sorry,` she texted. `Control room's a no cell zone. What's up?`

`Give me 2 secs to fix a drink.`

"Problem?" Winnie carried over a huge muffin on a square red plate.

Jade inhaled. "Nothing the smell of a warm muffin can't fix. I owe you big-time."

Winnie waved her off. "Honey, the good Lord's not keeping count and neither am I. But you best stay here until that storm's passed. Looks like we've got us a tornado watch."

"Won't get any argument from me." Jade peeled off the paper and took a huge bite of muffin. "You're the best."

"So you keep telling me, girl. I'll bring your cappuccino over while you wait out the storm."

Going into her contacts, Jade hit the number for the rectory. Gabriel answered on the first ring.

"Rough day?" Jade chose to not think about the cost of a transatlantic phone call.

"Where to begin? I've warmed up Marianne's supper twice, and I think it's no longer edible; I have the strangest desire to roll around on the floor kicking and screaming like a child whose teddy bear has been dismembered; and I'm drinking pink gin because gin diluted with tonic isn't up to the job. Oh, and I can no longer find time to empty my compost bin. I had to dump the coffee grounds in the regular bin, which means I am now a delinquent recycler."

"*Oookay,*" she said. The dumping of the coffee grounds seemed to be the big issue. Was he losing it on her? "What's pink gin?"

"Neat Plymouth and a splash of Angostura bitters."

"Just what the doctor ordered?" Jade took another bite of muffin. *Hmm.*

"Indeed. It feels like a flamethrower on my throat, which is exactly what I need after an afternoon of shopping." Gabriel slowed to his normal talking pace. "The cupboard under my stairs is stuffed with bags from a lingerie shop called Agent Provocateur. I've had to hide them so I don't either give my cleaning lady a heart attack or start a village rumor that I'm a pervert."

Jade sat still. "What's Marianne doing right now?"

Winnie placed a huge porcelain cup of cappuccino in front of her with a heart-shaped swirl in the froth. *Thank you,* Jade mouthed.

"She's been conducting a one-woman fashion show for the last hour. Thankfully it excludes the underwear."

"How much stuff did she buy?"

"Enough to fill my boot and the entire backseat. Is Darius a millionaire?"

"No." Jade stood up. "Is that music in the background?"

Gabriel sighed. "Yes. Not content with buying up half an outlet mall, she also downloaded a ton of new music to my iTunes account. And bought me a speaker that looks like a tiny black ball. Hang on a sec. Marianne, could you please turn that down for the neighbors' sake?"

The music got louder.

"You might want to close the door," Jade said.

"I already did."

"Ah. Your turn to wait a sec." She asked Winnie for a to-go cup and then transferred the cappuccino from the ceramic cup into the paper one. With any luck Gabriel could deal with a Marianne crisis more calmly than Darius. Still, she would proceed with caution. You never knew with guys, most of them being such babies.

"Did this shopping, by any chance, include useless items purchased in bulk?"

"You judge. I'm now the proud owner of ten pairs of slippers. I don't wear slippers."

"Ten?" Hopefully Darius wouldn't discover that his wife had been buying personal items for another man. Certainly not now that he'd found the focus to become a producer at the top of his game.

"If I can't return them, I'll donate them to the next village jumble sale. At least she'll be supporting a good cause." Gabriel sipped his drink. "I spoke to my friend Hugh earlier."

"And what did he say?"

"If he had concerns, he kept them to himself, but he did tell me, twice, that I should not hesitate to call the police if I thought she was a danger to herself or me. He's working tonight, but he's coming over first thing tomorrow."

"How's her sleeping?"

"Nonexistent."

"Can you stay up with her tonight, until your buddy can get there?"

"Jade, the moment we hang up she's not leaving my sight unless she's in the loo. And don't worry, I've already removed the razor blades from the bathroom."

The good news was that he seemed to have coping skills. She could push harder. "I know she's told you numerous times that she's taking her meds, but you need to snoop. You'll have to find them and count them."

"Invading someone's privacy contradicts all my beliefs."

"I hate to break it to you, but you have to change your belief system for mania. I'm assuming Hugh agrees she's manic?"

"He's a professional. He's not going to offer a diagnosis over the phone. Why, what do you think?"

Great. Life always came down to what she thought. Jade peered out of the café windows. The rain was falling sideways. "If you want my opinion, she's manic. And my gut's telling me she's off her meds. Which means we need to get a handle on this. Okay?"

Jade shoved what remained of her muffin into her mouth and swallowed.

"I won't have her locked up, Jade. She's been institutionalized once because of me. I'm not putting her through that a second time."

"Back up a minute. I'm not talking about anyone going to the nuthouse, so no worries. We're both on the same page, and I'm going to get you through this." *As soon as it stops raining.* "You'll have to trust me, but first—confession time, Father." She drew out the word *Father*, heavy on the irony, and walked over to the counter to hand Winnie the Nightjar credit card.

"Do you have any respect for my office?" Gabriel laughed. A feeble laugh, but it was a start. He just needed to hold it together until she could get back to the studio, pull Darius out of the session, and set her backup plan in motion. The one she'd concocted after her first phone conversation with Gabriel, and the reason she had an overnight bag stowed in Ernie's trunk and her passport in her messenger bag.

"Truthfully? I'm not a believer, and you're still a man. A good man, I'm sure, but flesh and blood and full of human frailty."

Winnie gave her a look, and Jade shrugged.

"Few people make that distinction. Most talk to the collar. Some days I feel the weight of people's preconceptions—that priests are holy and wise and above reproach. And yet Christ was the suffering servant, and priests are wounded healers."

Shit. Was he going to give her Bible study next?

"Yeah. Listen, we need to get serious for a minute." She turned away from Winnie and went back to the window. "I've been waiting for this, for her to come off her meds. Nothing tangible, only the gut instinct I have with all things Marianne. Because whatever her endgame, I suspect she wants to do this the hard way. Lots of self-punishment for all the guilt."

"Endgame? As in suicide?"

Great, Jade, fucking great. Way to reassure him. "I was thinking more about psychosis. She's not hallucinating, is she?"

"No."

"Good, that's good."

Rain battered the café window. If it didn't ease up soon, she'd make a run for it and leave the coffees behind.

"Gabriel?" she said. "Talk to me."

"I'm hopeless at asking for help, but"—his voice competed with a burst of static—"Jade? Help?"

"You've got it." And then she ran back into the rain as her phone sounded a weather alert.

SIXTEEN

DARIUS

Cabin lights dimmed, blinds drawn, the plane rumbled toward his destiny with zero turbulence.

Darius pulled back his legs as Jade stumbled over him yet again to go pee. He should probably have cut her off after the second round of vodkas, which, he couldn't help but notice, she'd paid for using the company credit card. Maybe shrink number whatever had been right, and he was a classic enabler. At the time it was the word *classic* that had ticked him off. But thinking about it now, while squashed into the back row of an overbooked transatlantic flight and disturbed by the stereo of every toilet flush, it was the codependent tag that grated.

Behind him the flight attendants chatted; down the aisle a baby cried. He should have packed earplugs. He should have packed, period. But the second Jade had returned, soaked through and without the band's chai lattes, he knew there was no time to grab more than his wallet, passport, laptop, two changes of clothes, and his toothbrush. And download the new Stephen King, which he'd been meaning to read since June. He'd been meaning to do lots of things since way before June, but his life was disappearing down the sinkhole of another marriage gone south.

He threw his head back against the plastic headrest. This time was meant to be different, and it had been, because he knew the woman he loved was crazy when he married her. She never hid that fact. From the moment he scribbled his cell number on a paper napkin and tried so hard to play it cool—being Marianne, she saw right through him—he wanted to fall at her feet and say, "Love me for all eternity." Marianne was the real deal minus all the pretentious shit. Sexy, funny, smart, compassionate, she could spot talent better than half the people he'd worked with in LA. But she didn't want fame and glory. She chose to work with teenagers and unknowns. People who were as lost as Jade.

Everyone who ended up at Marianne's door—he and Jade included—was running from something. Jade kept her personal life private, but there was darkness in her backstory. He'd bet his reputation on it. Not that he ever delved into Jade's past, and he knew zip about her dating life. Come to think of it, he was always dumping on her, and she never reciprocated. Jade knew all about his long history of choosing the wrong women. Except Marianne wasn't the wrong woman. For the first time in his life, she'd been the right woman. She loved him, she accepted him; didn't care about his family name or his reputation. She wanted nothing but him. And he'd wanted nothing except unconditional love from her. And now? The restroom door crashed open and he covered his nose and mouth against a fresh assault of chemical toilet. Now? Despite the itching need to throttle her for giving him the worst case of déjà vu, he missed Marianne so much he was burning up from the inside out. Maybe that meant he too was crazy.

Jade lunged for him as she tripped over his leg. He really should have intervened instead of letting the flight attendant believe the two doubles Jade kept buying were for sharing.

"Can I ask you a personal question?"

"*Suuure.* Fire away, boss."

"You're a beautiful, talented woman. Why don't you date?"

"None of your fucking business." She pulled up her armrest and fell against his chest.

Easing one arm around her, he reached down to retrieve his blanket from the floor and tucked her in.

"Darius," Jade said quietly. "I've got this." And then she fell asleep while he stared at the covered windows, waiting for dawn.

SEVENTEEN
GABRIEL

Gabriel snapped awake to Marianne yelling inches from his ear. Wiping what appeared to be saliva off his cheek, he leaned back from the kitchen table into a pool of morning sunlight. Outside, council workers pushed wheelie bins down the lane. "Alright, mate?" one of them called; another one whistled. Bin day and he'd forgotten to put his out, but then again, the minutiae of life had ceased to exist. His world had tumbled into an abyss of two.

Marianne danced around the kitchen table in his U2 T-shirt. At what point would her body, poisoned by exhaustion and lack of food, cease to function?

All that shopping and still she slept in his old clothes. Not that she had slept. He glimpsed a ray of hope around two a.m. when she announced it was time to brush her teeth, and he managed to pull on his PJ bottoms before she flew out of the bathroom in the middle of a tirade. He never manage to put on a T-shirt. Not that he needed one. The house had been insufferably warm all night, the air heavy and stale.

Now what was she doing? She was riffling through the dumper drawer where he kept elastic bands, biros, and . . . Oh no. He'd hidden all the knives in the rectory and forgotten about his Swiss Army knife. And Marianne knew exactly what to do with a penknife.

Bugger it, where was Hugh?

Pushing back his chair, he walked over to open the kitchen window, and the moment she flitted off to something else, he closed the drawer with his hip. As soon as she left the kitchen, he would retrieve the penknife and toss it in the bin.

"Did you hear what I said?" Marianne screamed. "Brilliance!"

"Yes. Marianne. I was listening."

"Liar liar sleepyhead!"

Coffee, he would make coffee. Not for her—an appalling idea—but for him. Fill the kettle, plug it in, put the ground coffee in the *cafetière*. Yes, that was manageable. He stood by the kitchen sink and concentrated on the ping of water hitting the metal bottom of the kettle.

"What was I saying?" she yelled.

If they made it through the day, never again would he take his solitary existence for granted: the silence that hung in his empty house at two a.m. and that first cup of coffee before his phone started ringing and people appeared in his kitchen making demands. He needed a shower; he needed fresh clothes; he needed a gap in time to pray, to breathe, to fill his kettle.

"If I recall correctly, you're going to win the lottery, get me backstage passes to the next U2 show, and you're a prophet. Did I miss anything?"

"Global Girls In Motion! In Bedford. In memory. Simon!" She threw her arms wide.

Highly doubtful that Simon, dead or alive, would appreciate the gesture. His musical taste had started with Genesis and ended with Phil Collins. To this day Gabriel couldn't listen to a Phil Collins love song.

Marianne jabbered through a slalom race of incomplete sentences left hanging in nothing but air. If only she would stop: stop moving, stop talking. If only she would sleep. God help him, he wanted to grab her shoulders, get in her face, and scream, "Enough!" One more day of this and he'd be pleading with Hugh to book *him* into the nearest mental hospital.

"All work and no play makes Gab—" Disjointed fragments flew from her mouth.

Gabriel rubbed his eyes. Which was worse: the eyestrain from trying to watch her, or the splitting headache from trying to follow her thoughts? It was as if he were watching a ridiculously fast rally on center court at Wimbledon, with his telly on the fritz and multiple channels playing at once. Although her thoughts appeared to crash into each other with more topspin than a tennis pro's serve.

He plugged in the kettle and, tuning her out, picked up his mobile. Nothing from Jade, but their flight probably hadn't landed. In the meantime he was hanging on tight until Hugh could ride in and save the day. Conferring with professionals when parishioners were in crisis was standard practice, but he'd always maintained emotional distance. Everything Marianne-related, however, went straight to his core. Once again she'd shot down his defenses.

"Quit your job! Move to . . . Caribbean. Dance!" Marianne tripped and slammed into the fridge.

"Are you—"

"Gabriel has a girlfriend," Marianne sang over and over. "I saw you. Texting. Smiling."

"No, I don't, I—" Why bother to reason with insanity?

She turned the music back up and started singing in screeches of frantic energy blasted through a voice worn thin. The lyrics made no sense, and she jumped from one verse to another, her angelic voice perverted into a pneumatic drill shattering his skull.

Where the bloody hell was Hugh?

Marianne skipped into the living room. He followed—coffee unmade, penknife still in the drawer. She dropped to her knees, scribbling over the lined pad he'd given her when she announced she was writing the great American novel. Ripping out the page, she tossed it onto the pile of screwed-up balls of paper that had created a small snowdrift in front of the patio doors and started singing again.

"Marianne," he said. "I know you love to sing, but would you be so kind as to implement five minutes of silence?" *Before my eardrums explode.*

"Boring boring boring!" she sang, and started to pull off her T-shirt. Gabriel covered his eyes at the first flash of stomach. His U2 T-shirt landed on his head.

Marianne cackled—yes, cackled. And then ran upstairs like a torpedo and slammed the bathroom door. The doorbell rang and seconds later rang again. Hugh normally knocked and walked in, as did everyone who knew the rectory had an open-door policy between nine a.m. and nine p.m.

"Come in, Hugh," he called out.

The bell rang again. *Oh, for Pete's sake.*

"Hugh, I told you—"

The bell kept going.

With a glance upstairs at the closed bathroom door, Gabriel shrugged on the still-warm T-shirt in his hand and headed down the hall.

"Hugh, you don't have to—" He yanked open his front door, but Hugh wasn't standing on his doorstep. It was a couple who seemed more suited to a fashionable life in London than breakfast in Newton Rushford. The man, who glowered at Gabriel as if he were an insect worthy of squashing, had a mass of shoulder-length hair—dark but turning gray—and was wearing a black leather waistcoat over a tight long-sleeved T-shirt, rolled up to reveal tattoos on both forearms. Rather muscular forearms. He was also carrying a laptop and had a black duffle slung over his shoulder. The young woman had smooth caramel skin, hacked hair in the most alarming shade of clown red, and appeared to be weaving around. The knee-length black canvas boots laced with tartan ribbons and worn with a tiny black miniskirt were an interesting choice, too. Half falling against the doorjamb, she looked him up and down with huge brown eyes. The absence of makeup compensated for all the hardware stapled into her ears. But not the diamond stud in her cheek.

She dumped a leopard-print duffle bag at his feet. "Not bad looking for an older white dude. But don't worry, Father, I gave up men for Lent."

"Jade?"

"Yup." She reached into her jacket pocket and held up two pill bottles. "And we brought emergency supplies. Not easy to organize with only a few hours' notice."

Until that precise moment, Gabriel hadn't realized he'd pictured a woman to match the voice and the texts. Someone soft and pretty. Yes, she could have been beautiful—how surprising that she was black—but she'd worked hard to disguise that beauty. Jade in person was all jagged lines that said, *Leave me alone.* The hair was appalling.

"Where the fuck is my wife?" the angry guy said.

"Darius?" Gabriel extended his hand. Darius didn't take it. Instead he frowned at Gabriel's bare feet, and Gabriel nearly said, *I don't wear slippers, and I certainly didn't ask your wife to buy me a lifetime supply.* His cheeks burned.

Darius's eyes moved up to Gabriel's chest. "I hate U2," he said.

"Now, now, boss." Jade hiccupped. "Play nice."

Out of the corner of his eye, Gabriel spotted Bill Collins on his early-morning constitutional with his yappy Yorkshire terrier, Queenie. This would fuel local gossip for days—the vicar opening his door, while still in his jammies, to two people who looked as if they belonged in a traveling circus. Good grief, he needed sleep.

"Morning, Bill," Gabriel said in a too-loud voice.

"Morning, Bill." Jade swiveled round with a sloppy wave. "Friendly neighbors."

"Ignore her, she's drunk," Darius said, with a scowl.

Drunk? At nine a.m.?

"Our flight was super early. Strong tailwind or something." She moved forward and breathed on him. Yes, drunk at nine a.m. "But it was *sooo* bumpy at the beginning." Jade rolled her eyes. "And I saw the Concorde trailing fire on CNN before *kaboom!* When we landed I was so relieved I had to celebrate with a screwdriver. Or two." Jade threw up her arms as if to say, *What's a girl to do?*

"Maybe if you hadn't had the other ten vodkas on the plane you'd be sober," Darius said.

Jade hiccupped. "No way I had ten."

Queenie flopped onto her stomach and watched, doggy ears alert.

Darius sighed. "My wife? Please?"

"Of course, my apologies. Come in. I was about to make fresh coffee." Gabriel opened his arm to wave them through the front door but was swept aside by a hurricane of banshee shrieks. Marianne flew past him wearing a towel, which started slipping as she hurled herself toward Darius. Thank the Lord she was still wearing underpants. Darius's arms shot around her and he buried his face in her neck.

"I love you," he mumbled. "I love you so much."

Gabriel looked down at the grass.

"You came!" Marianne laughed. "So much sexy . . . to show. Shopping! Why did you come?" She pointed at Gabriel. "You ratted me out!"

"No, this isn't Gabriel's fault. I found you, Marianne." Jade stood up straight. "You must have known I would."

"Phone tracker?"

"No, honey." Jade shook off her mannish suit jacket with the sleeves rolled up and draped it around Marianne. A red bra strap was visible under Jade's sleeveless black T-shirt, and Gabriel glimpsed the edge of a tattoo on her shoulder. "I tracked *you*. I miss you when you're not slamming doors on me."

"What?" Darius said, but no one answered.

"And when I'm ninety percent sure you're off your meds, you leave me no choice but to come in person. And Dr. White wants to talk to you pronto. Although not at four a.m. American time. And we brought your phone charger. Tut, tut, tut. Never leave home without it." Jade wagged a bandaged finger.

"Who needs Dr. . . . Not me!" Marianne attempted to spin as Jade tried to push Marianne's arms through the sleeves of her jacket. "Look at me! Great. Better than great! On top of the . . . Media Rage . . . Going to make you famous, Ja—! Who needs pills? Haven't felt this great in . . . Going to win the lottery. God told me. Let's shop!"

"No," Darius and Gabriel said in unison.

"Marianne, honey"—Jade had wrestled Marianne's right arm into the jacket and was now working on the left—"you need to slow down so we can keep up with you."

Gabriel closed his eyes briefly, imagining the deadening escape of sleep. When he opened them, Bill Collins was leaning back against the telegraph pole, watching him.

Some days Gabriel suspected gossiping about him was all Bill had to live for. Truthfully that was the reason he engaged in their sport, which routinely involved launching a midweek counteroffensive in the butcher's. No, he didn't like the man and never had, but Bill's wife, a bit of an oddball, had died under horrific circumstances. If anyone deserved some leeway, it was Bill. But that didn't make him likeable. *Sorry, God.*

"Let's take this inside." Gabriel lowered his voice.

Marianne laughed and then pushed Darius away. "Love! Group hug. Now leave. Go home."

"No, I'm not—" Darius said, but Jade moved quickly, remarkably alert for a woman who had, evidently, drunk all the vodka on the plane's service cart.

"C'mon, honey. Let's get you inside." Jade wrapped her arm around Marianne. "Fuck, I think your house is spinning, Gabe."

Delightful mastery of the English language.

"Gabriel." He sighed. "My name is Gabriel. I'm fixing eggs and bacon and strong coffee for anyone who hasn't eaten breakfast."

Hugh! *Dear Lord, thank you.* Hugh was walking up the lane toward the front gate. "Hungry, Hugh?" Gabriel called over Jade's shoulder.

"Always," Hugh said. Thankfully he'd left the dog at home.

"A party and . . . Not dressed!" Marianne squealed.

"Rad," Jade said. "I'm starving. Can we have toast, too? Come on, Marianne."

Bill shot up, eyes wide.

"Rad?" Gabriel said. Was that drunk talk?

"I know you!" Marianne pulled toward the gate as Jade tried to do up the buttons on the jacket. "Bill Col—!"

"Radical," Jade said, fiddling with the buttonholes. "*Rad* means *radical.*"

Marianne pointed at Bill and laughed. "Remember me? I'm a prophet! 'Cept I didn't foretell you'd still be . . . Shit."

The answerphone clicked on in the hall. "Gabriel? Gabriel!" his mother said. "Mrs. Pinker, that miserable old biddy next door, is after your father. Chased him down the street in her electric wheelchair, yelling, 'Darling, you look delicious.' I called the police and reported her for lewd behavior, but the policewoman who came by and was fat, *fat,* Gabriel, as if she had no self-respect, said I had to stop filing bogus complaints, yes, I'm sure that was the word she used, *bogus,* and . . ."

She chuntered on until his machine clicked off. Crazy women, drunk women, angry husbands, Bill Collins clutching his bag of dog poo as if Christmas had come early, and now old people behaving badly.

Radical shit pretty much described his Friday morning. Was it too early to consider a pink gin? Or he could forget the Angostura bitters and go for a straight shot. No doubt Jade would join him.

EIGHTEEN
JADE

Most men couldn't multitask without blowing brain cells. But Gabriel was calmly talking to his mom on the phone while cooking enough breakfast to feed an invading army. Or four people plus one starving twenty-nine-year-old with a high metabolism. Jade chewed the inside of her cheek as she watched Gabriel's butt move around the kitchen in black slouch pants. And what was with the bare feet? Very hipster. Hipster wasn't normally a good thing, yet Gabriel made the look unbelievably sexy. She'd never paid attention to a guy's feet before. Must be jet lag setting in. Or the vodka buzz.

Was Gabriel the reason Marianne had run away? Had she kept tabs on him, known all along that he was still in the village and could wear the disheveled-bed-head look like a Greek god? Darius was hardly a male beauty. For one thing, his nose was far too big. But if you liked the darkly tortured types, Darius was sort of sexy when he stomped around, flicking hair out of those brooding eyes. She'd caught plenty of women—and men—watching the way he moved around the studio. But Gabriel? *Oh man. Sex on a stick.*

Upstairs, Marianne laughed.

Gabriel placed a loaded plate in front of Jade while continuing to talk to his mom. *Start,* he mouthed.

"No grace?" Hugh said, as he passed the butter and a jar of jam.

Gabriel shook his head, then handed another steaming plateful to Hugh.

Jade slathered her piece of toast with everything Hugh sent her way and chowed down. After a few minutes, she remembered to put her napkin on her lap, and then she paused to check out the non-Gabriel scenery. What a great space. Warm and cozy, light and cheerful with the perfect amount of clutter. The vase of flowers in the middle of the table was unexpected, as were the houseplants on the windowsill. And none of the mugs on the top shelf of the pine dresser matched. Some were funny, some serious, some had flowers on, a few advertised businesses, a couple were chipped, and one looked as if it had been made in pottery class by a kid. No way the same person had bought all those. Which meant people gave him gifts and he displayed them without selection. All were welcomed and accepted. Did he have to be a decent guy as well as a hottie? Seemed Darius's fears had been on the money.

Gabriel hung up the phone. "Sorry. I'm not normally this rude, but I have two aging parents, one of whom appears to be losing her mind. She seems to think the neighbor is out to seduce my father."

"Maybe she is." Jade shrugged.

"Maybe." He smiled. A warm, comforting smile that matched his kitchen.

"Like your kitchen," she said.

"Thanks, me too." He sounded exhausted. "The rectory comes with the job, so when I leave it'll pass to the next incumbent. Can't really claim this house as my own, but the kitchen has always spoken to me. It seems to change with the seasons: snug in the winter, light and airy in the summer, and"—he pointed to the window behind her—"you can watch the world go by."

Highly unlikely given that they'd seen no one except for some old dude with a cane and a little dog.

Jade shoveled in several forkfuls of scrambled eggs.

"Wonderful to see a young woman with healthy eating habits," Hugh said.

"Yeah, well. I do have a few strands of semidecent DNA," Jade said. "My birth parents were deadbeats, but hey, they were both size zero. Of course my mom was an addict. Don't remember my dad other than as a skinny white dude who chain-smoked."

"And Marianne's your real mother?" Hugh said.

"Word," Jade said through a mouthful of toast and jam.

"Word what?" Gabriel said.

"Dude!" She swallowed. "I might be a little drunk, but *word.*"

"Repeating something I don't understand isn't going to help."

"*Ohhh.*" Jade slapped her forehead. "Totally my bad. I forgot you guys are uptight Brits." Gabriel frowned at her. "*Word* is everyday-speak for *I agree.*"

"Thank you for explaining," Gabriel said, like a parent faking patience with his preschooler. Okay, so maybe he wasn't that hot.

"We never made it legal or anything. But she helped me become an emancipated minor at sixteen, and then I lived with her until—" Jade looked from Hugh to Gabriel. "Why are you both staring at me? Do I have something caught in my teeth?" She stuck a fingernail between her front teeth.

"What does it mean to be an emancipated minor?" Gabriel ruffled up his hair. Damn, no, he *was* that hot.

"In America, I believe minors can be legally freed from parental control under certain circumstances," Hugh said. "I'm suitably impressed, my dear."

"I can't take the credit. It was Marianne's idea, to make sure my mom couldn't come after me. Fat chance. She never turned up for the court date. No one wanted me except Marianne. So, yeah, if I had a mom, Marianne would be it. You got enough room to put us up here, or should I decamp to the nearest hotel? Do you have hotels in bum-fuc—around here?"

"You can use my bedroom," Gabriel said. "I'll take the sofa."

"Nonsense. I'll bring my blow-up bed," Hugh said. "I can have her sectioned, you know."

What the hell was he talking about?

"Not you, my dear, Marianne."

Bedsprings squeaked above them, and Darius swore.

"I should warn you guys"—Jade tore off a hunk of bread—"their makeup sex gets loud."

"Lovely. We do have a bread knife," Gabriel said.

"Sorry. I'm—"

"Starving. Yes, I gathered." He placed another plate of food on the table.

Jade picked up the knife and cut a thin slice of bread.

"Want that toasted?" Gabriel said.

"Nah. Just an excuse for more of that delish jam. Blackberry?" She pointed at the jam jar with the knife.

"I picked them myself last September, in the hedgerows along the lane."

"Let me guess, they were covered in early-morning dew. Did you also smear goat's blood on the lintel at the time of picking?"

"Wrong religion, my child," he said with an angelic smile.

"If you'll excuse me," Hugh said, "nature calls. And then I suggest we get Marianne and Darius down here for a meeting. I'm assuming you did not, in fact, persuade her to register with your GP, Gabriel?"

"Sorry, that was a no-go from the start. She resisted, and I mistakenly thought I could handle things."

Hugh gave a nod, then swiped a piece of bacon off Gabriel's plate. "Bloody good bacon," he said before disappearing.

Gabriel folded his arms behind his head and stretched, revealing a flash of navel. Jade crossed her legs.

"I'm sorry, Jade. I seem to have made an almighty mess of everything."

"Things can spiral out of control fast with Marianne. Some days we're all just along for the ride—and that's when she's medicated. Thanks for feeding the starving masses. Feel loads better."

"Has my house stopped spinning?" Gabriel scraped back a chair and sat down.

"Yup. Think so." She picked up her last piece of bacon and tried not to think about having breakfast across from Gabriel every morning. "Listen, also sorry for not texting when we landed, I was—"

"Drunk, I know. Is Darius always so brusque?" Gabriel cut up his bacon with a knife and fork.

People ate that way—for real?

"Darius? He's a puppy, but he gets pathologically jealous. If he threatens to pop you one, don't take offense."

"Right."

"While it's just the two of us, is there anything you want to get off your chest?"

"I'm sorry"—Gabriel put down his knife and fork and reached for his mug—"I know I'm intensely sleep-deprived, but I'm not following you."

Was she going to have to explain this via kindergarten sketch? "Look. Cards on the table. I know enough to assume you were Marianne's first love." She paused; he didn't contradict her. "Which means you guys once had intense feelings for each other. And you've just been shacked up together for a week. Unchaperoned. And neither of you were wearing a whole lot when we arrived. Which means if anything of a sexual nature happened, you should tell me so I can defuse the situation before Darius settles on pistols at dawn."

Gabriel spat out a mouthful of coffee.

"If I don't ask, Darius will. And he won't be so polite."

Gabriel grabbed a napkin and mopped up his chest. "Jade, I'm a priest and Marianne is married. Marriage vows are sacred."

"Yeah, right. I'm talking about carnal sex drive."

"And I'm talking about higher things." Gabriel clenched his jaw; a muscle pulsed in this neck.

"Oh please. You're not married. Are you gay?"

"No, I am not gay." He spoke slowly, as if physically laying out each word in front of her. "Jade, everything that happened between me and Marianne was a long time ago."

"Was? Seems to me some wounds never heal."

"They do. This one healed and scabbed over. I have no desire to pick it open."

"Don't shit a bullshitter. What about the scars that don't show?"

Gabriel rested his arms on the table. "The truth is simple. I never wanted to see Marianne again. I certainly never wanted her back in my life. You're acting out of love. I am not. I feel a certain responsibility—to my brother, to her parents. Possibly to the friendship we once shared." He took a shallow breath. "But she betrayed me, and I don't appreciate betrayal."

He stared at her with cold blue eyes. *Interesting.* He wasn't quite the pushover she'd mistaken him for. Ice and anger were slugging it out under that perfect surface. Seemed the vicar might actually be human.

NINETEEN
GABRIEL

Jade had been wrong. Marianne and Darius were clearly not having wild sex in his spare room. The raised voices suggested a full-blown argument, and then something smashed. With any luck it was the lamp inherited from Great-Aunt Millie. Gabriel had spent years hoping Mrs. Tandy would bash it with the Hoover.

He stood and scrubbed his face with his hands. His visitors could be killing each other, and he was thinking about furniture. Did he have no compassion left, not even for Marianne's rather unpleasant husband? *Sorry, Lord. Will try harder.*

Maybe he really was a small-minded weasel. Either that or the relief of no longer being responsible for Marianne had trumped benevolence. No part of him had objected to Darius running upstairs after Marianne. On the contrary, he'd dared to hope they might spend the day up there.

"One of us has to intervene," Gabriel said. "What if they're hurting each other?"

Jade, who seemed to be taking control of everything including clearing up the breakfast things—although time would tell if she had a drinking problem—opened the dishwasher, loaded in the plates, and turned to face him. Her red bra strap had slipped down over her bicep.

"You"—she poked him in the middle of his chest and held her finger there—"cannot interfere. This is between them."

"And suppose one of them has drawn blood?" He pushed her hand to one side and slid up her bra strap. One swift movement, no thought involved, and he had crossed a line. Gabriel braced for the slap he utterly deserved.

"Sorry. I didn't mean to . . ." His head and heart pounded in sync. "Lack of sleep. Poor judgment."

They stared at each other.

"Excuse me, chaps." Hugh waved. "Can you two stand down for my professional opinion?"

Her eyes lingered on his as she turned slowly to Hugh. "And what is it that you recommend?" Jade's tone bordered on derisive.

"I recommend hospitalization and treatment in tandem with her psychiatrist in the U.S.," Hugh said. "And if Marianne's noncompliant, I shall have to take the next step. Do you have her psychiatrist's number?"

"Yes to the phone number, no to the rest." Jade leaned back against the dishwasher and crossed her feet. "You are not admitting her. Darius will never give his consent, and I can handle this if I can get her back on her meds. Which I can. Do you have any reason to believe her old combo of drugs won't work?"

"No," Hugh said. "The rule of thumb is always to put the patient back on medications that have worked in the past, barring a good clinical reason to do otherwise."

"Assuming we, I mean Jade, can get her back on the drugs, how long before they work?" Gabriel said.

"That depends on the patient. I've seen it take days, and I've seen it take months. But it's my opinion, based on the admittedly limited time I've spent with Marianne, that she needs to be treated in a hospital setting. It would certainly be safer. Does she have a history of violence?"

"No." Jade slid her hand, the one with the bandaged finger, behind her back. What had she said during their first conversation about a broken finger?

"And she has a history of psychotic episodes?"

"Yes," Gabriel said, before Jade could lie again.

The spare room door crashed open, and Marianne tore down the stairs and shot into the living room. Moving quickly, Jade went after her, and Darius appeared holding the side of his face.

"What happened?" Gabriel said.

"I tried to get her to put some jeans on, and she slapped me. But it's fine."

"No," Hugh said, "it's not."

And then they ran onto the patio, where Jade was watching Marianne prance around in her underpants and the jacket. Arms outstretched like Frankenstein's monster, Darius moved toward his wife. She jerked back into a ray of sunlight that slid off the grease of her stringy, unwashed hair. A sight harder to stomach than the misbuttoned jacket. Old Marianne had cared so much about her impossibly thick strawberry-blond hair.

"You. Never listen! Hate you!" She lunged at Darius, pounding on his chest.

"Marianne, please. Stop this." Darius tried to hold her still. "Jade and I are here to help. You have to let us."

"Hate! Want divorce! You beat me you rape me."

"I—I didn't. You need to stop saying these things. They're not true." Darius glanced at Hugh. "Please believe me, I would never hurt my wife."

Hugh stepped in front of him. "Marianne, my dear, this is your illness talking. Mania is a highly treatable condition, which you know, but since your initial plan might be quite involved, it would be best to get you inpatient treatment. Psychiatric medicine has worked for you in the past, and it can work for you again. We just need to get—"

"The devil!" Clutching her head, Marianne turned in circles. "Rising out of garden." She pointed. "No! No! Not real. Make it stop. Stop!"

"Marianne, please—" Darius said, his hands shaking.

"Go!" Marianne leaped backward and tripped over Gabriel's terracotta pots. She landed in a heap on the grass.

"Hate you. No one. Loves me. Alone."

"You're not alone." And then Darius screamed that he loved her, as Simon had done right before he'd died.

Sound and movement in the garden slowed; air roared in Gabriel's ears. Was he going to faint? His heart tightened, tight enough to rip. Had Simon felt this unbearable pain as his heart ripped free of its aorta? Grabbing the support beam of his arbor, Gabriel did the only thing he could do: he prayed.

"Voices!" Still holding her head, Marianne rocked back and forth. "So loud. The devil. See him? Coming for me. He knows. I kill babies. No!" She screamed at Darius as he dropped to his knees beside her. "Fuck off! Hate you! Rapist anal hate." And then she attempted to scuttle away from him on all fours, but just spun in place.

"I love you," Darius repeated over and over, his legs folded back under him in a picture of abject defeat.

Gabriel kept praying.

Jade came up quietly behind Marianne and sank, slowly, to the grass.

"Kill you," Marianne yelled at Darius. "I kill babies. Get away, Dar—Gabriel! Help. I need hospital go. Not safe! Not safe. Get me hospital."

Gabriel jumped to attention. "Does that count as voluntary commitment?"

"Yes," Hugh said. "Darius, do you have health insurance so we can circumnavigate the NHS?"

Darius nodded. "But money's no object. Whatever she needs . . ."

Hugh pulled out his mobile and walked back into the living room.

Jade wrapped her arms around Marianne and began to hum a song Gabriel didn't recognize. Darius bowed his head and shook silently. Yes, hell existed, and here was the proof.

Hugh returned. "I've booked her into the Beeches, a private residential facility not far from Heathrow. It has an excellent reputation, and I have admitting privileges. They're also flexible about GP referrals and good at admitting in a crisis. Jade, can you help get Marianne in my car?"

They eased her into a standing position. Darius stood too, his eyes red. A wasp dipped close to his face but he ignored it.

"Not cheap. However, it is the best," Hugh said. "A number of music celebrities go there for treatment. I believe she'll find it a very supportive community."

Darius flicked back his hair. "I'm coming with you."

"I recommend against it." Hugh had his arm around Marianne's waist. "We need to keep her calm in the car. I can't have her yelling obscenities at you as I drive."

"No, she's not going anywhere without me. I'm coming."

Gabriel moved forward and rested a hand on Darius's back. "Might I suggest—"

Darius swung round. "Get. Your hand. Off me." Gabriel had never heard a person talk in a growl before.

Gabriel lowered his hand slowly but kept his eyes locked on Darius's. "I have a suggestion. If you're willing to listen?"

Darius narrowed his eyes until they were almost slits. Gabriel continued. "Jade should go with Hugh and sit in the back with Marianne. We can follow in my car."

"That's a good solution. He's right, boss," Jade said.

Darius didn't react.

"If I put my dog collar on"—Gabriel kept staring at Darius; Darius kept staring back—"we'll have no problem with admittance, even if we arrive after Hugh and Jade."

A thrush sang, Marianne muttered to herself, and Darius tilted his head back and then rolled it from side to side. Seconds ticked by before he turned to Jade. "Fine," he said. "But you're to text me if anything happens on the way there and the moment you arrive." Jade nodded. "Hugh—name of the place again? I want to do a Google search in the car."

While Hugh rattled off the address and Darius typed into his phone, Jade ran back into the house. She reappeared moments later holding up a pair of pink sweatpants. They had the word *JUICY* emblazoned across the bottom. "These are mine, but she can't go to the hospital half naked. Marianne, let me help you put these on."

"I'm going to get dressed," Gabriel said. He began to turn away, but Marianne ran across the patio and threw herself at him. Instinctively, he closed his arms around her.

"No! No! The devil. Don't let . . . Take me. Gab—don't." She grabbed his T-shirt and yanked. "Don't me leave." Then she muttered gibberish.

"I'm not going anywhere," he said quietly. "We'll get through this together. Just like old times, Nightjar."

"What the fuck?" Darius said.

Jade was between them and Darius in a second. "Darius, look at me." She pointed at her eyes. "Focus."

"He called her—"

"Marianne's needs come first. We're all in agreement here. I suggest we let the guys get her booked in and settled. We can visit tomorrow. That's a better plan. Right, Gabriel?"

Jade shot him a look that implied he was a first-class twit.

On the High Street, brakes screeched and a horn blared, and Gabriel tightened his hold. He had loved Marianne, he had lost her, she had returned. He didn't understand what it meant, nor did he need to. Because he would do what he had always done: keep her safe. Consequences be damned.

TWENTY
MARIANNE

Marianne opened her eyes. Not a prophet, then. *Bummer.* The room smelled like a generic workspace. A cubicle for the unbalanced mind. Gray daylight pinned her to the bed; rain pelted the window. What had they shot her up with this time?

Her eyelids drooped.

When she opened them again, someone was leaving the room. The door shut quietly, blocking out the artificial light from the hall. In the dark corner of her mind, singing echoed. Something about hushing a baby and mockingbirds.

She fell back into the black hole of dreamless sleep.

The next time she opened her eyes, the room was bright with sunlight, and a female voice was talking about individual therapy and the evening yoga class; about group sessions three times a day covering cognitive behavioral therapy, mindfulness, and self-awareness; about how she would start in module one and graduate to module two when she was ready; about how the therapy assistant would explain this in detail.

Sleep, apparently, was no longer an option.

A shower, the chirpy voice insisted, followed by a meeting with the therapy assistant and then breakfast. *Busy, busy.* What a shit job, motivating the insane to shower.

Voices passed the closed door and disappeared into nothing.

"I'm here of my own free will," Marianne said, closing her eyes, "and that free will is telling me to sleep."

"You're here because you were smart enough to realize you needed help. That only works if you comply."

Outargued by a medical aide. Marianne started to sit up, but a memory sideswiped her: Darius's face red from her handprint. And sounds of breaking glass. Had she thrown something at him? Yes, a lamp. Right after she threatened to kill him. She flopped back onto her too-firm pillow. Darius would insist on seeing her, and she would insist he not. He must stay away, for his own sake.

"What day is it?" Marianne said.

"Monday."

The Monday morning to end all Monday mornings. And it wasn't as if she had the memory of a fun weekend to live off. Drug-induced oblivion didn't count.

"Do you want to resume your old life?" Chirpy Voice said.

"Yes." Marianne sighed, since *no* would have brought a truckload of problems. Compliance was the name of the game in mental hospitals. "I want to get better for my family. I have a daughter. I love her."

That was the thought to hang on to. Gabriel believed in angels, and Jade was hers.

"Then you should get up and start your day."

Pushing down on her elbows, Marianne forced herself upright. Then she forced herself to put her feet firmly on the floor, and forced herself to stand. "Can you remind me of my schedule again?"

✳

Breakfast, buffet style, was better than anticipated, mainly because the dining room was abandoned—as empty as a tracking room filled with nothing but silent guitars. The décor was contemporary restaurant style, not institutional mess hall clone. All very soothing with floor-to-ceiling windows, linen blinds, and filtered light drifting between stone-colored furniture. The place settings were real. Last time, she hadn't been trusted with anything but plastic forks and knives.

Marianne stared at what remained of her fruit. Fresh, not canned.

Clearly most people were compliant with their timetables and ate early. But she'd done this so many times—voluntarily and involuntarily. Pushing the limits by a minuscule amount was the way to go. Overt disobedience brought unwanted attention, but minor rebellion worked like a charm. She should write a guide: *I Did It My Way—Everything You Need to Know about Surviving Mental Hospitals.*

She got up to leave, facing the rear of the room. Fascinating, she wasn't the only rebel. One young woman—no, a girl—was hunched over a table in the far corner, partially hidden by a pillar. The girl tugged at the skin on the back of her hand; orange hair, stripped of its shine, hid her face. Lost in a huge mushroom-colored cardigan, she could have been a street kid. She could have been a skinnier version of Jade, asleep on the sofa at Girls In Motion, her fiddle wedged under her arm.

Dragging herself through the medicated shuffle, Marianne homed in on her target. She sat next to the girl, who was humming. Dried blood had formed crusts at the edges of several gnawed nails; underneath the ratty cardigan, she was wearing a Media Rage T-shirt.

"Hey, I'm new here. My name's Marianne."

The girl kept her head down.

"You're a Media Rage fan? My husband was recording them last week." At least he was until she went postal. Had Darius bailed on the band? Had she torpedoed Jade's big career break? So many reasons piling up as to why they were both better off without her.

The girl glanced up with huge, empty eyes. "Yeah? You're in the loony bin."

Marianne leaned forward to hear better.

"Why should I believe anything you say?"

Definitely a younger Jade. She'd come with a ton of attitude, too. "We own a recording studio in North Carolina."

"How d'you end up in 'ere, then?"

"Quit my meds, saw the devil growing in a garden, threatened to kill my husband. The usual."

"That is sick," the girl said. Nothing in her expression had changed, but the rise in her voice suggested *sick* was a compliment. "I have a mood disorder."

"Which one?"

"Schizoaffective disorder, bipolar type." Her voice registered no more life than a flatlined heart monitor. "At least that's what they say this time."

"You don't believe them?"

"Been in and out of places like this since I was thirteen. First time my world went tits up they called it aggressive behavior. Then they said bipolar depression. They make up shit worse than we do."

"Visual or auditory?" Marianne said.

The girl wrinkled her nose as if she'd smelled fresh skunk.

"Your hallucinations. I'm assuming that explains the change in diagnosis."

The girl picked remnants of green nail polish off her thumb. "Mainly auditory."

"Mine are visual. More like faceless shadows, really. Sometimes with the odd voice thrown in. It only happens when I'm off-the-charts manic and psychotic, but you wish you could forget those bits." Marianne lowered her voice. "Being psychotic's like being possessed."

"I started hearing voices when I was twelve. Not so bad at the beginning. Sort of white noise. Then it became more like a radio left on in another room. Got deafening after that. Multiple voices talking over each other all the time. Criticizing, threatening. I stabbed myself in the thigh once. Made sense at the time. Wanna see?" The girl got up and slowly tugged down her sweatpants. She was so thin, so frail, like the kid Marianne had first mistaken her for.

"Once I hallucinated my dead teenage lover," Marianne said.

The girl pulled up her pants and reached for a squashed packet of Marlboro Lights. "I'm going outside for a fag before group."

"Mind if I join you?" Marianne said. "It's my first time, and I don't know where to go."

The girl sniffed, and Marianne reached down to grab her napkin off the floor. When she stood up, the girl had gone.

✳

Group therapy started at nine a.m. In other words, sadistically early when you were pumped full of drugs. And then she had to meet her assigned shrink at ten thirty. She'd forgotten that they kept you busy in the nuthouse. The last activity before lunch? The substance abuse session. *Oh joy.* She'd been clean and sober for fifteen years, but her medical file had been stamped. Once an addict, always an addict.

First up, group therapy.

Marianne pushed open the door to some place called the Rhododendron Room. A seated circle of eight women and two men stared at her. She shuffled into the one empty seat next to the guy with the clipboard. His black-and-red metal glasses were very hip, very *I choose my idiosyncrasies, unlike you people.* He crossed his legs casually. His socks matched his glasses. How distressing.

"Welcome to group, Marianne," Trendy Glasses said. "Everything we say in here is confidential, so please remember that. Why don't you tell us about yourself and how you're feeling this morning?"

A battalion of lawn mowers fired up outside. Grounds upkeep was, no doubt, important to a place like this, a subliminal message to maintain appearances. Perpetuate the British war mentality: keep calm and carry on cutting the grass.

"What's there to know?" Marianne said. "I'm insane."

The girl from the dining room giggled. Trendy Glasses gave a tight smile.

"If you want the full bio, I'm also a record producer; founder of a nonprofit group in Carrboro, North Carolina; and I have one daughter and no pets." She paused, Darius front and center in her thoughts. He'd walked away from all that success to find authenticity. What he'd found was her. "And I'm married. To an amazing guy who deserves better." Despite the meds, she had the strongest desire to bawl like a baby. Damned if she'd do that in a circle of strangers. She sniffed.

"I was thinking more about your diagnosis, Marianne," Trendy Glasses said.

Did he honestly believe a woman with her history didn't know that? But confessing her sins in public never got easier.

"Bipolar I, alcoholic. And I'm here voluntarily." Really—even in this setting she was embarrassed, wanted to distance herself from those who didn't have the luxury of choice? "Stopped taking my meds, and went, you know, raging psycho. I wanted to get somewhere safe before I hurt anyone because I've killed. In the past, I mean. When I've been manic."

"What's your method?" This, apparently, from a young guy with a gray hoodie tugged over his head.

"Excuse me?"

He sat up. "Of murder?"

"Car wrecks."

"Ace," he said, and began pulling out his eyebrows.

"How about we go round the room and introduce ourselves to Marianne? I'm Mark." Trendy Glasses pointed at his name badge as if she couldn't read.

"EmJ," the girl from the dining room said. "And since you're going to ask next how I'm feeling, *Mark*"—she glared at Trendy Glasses—"let's get it out of the way. I feel like shit. And I still miss the Molly. Only thing that keeps the void away. Happy?"

"Your full name, please," Mark said.

"Emmajohn Peel."

"John Peel?" Marianne said.

"Yeah. Got a problem with that?" EmJ stared at Marianne as if she were part of the zombie apocalypse.

"Emmajohn, please," Mark said.

"John Peel of the Peel Sessions on the BBC?" Marianne said. "I grew up with my radio tuned to that guy. He inspired me to want to record and produce. He was my hero."

"My dad's, too." EmJ shrugged. "He was some wanker musician who blew his face off with a shotgun. Mum liked that stupid TV show *The Avengers* with Emma Peel, so I guess they thought my name was pretty funny. Too bad they didn't spend more time thinking about parenting."

John Peel, the voice on the radio. Thanks to him, music had always been her first drug of choice. Was that a sign? Who knew, but fate had spoken and she was listening. Emmajohn Peel needed a friend, and Marianne Stokes was it.

TWENTY-ONE
JADE

Jade sneezed and raindrops sprayed off the end of her nose. If she had to fly home with the English crud, she was going to torture Darius for all eternity. Although he was doing a good job of torturing himself right now, keeping up the pace of their death march through the soggy English countryside. Halfway across the field called Dead Something, a light drizzle had started and then turned into steady rain. Neither of them had thought to pack a waterproof jacket, which was a whole new level of epic fail. Worse, Gabriel had tried to give them an umbrella. Darius had refused to accept it.

Gabriel had told her about this walk, said it was where he came to clear his head and be alone. That made sense. One of the things she liked about the rectory was the constant hum of traffic. *Grow up in New York and you never get used to silence.* For the first time since they'd arrived, she wasn't aware of the road. All you could hear out here was nature.

She snuck a sideways glance at Darius. His hair, limp and wet, could have been spray-painted onto his head; his expression was as unreadable as that of a squished possum. She didn't want Marianne in residential care any more than he did, but why couldn't he focus on the fact that Marianne was getting the help she needed? Yeah right, like that was going to make a lick of difference to either of them. It wasn't as if they could unsee what they'd seen in Gabriel's garden. She'd lived alongside untreated insanity on the streets—ex–mental patients with no health insurance kicked to the curb—but she didn't have a connection to those people; she didn't love them.

A huge brown bird shot from the hedge, making some weird coughing noise. Darius didn't react. Rain dribbled down her bare legs and into her waterlogged canvas boots. Her feet squelched with each step, and still they stomped onward. If Darius knew their destination, he wasn't sharing.

They'd made it through the weekend, although they slept most of Saturday, and Gabriel worked most of Sunday. On Saturday night they ordered in—Indian, food of the gods—and Hugh joined them to talk Darius through daily life at the Beeches. Last night Mrs. Tandy brought over dinner—steak and kidney pie, not half bad. Gabriel ate alone in his study, and Darius ate in silence, doing a stellar impersonation of a death row inmate hoping for a last-minute reprieve. This morning they'd gotten the word that Marianne would see Gabriel, but no one else.

Darius had not taken the news well.

They walked past something that could have been an old quarry, and still they kept going. The land was flat, the fields planted with something yellowy gold that looked ready to harvest. Wheat? She'd skipped Farming 101. Tough life, being a farmer; tough life being a manic-depressive. Being someone who loved a manic-depressive wasn't a walk in the park, either.

Not once had anyone asked how she was feeling. She'd had high hopes for Gabriel, but it was as if they'd all been beaten up in the boxing ring only to retreat to separate corners. The spouse came first, she got that, and Darius's feelings should eclipse hers. But Marianne was all the family she had, even if, in the eyes of the law, their only connection was Jade's paycheck. Yes, she had health care power of attorney, could sign off on a DNR and pull Marianne's plug any old time, but she didn't have what mattered: family visitation rights in a medical emergency.

What now? She and Darius couldn't stay indefinitely. Sasha had said Media Rage was pretty happy when she dumped them back at the airport, that the drummer had worked with Zeke before, so the transition was smooth. Still. Bailing on the next big stadium band a day early hardly reinforced a reputation of "We put the clients' needs first."

They reached a chained metal gate with a pint-sized wooden climbing structure at the side that probably had some fancy English name. Darius stopped and looked around as if he had no idea where he was or how he'd arrived there.

"Do you think she still loves him?" He leaned back against the gate, resting his elbows on the top bar. "The guy who named her studio?"

"Hell no. And he doesn't love her. I flat-out asked when we arrived."

"And you trust him?" Darius sneered.

"Oh, come on, we've talked this one up the wazoo. And every time you ask it's like you want me to change my answer and declare them to be the *Bachelorette* couple of the century. But let's get real. Yesterday he was wearing a black maxi dress and doing God's work. I'd bet my car on the fact that Gabriel's not wired for lying."

"So why him and not me? What am I missing?"

"You're asking me to attach logic to a mind that saw Lucifer growing in an English garden?"

He sighed; she sighed; the rain kept coming. In the distance, a dog howled. She had half a mind to join in.

"Marianne has unfinished business related to Simon's death," Jade said, "and Gabriel's part of it. Repressed memories, teen secrets, two brothers in love with the same girl, I don't know. But something else went down in that first crash—other than a young guy dying, which is bad enough. And I'm assuming we're having this conversation because you want my opinion, so here it is: we should go home."

"We're having this conversation because I've made a decision, and no." He shook his hair. "I'm not leaving."

"Darius, we've got to get back to the studio. While this is, without doubt, a family crisis that makes real life seem impossible, we have a business to run. Your reputation might survive, but I doubt Marianne's will." *Nor mine*, she added silently. Although that fact should bother her way more than it did. "I need to sort out the Girls In Motion budget crisis, too. Give me another week and I'll have those accounting errors dealt with and our 501(c)(3) status back." Never again would she let volunteers run the books. "Marianne will be ecstatic. It'll be her get-well gift. And you should take a break from crazy for a while. Work might be a good distraction."

"Not this time. I screwed up last week by putting work first, and look how that turned out. I'm seeing this through—to the end, if I have to." He raised his face to the rain. "She's everything to me."

"Honey, your wife rocks my world when she's in a good place, and when she's not, I do what I have to do to survive. Right now she needs serious medical maintenance that's way above my pay grade, or yours. We came here to make sure she was safe. She is and we need to retreat, leave her to the experts. It's what she wants. And this place she's staying at has a fucking awesome reputation. If there were a Yelp for mental hospitals, it would light up with five-star reviews."

"And when she's released, what then? She goes back to him?" Darius stood up straight. "I've been in touch with an old friend from LA days. He lives in London and has a guest suite no one's using. I have no choice, Jade. Not if I want to keep my marriage. Not while the ex-boyfriend is hovering on the sidelines, willing to minister to her every need."

"He's hardly an ex. They were kids, which means the statute of relationships has long expired."

"Now who's being dense? Did you ever stop to consider why he never married or why she ran back to him? Something still exists between them, I can feel it. And no, this isn't jealousy speaking. This is me facing up to the truth. I'm pitching my tent here. I bailed on one marriage without trying to fix it. I'm not going to be that guy again."

"You hated your first wife."

"Yeah, but I aggravated the whole situation by taking her to the cleaners in the divorce. Last I heard, she was broke and detoxing in jail."

"Damn. You've got a few secrets after all."

"Not as many as you." He tried to smile. "But the point is, I won't run away from the person I love."

His words stung worse than those nettles that grew in every neglected corner of Newton Rushford. Color it any way you liked—saving the business, balancing the Girls In Motion books—but her impulse had been to leave. Pull out the rug, and she was still a sixteen-year-old searching for the fastest escape route. *See Jade run.*

"And I'm putting Zeke on salary as chief engineer," Darius said.

"Hey, that's my job."

"Not anymore. Nightjar is yours until Marianne and I get back." He closed his eyes. "The clients love you and Sasha, and Zeke has great connections. The three of you just have to keep the regulars happy until I bring her home. I'll check in with you every day about studio stuff; Skype in with client meetings if you want. And you can call my cell day or night. I can't be an ocean away while she's in crisis, Jade."

"I know." Jade leaned forward and kissed his cheek. "Marianne's lucky to have you. But if you get arrested for stalker behavior outside England's premier asylum, I'm not posting bail."

Finally he grinned. "You look half frozen. I'd offer you my jacket if I'd been smart enough to bring one. Let's head back so you can take a hot shower under that puny showerhead. Can't believe he calls that water pressure."

"Next up on the agenda—what do we tell Gabriel?"

"That we're both leaving. I don't like him, I don't trust him, and I sure as hell don't want him to know where I am. And if Marianne wants me gone, let her believe, for now, that I'm doing exactly what she asks. But I swear, if he gets in my way, I'm taking that guy down. Even if he is Mother Teresa with a dick."

TWENTY-TWO

JADE

Jade popped open her bag of Walkers salt and vinegar crisps—*crisps, how quaint*—and munched as Gabriel said something she couldn't understand. He'd insisted the only way to get privacy for dinner was to drive deep into rural Buckinghamshire, far, far away from his three parishes. His restaurant pick, Ye Olde Fighting Cocks, was heaving with pubgoers. The sound of multiple voices, muddy like a bad recording, surrounded them. And the music made Jade want to stick her fingers down someone else's throat.

Using her menu as a privacy screen, she leaned across the small round table. "Who do I have to murder to get the Spice Girls' 'Wannabe' off the jukebox?"

Gabriel laughed.

"This is one sketchy-ass bar," she said. "You sure it's okay?"

He scooted himself and his chair round so they were sitting next to each other. Jade shifted in her seat; her thighs had begun to sweat.

"Best pub grub in the area." He grinned.

Then he reached over for his pint of some local brew on tap. He'd let her taste it and—*ick, ick, ick*—it had been room temperature. The only warm liquor to pass her lips was tequila. Bad enough to have only two ice cubes happily melting in her Jim Beam.

Gabriel took a slug of beer that left beads of froth clinging to his upper lip. "I was wrong, then," he said. "Hard to admit, but that does occasionally happen."

"About?"

"I'd assumed you'd feel right at home in a dark, seedy pub."

"Yeah? Want your bed back tonight?" she said loudly.

Gabriel spluttered through a series of coughs and then slapped his chest.

"You're not going to croak on me, are you?"

"Very funny." Gabriel gave another cough.

"It's almost too easy to wind you up."

"Touché," he said.

"Oh, I see what you did. Nicely done." She gave him a knuckle touch. "What I meant, in all innocence, is that I can take Marianne's bed since Darius has gone. And Hugh's air mattress got that puncture."

"And what I meant"—mischief lurked in that smile—"is that your work must take you to lots of dubious venues. But thank you. I will take you up on your kind offer and move back upstairs. The lumps in the sofa are beginning to play havoc with my back."

"You poor ancient thing. Middle age getting to you, is it?"

"Do you always say what's on your mind?"

"Pretty much." Except no way was she telling him what was really on her mind. Good thing she didn't believe in God, because if she did, she'd be due for a lightning bolt right around now.

"I find your directness refreshing," Gabriel said, which for some reason killed the vibe. "Most people work hard to not say what they mean."

The music shifted to Elton John. A minor upgrade.

The waitress appeared and smiled at Gabriel. "Ready to order, handsome?"

In a T-shirt and jeans he was another good-looking forty-something guy, not a card-carrying member of God's chosen ones. Gabriel's lack of reaction to the not-unattractive waitress suggested either he knew her, he was oblivious, or he was used to women ogling him. Jade's money was on option three. Gabriel moved through the world with a confidence that came from knowing his looks held power. At sixteen she'd known the same thing, which was why she'd worked so hard to disguise her face, her hair, and her boobs. Hadn't been enough, though. Her stepdad had noticed anyway.

"Ready to order?" Gabriel asked Jade.

"Sure, fish and chips. To celebrate my last night in England." That was so not what she meant to say. Now he'd think she was happy to be running out of Dodge. And sitting here with Gabriel, she kind of didn't want to go. And that kind of had nothing to do with Marianne.

"I'll have what the lady's having," Gabriel said with a smile, and handed back both menus.

"I hope you don't think we're abandoning you." Jade tugged up her V-neck, which seemed inappropriately low when they were sitting so close.

Gabriel gave an *ahem* and leaned away from her. "Not at all. You can do very little at this point. Leaving makes perfect sense."

"Yeah, but if it makes perfect sense, why does it feel shitty?"

"Because you're a good person, because you care."

A fat guffaw came from the bar, wiping out all the other vocal sounds.

"I'm a good person who's running away? Not buying it, Father."

Gabriel ran a finger up and down his glass; she hugged herself tight.

"I have limited experience with mental illness, but I spend a great deal of time counseling the bereaved," Gabriel said. Jade huddled further into her own embrace. "Most people cling to the negative, to the mistakes and the doubt. But from my perspective, for what it's worth, Marianne would prefer you and Darius not be here. She came back to the village for a reason, and I think she feels her journey is a solitary one."

"Then why pick you up, Mr. Hitchhiker?"

He gave her the same cold stare she'd seen on the day they'd arrived.

Jade relaxed her arms. Darius had been right; she was being dense. "Oh. My. God. How could I be so stupid? You know why she came back, and you're not sharing." They had come full circle, trying to figure out whether they could trust each other. Apparently he'd decided the answer was no.

"I have an assumption, nothing more. And it's Marianne's story to tell if she chooses, not mine. I can't betray secrets, but I will tell you this: your relationship with Marianne is probably the reason she's working so hard to make sense of everything right now. I doubt anything could ever be more important than you." He folded his arms on the table. "She loves you with a mother's love," he said, as if that solved all the problems of mankind.

Jade stared at an ugly-as-shit painting of a shotgun with a pair of dead birds. "You're never going to tell me what really happened thirty years ago. Are you?"

He shook his head. "But I hope you'll answer a question for me. I'm curious. Why did Darius fly home a day ahead of you?"

"Different flight." The lie fell into place easily. Yup, they were back to the beginning.

Gabriel nodded slowly. No way he believed her, not Gabriel. He was far too perceptive.

"By the way, dinner's on me," she said. "As a thank-you."

"What have I done to merit such generosity?"

"Come on, you." She elbowed him. "You've watered and fed us, put your life on hold for a woman who was, until a few weeks ago, a stranger. And you've been the butt of some serious village gossip all because my family decided to take its dysfunction global. Besides, Marianne's getting the help she needs because of you, and that's huge. This train wreck was coming long before she arrived in the village."

They fell into a bubble of silence surrounded by laughter.

"Thank you," Gabriel said. "For supper. It's much appreciated."

"No protesting, no fluffing up of male feathers?"

"Hardly my style, but this does mean that next time we eat out, it's my treat. I like to keep things even." He sipped his beer.

"You think there'll be a next time?"

He picked up his napkin and spread it over his thighs. "I hope that after Marianne's recovered from this episode, she'll return to the village regularly and bring you with her."

"And Darius."

"Let's not get carried away, since he appears to dislike me intensely." Gabriel grinned. He had the cutest grin. "But yes, Darius would be most welcome. Will you manage alone on the plane? You're not going to down another ten vodkas, are you?"

"I do declare"—she slathered on a southern accent—"are you worryin' about me, good sir?"

He blushed, which was sexy as hell.

"Hugh gave me a magic pill. I expect to sleep the entire way." Jade stirred her drink with her finger. "I wish I could have stayed here longer. Something about your village crept up on me."

"Newton Rushford tends to do that." Gabriel played with the salt and pepper shakers. "It's a community with a large heart."

"While you were at church on Sunday, your elderly neighbor came by to check on us. Poor woman heard every word of Friday's epic garden scene."

"Phyllis? Yes, she's a kind soul. She doesn't gossip and at eighty-four thinks it's her duty to mother me. When I had flu last winter she organized a rota of meals-on-wheels. It was all rather sweet."

"And intrusive."

Gabriel shrugged. "I'm communal property in the eyes of the village."

"Minus Bill Collins."

"Aha, I see you're a quick learner."

"Why does he hate you so much?"

"I wish I knew. Marianne and I played some pranks on him when we were children. Silly, thoughtless pranks, but not enough to explain a lifetime of animosity." Gabriel sipped his beer, picked up his knife, put it back down.

"Do you ever think about moving away, starting over? I mean, people here knew you as a kid when you—"

"When I was a shoplifter?"

Jade cocked her head to one side and smiled.

"Newton Rushford's a good place to live," Gabriel continued. "The village looks after its own, and there's some measure of security in knowing you're never really by yourself."

"Except when you lock the door last thing at night."

"There is that, yes."

"I get it, I do. I'm a loner, but I have the ghetto mentality."

"Ghetto?"

He laughed. So did she, but it disappeared into the acoustic chaos of the space.

"I think that's what drew me to traditional Appalachian music. It's all about community. Just a bunch of guys trying to create something beautiful."

"You play an instrument?"

"The fiddle."

"Not an answer I would have expected."

"Me neither, until I was moonlighting in a local bakery during middle school. One day someone left a fiddle in the store. The owner kept it for a year. Never got claimed so I figured it needed a home."

"Do you have an electric one?"

She shook her head. "I work with technology but I like my own music to have nontechno *feel*."

"Feel?"

"Hard to explain, but it's unique. When a musician has great feel, you fall in love. I mean, if you're one of those smushy people who believe—"

"You're not a smushy person?"

What the hell was she talking about? Music. Right. "Nope. Except when it comes to making music. Music isn't supposed to be perfect. It's about passion, about digging deep into your soul. That often means messing up and playing out of tune. But my job and the technology I use contradict that. Every day I manipulate and disguise faults. When I play, I want an undoctored sound." Jade watched the waitress walk toward them with two piled plates. "We've started going back to the old ways with some of our recordings at Nightjar—everyone crowded around two mics, jamming. Feeding off each other. Those sessions are my favorite. Do you have any vinegar?" she asked the waitress.

The waitress tugged a bottle from the pouch of her apron. "There you go, m'ducks."

Jade shook vinegar over everything on her plate. "I love English food," she said.

"That's not a common statement."

"Here, you'll need this, too." He passed her the salt.

"It's going to be strange, not knowing when—or if—Marianne's coming back. I assured Darius she would, but I don't know." Jade grabbed a soggy, vinegar-soaked chip. *Chip*, another new word. *Yum. Loads better than crispy french fries.*

Gabriel looked down at his plate, then back up. "I know Darius doesn't believe me, but I hope you will: nothing is going on between me and Marianne. She didn't return to Newton Rushford for me. And if she stays, it won't be for me, either."

"When we first met, Marianne often reminisced about being a messed-up sixteen-year-old who'd managed to survive. I realize now that the stories were edited—nothing about Simon—but I think it was her way of giving me hope. You were part of nearly every episode."

"How curious," he said, but gave her no emotion to translate.

"Yeah, a fair amount of Gabriel chatter packed into those pre-Darius years."

Gabriel said nothing.

Jade shoved two chips in because one wasn't enough. No way. She covered her mouth with her hand. "This is better than—" She swallowed the word *sex*. "Anything on earth."

"Bubble and squeak next time you come. It's a fried hash of leftover vegetables. With potato." Gabriel cut his fish delicately.

"Gross."

"Quirky, not gross. I think you'd like it."

Now he was making assumptions about her taste? Jade glanced at his chips. Would he leave any for her? When she looked up, he was staring at her. *Man, those eyes . . .*

"How did you and Marianne meet?" he said.

"She didn't tell you?"

"I like to get both sides of every story."

"I ran away with my fiddle when I was sixteen. And no, I don't want to talk about it. I headed south because it was March and fu—freezing in New York. I ended up in Carrboro and heard about this place that was safe for runaway girls, where you could go and jam and crash on the sofa and no one bothered you. Marianne was a street legend." She paused to trip on memories, until she realized Gabriel was watching her again. Couldn't he look at something else? "Never expected she'd turn out to be my salvation. One night she was working late, found me asleep on the sofa hugging my fiddle. I guess she decided then and there to make me her next project, because she wouldn't leave off until

I agreed to go stay at her house. It took three days, the offer of a home-cooked meal, and new fiddle strings."

"And you never had any contact with your biological family again?"

"Nope, which was fine. The only person I cared about was my baby brother, but I left him behind when I ran."

Gabriel sipped his pint. "Ah, guilt. Something I understand."

"You too?"

"My last memory of Simon is saying some rather unpleasant things to him."

"My last memory of Jesse is saying nothing at all. If you had the chance for one last conversation with Simon, would you take it?"

"No. You can't undo what's been done." He picked up his knife and fork and started eating again.

"I meant in a hypothetical way."

He chewed slowly, then swallowed. "I know what you meant."

His cell phone rang and he held up one finger. "Yes, Mum. I'm here. Let me get outside where it's easier to talk."

He threw her a tired smile, dropped his napkin on the table, and disappeared.

Jade ate her fish alone while his grew cold.

TWENTY-THREE
GABRIEL

The itching started on his scalp and spread. The thunderflies had disappeared as quickly as they'd arrived, and there were no other gnats around. That left only psychosomatic causes. At least he was in the right place, then. As he stood on the pea gravel, staring up at the white Gothic arches of the Beeches, every piece of clothing chafed. None worse than his dog collar. Gabriel tugged it away from his neck and scratched.

Marianne had asked him, with some urgency, to visit today. She'd hardly spoken to him on either of his previous visits. Would this be a case of third time lucky now that she'd been in residential care for a week and seemed to be making progress?

He glanced back at the car park. His leaving ticket, his out from Marianne, had long expired, but had it been a horrible mistake to encourage her family to fly home? In another life he had never been happier than when the world isolated the two of them from the crowd. But these days the ride was bumpy and lonely. He wasn't even sure he should be on the ride. What if the refusal to see her husband was somehow tied up with him? Did she still have feelings for him? He didn't know, nor did he want to. He had no wish to explore his own feelings let alone Marianne's.

The itching started up again, and his muscles tensed. His ears rang with the past: Marianne laughing and saying, "You stole for me"; Marianne dragging him onto a dance floor, insisting he "let it all hang out"; Simon announcing, "Your little girlfriend didn't tell you she was pregnant with my baby, did she"; carrying her unconscious and bleeding to the cottage where the elderly lady—long gone—used her old-fashioned phone to ring for an ambulance. She said she'd never seen so much blood.

Gabriel pulled up the gold chain that hung around his neck. Clasping the small crucifix that normally lay flat against the skin of his chest, he forced himself to walk across the gravel and through the main entrance.

A huge vase of lupines and delphiniums greeted him. There seemed to be a different floral arrangement on the front desk every time he visited. This was not a bog-standard NHS hospital with flowers banned for a slew of ridiculous reasons. Nor was it a bog-standard parishioner visit. No, this was in a different league on many levels.

I hope you've got my back, God, because I'm making this up as I go along.

The nurse at the front desk raised her eyes but kept her finger marking whatever she was reading. "Good afternoon, Reverend."

"I'm here to see Marianne Stokes." Gabriel tucked his chain back under his shirt. "She's expecting me."

"I believe I saw her heading to the patient garden. Do you know where it is?"

He nodded and thanked her; she returned to her work. No one ever questioned the collar. Gabriel kept his gaze lowered as he followed the circuit of pale corridors, each identical to the one before. Marianne had told him several famous people were in residence. Heaven forbid he accidentally gawk at a movie star.

Finally he reached the door to the garden. He hesitated, watching Marianne through the glass. Still painfully thin, she was less jittery. Only her hands trembled as she spoke to a young girl. He pushed the door open and breathed in the warm air. The garden was a little contrived for his taste—his preference would have been for less gravel and more green, less design and more wilderness—but Gabriel had yet to visit a garden that didn't soothe.

The itching stopped.

Marianne waved him over to the wooden bench. The girl turned to leave, a curtain of lank hair hiding her face. She was petite and fragile; a breath could snap her in half. Marianne grabbed her arm and spoke quietly. The girl remained, staring at her feet.

"What news of Media Rage?" Marianne said.

Progress, indeed. Last time, any mention of Jade and Darius had been taboo.

"Full steam ahead, I gather."

The girl raised her face slowly and fixed huge, haunted eyes on him. He was used to down-and-outs, to tramps and addicts, to people who had lost their way and needed a hand up. But this girl? It was as if life had chewed her up, spat her out, and said, *No, thank you.*

Marianne smiled. "Gabriel, I'd like you to meet my new friend, EmJ."

"You a real vicar?" EmJ stared at the collar.

"Yes, I am."

"So you have to tell the truth?"

"I hope everyone does that."

"But it's, like, eternal damnation if you don't, right?" Her monotone voice was so quiet he nearly asked her to speak up. He'd learned to read lips in the army, but hers barely moved when she talked.

"I'm a truthful person, if that's what you're asking."

"Shag me sideways. You weren't lying." EmJ turned in slow motion to look at Marianne.

"EmJ's a Media Rage fan," Marianne said. "I think she wanted to make sure I wasn't delusional when I talked about recording them."

"Got it." Gabriel smiled. "In that case I can confirm that yes, Marianne and her husband are recording the band's new album. And they're due back for mixing and overdub. Did I get that right?"

"Jade has taught you well, young Padawan," Marianne said.

"Who's Jade?" EmJ said.

"Someone I love dearly," Marianne said. "She's almost my daughter."

"Almost?" Gabriel said.

EmJ squinted as if the gray afternoon light were too strong. "Whatevs. Enjoy your reunion." She pulled her voluminous cardigan around her. The right sleeve was full of moth holes.

"More therapy?" Marianne said.

"Like it makes a difference."

"It does. You need to stick with it, honey, especially when you get out."

"Yeah," EmJ said, turning a positive into a negative. She started walking away, then stopped. "See you in a bit?" She scowled over her shoulder at Marianne.

"Dinner at six, honey. It's a date."

EmJ shuffled along the path like an elderly person who'd misplaced her walker.

Gabriel sighed with relief. While EmJ had been talking, it was as if he'd been trapped in that moment between sleep and wakefulness when movement seemed impossible. He sat next to Marianne and breathed in the scent of fresh rosemary from the huge aluminum pot by the bench. Tonight he would make fresh pesto with basil from his herb garden.

"Shouldn't she be in a children's hospital?" he said.

"She's eighteen."

"She looks as if she hasn't made it through puberty."

"Eating disorder." Marianne shrugged. "Plus a few other things. Her mom threw her out when she was sixteen, and her father killed himself in the room next to hers—with a shotgun. EmJ was five."

Gabriel shook his head slowly. He had no words.

"She's a National Health patient. Only ended up here because there wasn't a bed anywhere else."

"Maybe someone was looking out for her." He glanced skyward.

"Or she got lucky. I heard a news story, a few months back, about this teenager in a mental health crisis who was housed in a police cell because there wasn't a bed for her. In the whole country. How is that possible?"

Gabriel crossed his legs and leaned back against the bench. How refreshing to hear Marianne register indignation minus the histrionics.

"One of the nurses told me she hasn't had a single visitor. She has no one, Gabriel. And her only choice when she leaves here is to crash on the floor of her ex-boyfriend's apartment. He's a thirty-year-old drug kingpin."

A siren wailed in the distance, pulling closer to the front entrance, and Gabriel angled his face toward her. A single word hung in his mind: *No*.

"Marianne, I know where this is heading, but you can't adopt her like a stray. You need to heal, and I'm sure she does, too. I doubt doing that together will be healthy."

"I need to focus on being a force for good in someone's life, not a force of destruction. She wants to be a singer. I can mentor her, help her find her voice."

"And what happens when you return to the States?"

"Obviously I haven't dotted all the i's and crossed all the t's, because"—she held a finger to the side of her head like a pistol—"heavy-duty drugs kill the thought process, but I guess I'll take her with me."

Marianne was thinking about going back, then. Up until that point he hadn't been sure. He'd thought—well, he didn't know what he'd thought. With Marianne it was futile to map out tomorrows. That had been his biggest mistake as a teenager: daring to believe they had a long and happy future together that included a mortgage and a family. "And residency?"

"Hire an immigration lawyer. I mean, how hard can it be?"

"Is this about being a substitute mother to another lost teen?" He paused. "Or avoiding your own problems?"

"Did the guy in the parable of the Good Samaritan ask that question? If you're trying to pick up someone from the roadside, trying to be a ray of light, not a cloud of darkness, does it matter what your motivation is?"

"Marianne, it's not that simple."

"To see hope, not tragedy?" She held up her hands. "I thought you were the one who believed in God, not me."

"You don't believe in God?"

"Sorry. Stopped believing in fairy tales when I was sixteen, stripped naked, and hallucinating demons in a churchyard."

"Religion isn't a fairy tale. It brings clarity and peace; it helps people see in the dark."

"Or helps them avoid dealing with the mess of life." She laid a hand on his knee and gave a light squeeze. He stared at her fingers and, after she had moved them, at the place where they had been.

"You would have to share the spare room."

"That's a yes?" She beamed, the first real smile she'd shown him since falling back into his life.

"No. I'm thinking aloud. And, with your permission, I'd like to discuss this further with Hugh. Get his take."

"Yes, yes. What did you think? Did you like her?"

"Is she an addict?"

"Does it matter?" Marianne looked up into the sky and watched a flock of starlings.

"Not if she's clean. I have a no-recreational-drugs policy for houseguests."

"I'll make sure of it."

Her hand moved to find his. Such an inappropriate gesture for a married woman, but somehow it transported them back to innocence. How many hours, days, and weeks of his life had he spent holding her hand? A question he would never be able to answer.

"I can help save her, Gabriel, I can." The twinkle was back in her green eyes.

"Marianne—" Gabriel reclaimed his hand. "My other reservation is whether you're stretching yourself too thin. You passed Girls In Motion to Jade because you couldn't manage two jobs. Isn't trying to heal while helping someone else on a similar journey the equivalent of two jobs?"

"I can handle it. I'm fine. I mean, I'm in a mental hospital, so obviously I'm not fine, but my moods have plateaued out, and I have nothing else to do except talk endlessly about me. Which is not my favorite subject." Eyes lowered, she picked at something on her thigh. "And Darius?" Her voice turned soft at the edges. "Do you know how he is?"

"Only what Jade's told me." Which didn't add up to much, now that he thought about it.

Not that he wanted to be sexist, but Gabriel had never seen a grown man cry quite so much as Darius the night after Marianne was admitted to the Beeches. Marriage counseling wasn't his strong suit, and most of Gabriel's close friends were bachelors. The only marriage he'd ever seen up close and personal was that of his parents. And that seemed to be built on resignation, not devotion. "If you say so, my dear" was the most-spoken phrase in his childhood home. But marriage, under any circumstances, was sacred, and it was his duty to help repair Marianne's. Whatever his impressions of Darius, who was currently vying with Bill Collins for the title of least likeable person in the world.

Sorry, God. Sorry.

"Your husband is desperate to talk with you, to reassure you of his love. Will you reconsider, agree to take his phone calls?"

"I can't right now, and I have my reasons. Please don't push. But I need to know that someone apart from me has Jade's best interests at heart—can do whatever it takes to keep her safe if I'm not up for the job. And what I'm about to tell you is confidential."

"Absolutely."

Marianne turned away to watch pigeons settle around another patient who was tossing out bread crumbs from a small plastic bag. She turned back slowly. "When you asked if I had kids that first day, you never asked the most important question."

He leaned forward and rested his arms on his legs. "What should I have asked?"

"You should have asked whether I wanted kids."

"But I knew the answer. Two girls and two boys, if memory serves." He smiled. "You always did think big."

"Enough was never enough for me."

"I know." He'd known months before the accident that he would never be enough for Marianne.

"I picked the number four so as not to scare you, but I wanted more. A houseful of babies." She laced her fingers together and slid them back and forth. "My parents would never talk about my adoption. I knew only that my birth mother didn't want me, and that one day I would raise kids who were wanted."

"If I remember correctly, your birth mother was a child herself."

"She never tried to find me. Never."

"And did you ever try to find her? It works both ways, Marianne."

"How is that relevant? I loved my parents. As far as I was concerned, my birth mother was nothing more than a womb. But I wanted her to acknowledge my existence. Reach out with a sorry-I-abandoned-you message. Send me an eighteenth birthday card. I was an embarrassment.

A mistake. Something to be thrown away. You know she left me in the church, right?"

"Indeed. You were the baby a village took in, but you can't guess at the thought process of a teen in crisis. Giving you up could have been an act of self-sacrifice. Why else would she have left a note explaining she was unable to raise a child given her age and circumstance? I imagine the desire to want what's best for your baby is a strong one. But whatever her motivation, she made the right decision. Your parents raised you with unconditional love."

"But she should have wanted me, Gabriel. Our last night, at the party before the crash, I'd made the decision to keep the baby. Up until then I hadn't been sure . . ."

He reached into his pocket and pulled out the white linen hanky he kept for these moments. It came from a pack of three, a gift from the rural dean's wife, a woman who used few words but understood everything.

"Maybe the girl who gave birth to you knew she couldn't be a mother."

Marianne sniffed. "You mean like me?"

"Now you're contradicting yourself. And what about Jade? You treat her as a daughter."

She dabbed her eyes with the hanky. "I never meant to. She snuck under my defenses."

Under mine too, he nearly said.

"When Girls In Motion expanded beyond a summer band camp, I had this grand idea to help girls with no other options. Unwanted girls. I figured if I wasn't careening through the odd mood swing, I could help. I mean, it wasn't like I could make their lives worse." Marianne smiled. "Then Jade turned up with her fiddle case."

She blew her nose and handed him back the hanky. He was used to this ritual, too. He shoved it in his pocket, making a mental note to put it in the laundry basket when he got back and replace it with a fresh one. Rituals, habits were good. They kept a person grounded in the turmoil of the human condition.

I know, God. Marianne's current crisis is way more personal than the human condition.

"It's important that you understand my need to protect Jade. From me, if you have to. Darius cares for her, but he doesn't know the real reason I opened my life to my baby girl." She took a deep breath. "Her stepdad raped her. Repeatedly."

Gabriel shot up, his hand over his mouth. He was going to be sick.

TWENTY-FOUR
JADE

Perched cross-legged in her desk chair, hands wrapped around a double espresso, Jade tried to feel the sound of the guitar track. The lights were dimmed—exactly how they should be for mixing—but still there was too much sensory stimulation in the room.

She hit "Stop" and stared up at the acoustic ceiling cloud suspended over her console and computer. Mixing normally got her all tingly with the thrills of her job—she might hate tinkering with her own music, but someone else's was a different beast—and yet sleep deprivation kept her on edge. Nights were lost to catnaps littered with nightmares about empty rooms and the crying angel picture on Gabriel's bedroom wall. Hadn't he ever watched *Doctor Who*? Didn't he know Weeping Angels were evil predators?

Gabriel's texts, her only link to Marianne, shared information but gave Jade nothing to hold on to. And she missed Darius so much they'd established a nightly Skype session. Although that had also become a necessity after Darius had called her apartment at six o'clock two mornings in a row. Family crises should never come with a five-hour time difference.

She twirled a finger through her hair, which was longer than it had been for years, with the dye job growing out. Maybe she'd go au naturel for her thirtieth birthday. Experimenting with outrageous colors suddenly seemed as pointless as performing to an empty auditorium.

Her cell phone vibrated and she grabbed it. Yes, she'd broken her own rule banning cell phones from the control room.

"Hey." She swung her chair around so her back was to the board and the speakers. In the warm orange glow of lamplight, she could have been alone with him.

"Am I interrupting?" Gabriel said.

Did this guy even know how to be inconsiderate? People interrupted her work all the time: an intern with a question, an artist who wanted to micromanage his own sound, Zeke with his latest girlfriend fiasco. Darius used to be the worst of the bunch. She smiled, remembering the last note she'd taped to the control room door before their world had spun off its axis: *Do not enter. Do not think about entering. No exceptions and that includes you, boss.*

"Nope. Not busy." Jade stretched. "Just locked in my girl cave doing some mixing. You know, the musical equivalent of putting together a sandwich."

"Interesting visual," he said. "I was hoping to chat with you about something."

She glanced up at the studio clock. Ten minutes until a new client, the Arcadian Project, came in for a consult. "Sure. Chat away, Father."

"Jade?"

"Yo."

"Could you please stop calling me Father? It makes me feel old. Whereas I am merely maturing like a good Bordeaux."

She snorted out a laugh. "You're a wine drinker?"

"No. You?"

Clearly he hadn't paid attention to her drink order on their dinner date that wasn't a date. "Nah. Bourbon or tequila shots."

"Tequila? Oh, that's plain nasty."

"This from a guy who drinks pink gin."

Her eyelids drooped as she watched the up-down movements of the lumps of wax inside her lava lamp.

"It was the traditional drink of the British navy. As such, it proves I'm full of testosterone."

"Let me guess, honey. You're alone in your study right now with a glass of pink gin. Your door is probably closed and you have U2 playing through your computer. And because you're ridiculously thoughtful and don't want to disturb your elderly neighbor, you have it turned down low."

"Did you just call me honey?"

"Maybe. Or maybe you're going senile. I've heard that can happen once you hit the late forties."

"Very funny." He sipped his drink. "Thank you, for a much-needed reminder to not take myself so seriously."

"Anytime you need a dose of humility, I'm your woman."

"But you're wrong about U2. Hang on, let me—" Music replaced his voice, and she shivered. "Inspired by you, I have widened my musical choices."

"'I Need My Girl' by The National." She rubbed at the goose bumps on her arm. "Good choice. And what's the verdict?"

"Undecided. It takes me a while to accept anything new." He paused. "Did I update you on the latest village gossip? Apparently I had a torrid affair with a married woman that caused her to have a nervous breakdown. I'm anticipating an upswing in my dating life."

"You date?" Jade said, her voice disappearing.

"That was a joke. Relationships are complicated, and I like my life clean."

"And casual sex isn't in the cards for someone in your line of work?"

He cleared his throat. "Any contact yet from Marianne?"

"Nope. I'm keeping up with nightly 'Love you lots' texts. Sometimes I vary it with, 'How's the food in the luxury loony bin?' I'm forever hopeful she'll reply."

"So you don't know about EmJ?"

"Never heard of him. Who is he, an obscure English rapper?"

Gabriel laughed. He had the best laugh: rich and warm. How would it feel to mix that laugh, to add depth for a richer sound? She visualized his voice hitting the cloud and bouncing back down, wrapping around her; and then she pictured those pale eyes that could hold you in place like the stare of a king cobra. She grabbed her hoodie off the back of her chair and shrugged it on.

"EmJ is an eighteen-year-old fellow patient Marianne seems quite taken with. A girl."

"Ah, Marianne has a new project, that's good." Yes, yes it was, and that little spark of jealousy was irrational. But still, it burned. Was Marianne collecting reasons to not come home?

"She's at her best when she's focused on someone else. I'm assuming this is a girl who has no family, some musical talent—probably as a singer—and is down on her luck."

"Are you psychic?"

"If only. What a great sideline that would be for the studio: each recording comes with Jade's personal prophecy of success. But no, I wasn't Marianne's first project or her last, but I was the only one who stayed around. Other than Sasha."

"Do I detect some self-pity in that tone, Ms. Jones?"

"A touch, I guess. Before I found Marianne, my life was quite the tale of woe. I'm struggling a bit with *will she won't she come back.*"

"Growing up, your home life was bad, wasn't it?"

"Pretty bad. Never thought of it as home, though. My only real home has been with Marianne."

"I'm always here, if you ever need to talk about it." He paused, clearly expecting her to say something she couldn't.

"Thanks. Gotta love the sympathy cards you amass as a teen runaway."

"I'm serious, Jade."

"I know, and I don't mean to be flippant, but my adolescence is dead to me. So tell me about your childhood. All perfectly civilized and happy in darkest England?"

"Not really. I spent most of my time at Marianne's house avoiding my own family. My parents were strict disciplinarians, not exactly demonstrative, and Simon and I were close in age but nothing else. He was the gregarious one, the shining star. I was lost in his shadow. Everyone was drawn to him."

"Including Marianne."

Gabriel hesitated before answering. "Including Marianne. When we entered double digits, he made my life miserable, but I retaliated in unconventional ways. Stinging nettles in his bed come to mind."

"Nice." She paused. "Were you ever close?"

"I suppose when we were little. Come to think of it, we built some great sand castles together." His voice had risen. "You forget, don't you?"

"My brother and I were super close. I was more like his mother than bio mom." Red holiday lights glowed around her and a fantasy played: drinking eggnog—heavy on the rum—and exchanging Christmas gifts with Jesse. He'd be twenty-one now. Had he found a decent career, succeeded in love? Did he ever think of her?

"You miss him, don't you?"

"I don't know . . ."

"This from the person who told me never to shit a bullshitter."

"My, my, His Holiness said shit." As she shook her head, thoughts of her brother floated away.

"Your corrupting influence, I can assure you." He sighed. "Do you every wonder how different your life would have been, without Marianne?"

"Never, because without Marianne I wouldn't have a life. Why do you ask?"

"Her return has pretty much upset my apple cart. I never know what's she going to ask of me next. Each day brings a new challenge."

"Yeah, she does that. Our Marianne's a force of nature. Put her and Darius together and the drama never ends. It's like being on a roller coaster twenty-four-seven." That was a cheap shot, to bring in Darius, but right now she didn't want to hear about Gabriel's connection to Marianne.

"She's stripped my life of routine, and I'm not someone who's comfortable with spontaneity. I had it all figured out, Jade, and then—"

"Poof?"

"Poof."

Please let him stop there. Please let him not confess to still being in love with Marianne.

She needed more than sleep. A social life, that was the answer. A female drunkfest with Sasha and the executive director of Girls In Motion. Problem solved!

"And something about EmJ bothers me, but I can't put my finger on it." Gabriel breathed heavily. "I can't help wondering how healthy the relationship is for Marianne. Hugh doesn't approve. He warned her against making friends from the hospital. In his words, 'The people aren't necessarily what they seem.'"

"And how did Marianne take that?"

"She laughed and told him she met her first husband on a locked psych ward."

"All true. But she's a big girl, Gabriel. And since she refuses to talk to me, my hands are tied."

"I know, but Marianne is in such a fragile state."

A text came through from Darius: ANY NEWS. He'd reverted to all caps and no punctuation or emoticons. Jade ignored him, her five minutes with Gabriel too precious.

"What's really rattling your cage?" she said.

"I'm that transparent?"

"No, you sound as if you're thinking aloud. Stream of consciousness."

"You're getting to know me too well."

I wish. From on top of one of the speakers behind the console, her plastic two-inch-high Kiss guitarist stared at her, frozen in midscream.

"I'm not comfortable with the idea of EmJ living in my spare room," Gabriel continued. "And that reaction is heinous to me. She's a lost soul, and taking her in is the right course of action."

Jade uncrossed her legs and sat up straight. "She's coming to live at the rectory?"

This unknown girl was going to sleep in the same house as Gabriel. See him first thing in the morning when he padded downstairs with bed hair and bare feet.

"It would appear so, since she has nowhere else to go. Apparently her mother has disowned her, her father's dead, and her ex-boyfriend is the drug lord of Luton."

"O brave new world for you."

"Are you teasing me?"

She could hear his smile. "Possibly."

"I'm not enjoying these decidedly unchristian feelings I have about this girl."

"Wait a minute. Aren't you always telling me priests are human beings? Then this is a perfectly normal reaction. Taking in Marianne was one thing—you guys share a past. But this is a young person who likely has a truckload of issues. My guess is that she doesn't trust you any more than you trust her. Am I right?"

"Spot on. I knew talking to you would help me find perspective. Thank you."

Sasha poked her head around the door. "Meeting in five."

Jade held up a finger and mouthed, *One minute.* "I'm sorry, but I have to hang up on you. If Marianne decides she's ready to talk to me, I'll check out this EmJ chick. Let you know what I discover. My advice? Let this play out. And as you said to me, I'm here if you need to talk."

This time Sasha stood in front of the plate-glass window to the smaller tracking room, mouthing, *They're here.*

"Before I go, tell me one good thing about Marianne. Did she put some weight back on?"

"She looks better, less gaunt. And I overheard her tell EmJ that she loves you deeply."

Jade sighed. "Thank you. I don't mean to be insecure and needy, but I—"

"Need to feel loved. I understand. We'll talk tomorrow."

Darius sent another text: STOP IGNORING ME.

"Yeah. Chin up, Vicar."

And Gabriel hung up.

It took all her self-control to not fill her soundproof room with a battle cry of "You're loved too." Because there was no more escaping the obvious: in one weekend, Gabriel Bonham had stolen her heart, and she didn't know how to get it back.

TWENTY-FIVE
MARIANNE

Madness didn't take a break, and neither did therapy. Marianne stared at the framed family portrait on Dr. P.'s desk. His name came with a complex pronunciation that refused to stick in her brain even though she'd practiced it alone in her room. The first time she'd referred to him simply as Dr. P., his tired smile had suggested he was used to compromise. The precious little girl in the photograph probably had something to do with that. Marianne looked up.

"Are you having thoughts of dying or hurting yourself?" Elbows raised, Dr. P. created a triangle with his index fingers and thumbs in a let's-quiet-it-down-and-find-our-happy-place gesture. This psychiatrist had one speed: slow and deliberate, like a well-rehearsed performance that drew crowds but lacked heart. "Have you been thinking about death?"

Two tricky questions, since she hadn't been doing a whole lot of thinking. After talking with Gabriel, she'd been ridiculously happy. A little too happy, Dr. P. decided, and another week of endless meds-tweaking followed: *You put the right leg in, the right leg out, you do some hokeypokey and you shake the meds all about.* Meds shifts came prepackaged with their own quiet version of hell. Back to being a medical dartboard. But at least it had delayed reentry to life, given her time to think about her marriage. Not that she was. Thinking.

"No. I've been focusing my brain power on putting one foot in front of the other so I can leave my room each day."

He tapped his index fingers against his chin. "And does this have something to do with Emmajohn Peel? I gather you've become friendly."

"You've got the nurses spying on us?"

"It was a simple question, Marianne."

She tried to give Dr. P a withering stare, but her eyeballs ached with the need for more sleep. "Yes. When she leaves, she's coming to my friend Gabriel's house. Any strings you can pull to get us released on the same day would be much appreciated. She has nowhere else to go."

"Gabriel has agreed to this plan?"

"After pondering the complexities of his decision and, no doubt, having a tête-à-tête with the deity in the sky, Gabriel said yes."

"You think this a wise course of action, Marianne?"

Outside Dr. P's window, the grounds staff clipped potted privet into elegant topiaries. Lots of curved, round edges created by very sharp hedge shears. All with red handles.

"Yes, I do. I can teach EmJ to focus on her music. Music can save her the way it's saved hundreds of young women I've helped through my nonprofit group."

"Your idealism is noble, but encouraging a fellow patient to indulge in fantasies of fame and glory might not be advisable. She needs to live within the means of her illness, not stretch for stars she can't reach."

"Ah, but there, dear doctor, is the flaw in your argument. I'm not talking about fantasies. Music is my business and I can spot talent with my eyes closed. And with all due respect, the idea that *nutters*"—she smiled as she quoted EmJ—"like me have to live within the lines of our illness is utter bullshit."

He nodded as if in agreement. Marianne picked up his paperweight, juggled it between her hands like a Hacky Sack, put it down and crossed her arms. And her legs.

"I was told to lower my expectations of life, to give up hope of having a family and a career. But I've managed all those things despite my illness. EmJ doesn't have to think like a disabled person."

"I disagree. Accepting your limitations is part of the process."

"I do accept my limitations, but living within the confines of manic-depressive illness doesn't mean we can't reach for success. I can help her. Where's the harm?"

"EmJ is not your problem," Dr. P. said.

In the distance a phone rang. "If not mine, then whose? Who's going to make sure she doesn't end up living on the streets and back on the Molly? She's got no support system, and no one can do this alone."

"No, Marianne. You can't." He paused. "Your husband is calling the front desk multiple times a day. Have you taken any of his calls?"

Marianne shook her head.

"How were things between you and Darius before February's car accident?"

"Good. We used to fall asleep holding hands." Then she couldn't help herself. "Sex off the charts."

He stared back, unfazed. "When was the last time the two of you were intimate?"

She broke eye contact and shrugged.

"How have things been between you since the accident?"

"Bad. He hovers all the time, reassuring me it wasn't my fault. I don't want reassurance. An unborn baby is dead. I deserve to suffer."

"Next week is the six-month anniversary of the accident. Am I right?"

"Thanks for reminding me. That certainly puts a smile on my sedated face."

"Yesterday you told me you were responsible for what happened, but I gather you weren't charged with reckless driving."

Marianne slumped back in her chair. Verbal sparring was a brain drain. "I spooked the deer and started the chain reaction. Then I lost concentration for a second when Darius . . ."

"When he what, Marianne?"

"He turned down the music. I laughed and turned it back up. That's all I remember. I woke up in hospital with a head injury, and Darius told me the other driver was fine. But he lied." She reached across Dr. P's desk for the tissue box. "She was seven months pregnant, the other driver. Her baby was stillborn."

"Is this why you're mad at Darius, because you think he lied to you?"

"No! I'm not mad at him. The very opposite."

"Does he know about your baby?"

She blew her nose loudly. "No one ever knew except for me, Simon, Gabriel, and our parents."

"Why did you never tell Darius?"

"He was my do-over. My second chance. Technically my third. We both wanted a clean slate—no rehashing of past mistakes. His first wife was half-baked, and I was going to be everything she wasn't. For Darius, I was doing to do Stepford-wife normal." She screwed up what remained of the tissue. "Denial is a great drug, Dr. P."

"And now?"

"Now he wants to be knee-deep in madness and part of my treatment plan."

"And why does that scare you?"

"He and I made a deal to not share the past. To put it aside. My past with Gabriel and Simon represents the worst of me—everything I've tried to change. It's not just about the baby, it's about what I did to a family. My best friend's family. My best friend who then didn't talk to me for thirty years." She dragged her hands through her hair. "Simon shouldn't even have been there that night. Mrs. Bonham was supposed to pick us up, but she came down with a migraine and sent Simon in her place. And everything that followed was a direct consequence of my secrets, my lies."

"If you don't remember what happened, how can you blame yourself for the accident?"

"I remember enough to know that I'm the reason a mother has to live with the guilt of sending her son to his death. That accident is my Pandora's box. What if Darius sees inside and decides been there, done that, no effing way I'm reordering the T-shirt in a different size?" The merry-go-round was starting up again like a song set to repeat. "I can't lose him."

"Talk to him, Marianne. He may surprise you."

"I've worked hard to protect him and Jade from my past. I crossed the point of no return a long time ago."

"Protect them or shut them out?"

She didn't answer.

"And what about Gabriel? You seem to trust him more than your family."

"That's not fair." She stood, walked to the window, and stared out at the bench where she and Gabriel had sat, hands entwined like a pair of kids. "Our connection might be . . . a little weird, but we go back a long way." *We go back all the way.*

A light rain started to fall, and the grounds crew began packing up their tools.

Dr. P. was right. Ten days ago Jade and Darius had flown back to North Carolina, and with each day it became easier to not return their calls and harder to figure out the way home. The one relationship that didn't need fixing was with Gabriel. God's ultimate irony.

TWENTY-SIX

GABRIEL

Never before had Gabriel wished to be clairvoyant.

Using the rectory as a refuge for those in need was highly appropriate; his level of conflict over how long the situation would last was not. In the three weeks minus a day that Marianne had been in the Beeches, he'd fallen back into a blissful routine—dull except for his nightly conversations with Jade—but yet again he would be tiptoeing through uncertainty in his own house. Trying to piece together the puzzle of Marianne's plans was tougher than translating the new BBC weatherman with the Welsh accent. And EmJ, who sat in sullen silence in the back of Hugh's Volvo, was a closed book.

Hugh's car smelled of dog and was stocked with pear drops, a weakness Gabriel didn't share. As penance for being the sherbet lemon thief, he had avoided boiled sweets for the last three decades.

Marianne pulled forward in the backseat, nodded in Hugh's direction, and then fixed her focus on Gabriel. "Thought you needed reinforcements?"

"Do you recall how small my car is?" Even to him that made an unconvincing counterargument. He half turned in his seat.

Marianne, who had successfully petitioned for two extra days in the Beeches to ensure that she and EmJ were released on the same day, raised her eyebrows. Next to her EmJ picked off what remained of her nail varnish.

"Seat belts, ladies?"

EmJ ignored him. Marianne sat back and made a big show of strapping them both in.

"Happy?" she said, and squeezed EmJ's knee.

Gabriel turned back to stare through the windscreen. "Extremely. It's the law over here." How could she have such a cavalier attitude toward car safety? Sometimes he felt he knew Marianne better than himself; other times he didn't know her at all. He closed his eyes briefly and tried to imagine the soothing sounds of the indoor water fountain in Hugh's office, but it quickly transformed into the deafening roar of a mountainous waterfall.

Inhale, exhale; inhale, exhale.

As the car inched through the avenue of beech trees that led to the main road, EmJ muttered something that could have been, "Good riddance." They turned right and followed signs to the M1. Before long they were in a stream of fast-moving traffic. Whether he liked it or not, they were heading home.

"Do you mind if we drop you at the rectory and leave for a while?" Gabriel said. "Hugh and I need to meet with some members of the youth group."

Hugh glanced up in the rearview mirror. "They formed a band for a teen dance, but it all got a bit out of hand."

That was a humongous understatement. Despite having once been a key participant in teen melodrama played to the hilt, Gabriel had never before witnessed teen girls declaring war on each other. Hugh, however, had found the whole thing mildly amusing.

"The lead singer quit," Hugh said. "You should come with us, EmJ. Try out as a replacement."

Gabriel glared at him.

Hugh responded with a quick smile. "Why don't you pass around the pear drops?" he said.

Gabriel picked up the white paper bag of loose sweets and offered it to the backseat passengers. Marianne shook her head, and EmJ gazed out of the window at the concrete barriers. Gabriel waited, his arm held out. Slowly EmJ turned and reached for a sweet. She gave Gabriel a shaky smile that made her look about ten years old. He grinned back, and something settled inside. Hope.

"Are they snotty and all religious?" she said quietly.

"Hardly." Hugh laughed, and Gabriel kept his thoughts unexpressed—that the recent behavior he'd witnessed had been far from religious.

"And Marianne, you might have some good advice for them," Hugh continued. "The idea is to create a regular event for local bands. Village life can be deathly quiet for teenagers."

"Oh, I don't know," Marianne said. "We never had a problem finding our own entertainment, did we, Gabriel?"

Hugh glanced sideways at him, this time minus the smile.

✳

They walked across the wood floor of the cavernous village hall, their footsteps as loud as firecrackers. The boys, with the exception of Tom, were not subtle about watching EmJ. And EmJ, who had struck Gabriel as asexual up until that point, appeared to walk toward them with a slight sway in her hips.

"Are you sure this is a good idea?" he whispered to Hugh. Tom was a good sort, Jack too, but Charlotte—*Let's be honest, God*—was not an exemplary Christian, and he knew nothing about Matt, who lived one village over.

Charlotte greeted them with a too-wide smile. "Good afternoon, Reverend."

Gabriel nodded at the pretty blonde in the shortest skirt he'd ever seen. Did it even count as a skirt?

EmJ ignored the boys and looked straight at Charlotte. A wise move from one so young. "You, like, need a singer?"

"Yar," Charlotte said, her voice posher than usual, but then Charlotte enjoyed flashing her social class. "Why?" She looked EmJ up and down. "Do you know of anyone?"

"Might." EmJ shrugged and folded her cardigan around herself.

"EmJ's a talented singer." Marianne moved forward to stand next to EmJ. "And I have some experience with live musical performances. We're going to be in the village for a while with nothing to do. We'd be happy to help out, if you'd like us to. No pressure."

Marianne had also read the situation well.

"She owns a recording studio in America," EmJ said with a sniff. Finally she turned to the boys. "They're recording the new Media Rage."

Nobody moved, but Tom's eyes grew wide. Taking this as her cue, Marianne stepped toward him, hand outstretched. "Nice to meet y'all. I'm Marianne."

Oh, she was good. Whereas Charlotte had polished her accent, Marianne had turned hers southern. For some reason it made her less intimidating.

"She's in her element," Hugh whispered.

Tom shook Marianne's hand. "I'm Tom, the guitarist." He pointed at the others. "Matt plays the drums, Jack's on bass. Charlotte's our manager. She makes all the posters and stuff."

"Is there a Media Rage song you could play?"

"Too bloody right!" Tom said, his handsome face lighting up with the same impish grin he'd had as a small boy wreaking havoc during his brother's baptism. Gabriel couldn't help but smile. What a handful Tom had been as a youngster, but even so, he had such compassion, such generosity of spirit. Hopefully when he went up to Oxford in the autumn he would find someone more deserving of his affection than Charlotte. Good Lord, that was an inappropriate thought.

Sorry, God.

He tried to listen as Marianne quizzed Tom about Media Rage.

"EmJ knows that one," Marianne said. "How about you let her audition?"

"Why not?" Charlotte said, and tugged on the large gold-and-ruby cross dangling around her neck.

Gabriel leaned against the far wall of the village hall and watched the energy in the room shift from Charlotte to Marianne. As she talked and gestured, the band members nodded.

Marianne winked at him. "We've got this covered, Gabriel. We'll walk back when we're done."

"Would you mind terribly if we watched the performance?" Hugh said.

"Guys?" Marianne asked the band members. They all mumbled their approval. Much scraping of chairs and shuffling followed before the boys hopped up on the stage with an agility Gabriel doubted he'd ever possessed, even in the sixth form. EmJ took the stairs.

Hugh leaned in to Gabriel. "I think EmJ's more than capable of dealing with one Sloane Ranger, but I'd like to make sure."

"Me too. Since I appear to be responsible for her well-being."

"Come on, you old fogy. Admit it, she's bringing out your inner Papa Bear."

The band tuned up and exchanged a few words.

"I don't have an inner Papa Bear," Gabriel said.

"Balderdash and poppycock."

Gabriel laughed. "What?"

But before Hugh could answer, Matt tapped his drumsticks together, Tom plucked his guitar strings as if his life depended on it, and music—loud and wild—exploded.

Matt, a quiet boy who never looked Gabriel in the eye, started bashing the drums with a savage intensity. His hair flopped back and forth; his mouth hung open in a silent howl. EmJ stood alone, isolated in the middle of the stage in a trance. She held the mic close with one hand, and with the other, clasped her cardigan to her throat.

And then she detonated.

Stomping to the drumbeat, gyrating one way, then another with an uncanny sense for where the equipment and other band members were, she grabbed her hair and yanked it back to expose huge, black-rimmed eyes. Her voice—raspy and gravelly—unleashed its power, transforming her from a brittle, soft-spoken urchin into a fearless, screaming presence. She screeched the lyrics as if they were being ripped from her soul. Her performance was aggressive, ferocious, and unlike anything Gabriel had ever seen. The music jolted through his body, and his scalp tingled. What would Jade make of this? Blast, he should have been recording it for her on his phone. He sort of knew how to do that.

The band stopped. Tom and Jack rushed EmJ with high fives while Marianne clapped and Hugh whistled. But Gabriel stood still. This was a window into Marianne and Jade's life halfway round the world. Their real life that he didn't share.

"We don't really know what we're doing." Jack, who normally kept his face lowered due to acute acne, smiled at Marianne.

"Bull. You guys were rocking it! Name of the band?" Marianne said.

"We couldn't agree on one." Charlotte blushed.

Marianne rubbed her hands together. "No worries."

"Come on, old chap." Hugh slapped his back. "I need a cup of tea and a chocolate digestive. Please tell me your biscuit tin is full."

Gabriel snapped out of his reverie. "Marvelous job, everyone. Marianne? See you later?"

Outside he took a deep breath of muggy August air. In the horse chestnut tree at the edge of Bill Collins's garden, a blackbird sang.

"You might want to rethink your assessment of the drummer," Hugh said. "Matt's hardly as you described him, shy to the point of being nonfunctional."

"It appears I was wrong." Gabriel swatted away a bluebottle. "About that and my concern they'd pick on EmJ."

"And Marianne? Very impressive, I have to say. Those teenagers were eating out of her hand. This could be exactly what they both need. Did you see her face when EmJ started singing?" Hugh opened his car door. "I think something very opportune is unfolding in the Newton Rushford village hall this afternoon."

"I hope you're right," Gabriel said. He glanced at Bill Collins's front door, which mercifully stayed shut. Something huge had just happened, he wouldn't disagree with Hugh on that score, but the word *opportune* did not sit well in his stomach.

TWENTY-SEVEN

GABRIEL

Supper cleared up, Hugh and Gabriel sat under the pergola. From the open windows above, a duet—one voice sweet as a thrush, the other more folksy, more Celtic—drifted down to the garden. The singing stopped, and EmJ giggled. She had a quiet, sweet giggle. Hearing it for the first time along with more of Marianne's singing? He could get used to both sounds filling his house. Gabriel stretched out his legs and crossed them at the ankles.

In the navy-blue sky the last of the swallows circled. Soon they would be gone, and the hours of evening twilight on the patio would be replaced by curtains drawn at four p.m. The months of short gray days had never bothered him before. Every season had its own beauty. But this year when winter descended, he would be sealed inside his house, alone. And Marianne and EmJ would likely be in North Carolina with Darius and Jade.

"That was a rather big sigh," Hugh said. "Not enjoying the music?"

"I'm inhaling your secondhand smoke."

Romeo and Juliet cigars were Hugh's other guilty pleasure along with pear drops.

"I'm not losing my hearing yet, old chap. That was definitely not an inhale."

"This evening has taken me a bit by surprise, that's all."

"You were expecting female hysterics, not heavenly music?"

"Something along those lines."

Marianne called out words of encouragement. "You have a beautiful voice, rock it!" Followed by, "What's your instrument? I can't hear you. Louder! What's your instrument?"

"My voice," EmJ shrieked.

"Louder! Take up space! Be heard!" And they both started laughing again.

"They have such lovely voices." Hugh tapped his cigar in the glass ashtray Gabriel kept especially for him. "Different but equally lovely."

Gabriel rested his head on the back of his chair and watched for Venus on the horizon. "Marianne always had an amazing voice. She snagged all the solos in the church choir."

"You were in the choir with her?"

"With my voice?"

"That doesn't stop you from belting out U2 most enthusiastically."

"You're on thin ice, my ABBA-singing friend. But no, I didn't make it into the choir. The choirmistress refused to take me after I gave an abysmal rendition of 'Onward, Christian Soldiers.' We auditioned together, Marianne and I. It was the first time I realized she would, one day, leave me behind."

That was more than he'd meant to say, but it was too easy to lower his guard with Hugh. Gabriel sat up and stared into his chipped coffee mug, purchased from the bring-and-buy stall at the last Christmas bazaar. It was hard to support all the village fund-raisers on his salary, but he did his bit. Mainly he bought loads of rubbish he didn't need and provided prizes for the annual teddy bear jump from the church tower—a decent little fund-raiser for the leaking-roof fund. As opposed to the save-our-organ fund, although they were making progress with the heritage lottery people on that one.

Hugh puffed a thin column of smoke into the evening air. "And how are you doing with all this Marianne business?"

The light was fading fast. In Dead Woman, an owl hooted.

"Me? Not bad. A bit tired." Gabriel turned toward him.

"You put up a good front. Always have, always will. But this? This would be outside anyone's norm. The woman whom I suspect was your one great love pops back up after thirty years; has a psychotic break, which rebounds on you; and now appears to be living in your house with a teenager who has nowhere else to go. Have you thought about where this will lead?"

"No. I learned a long time ago not to plan my life around Marianne. I'm here for as long as she needs me. I have every assumption that, at some point, she'll return home."

"To her husband."

"If you have a point to make, Hugh, please do so." Gabriel put his mug down on the table between them.

"I know you would never compromise your faith, but Marianne is a married woman."

"Yes, I am fully aware of that fact."

"And unless I'm very much mistaken," Hugh continued, "earlier today she alluded to the fact that the two of you had had a sexually active relationship."

Gabriel crossed his arms and listened to the boom-boom, boom-boom of his heart pumping blood.

"Have you considered what could happen if she decides she's still in love with you?"

"Marianne is not in love with me. And I sincerely doubt she ever was, given what happened with my brother."

"And if you're wrong?"

"Thank you, Hugh," Gabriel said, "for questioning my understanding of my own past." Although he had been doing exactly that since the day Marianne had appeared in his church.

"You have to admit, this refusal to see Darius." Hugh shook his head. "Very strange."

"She has her reasons. That's all I need to know." Gabriel reined in his voice. He would not lose his temper. "And I'm continuing to offer counsel that encourages her to contact Darius and save her marriage. My mind is perfectly clear on this issue. I appreciate your concern, but I do not need your guidance."

"Gabriel," Marianne called from inside the house. "We need to use your computer to help EmJ find her front-woman style. We can't decide whether to go for the androgynous look or punk princess."

"It's all yours," he called back.

"Exceptional circumstances and all that, though," Hugh said.

"There are no exceptional circumstances. I'm thankful that we've been able to reconnect. And I'm thankful I've had a chance to help her. The end."

"Not the beginning?"

"No." Gabriel stood up and pushed back his chair. It grated on the concrete. "Now, if you'll excuse me, I need to go and check that my houseguests are not deleting my half-written sermon."

As he walked through the living room, his landline rang. A London number flashed up, not one he recognized, and Darius's voice blasted onto the answerphone.

"Marianne? I know you're there. The hospital told me you'd gone *home*." He spat out the word. "Pick up. Pick up the goddamn phone." Darius paused, and the machine recorded his breathing.

TWENTY-EIGHT

GABRIEL

Gabriel tugged on the locked bottom drawer of his desk and, against all reason, kept tugging. Tremors scurried up his arm and into his jaw, rattling his teeth. He knew the blasted thing was locked; there was no need to double-check. Unless he was running short on trust.

Retrieving his glass from on top of his printed-out draft, he stuck his bare feet up on his desk and leaned back in his chair. Marianne might be the reason he'd locked away his stash of alcohol, but she was not the reason he'd poured the second pink gin, the one that signaled death to the evening's sermon writing.

He glanced at his silent mobile phone. Jade hadn't called the night before and had remained quiet all day. No texts, no emails. Not so much as a smoke signal. Was this because she knew Darius had returned to England? Or had she been swamped running a business without her boss, the man with a rather nasty temper who was a forty-minute train ride away?

Chattering female voices filtered under his door. Marianne was giving EmJ another singing lesson, but in here, it was just him. Alone with his foul mood and his illicit booze. He should add gin to his shopping list. It might be a good idea to stock up. His cache was pitiful even for a bachelor: a bottle of sherry for the organist, whisky for Hugh and the churchwardens, gin for himself and his parents, although they visited less and less. Traveling had become increasingly difficult for his father. Mind you, that was probably a blessing. His mother's new confrontational personality seemed ill-suited to driving. A week earlier she'd been involved in an incident of parking rage at Tesco that had involved the police.

Gabriel picked up a biro and scribbled *"Call Mum's Dr."* on the back of his hand. It seemed his note-taking was slipping. Quite a bit had slipped in the last twenty-four hours.

He texted Jade again. `We need to talk. Urgently. Please call.`

Until yesterday he'd taken their brothers-in-arms mentality for granted: *I've got your back, you've got mine.* And without warning she'd cut him off at the knees. The possibility of their friendship had become a closed door with laughter on the other side.

The landline rang, and he swallowed a huge gulp of gin before snatching up his handset.

"Evening, sexy," Jade said. "Sorry for the radio silence, I've been underground with a new band."

Gabriel shot back in his desk chair, then wobbled to regain his balance. "Ow."

"Everything okay there in rural England?"

"Not quite the greeting I was anticipating." He rubbed his anklebone. "Bashed my ankle on the edge of the desk in the shock."

"Your fault. You told me not to call you Father, so I'm trying something new on for size. And you are quite sexy, except when you wear that dress on a Sunday."

He took another gulp of gin. This was not how he'd planned to start the conversation.

"Right. Thank you. Sexy is an upgrade from my usual compliments of 'Good sermon, Reverend.'"

"What's the emergency? You sound a little off-kilter." The fun had gone from her voice, but then again, she'd proved her skill at adapting to any situation. Or mood.

"We need to talk."

"I think you'll find we are, by most people's definition."

"Right." More gin. His computer screen became a little fuzzy; so did the room beyond. "What I meant is that I'd like to talk to Darius. Is he there?"

Brilliant, that was not what he'd meant to say, either. An honorable person would have let her explain, given her an out, not chosen the one question that cornered her in deceit.

Jade seemed to turn away momentarily to talk to someone. "He's not here right now."

"Don't you share an office space with him?"

Jade said nothing. A very long nothing.

"Jade?"

"Yeah. Sorry. Distracted by work stuff. Yeah, yeah I do—share a space with him. But right now we're working on different projects." She paused. "He's freelancing off-site. I can have him call you."

"From London?"

"You know, then." Her voice was small and distant.

"When did he arrive?"

"Gabriel, please don't ask me to betray a confidence."

"I'm not asking you to. I'm asking when he arrived."

"Can we let this go?"

Normally he would respect that phrase, *Can we let this go*. Gabriel flopped back into his desk chair. He'd engineered his life so it wouldn't be this way, so he didn't fill up on petty emotions. It was as if the last three decades fell away, and he was, once again, the jealous seventeen-year-old. As always, life circled back to Marianne when he'd hoped for a different story. Certainly one with a better ending. But this was a ruddy big roadblock.

"No, we can't. You neglected to tell me something, which, given Darius's combustible personality, I should have known. I thought we'd become friends."

The church clock struck the hour, and she gave a sharp laugh that was anything but funny. "Yeah, well, so did I. And now you're what, putting me in the witness box for a grilling? Life isn't tied up into good and bad, Gabriel. Sometimes we have to go outside our comfort zone to protect the people we love. My loyalties, in case you need a reminder, are to Marianne and Darius. No wiggle room in that mind-set. When it comes to them, I do what they need me to do. So take a number, why don't you."

His study was no longer fuzzy. It was a one-dimensional wall. In the distance, a horn blared on the A428, the road that sliced its way through the heart of the village.

"Is Darius in London?"

"I can't answer that."

"You just did."

"What do you want from me?" Jade said. "You want me to rat out my family? Since we barely know each other, I'll cut you some slack, but it's pretty fucking obvious that you don't understand the first thing about me. You want honesty? Here it is: the real reason I didn't call last night was because I wanted a break—from you, from Marianne, from Darius, from all of it. You think I'm having a rave over here trying to hold everything together? So here's the truth, *Father*. Last night I was out getting shitfaced with girlfriends, because I have a life that doesn't include you or running this studio. And today I'm juggling work with a mother*fucker* of a hangover. And wanna know what else? Nightjar has been mine since the day I flew home, because Darius didn't just arrive in England, you jackass. He never left."

Then she hung up, leaving him no one to apologize to.

In the room above, music started playing. As always, Marianne had turned it up too loud. He should remind her, for the umpteenth time, that Phyllis next door liked to fall asleep to *BBC News at Ten*, not the heavy thumping of Media Rage. Gabriel got up and walked slowly to the door but stopped by the mantelpiece to pick up the glass angel ornament with the damaged wing. He'd snapped part of it off, accidentally, that first Christmas after Simon's death, a grim affair short on presents and cheer. He had never attempted to mend his broken angel. It always reminded him of everything he'd survived, despite himself. Of the strength faith gave him. But sometimes—he dusted the angel gently with his hand and put her back—friendship mattered as much as faith. And sometimes, no mattered what you believed, you couldn't save yourself from your own stupidity.

TWENTY-NINE

DARIUS

A Berklee College of Music alum, with a master's, who'd once had Keith-fucking-Richards on speed dial, and his life had boiled down to chrysanthemum tea. Fifty years of sucky decisions and this, surely, was an all-time low.

Darius snapped the lid off his recycled paper cup. Flower heads bobbed in the no-longer-hot water. Yup. Losing his teeny-tiny mind. And if this crap was meant to help lower blood pressure, it wasn't working. His heartbeat was still a constant rhythm of stress, stuck in the hypertension zone according to the blood pressure cuff in the local drugstore. Marianne could, quite possibly, be the death of him.

Darius dumped out the tea in the long grass filled with jumping insects, missed, and got it all over his Dr. Martens boot. His favorite Dr. Martens. Tomorrow he was going back to espresso. If he was going to collapse with a heart attack, let his body at least be caffeinated.

The beautiful au pair, the one who kept trying to talk to him, waved. He raised his hand and looked away. Hampstead Heath was teeming with kids on tricycles and bicycles, kids flying kites and tossing

Frisbees, kids eating ice cream cones stuffed with swirls of vanilla ice cream and Cadbury Flakes sticking out of the top—chocolate flakes, best food invention since espresso gelato—and this was so not his world: kids, parks, and fucking dogs. Literally, there was a dog to his left humping another dog.

Fear of dogs was a shared fear, and the one part of her inner psyche Marianne had shown him. Damn his insistence, when they got hitched, that their pasts stay buried. It had all come back to fear. Fear that he didn't deserve their life at Nightjar, that he wasn't good enough for her. Fear of losing her love. She was the first woman who had never wanted anything from him. Even when he was a teenager, his sisters had carved out his role: you're the man of the family, you deal with Dad. Just because he was physically able to haul a drunk up the stairs didn't make him the right family member for the job. And after his sisters left home, he'd helped his mother perpetuate the pretense that his father wasn't a drunk. Did that bring him back to being an enabler?

A color-coordinated jogger trotted past. He should probably return to a regular exercise regime. Elevate that serotonin level; get those endorphins flowing. Maybe if he worked his body to exhaustion, it would forget to crave. Marianne was his drug; he'd known it from the first time he'd woken up in her bed. And this was where it had led—to a strange limbo of oversexed dogs and the obsession devouring his insides: he had never been the love of her life. That role belonged to Gabriel.

At least on Hampstead Heath the abundance of professional dog walkers meant the mutts were mostly controlled. Thankfully the humping and the being-humped dogs were on leashes while their owners discussed the chore of sewing name tags into school uniforms. Also, the mom on the left had a huge crush on her kids' piano teacher. This was his life now: eavesdropping on the humdrum existence of others to take his mind off the implosion of his marriage. Divorce the first time around had cost him a fortune in therapy and acupuncture. Divorce the woman he loved? He couldn't go there. But he was out of options and tolerance. The proverbial straw had broken the proverbial camel's back, and it was time to stop acting the fool and grow a pair.

Marianne had been released from the hospital two days earlier and still refused to see him, talk to him, listen to him. Not one day but two. Two. Was it too late to become a monk? Not really an option for an atheist. But he'd walked away from his life once, started over. Doing it a second time should be a breeze. Especially since he'd been offered a lucrative gig in London that could take him out of circulation for six months.

His phone announced a WhatsApp message, the app Jade had insisted they download after he'd announced his intention to stay in England because it allowed them to text for free.

Gabriel knows where you are, she'd typed.

Yeah, I screwed up. Used my friend's landline to call la maison de Dieu instead of my cell. It must have come up as a London number.

His life might be over, but at least he could still talk French. Although that took him back to another spectacular mistake in the shape of a French singer who had failed to mention she was married. It would have been so much nicer to discover the truth from her instead of the paparazzi. If you needed a passport to travel to this strange country called love, his stamps would read the same two words over and over: *denied entry.*

Now what? Jade texted.

Who knew? He didn't. Marianne sent a message last night. Says she's sorry and needs more time. I answered and she ignored me. How much fucking time does she need, Jade?

IDK, I got the identical text.

With a pulsing red heart at the end?

Mine was pink. Didn't pulse.

Think he put her up to it?

How should I know? Gabriel's pissed at me. Which is fine, because I'm pissed at him. He accused me of not being honest.

Interesting turn of events. Jade had laughed off far worse insults. Please tell me you haven't got the hots for this guy.

Fuck off.

Yup. He was on the mark. Well, well. Gabriel had become the cuckoo in his nest. Now he knew he was losing it: he was thinking about birds as well as flowers.

Has Gabriel come on to you? He texted.

NO!!!

Good because if he's messing with you, I will fucking kill him. Slowly.

Love you too. Can we forget Gabriel and get real. What's your plan, boss?

Wave a white flag?

After all you've been through? Are you a
man or mouse?

Squeak.

Come on, you're tougher than this.

I guess. I have one last idea. Working
on it.

You're not going to do anything stupid,
right?

A man's gotta do what a man's gotta do.

You going to hire someone to steal his
U2 CDs?

Fantastic idea. But no. I'm going to send
her flowers. Every day. Enough flowers for
her to open her own flower store.

Have you forgotten that the Beeches
is costing you $1,700 a day? We're
hemorrhaging money right now. Plus I
just opened her credit card statement.
Bread and water for you guys.

Jade, the leading authority on Marianne, was talking as if his marriage had a future. Bread and water wasn't so bad. Not if it meant he

could get his wife back. Marianne was worth a life of poverty; she was worth a heart attack, although he really should get the blood pressure under control; she was worth the excruciating blend of pain and joy, because she was his muse—his goddess—and he was not giving her up without a fight.

He stood and shook a bedraggled flower head off his boot. He would go back to the house, strum his new Gibson Les Paul, purchased on English eBay, and brainstorm. (Not Absalom, but an adequate substitute, this guitar was named Beelzebub.)

Jade had a point, though. It might take more than flowers. He needed action, big action, a huge statement that screamed, *For you, I would die.*

THIRTY
MARIANNE

Marianne rolled her neck one way, then the other. Imagine that—the crunching between her ears suggested screws really were loose inside her brain. She chewed the end of Gabriel's pen and then returned to the press release she'd been writing on the pad swiped from his desk. Gabriel wouldn't care. He'd never been possessive about anything except her. Was he still? Hard to tell. She was racking up more and more Gabriel debt with less and less thought about how to repay him.

Bleh. What she'd written was utter crap. Marianne ripped off the piece of paper, screwed it up, and tossed it to the floor. She hadn't come close to capturing the uninhibited, fierce presence of EmJ the performer.

In ten days those kids had figured out how to create a cohesive, powerful sound, looking to each other, not Marianne, for validation. And Tom was a better lyricist than most guys twice his age, which he should be since he was off to study English at Oxford. But central to their magic was EmJ. Singing was a transformative experience for her, and the boys fed off her energy the moment she stepped onto the stage with her yeah-well-fuck-you attitude. She gave a group of preppy, privileged kids authenticity.

Marianne had seen many teen bands perform, many rising and failed rock stars stand up in front of an audience—mainly on YouTube or at the Cat's Cradle these days, since she couldn't do huge crowds—but EmJ was a genuine artist. Darius would be mega impressed.

Yesterday she'd spoken to him for the first time since her rectory breakdown—as opposed to her churchyard breakdown or her UNC campus breakdown. Their conversation was clipped: "I love you, I love you too; I miss you, yeah me too; I need you, I need more time." But it gave her the courage to call Jade with a full apology. As it turned out, Jade didn't expect or want an apology, and they'd picked up as if nothing had happened.

Jade. She needed Jade right now! The band was lacking a signature style, and Jade was the person to consult. Marianne pulled out her phone and started typing.

Hey girlie. Miss you. She hit "Send."

Hey yourself.

Gabriel walked in, wearing shoes for once, and dressed head to toe in black, except for the strip of white dog collar. Today was Monday, so he had either a funeral or a hospital visit. And he was going to boil. It had to be pushing eighty and humid as hell. He zapped his coffee in the microwave. He did that a lot: warmed up half-drunk cups of cold coffee.

"You're looking very pensive," Gabriel said.

"Thinking about a spectacular present for Jade—as a thank-you for pulling double shifts at Nightjar and balancing the Girls In Motion books."

Gabriel did that little thing he did with his lips when he was uncomfortable.

Another text came through. `Yo. Still there honey?`

`Sorry. Gabriel walked in.`

`K.` There was a pause. `Tell him hi. Call me later.
Xox`

"Jade says hi." Marianne looked up.

The muscles in his cheek tightened, as if he'd clenched his jaw. The microwave dinged and he turned his back on her. "How about joining me for cream teas at the Chantry later?"

"Cream teas?"

"The village fete." He retrieved his coffee and slammed the microwave door shut. "Did you forget? Today is August bank holiday, and our annual cream teas have quite the reputation. Excellent write-up last year in the *Beds Times*."

"I haven't had a cream tea in thirty years." She twirled his pen. "But I can't cope with large, noisy groups of people. EmJ's the same. Unless she's performing, she naturally isolates."

"There'll be enough clotted cream to clog your arteries. Plus Mrs. Tandy's homemade coffee-and-walnut cake, which has been known to cause a mob scene." He gave his boyish smile. "Did I mention that the tables have been set up in the Chantry's award-winning garden? The herbaceous border should be lovely."

"You sure this isn't about me flashing my wedding ring to Bill Collins?" She held up her left hand and wiggled her fourth finger with the obscenely big engagement ring. So over-the-top. So Darius. She imagined his hands on her, his breath on her, a whispered *I need you.*

"The creative process not going smoothly?" Gabriel's voice cut across her daydream.

"Not exactly. I'm trying to write a press release for the gig."

"Marianne, they're a bunch of teenagers out to have fun. Don't put too much pressure on them. Or yourself."

"Yeah, yeah, yeah. You're going to have to trust me when I tell you the meds are working. Seriously. I know the signs—a subtle easing of the heaviness and then the colors return. Muted, but muted is good. And look, they've got me on such a strong dose of lithium, I keep dropping the pen." She tried to hold her right hand level as it trembled.

"Where's EmJ?" Gabriel said.

"Having a lie-in. She didn't sleep well last night. Think she was too wound up after band practice."

"And the reason that kept her out until midnight?"

"She was hanging with the band. I told her she had to be back by then and she was."

"Is she taking drugs?"

"I sincerely hope so. Without them she's as psycho as me."

"Very funny." He sipped his coffee. "You know how I feel about gossip, but I should warn you that I've heard a rumor about Matt, the drummer."

"Such as?"

"That his best friend deals Ecstasy."

Marianne swallowed. Ecstasy—also Molly or MDMA—was EmJ's drug of choice. "You told me they were stand-up kids."

"They are. Tom especially."

"And you didn't think to warn me one of them might have a drug connection?"

"I am warning you. Given how much time EmJ is spending with the band, I took it upon myself to do a little digging. I've known the others since they were little, but Matt's not a parishioner. And this is about his friend, not him. Still, I thought you should know."

Marianne sighed. "Thank you. I'll tighten the reins." Maybe while walking through the village to the Chantry for cream teas. "So, what's going on between you and Jade?"

There it was again, that tightening of his jaw. He finished his coffee and then put the cup in the sink. "We had a minor disagreement. Since then she's refused to talk to me."

"Jade's a sucker for an apology. Were you a jerk?"

"Quite possibly. I tried to make amends with several groveling texts, which she ignored."

How un-Jade-like. A lawn mower started up next door, followed by a weed whacker. The sounds of summer.

"I hope I wasn't the cause of the argument."

"Darius was."

"Aha, now I get it. This happened after you discovered he was in London and you coerced me, under threat of memorizing the entire New Testament, to text them both."

"Yes." He tugged on his shoulder.

"Need a shoulder rub?"

"No."

That was a resounding rejection. "If it's any consolation, I was as surprised as you were to learn that Darius had been in London this whole time. Every call he placed until that night came from his cell. They kept both of us in the dark. But if I know Jade, which I do, she was protecting Darius the same way you've protected me."

Gabriel scowled at her and then fished through the contents of his fruit bowl and pulled out a chocolate bar. He snapped off a square of milk chocolate. "Since we're giving each other advice, how about letting Darius come for a visit?"

"Last time I saw my husband I threatened to kill him."

"So that explains what happened to Great-Aunt Millie's lamp."

"Sorry about that. I am going to replace it, honest."

"With something more tasteful, I trust."

She smiled. "Darius is an intensely emotional being, which I'm sure you've guessed by now. And I can't make the progress I need to make if I'm worrying constantly about his feelings."

"Fair enough." Gabriel walked to the door.

Marianne stared down at the pine table, covered in scrapes and pen marks. Maybe it was time to tackle the big fat elephant hogging the space between her and Gabriel. "Being adored"—she spoke without turning—"it's not always a blessing. On days like this one, with no hope of a breeze or rain, it's suffocating."

"I wouldn't know," he said.

The mower next door stopped; traffic rumbling on the A428 filled the silence.

"Darius loves ferociously," she said quickly. "His passion is intoxicating, and I need to dial back on extremes right now."

"EmJ is also a person of extremes."

"But that's a version I get."

"You're lucky," he said. "To be so loved."

She looked up at him. "Darius takes Xanax because the stress of being my husband gave him panic attacks. I know what I do to people." She picked up his pen and doodled on the pad. "And I smell alcohol on your breath most evenings. More than when I arrived."

"True. I have fallen into a new gin pattern," he said. "But I also knew the old you, and I remember her well."

"She's long gone, and the mental health professionals can't glue her back together."

"Fascinating as this conversation is, Humpty Dumpty"—he glanced at the kitchen clock—"I have to go do vicar things."

"See and be seen?"

"And supervise the teddy bear parachute jump from the church tower. Last year some poor stuffed rabbit got caught in a yew tree. It wasn't pretty."

"So this is a very PC event. All cuddlies allowed, whatever race, gender, or animal affiliation?"

"Indeed. Now, about our cream tea. Shall we meet at the Chantry at four? First one there nabs a table?"

"It's a date."

"Can you rephrase that, please?"

"Sure. Tea for three. You're on."

"Righty-ho, off into the wilds of Newton Rushford." Gabriel made a motivational fist. "You two behave while I'm gone. I'll leave the front door open to get a through draft."

But it would make no difference. There wasn't a hint of air in the rectory. If only she was inside her home, listening to the air-conditioning click on. And what about her poor, neglected garden? How was it surviving the August heat and, presumably, drought? No doubt Jade was taking care of that, too.

Marianne picked up her phone. Please don't fight with Gabriel. He wants to kiss and make up.

A minor exaggeration, but left to Gabriel there would be no reconciliation. He took defeat far too easily. Jade didn't answer. Marianne put the press release aside. If she'd missed a whole undercurrent between Gabriel and Jade, she could have missed worse with EmJ. She needed to be more vigilant, pay more attention to EmJ the suicide survivor, not EmJ the performer. And she needed to start asking the right questions, because whatever she'd told Gabriel, she knew something was up. At band practice she'd overheard Tom and Charlotte talking about a date.

What if everyone was right, and she wasn't well enough to take on someone more damaged than she was? She'd never been able to stop, look both ways, and then cross the street. That had to change on the walk down to the cream teas, because EmJ was not someone she could screw over. That first day in the Beeches dining room, she'd wrongly assumed that EmJ was another Jade. But EmJ's attitude wasn't about self-protection, it was about lack of affect. Which was the real reason she was sharing a bedroom with EmJ—to keep her alive.

THIRTY-ONE
MARIANNE

A heat haze shimmered over the surface of the A428, and EmJ set a pace that said, *Existing takes too much effort.* In this sticky humidity and on this road, Marianne couldn't agree more.

Nothing moved across the watercolor sky except for a hot-air balloon, drifting lazily. The mugginess, tame by Carolina standards, came without the chance of reprieve, although the distant grayness suggested clouds were building. EmJ had left the cardigan behind, but without it her bare arms looked like toothpicks, and the sleeveless tank she wore over the bandeau top hung off her shoulders.

The entire village appeared to be on the move. So many people, too many people, greeted them with a cheery "Afternoon." Marianne tried to smile in response; EmJ kept her head lowered. As they passed the bus stop, a bunch of teen girls gave a muffled critique of EmJ's hair and clothes. The gist was obvious: EmJ was a townie from the wrong side of the tracks. She huddled closer to Marianne, and they linked arms.

"I was thinking," EmJ said, "'bout you and me getting a flat in Bedford. I mean, Gabriel's nice and all, but I'm living in a rectory."

Every muscle tightened. "We should talk about that."

"You are staying, right, I mean in England?"

"Honey, I—"

EmJ pushed her away. "You're going back to America, aren't you? Abandoning me like a stray kitten you've lost interest in."

Marianne reached out and pulled EmJ back from the edge of the sidewalk as a huge truck belted through the village, defying the speed limit. The backdraft whooshed over them. "I haven't figured out anything about the future," Marianne said. "But I'm not leaving you behind. Promise." Seemed she was making promises once more.

They started walking again, although EmJ lagged behind. No, it had not been the best plan to tug someone else into her world when she didn't know where home was anymore. Or if she had one. But that wasn't going to stop her from trying to save a girl everyone else had thrown away.

Marianne slowed down, waiting for EmJ to catch up. "Whatever happens, we're in this together. But our journey's going to be bumpy for a while, because I'm convalescing, too."

"You make it sound like we've got some nasty disease."

"We have," Marianne said softly. "One that needs managing. And honey, you can't add alcohol and recreational drugs to the mix. That's like playing Russian roulette."

"So what if I party? I'm a teenager. I'm meant to be a mess."

"Yes, you are." Marianne stopped and gave her a quick hug; EmJ stiffened. "But you need to make better choices about drinking and drugs. You can't afford either right now." Actually she couldn't afford either for the rest of her life, but that was a battle for another day.

"What part of 'I'm a teenager' didn't you get?" EmJ said with a crooked smile.

"Were you with Matt last night?"

The smile disappeared, and EmJ shrugged.

"Matt strikes me as a decent guy, but I know he mixes with the drug crowd. And you can't, not unless you want to end up back in the hospital. Do us both a favor? Stay off the Molly?"

"Yeah, whatevs."

Marianne elbowed her. "Don't be such a teenager."

They continued on in silence, passing the village shop with Union Jack bunting festooned over the doorway and the dusty window display of water guns and Barbie clones lounging in bikinis around a doll-sized swimming pool. Traffic slowed to a crawl as cars, turn signals blinking, joined the line waiting to exit off the A428 at the folding sign advertising pony rides. Someone had worked hard to decorate it with hand-drawn Thelwell ponies.

"Why can I hear sleigh bells?" EmJ asked.

"I'm guessing Morris dancers." They stopped at the pedestrian crossing with flashing orange lights. A modern eyesore on a historic street. "Want to go watch?"

"No."

Marianne made a point of looking both ways before they followed a small group into the crosswalk. "If I were thinking about moving into an apartment, I'd want one down by the river. The original mill is in the Domesday Book. How cool is that?"

EmJ's silence suggested not cool at all.

"They've just finished renovating the old building, converting it into swanky two-bedrooms. Mrs. Tandy was called in to clean the showcase apartment and told me the developer can't sell any of them because he's asking a fortune—holding out for wealthy commuters. Want to go look sometime?"

EmJ shook her head and took Marianne's arm again. "I'm scared," she said in little more than a whisper. "The monsters are loud right now. I feel like I'm waiting for the void to open up again."

"Let's call the Beeches when we get back. Get you an earlier appointment."

"Nah, it's only two days." EmJ leaned her head against Marianne's. "How do you do it? Stop yourself from going mental?"

"It's a slow process, and I'm on the learning curve same as you. But drugs and alcohol don't help. I know that from firsthand experience." Marianne paused. Constantly repeating herself would only push EmJ away. "Lesson over, sweetheart. We're getting way too serious. Right now all that matters is stuffing our faces with scones and clotted cream and drinking gallons of tea so we can be terribly, terribly British. And while we sip our tea with our pinkie fingers stuck out"—Marianne demonstrated—"we can rethink the set list for your gala performance. I disagree with Tom's lineup."

"Is it that simple?" EmJ said.

"Tea and music? Why not? God knows you and I got shortchanged in the area of nonmanic enjoyment. Cream teas rock, and performance is in your blood. Give yourself permission to enjoy both." Marianne swallowed the imagined taste of a homemade scone slathered in home-made strawberry jam with clotted cream oozing over the top. It was enough to turn the most hardened carnivore into a dessert queen.

"If performance is so great, how come you gave it up?"

"It gave me up," Marianne said. "Too much alcohol. The one time I came close to making it, I was barely functional. No way I could have coped with touring. I had to learn my own parameters, narrow my world while I tried to heal. And then I started Girls In Motion and discovered my real gift was working with teens who couldn't see their own potential. I guess"—she thought of Gabriel—"you could say it was my calling. And you, girlfriend, have got it in spades. Those guys won't hold you for long. This is only your first band—a stepping-stone to bigger things."

"Why do you have such faith in me?"

EmJ spoke with too much weariness. Maybe forcing her out of bed after she'd expressed a desire to sleep the day away had been a mistake.

"Because you have extraordinary talent and I'm sure no one's ever told you that."

They rounded the village green and joined the stream of people moving toward the Chantry gates.

"I'm really fucked up, Marianne," EmJ said.

"Newsflash—so am I. Need I remind you we met in the loony bin? And there's a chance I've screwed up my marriage and my business in one quick tango with mania. I'm a three-time suicide survivor and an alcoholic, and I can't ever risk going off my meds again. I'm far from having my life together. But that's not going to stop me from trying to figure out how the pieces fit. I want to live. And I want you to live, too. You've got so much going for you. I know it's hard to see that right now, but you have to believe."

Marianne hadn't said that out loud in a long time. It used to be her daily mantra, recited into the bathroom mirror: "My life is worth living; I want to believe I can live."

"But you're not angry all the time like I am. Everything pisses me off, and things matter to you." EmJ chewed her thumbnail. "I'm not sure anything matters to me."

"Please don't say that. You have your music. Music matters. It can change lives, including yours."

"I don't think that way. Music is what I do. That's all."

Bill Collins overtook them, walking remarkably quickly for someone who clearly needed a hip replacement. "Afternoon, *Marianne*." He raised his stick a few feet off the ground and aimed it at her before disappearing.

"Afternoon, Bill."

"Tosser," EmJ whispered. "What's his problem?"

"I did unspeakable things to his daffodils a long time ago. As payback after he ratted out Gabriel for stealing candy from the village store. He and his wife were ridiculously proud of their garden, which was open every summer for the Red Cross Garden Tour. I ruined it. Guess he never forgave me."

"Shut the fuck up! Gabriel was a shoplifter? *Amaze*."

"Yup. It is amazing—the stupid things guys do when they think they're in love."

"I bet Gabriel would still nick stuff for you if you asked," EmJ said. "Long-lost love. It's so romantic."

"Our boat sailed a long time ago, honey, and I'm happily married to someone else." *Please let that be true.* "My relationship with Gabriel's complicated, in part because of decisions I made when I was younger than you. Life would be great if we could hit the 'Rewind' button and fix things, but we can't. And don't be fooled by his dog collar. Gabriel has demons. He just doesn't know what they are." *And neither do I.*

They turned onto a gravel driveway between high stone walls and artfully trimmed privet. Bunting was looped around the open gate, and sparrows and finches flitted in and out of the hedge. People swarmed: chatting, laughing, sitting, walking people. Couples sauntered around inspecting the gardens; some of the older women wore hats. The noise level rose, and EmJ sucked in her breath.

The lawn was dotted with individual tables covered in white table-cloths. Bumblebees buzzed over the daisies embedded in the lawn, and china teacups chinked. Blue tits hopped between chair legs looking for crumbs, and at an abandoned table to their right, wasps hovered over a half-eaten slice of cake. The Chantry, a sprawling, two-story historic home that couldn't decide whether it was a cottage or a country mansion, spread out in front of them.

Gabriel ducked as he walked through the front doorway with a tea urn in his arms. He lowered the urn onto what appeared to be the serving table, then spotted them. With a broad grin, he pointed to a table isolated under the shade of a huge chestnut tree and wandered over.

"Bit close this afternoon, isn't it?" He raised his arm to fan his face, revealing a large sweat stain under his arm. "Not likely to storm till tonight, though."

Heads turned; eyes watched; Marianne's skin prickled. EmJ pulled closer.

"It's okay," Marianne said. "We don't have to stay."

"Hey, EmJ," a quiet voice said behind them, and EmJ yanked her arm free of Marianne's.

Marianne turned to smile at Matt. He was wearing a Media Rage T-shirt that matched the one EmJ owned. And he had a new ear piercing that looked red and slightly bloody. Home done, no doubt. He wasn't a bad-looking kid when he smiled. Bit pimply, but cute.

Gabriel caught her eye. "Great timing, Matt. I have to go back inside to help Mrs. Tandy for five more minutes. Could you and EmJ get tea for all of us?"

Matt grunted; EmJ caught her lip with her teeth and shrugged, and they walked off.

"Good idea, inviting Matt to have tea with us," Marianne said.

"I thought you and I should get to know him better."

Marianne watched the kids walk toward the serving table. "Were our social skills that rough around the edges?"

"Undoubtedly." He glanced toward Bill Collins. "Will you be alright by yourself for a few minutes?"

"Gabriel, I'm not a helpless damsel." She leaned in. "I'm way tougher than I look when I'm sedated in the nuthouse."

He smiled. "I'll be right back."

Marianne moved a chair around to face the flower bed and sat with her back to the villagers. Fat hostas, deer food in her garden, lined the front of the border, then astilbes with lacy plumes of white and red—blood and bandages, never plant those two colors together—and behind, black *Sambucus*, lacy elderberry shrubs masquerading as small trees. She'd tried to grow them in the ground and in pots. Not one had made it through a Carolina summer.

A pair of peacock butterflies danced over the posy of garden flowers in the middle of the table. A moment's peace . . . until a kid collided with the back of her chair and shouted, "Sorry, miss!" before scampering after his friend.

Marianne turned with a smile and froze. Stalking up the driveway, his hair wilder than usual, his designer stubble closer to a real beard, was Darius. He flicked his hair back from his face and locked his sights on her. Her heart clutched the way it always did when she looked at this man who loved her with such devotion.

Gripping the back of the chair, she stood slowly. Without missing a beat, he stepped off the path and made straight for her. As he wove through the crowd, putting his hand on people's shoulders to push his way across the lawn, his eyes never left hers.

Marianne forgot how to breathe.

Darius stopped in front of her, and neither of them moved. The bags under his eyes were purple like bruises, his face thinner than she'd ever seen it.

"Darius, I—"

He grabbed her hands. Pinning them behind her back, he crushed her against his chest. "I was going to hire a plane to write *I love you* across the sky, but it was taking too long. So I'm delivering the message in person."

Arms locked around her, he tugged her closer still. "Please, Marianne," he whispered, his words warm on her cheek, on the edge of her mouth, on her lips. "All I want is to love you. Please let me love you."

Her mouth yielded to his, and she tasted desperation. His. Hers. Theirs.

Voices around them fell away except for EmJ's, coming from a distance and closing in fast. "Get off her!"

Darius pulled back. "Who the hell are you?"

A flash of steel. Darius pushed her away, and Marianne stumbled over a chair and fell to the grass. She scrambled back up to see EmJ, legs braced, glaring at Darius. And she had a knife. A very long, very sharp-looking knife.

"Give me the knife, honey." Marianne put a hand on EmJ's arm. "This is Darius, my husband."

EmJ swung around, and Marianne took a step back. Everyone had stopped moving; the crowd was as silent as it had been when she was sixteen, psychotic, and naked.

"He's going to take you away from me!" Knife held high, EmJ turned back to Darius. "No one wants you here! Go!"

Darius raised his hands in the universal sign for surrender, but EmJ didn't retreat, she advanced and slashed. One vicious movement that sounded like death itself slicing through Darius's skin. Darius groaned and crumpled to his knees, clutching his arm. EmJ raised the knife for a second swing, and Marianne shot between her and Darius.

"EmJ, no!" Marianne screamed. She grabbed EmJ's wrist and held on tight.

"We both know you're going to leave me. Why'd you even bother to pretend?"

"Stop. Please. I do care, honey. But Darius is my husband, and I love him."

"No, you're meant to love Gabriel."

Gabriel appeared behind EmJ. "Drop the knife, EmJ." The voice of reason and calm.

Marianne glanced down at Darius, now lying on the grass, his black T-shirt and black jeans stained with fresh blood. And in those five seconds that she was distracted, EmJ wiggled free and ran.

THIRTY-TWO
GABRIEL

EmJ tore down the driveway, bloody knife in hand, and disappeared into the village.

"EmJ, wait!" Matt shrieked and started running after her. Two youths Gabriel didn't recognize joined him.

"Matt!" Gabriel yelled. "Stop, all of you. She has a knife."

Ian, the retired-army-sergeant churchwarden, appeared in the gateway. "Listen to the reverend, boys," he said. Then he crossed his arms over his chest and gave Matt a smile that said, *Don't even think about trying to get past me.*

Gabriel yanked a tablecloth off the nearest table and ripped the thin fabric into strips. Dropping to his knees, he leaned over Darius. "Darius, raise your arm." He wrapped a piece of cloth round the wound and then grabbed Marianne's hand. "Keep the pressure on."

She was kneeling on the other side of Darius, her lips pale, her face ashen.

"Stings like a bitch," Darius mumbled.

"Focus on how much you dislike me instead," Gabriel said.

"Yeah, you're a dick."

"Rayne." Gabriel called out for the Women's Institute matriarch, a former school matron. "We need you."

He turned back to Marianne. He would prefer to not do this with an audience, but clearly she hadn't told him everything. And EmJ was now loose in the village with a large knife. And children were having pony rides in the Abbey park.

Behind him a mobile phone rang, and hushed voices gathered. He heard the word *stabbing*, and someone said, "Did you see what happened?"

"Does EmJ have a history of violence?" he asked Marianne, but she didn't answer. "Yes, or no? There are children everywhere."

She glared at him, her green eyes defiant. "She's a child, too. A scared and unloved child who deserves a second chance. Her family failed her; the mental health care system failed her. We can't fail her."

"I won't ask a second time."

"She was hospitalized at thirteen for aggressive behavior. At *thirteen*, Gabriel. Who isn't a powder keg at that age? But with that first incident on her record, the cops won't take any chances, and neither will her psychiatrist. Any way you look at it, they'll label her a mental patient with a history of violence. She'll end up in the criminal justice system."

"She's right. Happened to my first wife after she attempted to brain me with the meat tenderizer." Darius closed his eyes. "Never told you, babe. Sorry."

"Someone call the police," a voice yelled, "that girl is—"

"No." Marianne's head jerked up. "No. I'm begging all of you. Please, don't call the authorities. She's not dangerous."

"No cops," Darius said, his voice loud but shaky. "I'm not pressing charges."

"Everyone, please. Stay calm," Gabriel said.

Marianne turned to him. "We can find her, bring her back to the rectory, and keep her safe. Tell them not to call the cops, Gabriel. They'll listen to you."

He glanced up. One of the choirboys was filming the scene with his phone, and an older parishioner, who had recently lost her grown son to a mugging turned fatal, watched Darius, her eyes watery. Gabriel scanned the crowd of people who looked to him for moral and spiritual guidance; people who trusted him to make good decisions for their community.

"I can't do that. And I won't"—he softened his voice—"I'm sorry, but that would be an abuse of my position."

"So once again you're taking the moral high ground. Must be great to feel so certain of your own righteousness."

"Marianne." He lowered his voice. "This is not the time."

"Guys. I'm not feeling so good," Darius said.

"Now, now." Rayne appeared and patted Marianne's shoulder. "I think we've got this, haven't we, dear? Let's have a look." She pulled her multicolored reading glasses from the top of her head, slipped them onto her nose, and peeled the bloodied rag back from Darius's arm. "Oh yes, definitely needs stitches."

"I'll call for an ambulance." Gabriel pulled out his phone.

"Heavens, no need." Rayne pushed her glasses back up. "We'll take him in my Discovery. Got the dog crates in the back, though. Has anyone seen my car keys?"

Mrs. Tandy ran over, red-faced and coughing, and rattled a bunch of keys attached to a crocheted, heart-shaped Union Jack.

"Ian?" Gabriel called out, not expecting Ian to be standing behind him. Gabriel glanced toward the gate, but there was no sign of Matt and his friends. "Call Hugh and ask him to contact EmJ's psychiatrist at the Beeches. Have you got his number?"

Ian nodded.

"Ken?" Gabriel looked around for his other churchwarden. A hand shot up in the crowd. "Call the police. Tell them we have a missing teenager in crisis, recently released from psychiatric care, and that I've gone after her."

"Wait, man." Darius reached out and tugged on Gabriel's arm with remarkable strength. "I hate hospitals. Really hate hospitals. Isn't there some country Doc Martin around here? I love British imports. BBC America rocks my world."

Good Lord, what was the man prattling on about? "Darius, you need stitches."

Then Darius smiled up at Marianne, his face white. "Wounded in the line of husbandly duty. How fucking cool is that? For the record, I would die for you, my goddess."

"I love you too." Brushing back his hair, she kissed his forehead. "Please be okay."

"It's just a scratch," Darius said, attempting to pull himself up. And then he fainted into Gabriel's lap.

✳

As the church clock struck the hour, his shoes pounded on the pavement. His lungs were about to explode—running in this humidity was ludicrous—but the moment Darius and Marianne had left for the hospital, Gabriel had been haunted by an image of EmJ alone with a knife in the only place she knew to go other than the village hall: his house.

He turned the corner to Nell's Lane and flopped, wheezing, against Phyllis's stone wall. The front door of the rectory was flung open, and his car was missing. Gabriel doubled over, fighting to control his breath and confront the stark reality of his own ineptitude.

Simon had always accused him of being a pushover, saying that anyone who trusted others as much as his baby brother did was begging people to take advantage. Apparently that was still true. Even Marianne, who never thought her actions through, had questioned the wisdom of perpetually leaving his front door unlocked. With his car key on the hook inside the door. And if that wasn't bad enough, he'd filled up on petrol the day before. That car could go hundreds of miles on one tank.

EmJ's duffle might provide some clues: an address book or a phone. He ran into the house, up the stairs, and into the spare room. The duffle, the only thing EmJ had brought with her, was gone. Briefly he wondered what else was missing. Had she found the fake Bible safe where he kept his cash?

Sunlight hit a single cobweb strand, hanging in the air, attached to nothing. It shimmered, floating without beginning or end. He collapsed onto one of the unmade beds and visualized EmJ wandering around his house in her boyfriend's boxer shorts and a tatty white T-shirt, her legs like matchsticks. He saw all the elastic bands and bits of goodness-only-knows-what tied around her tiny wrist, small enough for a christening bracelet. He hadn't wanted this teenager in his house, but now he would give anything for her to be in this room. Safe. This wasn't about Marianne, this was about a young woman—no, a child—in danger. A child he should have paid more attention to. Instead he had fallen behind Marianne's lead, knowing that she was barely able to look after herself, let alone a disturbed girl. He should have asked for details of EmJ's medical history; he should have monitored her behavior. He had fouled up big-time.

Life had been so much easier in the army. Maybe he should think about going back. He'd never questioned his ability as a vicar, always knew he could rise above the petty gossip and the endless flack. But he'd hit a concrete wall of his own failings. What if he was no longer the best man for the job? And take away his job, and what remained?

Slowly he stood up and walked downstairs. When his mobile rang, he answered immediately. "Hugh?"

"Bloody big cock-up. I've called her psychiatrist, but off the record, I have no doubt he'll recommend she be sectioned. He would have no choice with her history." Hugh knew her *history*? "The most important question is whether Darius is safe. Will he be in danger if he comes back to the rectory?"

Gabriel pinched the bridge of his nose. "I never thought about that. But EmJ may be some distance away. She took my car."

"Do you think she's dangerous?"

"Honestly, Hugh, I have no clue. If you'd asked me the same question this morning, I would have told you no. But she's highly unstable and I suspect still on drugs. I'm going to wander round the village, see if I can spot my car."

"I'll get the dog sorted and come over. Keep your mobile on, and for God's sake, man, lock your house. Leave a key for me in the garden shed under an upturned flowerpot." Hugh's voice had shifted. The professionalism had gone. He sounded, for want of a better word, afraid. Or had he also dared to hope that they could make a difference in EmJ's life?

"I'll see you later," Hugh said, and hung up.

Throat dry, Gabriel pushed open the kitchen door. He would grab a cold drink before heading back out. Marianne's half-written press release was still on the table, and her balls of paper were on the floor. And dropped in his sink, covered in blood, was the knife.

He turned the tap to hot and watched Darius's diluted blood circle down the drain.

Marianne didn't know him as well as she thought. This had nothing to do with taking the moral high ground or putting his parishioners first. What it did mean? That wasn't quite so clear.

Any advice you have, God, would be much appreciated. Since I appear to have started on a path of no return.

THIRTY-THREE

MARIANNE

A reformed addict was now responsible for feeding her husband opiates. Neither Gabriel nor Hugh had clocked that Marianne was in possession of enough pain meds to give a woolly mammoth the trip of a lifetime. But her objective was to fly under everyone's radar. And be strong for EmJ. *Lead by example.* Marianne eyed the pill container on the bedside table and muttered, "Stay over there, guys."

Hugging her knees to her chest, she watched Darius from the small wicker chair with the floral slipcover. Hard and uncomfortable, it was an old nursing chair from the sixties, and the drawer in the seat had once been Gabriel's hiding place for everything from her love letters to their weed. Since Mrs. Bonham nursed both her boys in the chair, she always treated it with the same reverence as the stuffed dog on wheels they used to push around the house. Which had made it the last place she would have gone snooping.

Muffled voices rose up through the floorboards and thin carpet, and then chairs scraped across the kitchen floor. Hugh and Gabriel were still up, although it was past midnight. Gabriel had remained out, searching, until the light began to fade around nine o'clock. Blessedly late by North Carolina standards, but not late enough. And she and Darius had returned from the hospital to find Hugh chatting with the police. Apparently the fact that EmJ was missing superseded concerns about a possible criminal investigation, but a chain reaction was in place that would have serious repercussions for EmJ.

Thankfully EmJ had money—Marianne hadn't told anyone that her wallet was now empty—but she was out there scared and alone. Even on psych wards, Marianne had never been alone. Her parents were always there, on the other side of double-locked doors, waiting to hug her and take her home. Never once had they said, "We didn't sign up for this. Give us the out clause."

EmJ should have the same guarantee. Every kid should. Marianne rested her cheek on her knees while a band of pressure tightened across her chest. Man, this time she'd earned the I Screwed Up Girl Scout platinum badge. But she could fix this, and the second an opportune moment came, she was on a one-woman rescue mission. Failure was not an option, because if roles were reversed, she knew the emergency exit she would take. EmJ had nothing except for the most lethal weapon of all. A car.

In the black night the wind picked up, blowing through the open sash window, ruffling the curtains and carrying in the smell of rain. Marianne got up and closed the window. Then she sat on the edge of the bed—her back to the pill bottle—and took Darius's hand.

He looked impossibly peaceful for someone who slept only in snatches. Often he would thrash around until she kicked him out of bed to wander the house like a roving gypsy. And in the morning she would find him asleep on the sofa or the bedroom floor. She never figured out where his nightmares came from. The meat tenderizer incident he'd never mentioned before today?

There was so much they hadn't told each other, filling in the blanks with words of adoration. Darius always labeled his marriage to the ex, an alcoholic with violent outbursts, as the worst decision of his life. After today Marianne was in little doubt the woman had also been abusive.

A flash of lightning illuminated the room, and a boom of thunder, directly overhead, rattled the windowpanes. Torrents of rain lashed the roof and battered the gutters. Darius stirred and Marianne glanced at her watch. Time to give him some more Tramadol. Keeping her mind blank, she snatched up the pill bottle, screwed off the top, dumped one pill into her hand, screwed the top back on, and hid the bottle behind the digital clock. Then she slipped an arm under his head and raised him up.

"Darius, sweetheart, it's time for more meds." He opened his mouth; she popped in the pill and brought the water glass from the nightstand to his lips. He gulped, and she eased him back down.

"I don't suppose you'd consider getting a nurse's costume with a garter belt and a push-up bra?" His eyes were still closed, but he sounded remarkably lucid.

"How long have you been awake?"

"Long enough to know you're holding my hand." Wrapping his free hand around the back of her neck, he pulled her down for a kiss. A warm kiss, a gentle kiss that said, *Stay with me, love me, don't make life so hard.*

"I guess sex is out of the question?" he mumbled.

She laid her palm flat across his chest and tried to remember desire. His naked chest was as perfect as it had always been—clichéd in its ruggedness—but the new dose of lithium had annihilated her libido. Pluto, that frigid little ball of ice and rock, probably saw more action. Her hand slipped down to the eiderdown at his waist and tugged on a feather sticking half in, half out.

"You should have stayed away," she said. "What if you can't strum Absalom ever again? I asked you to go home for a reason. I wanted you safe and away from all this craziness. Why didn't you listen to me?"

"Can't stay away from you, my goddess." He started singing the Troggs' "Wild Thing" off-key. Marianne couldn't help it, she broke into a smile. Darius, it seemed, was a sweet drunk.

He opened his eyes, blinked several times, and licked his lips. "Water?"

She handed him the glass, and he half pushed himself up, drained it, and flopped back down. "Hey, you're my hero. I mean heroine. You saved my life. And when I'm better, I'll show you my gratitude. I'd like to prove it now. Not sure the junk's up for the job, though. Feel kinda smashed. What did they give me, horse tranquilizers?"

"Tramadol. A morphine-based opiate."

"Nice. If I play the sympathy card, will you come home with me?"

"I love you, Darius, but I'm not ready to go home, not yet."

"Because of ex-boyfriend in the God squad or his brother, the teen stud?"

"This was never about Gabriel, or Simon, or anyone but me. It shouldn't always be about me, but right now it has to be. I have to get well for both of us, and I can't until I've figured out all the broken pieces of my past. Have you ever considered that I'm a danger to your health?"

"I like my health dangerous."

"Darius, what EmJ did? I have that same potential. In case you've forgotten, I threatened to kill you with a lamp."

"Yeah, but you throw like a girl. I can't lie, though; you've got a spicy temper. Worse than mine half the time. You should take that anger management class I flunked." His eyes closed. "Twenty-four stitches? That's gonna leave one badass scar. I'll be fending off hot-blooded middle-aged women and drag queens for the rest of my days. You'll have to learn to deal with the jealousy, babe."

"*Grrr,*" she said, "you're impossible."

"You're growling at me. That's kind of a turn-on. About the nurse's costume . . ." His words trailed off and he fell back to sleep with a lopsided smile tugging on his lips.

*

The thunder rumbled off around two a.m.; the rain didn't. It continued like a biblical deluge. When she was a kid, the village was frequently cut off after this kind of rain. The River Ouse would rise over the bridge, and the flood level wouldn't recede for days. They could be trapped; she would never find EmJ.

Gabriel was carless, which meant she was carless, but Hugh, who was snoring on the living room sofa, was not. And last night she'd overheard him tell Gabriel that he'd canceled his appointments for today. So why did he need a car? He didn't; she did. The conjoined facts—that she'd barely driven since the accident and never on the wrong side of the road—were irrelevant.

Rain pummeled the glass patio doors as she slid Hugh's car keys off the coffee table and into her jeans pocket and tiptoed back upstairs. Darius was lying on his back with the eiderdown kicked to the floor and his bandaged arm resting where she'd positioned it at three a.m. on a puffed-up pillow.

"Where did you go?" Darius said quietly.

"Downstairs to get something. How are you feeling?"

"Woozy, and I had the worst nightmare. Some towering banshee was coming at me, screaming and waving a machete. I expected better from the Brits than allowing weapons into a church gathering."

"I hate to destroy your fantasy, but it was a serrated-edged cake knife with a decorative porcelain handle. Very beautiful. And EmJ's tiny. She weighs ninety pounds tops."

"Can we keep those details between us?"

She took his hand and kissed his wedding band. "I'm sorry. I should never have dragged another crazy person into my orbit."

He rolled his head sideways to examine her with huge dark eyes, penetrating eyes that she'd fallen in love with during an AA meeting. "You dragged me into your orbit."

"You're intense, not crazy."

"I'm flattered you think so, but the dividing line's a bit blurred for me where you're concerned. Coming here to announce I would die for you doesn't seem entirely sane to me this morning . . . especially since my favorite tattoo has been sacrificed to prove my point."

"I love you too, honey. And no, I don't deserve you. And yes, I owe you an appointment at Tattoo Asylum to fix Cthulhu's face."

"Damn right, woman. What time is it?"

"Early. You need to go back to sleep, but I have to tell you something first."

He wove his fingers around hers and squeezed. "Anything except that you're leaving to go after her."

"I'll be back for dinner."

"Don't do this, Marianne. She's not stable."

A thrush welcomed daylight in the plum tree outside their window. Time was ticking. "I'm all she's got. Her boyfriend abandoned her, her mom kicked her out. Gabriel, Hugh, and Dr. P. all warned me off. But how can that be right, to give up on a kid?"

"It's not, but you can't save every unloved teenage girl."

"I don't want to. I want to save *this* girl. She needs to know that I won't give up on her."

He let go of her hand and turned to look at the bedroom wall. "You're thinking about bringing her back to North Carolina, aren't you?"

"Yes."

"God help me, I love you more than makes sense."

"Ditto, which means we're stuck with each other." Reaching over the bed, she eased his face toward her and kissed him. "Do you need anything? I've written Hugh and Gabriel a note, asking them to take care of you."

He shook his head. "But I was serious about the nurse's costume."

"I'll buy one online when I get back. How's that?"

He grinned. "What are you doing for transportation?"

"I'm taking Hugh's car."

"Without his permission, I assume."

"Sleep. I'll check on you later." She tried to stand up, but he seized a fistful of her T-shirt and pinned her in place.

"I'm letting you go because I'm trying to understand, but no heroic actions on your part. If you find her, call the cops. And if you don't agree, I'll scream loud enough to wake up half the neighborhood. She's dangerous, and you're not to risk upsetting her. Are we on the same page?"

She said nothing; he continued. "It's simple math. You agree equals you can commit grand theft auto. You don't agree equals I scream, and three guys keep you hostage."

"But—"

His index finger waved in front of her nose like a metronome beating *no*. "Place your left hand here"—he grabbed it—"on my heart. Good. Now raise your right hand, and say after me: I, Marianne Stokes, do solemnly swear on the life of my amazing husband . . ."

And she did.

THIRTY-FOUR
GABRIEL

"We have a new wrinkle." Gabriel shook Hugh awake. The grandfather clock in the hall chimed seven a.m.

"Did you forget that you're meant to remove your clothes *before* taking a shower?"

Gabriel continued drying his hair with the kitchen towel. "I was attempting to prevent Marianne from stealing your car. I was unsuccessful. Also, it's still pouring."

Hugh fumbled for his glasses, which were on the coffee table next to a torn scrap of paper. He sat up, yawned, and read the note. "Marianne apologizes and asks me to check on Darius. I do hope she fills up with petrol. I drove here on fumes."

Gabriel flopped down in his battered leather armchair and then shot up when he realized his bottom was soaking wet. "I specifically told her to not go after EmJ. What was she thinking?"

"Probably wasn't. Bipolar disorder does tend to make one a tad impulsive. She's not covered under my insurance, though, so let's hope she knows how to drive on the left. Then again, no point worrying about things you can't control."

The phone rang, stopped, rang again.

"Don't you think you should answer that?" Hugh nodded at the phone on the coffee table.

Gabriel shrugged. When his phone rang, the number of fires to put out tended to grow, and his problem list was officially full. Hugh, however, picked it up.

"Newton Rushford rectory, good—" Hugh looked at Gabriel and made sympathetic noises that included *uh-huh, oh dear,* and *my, my.* Then he held the phone out so Gabriel could hear the squawking female voice.

Gabriel stared through the patio doors. The lawn was covered in huge puddles of standing water, his hollyhocks were on the ground, and the blasted pigeons huddled on the birdbath had nothing to coo about this morning. He would include farmers in his morning prayers, especially those who had yet to finish harvest. (The combines had been out late last night.)

"Mrs. Peel," Hugh said loudly and deliberately. "Yes . . . I'm sorry the police woke you in the middle of the night. Yes . . . Yes, I can confirm that they are investigating this as a missing-person case. Hopefully she'll come back today and this will get cleared up quickly . . ." Hugh nodded. "As a psychiatrist who's been involved with your daughter's treatment, I'm not at liberty to discuss . . ." He looked at Gabriel. "I'm sorry to hear that, Mrs. Peel, but what a shame you never felt the need to express any of this concern before your daughter left residential care. In my experience, the full support of loved ones at such a time is crucial."

More screaming and then Hugh put the phone back on the coffee table. "EmJ's mother appears to have hung up on me."

"Bloody well handled, Hugh. I would not have been half as tactful. What did she say?"

"Mrs. Peel plans to 'sue your arse off' for not taking better care of her only child. One assumes she's been watching too much American television."

"Sue me on what grounds?" Gabriel started walking toward the hall. He needed to get out of his wet pajamas, and a hot shower might be an idea. Stave off the chill.

"That, my friend, is a mystery. The only thing I can tell you with certainty is that EmJ's mother has a rather shrill voice. Now. What's up first?"

"You don't want to report your car as stolen?"

"Most definitely not."

"Good. One less problem. I'm going to make coffee, put on dry clothes, and then have a conversation with Darius to establish what he knows about his wife's latest escapade. After that I was thinking bacon and eggs."

"I know you enjoy pottering around in the kitchen, but you really don't have to keep feeding us all."

"It calms me," Gabriel said, "and cooking for a horde is a perverse treat when you normally cook for one."

"Should I accompany you upstairs as a bodyguard?" Hugh said. "Darius does seem to harbor strong opinions about you."

"Thank you, but no. It's time Darius accepted the fact that I have never been, and never will be, an adulterer."

✳

Gabriel climbed the stairs with a cup of coffee. Strong and black, the way Darius had asked for it on the day he and Jade had arrived. Clearing his throat somewhat theatrically, Gabriel rapped on the door. No answer. The second time, he knocked and turned the knob.

Darius stirred. A grown man in a dwarf's bed, he seemed to spill over the edge of the single mattress. It might be time to replace the hand-me-down twin beds with a double. They weren't exactly welcoming, especially for men. Darius wasn't even that tall, although he was certainly—Gabriel swallowed—solid.

"Morning." Gabriel tried to sound jovial. "I brought you coffee."

"Thanks." With a groan, Darius heaved himself up to sitting. Since he was bare-chested, it was possible to see the full extent of the man's tattoos. Gabriel had a strange desire to ask which one had hurt the most. Hopefully it had been the satanic pentagram.

"How's the arm?"

The mobile phone on the bedside table started playing the Clash, "Should I Stay or Should I Go." Highly ironic under the circumstances. Darius picked it up and made awkward one-handed movements. "It's a text from Jade. She's lying awake worrying that I'm going to do something crazy. Guess it's a bit late for that." He mumbled a few colorful obscenities as he tried to text.

"Here, let me." Gabriel put the coffee down on the bedside table. "You dictate, I'll type. Does she know about yesterday?"

Darius shook his head.

"What would you like to say?"

"*Hey, doll. I'm fine. Spoken with Marianne. She's fine. Will call tonight.*"

"That's it? You're all fine?"

"It's what she needs to hear right now."

Gabriel typed as directed. When Jade sent back a row of stickers that included the Union Jack, he smiled. He typed, `Nighty night, you,` and then deleted it. Jade would know it was him. He'd send her a text tomorrow, on his own phone, one that said, *Long time no speak. Friends again?*

"Would you like to wish her good night?" Gabriel said. "Since it's two a.m. over there?"

Darius squinted. "Sure. Type this—'*Sweet dreams. Love, love.*'"

Gabriel hesitated.

"Is there a problem?"

"No." Gabriel swallowed again. When he was done, he put the phone down and retreated to the old nursing chair. "Would you mind if we talked?"

"Sure. I won't give Marianne up without a fight. The end. Anything else you want to know?"

"Glad to hear it. There's nothing I respect more than the institution of marriage. And I would like to assure you that I was not an active participant in events leading up to her return."

Darius remained silent. Right, then. In the immortal words of Sir Winston Churchill, *Keep buggering on.* "No one was more surprised than I when she appeared in Newton Rushford. I'm still not entirely sure how all this happened." Gabriel waved his arm around his spare room, which appeared to have become a woman's dressing room with more pairs of shoes than he'd seen in his entire life. "My brother was in love with her at the time of his death, and when she arrived in my church, clearly in need, I felt I owed it to him to help."

"You're acting out of brotherly duty? Not buying it, man. I have three older sisters and as much as I love"—wincing, Darius grabbed his elbow and stretched the fingers on his wounded arm—"and admire them, I certainly wouldn't upend my life on their account. Unless you're gay, which I'm one hundred percent sure you're not, I'm betting you're in love with my wife and always have been."

"Innocent on all counts."

"And when you were younger?"

"How is that relevant? Who were you in love with at seventeen?"

Darius rubbed his Robinson Crusoe beard. Was he in need of a razor? "I'll give you that one. I was in the school marching band and working my way through the baton twirlers. It's the costumes." Darius shook his head. "But I imagine Marianne would be hard to forget at any age. She can get under your skin."

"I'll take your word for it."

Darius shifted. "Can we cut to the chase? I'm in pain and holding on to my marriage by my teeth."

"Do you need some paracetamol?"

"No idea what you're talking about."

"Same thing as Tylenol."

"Appreciate it, but no. I'm not much of a pill popper. Can't be, with my family history of addiction. The odd Xanax is about it for me. Killer good for lowering anxiety." Darius reached over awkwardly for his coffee mug. "And I should tell you—my first wife was a violent drunk. She's the reason I don't drink. I'm not an alcoholic, but dammit, I'm a fan of the AA philosophy."

Oversharing was typical in his line of work, but Gabriel sensed strategy in play: *I told you mine; now you tell me yours.* He crossed his legs and glanced up at the exceedingly ugly lampshade that had always reminded him of a suet pudding. He'd inherited it along with the house. "You're correct, I was in love with Marianne. At least I thought I was. But we were barely out of childhood, and she was also my best friend. Our lives were bound together in such a way that I mistakenly believed we had no secrets, that nothing could ever come between us. But the night my brother died, he informed me that they were lovers. I was badly injured in the crash and had plenty of time in hospital to relearn everything I knew about Marianne. Cutting her from my life became intrinsic to my recovery. It's not a decision I regret, especially when she then tried to kill herself on my brother's grave."

Darius's eyes grew wide. Did he not know that detail?

"And that's more than I've ever shared with anyone about our history." Gabriel stood.

"Thank you—for the truth and the coffee. Let's start over." Darius held out his hand. "Hi, my name is Darius. A pleasure to meet you. Make a move on my wife and I'll kill you."

"Message received and understood." Gabriel shook Darius's hand. "Talking about your wife, it appears she's taken Hugh's car to search for EmJ. Should we be concerned?"

"I spend my life being concerned. This is nothing new."

"So we shouldn't worry?"

"The only person who can anticipate Marianne's moods is Jade, but when Marianne's on a fully fledged aid mission, a packed stadium of headbangers couldn't derail her. I did, however, remove her wallet from her purse." He reached under the bedclothes and pulled it out. "So if Hugh doesn't have a full tank of gas, she's not going very far. Although there's no cash in it, so I might be wrong." Darius paused. "I'd like your permission to stay here, in your house, until I can persuade Marianne to come home with me. And I guess I'll have to call my buddy in London, get him to overnight my stuff. Yesterday's clothes are trashed."

"You're welcome to borrow anything in the meantime. And yes, please stay as long as you need." Without thinking, Gabriel bent down to pick up a towel from the floor. It was still damp. He draped it over the back of the nursing chair. "How long before the stitches come out?"

"A week, I think. The details are a bit hazy. I was barfing like a spigot when they told me. I hate hospitals, did I mention that?"

"Yes, I believe you did." Gabriel tugged on the back of his neck.

"And thanks, for letting me stay. You don't play tons of U2, do you, because I really—"

"Dislike U2, I know. Is there a point at which we should call the police and report Marianne as missing?"

"Hell, no. Bringing in the cops is the last thing I want. Marianne would never forgive me." Darius pulled back his hair, revealing a squarish, piratical face. Truthfully, a tad menacing. "My official response is no, I'm not worried. And I assume you know that's a lie. However, she promised she'd be back by dinnertime. And my wife's a woman of her word. Which you probably know."

Rain shot down the guttering. Gabriel nodded. "Can I make you breakfast?"

"Seriously? That would be fantastic, man."

Darius swung his legs to the floor but shook his head as if he was dizzy.

"What are you doing?" Gabriel said.

"Coming down to the kitchen."

"Most ill-advised. Stay here and I'll bring you up a tray. Bacon, eggs, toast, sausage, a grilled tomato?" Six months ago, if anyone had told him he'd be taking breakfast in bed to Marianne's husband, he would have assumed he was having a nightmare.

"Music to my ears. So you can cook, I mean really cook? I know some of the best chefs in the world are men but not in the Montgomery family. Mom never let me near the kitchen. Mind you, she hid the cooking sherry in there. My dad, who ran the family business like a mafia boss, was a drunk. A mean one. Not much of a role model and probably the other reason I don't drink."

Who knew Darius could be so chatty? "Mine was a lieutenant general. He had high hopes that at least one of his sons would carve out a career in the British army."

"I guess we were both disappointments, then."

Gabriel frowned. Had that been intended as an insult or an olive branch of male bonding?

THIRTY-FIVE

GABRIEL

Gabriel examined the fresh produce in the navy-blue plastic crates outside the butcher's shop: potatoes, carrots, and runner beans. All from the Abbey's garden and normally sold out at this time of the day. Luckily for him the nuns must have recently replenished the stock.

The rain had stopped and the afternoon sun tickled the back of his neck. He should have been worrying about Marianne, about EmJ, about dealing with his mother's latest crisis—something to do with the neighbor's hedge not being trimmed—but the lull of drama post–tea time had left him strangely peaceful and almost drowsy. The rectory phone had even remained silent for several hours. Although silence wasn't necessarily reassuring when a teenager was missing. And he had yet to inform Marianne that EmJ's attack on Darius would be noted under the National Crime Recording Standards, whatever the outcome of any criminal proceedings. And there was the lingering question of the missing forensic evidence . . .

After Hugh had taken a taxi home, Darius made it down to the living room, where he'd parked himself on the sofa to enjoy his get-well

Cadbury Roses from Mrs. Tandy and—in Darius's words—binge-watch British TV while stuffing his face with English chocolate.

Gabriel grabbed a small brown bag hanging from a piece of string and, picking up a fistful of runner beans, planned his menu: beans, mashed potato, and lamb chops. He might splurge and buy an orange-and-rhubarb pie from Puddings Galore.

A tractor pulling a trailer of grain lumbered down the A428, leading a long line of cars. On the other side of the beaded curtain that hung across the open doorway of Len's shop, a fan whirred and women chatted.

"It's shocking, isn't it?" Gladys Crowley said in her high, squeaky voice. A lapsed churchgoer, she managed to attend Matins whenever she needed a favor for the gardening club. "He left Ian and Ken to deal with the police, you know."

Gabriel leaned forward to listen.

"Just the chipolatas, m'ducks?" This from Len. "That'll be seven pounds and fifty pence, please."

"The wife of the injured man is that Marion girl, the one who went psycho in the churchyard when the reverend's brother died. Stripped naked, she did. Mad, quite mad. I was in the choir in those days. Saw the whole thing."

"I'd forgotten that about you, Audrey," Gladys said. "You had a lovely voice. Lovely."

"I still do." Audrey Pike sounded more than a little peeved. "But who has time for choir? Not me with the coffee mornings to organize and the demands of being on the village school board. I barely have time to listen to the omnibus edition of *The Archers*."

"They always said"—Gladys lowered her voice—"that she was messing around with both the Bonham brothers. I remember Simon. Bit of a looker, that one. All of us had a crush on him. He could have done so much better than Mary."

Gabriel clenched and unclenched his right hand, and repeated the Lord's Prayer silently.

"Marion, her name was Marion. We were in playgroup together. Had a wicked temper. She once threw a proper fit during the nativity play and ripped down a curtain. Her mother—sweet woman, blanking on her name—had to carry her out kicking and screaming."

Gladys tutted. "But who's the girl, that's what I want to know?"

"Bill Collins thinks it might be her love child."

"With the reverend?"

"That's the thing, isn't it?"

"Well I never. I think it's high time someone called the bishop."

Enough. Gabriel pushed the beaded curtain aside.

"You alright, then, Reverend?" Len said, wiping his hands.

"Yes, thank you." Gabriel inhaled the familiar smell of blood and bleach. "Ladies, I'm delighted to hear you have constructed such a colorful love life for me, but I'm afraid I must disappoint. With great regret I can inform you that I have fathered no children in my time on earth, and I have, in fact, been celibate for many years. I believe I still have the name of my last sexual partner in my old Filofax, should you need to check references."

Gladys fiddled with the clasp on her purse and then dropped it. Gabriel's smile contradicted his inner thoughts, which were quickly followed by a brief prayer of repentance. A motorbike roared on the A428.

"Her name is EmJ, by the way, and she's a remarkable young lady who has no family support and has fallen on hard times. Mari*anne* has been trying to help her, as any Christian should." He emphasized the word *Christian.* "Facts are important, are they not?"

"Quite so." Gladys retrieved her purse from the floor and stood up. "Better be getting along." Audrey followed her out, head bowed.

"I'm sorry you had to hear that," Len said.

"Let me guess, I just missed Bill?"

Impressive color rose up Len's neck. No one blushed quite like a redhead.

"I didn't mean to pry. Just thinking out loud."

"Any news of EmJ?" Len said. "I heard she nicked your car. Did the coppers find it yet?"

"Both still missing." Gabriel looked into the glass case with all the gleaming metal trays of bloody meat edged with flat plastic grass. "How does Bill know these things?"

"He's a sad git with nothing better to do. Sorry, that was uncalled for."

"We each have our cross to bear," Gabriel said. "Bill appears to be mine."

"How's that bloke with all the hair?"

"Darius? Recovering admirably. I'm trying to feed him up, though. I was thinking three lamb chops? And can I get half a pound of corned beef and the same of ham? Oh, and I need more eggs." Gabriel walked over to the shelf and grabbed two egg cartons and a jar of Mrs. Darlington's mint sauce—made with love, according to the label.

Behind the counter, Len picked up a shiny cleaver and thwacked off three chops. "On the house."

"Absolutely not." Gabriel reached for his wallet.

"Your money's no good in here today, Reverend. Think of it as an apology for the bad smell in the shop. Next time call and I'll deliver on my way home. Save you a trip."

"And how would I know what's happening in the village if I didn't stick my head inside the shops several times a week?" Gabriel put away his wallet. One single act of kindness could restore a man's faith in humanity. "Thank you. I graciously accept your most excellent customer service."

"I should warn you," Len said, as he sliced the corned beef, "Gladys was right about one thing. There was talk earlier—I'm not naming anyone—about calling the archdeacon."

"Are you hiring if I lose my job?"

Len turned from the metal slicer. "They fire you, I'll lead the revolt. Haven't been in a riot since Thatcher's day. I was in Brixton in the early eighties."

"Were you indeed?" Every day he learned something new about his parishioners. Gabriel would have told anyone who asked that he knew Len reasonably well—worked for his father, officiated at his daughter's wedding, buried both his parents—but if he'd missed this rather large detail about one parishioner's life, what else had he missed? He had grown far too complacent about his ability to judge and understand others. And there was one person who still deserved a full apology.

While Len wrapped up the meat packages in white paper, Gabriel pulled out his phone and started typing.

```
Am I forgiven for being a small-minded
pillock? Please say yes because I miss
our chats.
```

Jade texted back instantly. `Miss you too, pillock. (Is that English for jackass?)`

He smiled. `Close enough.`

Errands completed, Gabriel ambled back up the High Street with a heavy canvas bag and lighter thoughts. But as he turned into Nell's Lane, the good mood evaporated. Bill Collins was hobbling past the rectory with Queenie and his stick. Instead of ignoring Gabriel, as usual, Bill slowed to toss out a sneer. It seemed the phone call to the archdeacon had already been placed. And since the archdeacon had the bishop's ear, the wheels must be in motion.

THIRTY-SIX

MARIANNE

Marianne had never been a conspiracy theorist—too hard to keep her own truths straight let alone worry about everyone else's—but a teenage plot was definitely afoot in Newton Rushford. The moment she'd pulled out of Nell's Lane and hesitated about turning right or left, she realized EmJ couldn't have bolted for some remote corner of England, Scotland, or Wales. Teen bands frequently formed intense bonds during their weeklong summer camp at Girls In Motion, and EmJ's band, newly named Shadowbox, was no exception. The big question was how far three of the members had gone to protect their greatest asset.

After grilling Charlotte and the boys—except for Matt, who was having his wisdom teeth pulled, or so Tom said—Marianne became convinced the kids were up to something. What else could have explained Tom's uncharacteristically twitchy behavior with his keys? And if EmJ was still in the village, someone had helped her hide Newton Rushford's most recognizable vehicle. In a barn on one of the outlying farms, no doubt.

She was close to finding EmJ, and Marianne Stokes stopped being a quitter the day she understood her life was about providing a stable home for a young runaway. But her rumbling stomach reminded her that she had a dinner date with Darius, and he'd suffered enough in the last twenty-four hours. All summer she'd been bouncing up and down saying, *Me, me, me.* Now it was time to start acting like a wife.

Besides, she'd searched as many outbuildings as she could without reinforcements, and if the kids had gathered around, EmJ was safe, although probably living on iced buns—the band's snack of choice. It was time to update Jade, too. That was going to be a toughie. Jade would not appreciate being left out of the loop.

Marianne retrieved Hugh's car—tucked away in a secluded dead-end lane on the other side of the Abbey—and drove back to Nell's Lane. Slowly enough to be honked at. Her brain, running on empty from lack of food, repeated over and over, *You're on the wrong side of the road.*

She parked in front of the rectory and pulled out her phone. `Sorry for the radio silence. Lot going on here.` She hit "Send."

`Ditto. Been swamped at the studio. How's the next Madonna?`

Marianne took a deep breath and typed quickly. `About that . . . Darius turned up yesterday, EmJ freaked out, cut his arm with a cake knife, ran away. He has a few stitches, but I'm taking good care of him. Promise.` At least she had been last night. Did that count?

Her phone rang.

"What the fuck?" Jade yelled. "Darius is with you and EmJ stabbed him?"

"It was more of a slash. But yeah, that's the gist."

"Holy shit. Does he have enough Xanax with him? He's such a wuss about anything medical."

"Fortunately yes, and they gave him killer pain meds. He puked a lot in the hospital, but he was lucky. The knife didn't sever anything important like a tendon, so he didn't need surgery or general anesthesia. He'll probably tell the world he was attacked saving me from a marauding gang of English muggers. I have a feeling the story will grow."

"Another Darius legend for the books. It's quite the summer you guys are having. Can't wait to see what you do for your tenth wedding anniversary. But he is okay, right?"

"Yeah, he was pretty cute and loopy on the meds last night. It melted my heart." Marianne pulled out the car keys and for good measure put the parking brake on, which she never did in her own car. "But I have no illusions. I'm responsible for one impressive scar on my beloved's arm."

"We scar people we love all the time," Jade said quietly. "Mostly it doesn't show."

"It's on his left arm."

"On his full-sleeve Lovecraft tat? His favorite thing in the world after you and Absalom?"

"Uh-huh. Slashed Cthulhu's face."

Jade made a strangled noise. "Glad I wasn't around when he figured that one out. What about EmJ?"

"Still missing, but I think the band members are hiding her. Now I just have to figure out where."

"Oh, that's totally the scenario I would go with." Jade hesitated. "How's Gabriel doing with all this?" she asked casually, too casually. A thought to be continued.

"You know our friendly neighborhood vicar, very little disturbs his om. However, I'm intrigued to see whether he and Darius slaughtered each other today. I left them alone while I went out to search for EmJ."

"Does she still have the knife?"

"No. Gabriel disposed of it."

"As in tampered with evidence? Wow. Mega"—Jade yawned—"shocker."

"You getting enough sleep?"

"Not really."

Marianne stared through the windshield to the sparrows cozied up for the approaching night on the telephone wires. "I'm sorry, I—"

"Na-ah, stop right there. I know you're feeling shitty about yourself right now, and I'm going to tell you—"

"Am not."

"Are so. You do everything magnified, including guilt. Two facts to digest: I am perfectly happy running your studio. So happy I might never hand it back. And without you, EmJ would probably have returned to her druggie boyfriend and opened a his-'n'-hers meth lab. You showed her another way. It's not your fault if she chose not to take it."

"You're too wise for a not-quite-thirty-year-old. Sometimes I feel as if you're the parental figure and I'm the teenager."

"I was never a teenager."

"I know, sweetheart. You grew up way too soon."

"Whereas you never grew up at all. Jump off the ride, Mama Bird. You saw someone who was more broken than you, and you tried to help. That was a good impulse. The right one, and I'm proud of you."

Gabriel tapped on the car window.

"Oops. The day of reckoning has arrived. I have to go and make amends to Gabriel for stealing Hugh's car."

Jade snorted out laughter. "Are you fucking kidding me? On top of running a soap opera you stole a car? Forget about music—you should write a memoir."

"Like anyone would believe it." Marianne got out of the car. "Can we talk later, baby girl?"

"Go. Deal with Gabriel. Love you lots, you loon."

"Love you too." She looked up at Gabriel. "I was updating Jade on the cake-knife incident."

"I gathered. How did she take the news?"

"Fine. Like you, she's one of life's fine people. Mainly she was worried about Darius. Have we reached the part in the story where you lecture me on being irresponsible?"

A fighter jet roared low over their heads, and Marianne covered her ears. Gabriel, waiting for it to pass, didn't flinch.

"No. This is where I tell you supper's ready. And ask for Hugh's car keys back." He held out his hand, and she dropped the keys onto his palm.

"You would have made someone an amazing wife. How's Darius?"

"Quite perky. He's discovered my chocolate supply and no longer wants to do unspeakable things to my manhood."

"Any news from the police?"

Gabriel shook his head and turned away.

Marianne followed. "Doesn't matter, I've figured out something huge."

As they entered the house, the hall phone began to ring, and the deafening boom of a barrage of military planes filled the sky and quickly disappeared. With a deep sigh, Gabriel picked up the phone.

"Good evening, Bishop," he said. "Yes, I've been expecting your call."

THIRTY-SEVEN
JADE

Sitting in the control room, Jade stared at the black console with the little knobs that could tweak any sound into a polished version of the truth. But what if you couldn't add or subtract? What if truth held you, suspended in time, and said, *This is it. No easy fixes. Learn how to deal?* She could no longer avoid talking with Gabriel. Not now that they'd kissed and made up—without the kissing part. Her phone connected to his, and he answered immediately, his hello more of a declaration of war than a greeting. Time to slip into the overdubbed role of Jade Jones.

"Whoa there. Don't shoot the caller."

"Jade." He blew out her name.

"Yup, me. I called to see how Darius is doing. He's a big baby about all things medical, but what's up with you? You picked up that phone sounding pissed as fu—very angry."

He didn't reply.

"Time is money. Spill."

His breathing changed, as if he was walking. Or retreating into his study. "Someone called the archdeacon, who called the bishop, who wants to know if, in fact, I have been living in sin with a married woman and have a psychopathic love child who attempted to commit murder in full view of the village. I think that's the gist."

"Let me guess, Bill Collins?"

"Jade"—she heard his smile in his voice—"I've missed you."

She nearly said, *I've missed you more.* "I could arrange for someone to kidnap his dog. I know plenty of scuzzballs."

"I don't doubt that." Gabriel laughed. A few weeks earlier she'd imagined taping and enhancing that sound. But that was before he'd withheld it from her. No, she wouldn't change a thing. His laughter was perfection.

"Tempting as your offer is," Gabriel said, "I'm turning the other cheek."

"Let me know if you change your mind. I'm always game for a little covert revenge ops. What's the bishop's take on our family drama, then?"

"He's clearing his calendar so we can meet later in the week. I anticipate a private slap on the wrist followed by a clandestine period of parole. The bishop protects his own and strongly dislikes scandal, but he's not my number one fan."

"Well, fuck 'im. Shit a brick—sorry, that came out wrong."

"Are you alright?" Gabriel said.

"No, not really. Can we back up for a moment so that I can apologize? About before, when we had our falling-out. I'm not normally such a loose cannon, but this has been the worst summer of my life, and I've had some bad ones."

"The fault was mine, Jade. My reactions were petty and arrogant."

"Far from it. You thought I'd lied to you, and I get it, I do. Sometimes you just want to be one person's priority." She added five hours to the studio clock. Did Gabriel have his postdinner pink gin in hand? "Darius is good at that. He always puts Marianne first, no hesitation. I used to think he was out of his ever-lovin' mind, but you've got to admire his devotion." A first for her. Never again would she tease Darius about being henpecked. "How is he?"

"Doing rather well. Want to chat with him?"

"In a minute. Can you just listen to my ramblings for a bit longer? Now that I'm the boss, the only thing everyone wants from me is certainty, and I'm wearing thin in the department of making sense."

"Then you shall have my undivided attention. I'm sitting at my desk with a pink gin, about to make you my number one priority. What ails you, my child?"

Jade smiled and got up to leave the control room, but she paused and leaned back against the open door. The doorknob dug into her spine. "I'm struggling," she said, "to figure out how all this impacts me, which is selfish, I know, but with everything that's gone down between your world and mine, I'm kind of unanchored. Like I don't know what I want anymore. I mean, I'm working to exhaustion every night, and once upon a time that would have been enough. I—I dunno what's got into me." *Big fat lie, girl.*

"Jade, you've been under extraordinary stress. You need to look after yourself."

"I don't have the energy right now."

"Who looks after you when you're sick?"

"I'm low maintenance. Don't get sick."

"Everyone gets sick."

"Not me. I'm a self-contained pro."

"Well, Ms. Self-Contained Pro, make time for a regular activity that gives you emotional space. For me it's those long, solitary walks across Dead Woman."

"Reading for me, but not so much lately. I was on a Daphne du Maurier kick until this all blew up."

"Have you read her short stories: 'The Birds,' 'Don't Look Now'?"

"She wrote 'The Birds'? Wow."

"Short fiction is an excellent balm for the stressed. Poetry too. I'm sure you could fit one of those in before bedtime."

"I've never read much poetry."

"Then I'll send you one of my favorite anthologies—as a delayed thank-you for the headphones. And remember, I'm only ever a text message away."

"Thank you." She held the phone to her cheek and ran out of things to say. Silence, as perfect as his laugh, spread between them.

Gabriel cleared his throat. "I'll get Darius for you."

And she wanted to say, *No. I can keep talking if you can keep making me your number one priority.* But he'd gone, and she was losing it. Gabriel was a man of God. Who'd likely never been laid. Who likely didn't believe in nonmarital coitus. Who, whatever he told himself, was likely still besotted with his first love.

Then she hit the red "End Call" button, locked the studio, and walked through Marianne's garden to Ernie, *her* first love. A black snake, lounging by the pond, shot behind the metal sculpture of a praying mantis.

"That's right, you big frog-eating loser. Slither off and hide." She would if she could.

Jade started the engine and then, rummaging through her messenger bag, fished out the CD of a track she was mixing. She could con herself into believing this drive was about work, since she listened to all her mixes through the bass of the car stereo, but really, what she needed was thinking time.

Finally she understood why Darius had stayed in England; finally she understood what it meant to stand your ground for someone you loved. To not retreat—whatever the personal cost. Jesse had deserved better, and yet she bailed on him. But Marianne? She owed Marianne her life. Which meant Marianne must always come first; which meant these feelings for Gabriel should be napalmed.

She crisscrossed the county until the light faded to dusk and fireflies sparked at the edge of the forest. Adult fireflies, Marianne had once told her, spend most of their lives searching for a mate, and after the females lay eggs, they die. *Their sole purpose is to reproduce.* To reproduce, but not to mother. What a sad existence. Reproduction and motherhood weren't necessarily connected. Marianne had always been her real mother and the only person Jade had ever truly loved.

Jade gripped the steering wheel. "Okay, God. We've never talked before, but we have a mutual friend, and I think it's time we had a chat. I'll be honest, I'm more than a little skeptical that you exist, but given that Gabriel is the most upstanding human being on the planet, I'm willing to give you the benefit of the doubt. So here it goes: I'm in love, and it can only hurt the person I care most about—Marianne. I'd be grateful if you could take these feelings for Gabriel and trash them. Deal?"

She didn't know what she'd expected, but just saying those ludicrous words out loud—*I'm in love*—was empowering. Yeah, it was all good. She was so over this whole thing. Definitely going to follow through on that invitation for coffee from Ricky Tanner, former UNC basketball star and best friend of Winnie's son. He was a total hunk.

As darkness descended on the unlit country roads and the tiny pulses of light from the fireflies vanished, she stayed alert, watching for deer. When her stomach growled, she turned onto Highway 54 toward her favorite Mexican restaurant, Fiesta Grill. She would order nachos and chicken fajitas with corn tortillas. It wasn't until she'd parked and inhaled the symphony of a Carolina night, with tree frogs and katydids, that she remembered why she'd called the rectory: to talk with Darius.

THIRTY-EIGHT
GABRIEL

Morning prayer was no longer sacred, and a closed door in the rectory meant nothing. Gabriel sighed. *Forgive her, Lord, she knows not what—*

"I've figured out where she is!" Marianne waved at him to get moving, which accentuated the fact that she wasn't wearing a bra under her rather skimpy top.

Darius appeared behind her, wearing boxer briefs that left nothing to the imagination, and slipped his arms around her waist. Gabriel stared at the spines on the top row of his bookshelves and focused on his P. D. James collection. What would Commander Adam Dalgliesh, his favorite literary hero, have made of Darius's constant need to touch Marianne in front of others? Or was the show reserved for Gabriel's benefit?

Gabriel picked up a copy of the *Church Times* and fanned his face.

By seven a.m. the heat in the house had been unforgiving, prompting him to ransack his chest of drawers for a pair of khaki shorts not worn since his last trip to Cornwall, circa 2005. Fortunately they still fit, and not as snugly as anything his houseguests were wearing.

"You"—Marianne twisted free of Darius, who was now nuzzling her neck—"back to the sofa with *Sleepless in Seattle.*"

"C'mon, babe. I haven't spent this much time lying down since the weekend we met. And that was a whole lot more fun."

Gabriel imagined Jade's voice: "Dude, too much information."

"You're staying here to continue your recuperation. Gabriel's with me," Marianne said.

"No, neither one of you is going anywhere. If you know where she is, call the cops. The authorities should handle this."

"He's right," Gabriel said, although no one had asked for his opinion. With God as his witness, he was trying to fall back and follow Darius's lead. Unfortunately second place was not a position he was used to these days, and certainly not in his own house. To Marianne's husband. Who was practically naked.

I'm trying, God. I am.

"What planet are you two living on?" Marianne jerked back and glared at Gabriel. "You really think you can stop me?"

Darius tugged a fistful of hair back and then let go. "I swear, woman, you'll be the death of me. You are not to leave Gabriel's sight. Do you understand?"

She darted at her husband and kissed his cheek. "Promise."

Darius stared at Gabriel. "I'm trusting my wife into your care, man."

"I know. Look after her, or you'll kill me," Gabriel said.

"At last we understand each other." Darius cocked a smile.

"Mrs. Tandy will be here at nine and she has a key, so you can lock the door behind us. And might I suggest a pair of jeans and a T-shirt? She gets upset by anything too personal."

"I don't know pants'll make too much difference. I think your cleaner's got a crush on me." Darius turned to Marianne. "I'm telling you, this wound is a middle-aged chick magnet."

"Mrs. Tandy's a grandmother," Gabriel said.

"And she doesn't look a day over sixty-five," Darius said.

"We'll leave you to your fantasies of Mrs. Tandy in a maid's outfit," Marianne said, "which I'm sure will far surpass the nurse's one."

Really, too much information.

As they walked down the hall, Darius muttered, "Hmm. Maid's outfit . . ." Then he called out, "You be careful, and that includes you, Gabriel. Wait! I need to know where you're going and whether you both have charged phones."

"Yes, and the Mill." Marianne opened the front door and then turned to Gabriel with a triumphant smile.

She chattered away while he shoved his bare feet into his trainers and tied the laces. "I was telling her about the Mill conversion on the way down to the cream teas, jabbering to distract her. But EmJ's a smart girl; she must have figured out an empty high-end apartment meant an empty garage where she could hide your car. Come on, already. Jade taught me a few things about breaking and entering."

"Did she now."

Gabriel shut the front door, and Marianne broke into a run. He did his best to keep up, his gold cross bumping against his heart as one thought repeated in a loop: *Why would EmJ stay in the village unless she'd never planned to leave?*

When he reached the war memorial, Gabriel put his hands on his knees and gulped air. The bunting from the fete, still draped around the lych-gate, waved merrily. The ghost of celebrations past. Huffing out a breath, he chased after Marianne, who had turned toward Bridge Lane. Once again the crenelated bridge, parts of which dated back to the twelfth century, was under repair and down to single file. The temporary light turned to red, halting traffic leaving the village.

"Wait," he yelled. "We need to do this together."

She nodded—her face flushed—and suddenly looked ridiculously young. She was also barefoot and holding up her flip-flops. At some point she must have taken them off, which seemed extremely risky and utterly teenage Marianne.

His mind rewound thirty years. It had been impossibly hot that July, like a Mediterranean summer. How different would their lives have been if she'd waited for him? How different would their lives have been if he'd put her first, so she wouldn't have needed to?

He wiped beads of sweat from his face.

"Come on, already!" Marianne slipped her flip-flops back on and walked toward the Mill's gravel driveway. Neither of them spoke.

Under the arched entranceway, they confronted a complex system of buzzers incongruous to a building that had stood for centuries.

"Which one do we push?" Marianne whispered.

"Absolutely no clue. What else did Mrs. Tandy tell you?"

"That the views of the river were outstanding."

"So the flat she cleaned must be on the side."

"And it was on the second floor with a wooden deck. And it had stairs down to the river!" Marianne held up her hands in triumph.

"Ergo there must be a back access."

"But how do we get around those gargantuan fences?" Marianne pointed at fortifications more imposing than anything on a medieval castle.

"I have an idea. Follow me." He led the way back to Bridge Lane.

She smiled. "Are we going to do what I think we're going to do?"

"I think we are."

"Like old times," she said.

"Except that we're now middle-aged, and clambering over the side of the foot causeway and jumping to the grass below might result in serious physical impairment."

"Wuss," she said.

The bridge had been widened to accommodate the traffic after the war, but the foot causeway still remained on the medieval side. When they reached it, Gabriel peered over the limestone wall. There was less riverbank than usual, given the water level. Beneath them, the swollen

River Ouse roared through arches that had seen seven centuries of life and death, including numerous drownings.

"Scared?" Marianne said.

"Terrified. I'm not a teenager anymore, and that ground looks awfully unforgiving." What they had once done without forethought now seemed positively dangerous. Surely they would break limbs.

"Oh, Gabriel!" She grabbed his arm. "A pair of swans. Remember the swan's nest?"

Please don't ask me that. Had she forgotten what else happened that day—the moment that changed everything between them? Her mind had erased the worst moments of their past. Had it also erased the best—their first kiss?

"Okay, I'm doing it," she said. "Call for backup if I break something."

She tossed over her flip-flops and then followed, landing as gracefully as he'd known she would. He, on the other hand, clambered down inelegantly, and landed on his bad knee with a loud *ooff.* She smiled and reached for his hand. Once again, the years stripped away.

They raced across the sodden grass, under the low-hanging branches of a willow tree, past a wooden bench angled toward the river, past the rushes that had made the village famous, past the imposing statue of Jonah that had guarded the millpond since the mid-nineteenth century. Bought by a former lord of the manor in what amounted to an aristocratic car boot sale, it was an anachronism. Phony history that didn't belong.

They approached the back of the Mill and slowed. During the last year, Gabriel had chosen to not pay attention to the conversion, averting his eyes in protest every time he drove across the bridge. But up close it was obvious, even to someone who was not a fan of adaptations, that the work on this historic building had been carried out with care and attention to detail. Some of the flats had imposing doors; others had huge barn-style windows. Round the side, a cluster of wooden balconies extended toward the water's edge. One was covered in terra-cotta pots filled with begonias and appeared to have been recently stained, or treated, or whatever one did to wooden balconies.

Ignoring Gabriel's signal to get behind him, Marianne grabbed the railing and mounted the stairs. He followed, pausing when he reached the top to glimpse the village from an angle never seen before. The church, in his mind, had always been the most imposing structure in the village, but from up here it was dwarfed by the Abbey. And Newton Rushford, a place that pulsed with the constant echo of traffic, was silent. A mallard duck quacked, and the two swans Marianne had spotted earlier glided toward the sluice gates, leaving ripples in their wake.

Turning away from the view, he watched the woman who had once been the love of his life peep through the glass door and then slide it open.

THIRTY-NINE
MARIANNE

"Honey?" Marianne kicked off her flip-flops and walked into a huge open-plan loft, which was hot like a sauna. "It's Marianne and Gabriel. We just want to talk."

Nothing. With a quick glance at Gabriel, she swallowed the smell of paint fumes and meat gone bad—a screeching juxtaposition of renewal and rot—and reached for his hand. His calm had always been her lifeboat. Let that still be true, because she was going to either throw up or faint. Which seemed irrelevant because the ringing in her ears suggested she was about to become the first person to drown on dry land.

White gauzy curtains, looped back, exposed large windows flanking a high-tech fireplace. A solitary sound bounced off the white walls and the exposed wooden beams: drip, drip, drip in the steel kitchen sink. Indian take-out containers were scattered over the breakfast bar, and there was a topless half-empty bottle of vodka. Two black flies hovered over the food, and an ashtray overflowed with cigarette stubs.

Matt smokes.

Marianne released Gabriel and clenched her hands together in a silent clap. They had found EmJ, and she was living on real food, not iced buns.

"Darius is fine, honey. We're not pressing charges."

EmJ and Matt were probably out cold recovering from drunken sex and hangovers. Let them at least have underwear on. Or be covered by a blanket. Was EmJ on the pill? They'd never had that conversation.

"Marianne." Gabriel nodded toward a dim hallway.

Two doors on the left, closed; one set of sliding doors on the right. Also closed. Marianne went to the sliding doors.

"Honey? Are you decent?" She knocked. "Can I come in?"

She opened the doors and stared at the scene staged between her and the wall of glass framing a tranquil river view. A macabre Madame Tussauds display. That wasn't EmJ, lying on an inflated pool float, wearing nothing but a pair of panties with a hole in the side. That wasn't EmJ, spread-eagled on her back, the skin on her calves covered in dark red patches, her mouth crusted with dried vomit. That wasn't EmJ. It was a wax model, an imposter. It had to be, because if that were the real EmJ, she'd be wearing the new panties Marianne had bought for her.

Pills were scattered on the floor, and a small vodka bottle lay on its side, empty. In the distance, at the end of a long tunnel, Gabriel's voice told her to stay put.

He squatted down and pressed three fingers to EmJ's wrist. Did the same on her neck, then glanced up, shaking his head. One word: *Sorry.* But that was wrong, all wrong. He shouldn't be touching her; EmJ was practically naked.

Falling onto hands and knees, Marianne crawled across the floor. Pills crunched under her.

Gabriel stood, pulled out his phone, and started talking.

"Please, sweetheart." She smoothed the tangled mess of EmJ's hair. "Don't do this. You have to meet Jade, you have to live. Please, sweetheart," she whispered. "You have to live."

She tried to hug EmJ, tried to cradle her. Stiff, unyielding. Cold, so cold. The smell—rancid. Marianne gagged.

"I'm sorry. She's gone." Gabriel crouched down behind her. "I've called the police." He touched her shoulder.

"No!" Marianne shrugged him off and threw herself over EmJ. "You know CPR. You can save her the way you saved me. Start compressions. Give her the kiss of life."

His hands pulled her back.

"Get off me, Gabriel." Marianne struck out with her elbow. Hit air.

"There's nothing you can do here," he said. "EmJ's at peace."

"No!" She twisted around. "There is no peace. Do you hear me? That should be me, not her. She has her whole life ahead of her. Do something. Tell God he can't have her. Pray. Bring her back."

"Marianne, I can't."

"Then I will!" She squirmed and pummeled his chest. He lost his balance and they fell with a thud. She managed to wiggle free, but he grabbed her around the waist.

"Let go, you bastard! I need to save her. This cannot happen to us. Not again. Not twice."

"Marianne, we mustn't disturb the scene."

Too late. I already did that. I did that in spades.

She kicked backward and made contact with his leg. A weird crunching noise, and he groaned but wouldn't release her. She clawed at his arms, scratched his skin. Drew blood, but God help her, she would bite him if he didn't let go. She would not be powerless, helpless. For once in her life, she didn't need restraints. But his grip was strong, unyielding. Unbreakable.

She slammed her head back into his chest. Screams poured from her lips; insults spewed out like rapid gunfire. Inhumane, cruel. Bitter words aimed to maim, they tasted like blood, like desolation. Deafening, hateful words that would never make any difference because the one sound she craved, she would never hear again. It was gone forever.

"EmJ, talk to me. Tell me this is a hallucination." She collapsed into sobs. "Please don't let the monsters be real."

"My darling Nightjar"—a voice from the past—"you can't save her. She's with God now."

Gabriel stood and lifted her with him. He eased her around in his arms as if she were a rag doll, and maybe she was because she was done. Done with pushing back—with or without meds. Her own baby had died because of her, and she was stuck on repeat, trying to create a family out of nothing more than echoes. Past and present crashed into each other. There was no future. Everything stopped except for Gabriel's heartbeat and a distant siren. Insanity—ugly and twisted even in death—was the devil that couldn't be defeated. Madness was the victor; she quit.

FORTY

MARIANNE

It wasn't a conscious decision to stop talking, but after she'd formally identified EmJ and given her statement, after she'd learned the police had found a half-written suicide note, Marianne ran out of words. The stench of EmJ's vomit lingered, filling her nostrils and her mind. Eating away at her like acid.

As she walked into the rectory, Darius ran toward her, arms wide open. Gabriel, scratched arms hidden behind his back, retreated with Hugh and a bottle of brandy. A changing of the guards.

Darius helped her upstairs, where she lay down on her bed, fully clothed, and watched a memory collage of flashing lights. So many emergency vehicles over the years, but the memory of the first ones, on the A428, remained unaccounted for. Stolen by treatment to mend a broken mind.

But there was no treatment for a broken heart.

Darius sat in the old nursing chair, pulled close to the bed. Crumpled forward, his hair hiding his face, he held her hand. When darkness fell, he undressed her. She rolled toward the wall, and he spooned behind her.

The shadows of time moved across the bedroom wall.

She fell into a sinkhole of pain—in her stomach, in her muscles. In her head. A pounding migraine drummed louder and louder until it threatened to steal her vision and split open her skull. She didn't move; she didn't tell Darius.

Again, he lay with her when night fell. In his arms, she welcomed death. All those years wasted planning suicide, and it was so much easier to give up. To lie still and stop eating. But the next day came anyway.

She asked in a scratchy voice for a bowl so she didn't have to go to the bathroom to pee; Darius refused. Instead he picked her up, carried her to the commode, and held her in place. When she was done, he carried her back, tucked her up in bed, pulled out his phone, and pressed it to her ear.

Jade whispered, "I love you, Mama Bird. Please come back to me."

Please come back to me.

FORTY-ONE
MARIANNE

The next morning she started eating.

A routine began: Darius gave her sponge baths, made her take her meds, fed her. If he could have breathed for her, he would have. Whenever he left her, which was only to get coffee or bring up food, he propped the bedroom door open. One time he was gone for ages. Mrs. Tandy sat in his place, playing games on her phone. When he returned, the stitches had gone.

After that Mrs. Tandy came in every afternoon and sat with her while Darius showered and called Jade to discuss business. In the mornings and evenings he read to her. The classics she had loved as a teen: *Jane Eyre* and *Wuthering Heights*. After he declared himself Victorian'd out, he chose a Terry Pratchett novel and laughed loudly. Sometimes he stroked her hair, disgusting as it now must be.

He told her he loved her.

Love—a strange word. It tasted of dust.

Gabriel stayed away.

At the end of each day, Jade called with the same message. "I love you. We'll talk tomorrow, Mama Bird." For her baby girl, Marianne tried to believe tomorrow existed.

The funeral service came and went. Gabriel—owner of the disembodied voice outside her door—told Darius it had been held at the local crematorium. EmJ's mother had come and some aunt. The ex-boyfriend and the band had stayed away.

The local GP visited, and the district nurse. Dr. P. came once. Probably because she'd missed her follow-up appointment. He prescribed an SSRI, telling Darius, "We're going to increase the dose faster than I'd like, given her level of distress. Watch her carefully."

Didn't he know she'd flunked out with every antidepressant on the market? *Read my file, Dr. P.* An SSRI couldn't take away the truth: she had killed her baby; she had killed someone else's—twice.

She had nothing left to say.

✳

Days became night became days. Thoughts filled the void. This new antechamber of purgatory allowed no wiggle room for distraction.

While she lay awake, staring, while Darius read in his rich voice, while Mrs. Tandy played *Angry Birds*, Marianne's mind wandered. Roved endlessly in search of thoughts to lasso. And what she discovered one morning as she watched light creep around the edges of the curtains and listened to birds heralding another day might have been the ugliest truth of all.

For decades she had sought excuses, and medicine delivered: *You need to live within your psychiatric means, Marianne.* Gotta love scapegoats: blame the pills, blame the doctors, blame Gabriel for leaving her alone with Simon. Demonize her illness. Blame everyone but herself. Because to blame herself meant to revisit decisions made in the months prior to her baby's death. Decisions made of her own free will. She had released herself from complicity. Had given her past a Viking funeral, pushed it out to sea on a burning boat and said, "So long."

Events leading up to that night on the A428 had come from one starting point: the first time she slept with Simon. And she wasn't manic or hypomanic when she made that colossal mistake. She was bored. Mania didn't destroy her chance at motherhood, teenage boredom did—a stupid, secret game started with Simon because she had no one to play with.

Clean out of scapegoats, Marianne sat up, slowly. Darius was asleep in the other bed: on his back, arms flung out, hair spread across the pillow. He was snoring through his twice-broken nose. He'd never told her how the first breakage occurred—ex-wife, no doubt—but the second break had been caused by a singer throwing a mic.

Quietly Marianne got up, tiptoed to the bathroom, and peed. When she pushed back up to standing, her legs wobbled. As she clasped the sink, she accidentally glanced in the mirror. Defeat and neglect stared back. She had committed the number one sin of the deranged: allowed her illness to define her, to whisper, "Give up the fight."

But she wasn't her illness, and manic-depression was not responsible for the worst decision of her life. She had tried to reinvent herself by leaving the past behind and never looking back—until the accident in February.

Reinvention wasn't acceptance. It was denial.

Marianne leaned closer to her reflection. Bad enough that she'd given up on herself—and all that meant for Jade and Darius—but she gave up on EmJ, too. Worse, her inaction allowed the memory of Emmajohn Peel to disappear into statistics. A young woman committed suicide and no one cared. Almost no one had come to her funeral.

But she cared, and today she would find words to express that.

Gripping the sink tight with her left hand, Marianne gave defeat the finger. Then to make sure he'd gotten the message, she stuck out her tongue.

After she climbed back into bed, exhausted from being a rebel for the insane, she lay awake, watching and waiting. When Darius opened his eyes and looked straight at her, she whispered, "I love you with all my heart."

When was the last time she had said those words and meant them?

FORTY-TWO

JADE

Jade was about to say, "From the top, guys," but the singer, who'd chewed off his nails between each take, was now picking apart the rip in his jeans, thread by thread. Would it be totally out of order to offer him the Xanax she kept in the control room for Darius? Or Sasha could run to the touchy-feely gift shop on Weaver Street and buy some scented candles. Or Zeke could offer the dude a foot rub. He'd certainly kneaded the tension knot in her shoulder into melted butter.

"How are you feeling in there?" Jade spoke into the talkback mic. "Want a beer break?"

The singer looked up and smiled. *Bingo.*

She turned to Sasha to say, *Take my wallet,* but the control room door was wide open. Jade glanced through the plate glass into tracking room B, and there was Sasha, taking drinks orders. Zeke came up behind her and discreetly squeezed her butt. Sasha smirked at him. *Fantastic.* What the hell would happen to the studio chi when that little tryst went *kaboom*?

Jade pulled out her phone and called England. By now AT&T probably owned her soul, her savings, and what was left of Ernie. Gabriel picked up straightaway.

"You sitting on top of the phone?" Jade said. Since God hadn't listened when she'd asked Him, sweet as pie, to lobotomize the part of her brain that insisted she was in love, Jade had developed a new ploy for making it through phone calls with Gabriel. She concentrated on images from the movie *This Is Spinal Tap*, when the drummer spontaneously combusted on stage.

"I didn't want to wake Marianne," Gabriel whispered.

"You think she's asleep?"

"I insisted Darius take a night off and go to the pub with Hugh. I'm Marianne-sitting from the bottom of the stairs, but Darius left the bedroom door open. I'm checking to make sure"—his voice got quieter—"yes, her room's still dark."

"She is going to snap out of this, right? I mean, I know it's been eleven days, but Darius is husband of the century. He wouldn't let anything happen to her. Right?"

"Jade, he continues to win my utmost admiration, but what happens next is not up to Darius. Only Marianne can find the will to fight. The decision is hers alone. But she did talk to Darius this morning. I think that's the only reason he agreed to go out."

"I'm scared." She hadn't said that aloud before, but now it was September. Marianne's mental collapse, or whatever it was, had sucked up the entire summer. October wasn't far off, and that was never a good month for Marianne. What if she couldn't pull up from the nosedive before then?

"I know you're frightened." Gabriel paused. "Honey."

To hell with the exploding drummer. "Did you just call me honey?"

"Indeed, and it worked. You're laughing. Although I have to say, I find it a very empty endearment."

"What would you use?'

"I'm old-school. It would have to be *darling*."

Jade started to groan and turned it into a fake cough. "Allergies, sorry. We get them year-round in North Carolina. It's total shit. Must stock up on antiallergy meds." Maybe love was an allergy. If only there was a pill for that. "What happens next?"

"That, my dear Jade, is the question."

Dear. Where did that fall on his endearment spectrum—anywhere close to *darling*?

"Hugh thinks some sort of fund-raiser for teens in crisis might help the band members heal. To be honest, I'm worried about Matt, the drummer. His parents have him on lockdown, although his mother has allowed me to visit. He's made bad decisions, but I believe he cared deeply for EmJ. I don't want him to carry this guilt for the rest of his life."

His voice had hardened, and he was no longer whispering.

On the other side of the glass, Zeke sat on the floor and rolled a joint. The band members formed a circle around him. Therapy Zeke-style. Maybe she should start getting stoned. Medicinal marijuana for the pain of love?

"Do you think an event with music could help Marianne heal?" Jade said.

"I'm out of ideas at this point." Shuffling noises came down the phone. "Jade, I'll have to call you back. Marianne's out of bed."

FORTY-THREE
MARIANNE

She blinked, the light coming up from the downstairs hall too bright. Gabriel rushed toward her but stopped with one foot on the top stair and one on the landing. His hand shot to his throat. An oddly self-defensive gesture that protected his jugular.

"I don't bite." Her voice came out croaky and rusty. Not even Darius could fix that sound.

Gabriel frowned. "Do you need something?"

"A new mind? You not to look at me with fear?"

"I'm concerned, not afraid."

If she had the energy, she'd call him a liar. But that might lead into a discussion about the words *my darling Nightjar.*

"Did your skin heal where I clawed at you?" she said.

"Gracious." He rubbed his arm. "That was nothing."

Liar. She turned, and Gabriel moved quickly, blocking her path.

"Sorry if we disturbed. Jade was checking in. She's worried about you, as we all are."

"I need to get back to bed. I'm feeling a bit shaky."

"Absolutely." Taking her elbow, he guided her back to the bedroom doorway. "Wait there a minute."

He straightened her bedding and puffed up her pillow while she leaned against the door frame. Standing took such effort, such concentration.

"You were talking to Jade about a fund-raiser for EmJ?"

"An idea Hugh and I are batting around." He started to smooth out her bottom sheet and then jerked back his hand. Had he discovered it was still warm? "Would you like to be part of the discussion?"

"Discussion takes work. But could we talk tomorrow?"

"Absolutely." A second absolute. Gabriel had always thought, talked, and acted in black and white: *This is right, this is wrong.* If they played their old game with daisy petals—*He loves me, he loves me not*—where would it stop?

"Are you going to tuck me in with your old Winnie-the-Pooh hot-water bottle?"

"Heavens, no. I don't lend him to just anyone."

Finally he sounded like Gabriel, but she couldn't read his eyes in the darkness. She shuffled toward the foot of the bed and dragged herself up to the pillows. With a grunt, she flopped down to watch the shape in her doorway, lit from behind.

He buried his hands in his pockets. "Need anything? How about a hot chocolate?"

"No, but thanks. I'm going to take the sleeping pill Darius left out."

"Right. Night, then."

"Gabriel?"

He bobbed back into the doorway.

"Next time Jade calls, I'd like to talk to her."

"Excellent plan," he said, and pulled the door shut.

✳

When she woke, having apparently slept through until dawn—rare to not remember her dreams or wake up to pee—Darius was snoring, and the room smelled faintly of pub. She sat up and wiggled her toes on the prickly short-pile carpet. Slowly she stood and walked to the bathroom, this time avoiding the mirror.

"Would you like to be part of the discussion?" Gabriel had asked.

Yes, she would. But a fund-raiser was a nebulous event that took planning. Took energy. And her brain hadn't done much work in a while. The only thing it told her right now was to go outside and see the day wake up.

She tiptoed back to the bedroom, found a pen and a piece of paper, and scribbled a note: *Need fresh air and a clear head. Going for a short walk. Don't send out the cavalry. Back soon. Love you.*

Angling the note toward Darius so he would see it the moment he opened his eyes, she secured it with the alarm clock. Then she pulled on a cardigan and a pair of jeans and picked up her flip-flops. She went to the door, hesitated, and returned to the note, tacking on a row of kisses and a lopsided heart. Definitely fatter on one side than the other.

Downstairs she found Gabriel's green-and-gold baseball cap for the Northampton Saints, his favorite rugby team since they were kids. Everything about Gabriel traced back to childhood.

Holding her breath, she stumbled as she eased open the front door and then clicked it closed. Damn meds had stolen her stealth. Sneaking out of houses in her teens, she was quieter than a cat burglar. Gabriel had been the heffalump.

She walked slowly, head lowered. A local celebrity, the lunatic who'd caused two scandalous deaths. When she left Newton Rushford this time, it would be for good. No way was she game to leave her mark on village history with another repeat performance.

The part of the A428 that became the High Street was deserted.

Memories swirled: pedaling frantically down the broken white line at two a.m., leaving Gabriel behind. He'd never joined her in the middle of the road, preferring to cycle where he should—at the edge. She'd forgotten that about Gabriel, how he followed her lead but always hung back. How when mania began to consume her, he chose to walk away. But if he hadn't, she might never have found Darius and Jade. Although Simon would still be alive. Was his death the price of her happiness? How could anyone—let alone an insane person—make sense of it all? Maybe Dr. White had been right all those months ago, and there was no reason. Or maybe everything that happened, including tragedy, concealed reason. And Dr. White needed to brush up on his Aristotle.

Down by the village green, a car door slammed and an engine revved. She stopped and waited as the car turned onto the A428, and then she watched its taillights heading for the spot that had changed her future. Or created it.

A flock of geese flew over in perfect formation, honking, and the church clock struck seven a.m. Marianne kept walking until she reached Puddings Galore, a place she had yet to scope out. But then she had no interest in things that tasted too sweet. It was the reason she liked English cream. No sugar spoiling the taste.

To her left, the war memorial pointed into the pale, clear sky where the outline of a crescent moon was still visible. Stepping closer, she stopped by the low black chain around the base of the plinth. It had been freshly painted and the stone of the Celtic cross scrubbed clean. The village took care of this memorial dedicated to the young men who had died for king and country in two world wars.

"'Their names liveth forever more,'" she read aloud.

Unlike EmJ's. And while she was on a riff about reason, how the hell could she find any in the suicide of an eighteen-year-old?

A robin sang, and a silent movie played in her mind: young soldiers enlisting for the front lines, getting on trains, traveling into battle. Living and dying in the inhumane conditions of the trenches in France. Then her mind flashed to the posters on the display in the back of the church. Posters for the women's land army. How many of those women had seen their loved ones return with broken minds? Shell shock, the grandfather of post-traumatic stress disorder. Seemed she shared something with professional soldiers.

And so did EmJ.

Neither of them had signed up for their private wars. Conscripts, they were dumped down in their own trenches without ammunition. EmJ went over the top only to die alone in no-man's-land. There would be no well-kept memorials for people like EmJ. No accolades or medals for their victories; no words carved into stone; no shiny commemorative plaques. But their deaths mattered, as did their courage. The courage to get out of bed and make it through another day. The courage to not slink off to America for a second time, leaving behind gossip and shame. The courage to keep fighting the monsters.

As always the Marianne Stokes strategy had been flawed, but facing the devil within had been a good, solid idea. Stopping her meds was the catastrophic mistake. Without them she couldn't think straight. Tugging off the baseball cap, Marianne shook out her greasy, matted hair and walked back to the rectory. Once again she was going to stand up to the devil. But in front of a captive audience with her brain tanked up on meds. And this time she would be fully rehearsed and fully clothed.

It would be her memorial to EmJ.

FORTY-FOUR
DARIUS

He was finishing up the Cadbury chocolate he'd found in the fruit bowl when Gabriel shuffled through the kitchen door and threw a proprietary glance at the wrapper. Darius shoved in the last strip of milk chocolate with a flash of finders-keepers attitude. Given that warring factions of his psyche were slugging it out over his next move—steam-releasing visceral anger or old-fashioned spousal patience—the last thing he needed was grief from the vicar.

"Marianne still asleep?"

"My beloved went for a walk." Darius swallowed hard, and a lump of chocolate stuck in his esophagus with a nice left hook. He swallowed again, making a strange gulping sound.

"Need a glass of water?"

Darius shook his head, and the chocolate started its slow descent into his churning stomach. Gorging on chocolate might not have been the best idea, but when you didn't drink, didn't smoke, and didn't do drugs, how else could you get a quick fix?

"Marianne left a note saying not to worry." Darius shredded the chocolate wrapper. "This is me not worrying."

"And chocolate is always an excellent choice for breakfast."

That, apparently, said without sarcasm.

"According to the *Huffington Post*, if you eat the equivalent of twenty-two Hershey's kisses a day, you lower your chance of heart disease and stroke. Not much of a facts-and-figures guy, but that's a number I can live with. And the best part—it includes milk chocolate. I mean, no one really likes dark chocolate, right?"

Mail plopped through the slot on the front door and landed on the hall floor as a voice said, "Morning, Reverend!"

This place was ridiculously busy and chirpy. The amount of people traffic would do his head in if he lived here. A room of one's own shouldn't be the exclusive right of feminists.

"Do you have any idea when Marianne left?" Gabriel pulled out a chair and sat on the opposite side of the table. As far away as possible.

"That would be a negative. I was asleep."

"And you're not concerned that she's gone walkabout after not leaving her bedroom for over ten days?"

Seriously? The guy didn't think he was freaking out in a thousand ways amplified? Despite everyone's best efforts, the offbeat vibe between him and Gabriel remained, and he wasn't entirely sure why. It didn't bother him that Marianne and Gabriel had been in love as teenagers— okay, so perhaps a teeny bit. But he was curious as all fuck to know how Simon fit into the picture. Did his wife have a fetish for brothers, or had the love triangle really been about Simon and Gabriel's relationship?

No, it wasn't the past that bothered him; it was the now. Gabriel protested a helluva lot for an innocent, and Marianne had said nothing at all. Did she keep the home fires burning for this guy? His mind skittered through a kid's taunt: *Marianne and Gabriel sitting in a tree, K-I-S-S-I-N-G.*

"Look, by now you know that Marianne is my life, but marriage isn't all nonalcoholic champagne and roses. I'm simply trying to respect her wishes."

"You're a good husband." Gabriel sighed. Was that with regret, longing, or jealousy?

Darius sucked chocolate off his finger. "Thanks. You ever consider tying the knot?"

"You've got a smear of chocolate on your cheek."

Darius wiped at his cheek.

"No, other one."

"Gone?"

"Indeed." Gabriel got up and went to fill the kettle. Seemed this was not a conversation the vicar wanted to have face-to-face.

"To answer your question," Gabriel said behind him, "no, I've never asked anyone to marry me, but I've seen enough marriages implode to know that I'm not wired for that kind of intensity." Gabriel flicked on the kettle.

"And what have you learned from watching so many marriages fail?"

"That the trick to surviving as a couple is not tearing each other apart when you're fighting the same battle. When there's a family crisis, you have to come together. Marianne's parents were good at that, being a team."

"Her mom died before we met, but her dad's a great guy. I get peculiar looks in the retirement home—with the hair, the earrings, the ink. He's never blinked, though. Treats me and Jade like his own."

"He was always a generous, kindhearted man." Gabriel walked to the fridge and pulled out the coffee jar.

Darius focused on a gouge in the pine tabletop. He liked to see a guy's eyes when they talked, but maybe Gabriel had been wise to turn his back. That throb of anger had faded into a steady pulse. A distant vibration. A curiosity. After all, Gabriel had known a different Marianne.

"What was she like, as a kid?"

"Exhausting and fiery. Her temper was quite vile. She wasn't the prettiest girl on the playground, but she charmed everyone like an exotic bird. She was untamable, unpredictable, and mesmerizing."

"Yeah," Darius said. "I figured."

"Fearless too. She would suggest we climb the tallest tree, and I would say 'I can't' and do it anyway because she'd dare me until I had no resistance left. And she was loyal to a fault. We both went to public—I believe you would say private—schools in Bedford and came home together on the 128 bus with children from the state schools. One day a gang of boys picked on me because of my school blazer. Marianne got up, ordered the ringleader to stand, and then kicked him in the groin. They never bothered us again."

"That's my girl. She once tossed some famous bass player out of the studio midsession because he called Jade a bitch. But that wasn't enough, so Marianne banned him for life. The manager was seriously pissed, and I predicted the end of Nightjar. But news traveled, and our bookings of female artists doubled."

"When we were growing up, she never saw consequences, only actions."

Darius glanced up at the kitchen clock. As the minute hand moved slowly, his stomach started gurgling. "Backing off doesn't come instinctively, but I'm trying. Got any more chocolate?"

Gabriel leaned over to peer into the empty fruit bowl. "Nope. It appears you ate my entire stash."

"Sorry, man. I'll replace it." Darius threw himself back into his chair. "She's doing too much again. Making bad decisions. How can I give her space if she won't look after herself? I feel as if this is her new pattern, and it terrifies me."

"One, two, three . . ." Gabriel counted out scoops of ground coffee with a slow precision that seemed unnecessary. Was he uncomfortable talking about male feelings in general, or was it Darius's feelings that set his teeth on edge?

"What's that old adage," Gabriel said, as he poured boiling water onto the coffee, "about if you love someone, let her go, and if she doesn't return, she wasn't yours to begin with? Or something along those lines."

Was that a hitch in his voice, one that screamed *I'm talking from personal experience*?

"But if it would ease your worry," Gabriel said, "I'd be happy to go and look for her. I know her old haunts and have no objections to playing the villain."

"Would you? Thanks, man. That'd be—"

The front door opened and closed. They exchanged glances, and Darius shot to his feet.

"We're in the kitchen," Gabriel called out.

Marianne appeared and handed Gabriel the mail; Darius rushed forward and kissed her cheek.

"Just in time for breakfast," Gabriel said. "How about a boiled egg with soldiers to dip in? Mrs. Tandy brought me some fresh farm eggs that are out of this world."

"I haven't had a boiled egg in forever." She and Gabriel exchanged smiles. Exclusive smiles that shut him out.

Darius put his arm around his wife. "What are soldiers?"

"Strips of hot buttered toast you dip into the yolk."

"Cool. Can I get some?"

There was another knock at the door. "Come in!" Gabriel bellowed.

A guy Darius vaguely recognized from the knife incident appeared. Was it the man who'd helped him into the backseat of the muddy Land Rover that stank of dog? Former military, if he had to guess. Something about the way the guy carried himself.

"Apologies for the early intrusion, but I need to clarify a few things for Saturday's wedding service."

"Morning, Ian. Can I offer you a boiled egg?"

"Gracious, no. The missus already made me a fry-up." Ian patted his flat stomach.

Another knock, but this time Gabriel went out into the hall and answered the door. And then the phone. Ian shifted and commented on the weather.

"Coffee?" Darius said, since someone had to act the host.

"Don't mind if I do." Ian sat down. "Milk and two sugars." He glanced at Darius's arm but didn't say anything.

Given all that had happened since the village fete, a knife wound seemed to have lost significance, and yet the churchwarden had stepped up to the plate for a stranger. Some form of gratitude was in order. "By the way, thanks for helping get me to the ER that day. Didn't really enjoy bleeding out in front of the womenfolk."

Ian nodded slowly. "Of course."

Shit, the guy didn't realize he was joking. In Darius's experience, if you were going to bleed out, it should always be done in front of women. His sisters had patched him up more times than he could remember.

"Coffee, babe?"

Marianne nodded as Darius forced the plunger down into the french press and then poured three cups. They drank in silence, Marianne leaning against him. Her first day up, and as he'd suspected, she'd done too much.

"Sorry for all the interruptions." Gabriel appeared and frowned at the french press.

"Sorry, man, we killed the pot. You really need to buy a machine. One that makes twelve cups minimum."

"Right," Gabriel said. And put the kettle on again.

"I'd like to float an idea by all of you," Marianne said. "Gabriel got me thinking when he mentioned a fund-raiser, but what if we did a memorial for EmJ at the church?"

"Uh-huh." Gabriel dumped out the coffee grounds in the tin labeled "Compost." He wasn't the neatest guy, but he was fastidious about recycling.

"We could celebrate her life and her music," Marianne continued, "but turn it into a community event to raise awareness of mental illness. Get the word out to local nonprofits that help teens in crisis. Shadowbox could play. And I'd like to be involved."

Gabriel turned. "By singing?"

"No, I'd like to give the address."

"Marianne," Darius said. "Are you strong enough for that?"

Ignoring him, she locked eyes with Gabriel. Darius watched their game of chicken. Marianne had no friends outside the Nightjar family, and Darius had always kept his inner world small. It meant you never had to second-guess whom to trust in a world of charlatans. Yet here was some guy he didn't know who could communicate with his wife via secret sign language. And it bugged the shit out of him.

"Can we do this for EmJ, in your church? Please, Gabriel?"

"You're asking my permission to do something?"

"Am I really that bad?" Marianne smiled.

"Yes, and my answer is yes," Gabriel said.

"Reverend—" Ian fiddled with the collar of his tightly buttoned shirt. "Our calendar is full until after harvest festival."

"Short notice, but how about this Saturday? Sadly the wedding just canceled. Off the record, I believe the groom has some emotional issues to work through."

"Serendipity," Marianne said, and stared at Gabriel. This time he was first to break eye contact.

Darius shot up. "Think I'll skip the eggs and go stock up on chocolate. Any requests? How about you, my goddess?"

And before she could answer, he twisted his hand into her hair and pulled her into a kiss.

FORTY-FIVE

MARIANNE

Marianne did something she rarely did: she wiggled into a dress. A Jackie O black shift that was too figure-hugging for church but made a screeching statement: *I am powerful, I am in control, I am not the madwoman in the attic.* If she was taking center stage, she was going to own it.

Right, EmJ?

Gabriel had taken them to the outlet mall the day before, but this time the shopping was restrained. Darius bought a Paul Smith suit and a black shirt, but balked at buying a tie; she bought the dress, simple black power heels, and a clutch bag; Gabriel bought a coffee. He said it was the only thing in the place he could afford. After they got back to the village, Darius disappeared and returned with supplies to restock Gabriel's fridge, freezer, pantry, and fruit bowl. He'd enlisted Mrs. Tandy's support.

Her phone vibrated with a text.

You've got this. Knock 'em dead. Jade added a
heart and a smiley face.

Knock 'em dead. Yeah, if she didn't throw up breakfast first. The
church could seat hundreds. A full house would be wonderful for EmJ,
awful for herself. She hadn't told EmJ the entire truth about why she
quit performing: debilitating stage fright. What if she got up to the
pulpit, saw a sea of faces, and had to run?

She glanced toward the bathroom door and pictured the bed a few
feet away. Five days ago she'd done a Lazarus, and Darius reprimanded
her repeatedly for overexerting herself. No one would criticize if she
retreated back under the covers and stayed there.

Turning to check her rear view in the mirror, she caught a glimpse
of the tattoo peeking out on her right shoulder blade: the single rose
half strangled by barbed wire. A daily reminder of how her mom had
tackled every bipolar barb without complaint. It had been a memorial,
a eulogy, for her mom. Her mother had never curled up into a ball and
said, "I can't do this." And neither would she.

Marianne attempted to tame her mane of hair, which had broken
free of its well-maintained layers and expensive color treatment. When
had it last been this long? Probably not since she was a teen. She twisted
her lucky earrings, the peridot studs Darius had given her for their first
wedding anniversary—"because they match your eyes"—and tried not
to imagine a guillotine with Mrs. Tandy sitting next to it sobbing into
one of Gabriel's white handkerchiefs.

Her stomach was on a slalom course. Hurling was not an option
and neither was quitting, because this was about EmJ and making
amends to Gabriel.

She opened the bathroom door, retrieved the scarlet clutch filled
with tissues from her bed, and began to walk the longest plank in history. She refused to think about what waited at the end. Right now she
merely had to make it downstairs to where Darius patrolled the hall like

a nervous prom date. As she reached the last step, he gave a low whistle. Darius never wore aftershave, not with his allergies, but he smelled of coconut soap and summer rain. His hair was restrained in a ponytail, which accentuated his huge, dark eyes.

"Ready to do this thing, my goddess?"

"No. But when has that ever stopped me. You look"—her eyes roved over his body—"omigod, totally hot."

"Hot enough to get lucky tonight?"

"I think that could be arranged," she said.

"Such a tease." He frowned. "You're not wearing your wrist cuffs. Want me to get them?"

"No. I'm not hiding anything today."

"That's my girl." He waved her around the banisters but hung back to watch her buttocks. As always. Which did she value more: his predictability or the way he could surprise her with unexpected moments of passion? The memory of that territorial kiss in the kitchen, in full view of Ian and Gabriel, still made her shiver.

"Come on, Mrs. Montgomery. We've got a date with God." Darius slapped her bottom and snuck in a quick squeeze. "Damn, woman. Now I know you've got your groove back. Going to church commando?" He kissed her neck. "Only my wife."

"I thought you might appreciate a return to my old ways."

"You do realize if we weren't running late and you hadn't slathered on all that lipstick, I would take you right here. In the vicar's hallway."

She smiled, and her stomach settled. "Love you too."

But as she grabbed her black cashmere shawl from the wooden chest in the hall, one of her many possessions littered throughout the rectory, the unease returned. Without meaning to, she'd taken over Gabriel's home. Leaving him wouldn't be quite as simple as walking out the front door.

✳

Clouds the color of mourning hung low but held on to their moisture. Marianne wrapped her shawl around her shoulders. September 13, and already the air carried a hint of fall.

Traffic on the High Street was heavier than usual, which suggested the motorway was closed. Hopefully not because of an accident. She and Darius walked slowly, given the height of her heels. Coming back she would carry, not wear, them. *Coming back.* In an hour and a half, this would be over. She would think of it as a performance, although performing had always been about pretending to be someone else. That was her cure for stage fright. Today she was going to be one hundred percent Marianne Stokes. The real deal. Stripping her soul naked had been easier at sixteen and batshit insane.

A steady stream of villagers filed ahead of them toward the church. A silent migration of people seeking what—healing, truth, comfort from Gabriel? Were they the same people who had headed to the cream teas on the August bank holiday?

As they moved under the lych-gate and up the cobbled path to the church, Marianne's thoughts returned to that cold day in July when she'd been running from herself and her husband. His hand was now pressed against the small of her back, gently propelling her forward. Everything she had put this man through, and still he loved her. If she believed in God, she would say a prayer of gratitude.

They stepped down into the church and Ian handed them an order of service. "I hope you don't mind sharing," he said. "We vastly underestimated the size of today's congregation. Standing room only, but Hugh has reserved seats for you in the front pew."

Marianne gulped.

"Thanks, man," Darius said, and pulled Ian into a quick hug. Ramrod straight, the churchwarden stared ahead, eyes wide.

Oblivious, Darius slotted his arm through hers, and they began their procession. Was it her imagination, or did everyone stop talking to watch? Marianne's mind flashed back to doing the same walk in a broderie anglaise confirmation dress and holding in giggles as Gabriel marched solemnly beside her. To her it had been a lark; to him it was destiny.

Her heels clacked on the Victorian-tiled floor—her history professor mom had called those tiles sacrilegious—until they stepped onto the long strip of blue carpet that led up the Saxon nave. Artificial light the color of the gloaming filled the packed church, and Marianne held her mother in her thoughts and her head high. Staring at the altar, she ignored the heat of stares and the darts of whispers.

When she stumbled—*stupid heels*—Darius caught her.

"Careful, my beautiful wife," he said in a loud stage whisper, then gave her a wink that nearly caused her to stumble for different reasons. And for thirty seconds she forgot that the front pew was still an ocean away.

Finally they reached it, and Hugh stood to greet them. He shook Darius's hands and kissed her cheek. In between the choir stalls, the band had set up the drums and the amps. Tom's guitar and Jack's bass waited on their stands. Only two mics when there should have been three. Marianne sat quickly and glanced up at the wooden angel ceiling. If she'd ever needed a drink, it was now.

Within minutes the organist started playing and the congregation stood. She rose with everyone else, her stomach muscles clenched into one humongous punching bag. The choir seemed to glide up the nave far more effortlessly than she and Darius had done, and Gabriel brought up the rear, his white starched surplice rustling against his cassock. The layers of clerical garb added bulk and stature. His face unreadable, he bore no resemblance to the boy she'd loved or the man who wandered through the rectory in bare feet, slouch pants, and shrunken T-shirts. This Gabriel was an intimidating presence, a man who held people's souls in his hand. This, she supposed, was the real Gabriel.

And she didn't know him at all.

FORTY-SIX

GABRIEL

Gabriel stood in the vicar's stall and waited for the choir to settle. His heart beat steadily, even though Marianne was watching him officiate for the first time.

"Please be seated." A voice flowed through the microphone and over the congregation like sea mist, but it wasn't his voice. It was the voice of a performer. Marianne had taught him more than she realized.

He had never seen the church so packed. There were plenty of strangers and young people who he assumed were friends of the band, but the congregation was also full of villagers paying tribute to a young woman who had become part of their community in death. Possibly some of those present felt as responsible as he did. Mrs. Peel sat hidden behind large sunglasses, halfway back. She had refused to see him when he called on her, but he would take it as a good sign that she was present today.

After his welcome, Gabriel concentrated on his words and the order of events. His eyes did not stray to the front pew. Hugh would, no doubt, comment on it later. Or maybe he'd see it for what it was: survival.

They sang "Onward, Christian Soldiers," and EmJ's best friend from primary school read a poem. He stood, he sat, he played his role, and then it was time for Marianne. Orders of service shuffled, and someone sneezed. When the church fell silent, he allowed himself to glance at her. She was clasping Darius's hand as if her life depended on it. Would he have to step in and give an address off the cuff? It wouldn't be the first time, but the moment called for something big, something healing, something prepared. Marianne looked at him, her sad eyes asking for help. He smiled, and the room stripped away to the two of them.

You can do it, he said silently.

She gave a nod and stood; Darius tugged on his lapels.

Gabriel expected Marianne to come to the lectern and stand in front of him, but no, she went to the pulpit. As she climbed the winding steps, so graceful despite the dangerously high heels, his eyes skimmed up the body he could have once outlined in his sleep. He picked up his reading glasses and pretended to study the order of service.

"Hi," Marianne said into the microphone, her voice hesitant. "I'm Marianne Stokes, the infamous wild child of Newton Rushford, which means every story you've ever heard about my teenage years that involves sex, drugs, vandalism . . . and stolen sherbet lemons is probably true. And under that fine mural on the bus shelter wall is my first and last attempt at graffiti. It was spectacularly bad."

The tension in the church loosened. People laughed and settled into more comfortable positions. Gabriel removed his reading glasses, folded his hands into his lap, and fixed his stare on the organ pipes behind Marianne.

"I'm also a manic-depressive and an alcoholic. And it's a first for me, saying those words to a gathering that isn't a group therapy session on a mental ward. So I guess you could say this is my coming out as a crazy person. And it's only by the incredible character of Reverend

Gabriel Bonham"—she glanced in his direction—"that I reached adulthood. Growing up in this village, Gabriel was my best friend. I chose to wear a sleeveless dress today because I wanted to show you what he did for me when I was sixteen and terrified of the monsters in my head." She held up her wrists; a few people gasped. "I'm a three-time suicide survivor. The doctors don't know how I survived the last two attempts, but I know why I didn't die as a teenager. Gabriel saved my life." She lowered her arms, and someone coughed. "I hope you realize how blessed you are to have this man as your vicar. And I hope the rumors about him and me end here and now. Otherwise my adored husband"—she waved at Darius—"will have to threaten each of you with a pair of boxing gloves."

Another round of laughter. Marianne glanced down at the floor of the pulpit; Gabriel glanced up at the pattern of acorns on the chancel ceiling and willed her to talk about anything other than him.

"I stayed away from the village for thirty years because I was too ashamed to show my face here. But I hit a downward spiral and, like a homing pigeon, came back to where I'd been happy as a child. Gabriel took me in, no questions asked. That's the kind of guy he is. I think that also means he saved my life twice." She swallowed. "Things got a bit rocky from that point. You expect that when you're as messed up as I am, but I also make more silly mistakes than most toddlers. Part of that's my illness and part of it's me. I made a disastrous decision to come off my meds and ended up in the loony bin. Not a bad one as loony bins go. I'm happy to give references if anyone is in need of five-star residential care."

A ripple of laughter.

"That's how I met EmJ. Emmajohn Peel. A young woman who made my past seem like a stroll in Bedford Park. Some of you witnessed my first psychotic break outside in the churchyard when I was sixteen. That was the beginning for me. But EmJ told me she'd been hospitalized at thirteen. What were you doing at thirteen? I was climbing trees with your future vicar and ripping up daffodils in your garden, Bill Collins."

Marianne paused and cleared her throat, and Gabriel wished he'd left a glass of water out for her. "You're told to expect failure when you have a mood disorder. My life has been filled with failure: destroyed friendships—Gabriel was my first victim—two collapsed marriages, the suicide attempts, and years lost to alcoholism. How I ended up with a devoted husband who puts up with everything I throw at him—quite literally—I have no idea."

"I'm a saint," Darius said loudly, and people laughed again.

"Yes, my love, you are. But not everyone can be as blessed. And not everyone in my position has someone who can say, 'Congratulations, you kept living.' For five years, EmJ kept living, and that took heroic courage. As it did to get up on stage and sing her heart out in that beautiful voice.

"We're here today to honor this amazing young woman. To remember her and her extraordinary musical talent. But I also want to thank her for the lessons she taught me. Finding acceptance comes in stages, and thanks to EmJ, I've reached a new level of acceptance. Yes, I love my family. But I have taken their support for granted and shut them out when they've tried to help. I realize now that I can no longer do this alone. At the risk of sounding like a trailer for a B-list horror movie, it takes a village to keep you safe when you have demons gnawing at your brain. So please, if you know people battling mental illness, don't judge them when they fail, which they will do. Help them get back up, as Gabriel and my family have done for me.

"I wanted to help EmJ—teach her coping skills and guide her into a career in music. And in that too I failed. EmJ and I have both failed. But we are not failures. We are and always will be—even in death—soldiers."

Someone blew his nose loudly. Another person sniffed.

"On the way here, I passed the war memorial. I'm sure many of you did. That column of stone is a testament to the courage of young men who died fighting for their way of life. People like EmJ—and me—fight equally hard every day for the right to exist. She lost her life to a fatal disease because the noise in her head had taken over, like an invading army. But she never made a decision to enter the war. Untrained and without weapons, she was thrown down on the front lines and told to fight. There is no reprieve when you have a broken mind; cease-fires are rare. Even on good days, you know everything could change on a dime. Fear is your constant shadow.

"Some people think suicide is the ultimate failure, but don't judge her that way. EmJ was a young soldier in a silent war, fallen before her time. I will never forget her, and I hope you won't, either." Marianne paused and turned her head slowly, scanning the congregation, trying, he assumed, to make eye contact with as many people as possible.

"Emmajohn Peel was my sister-in-arms. She didn't make it. But I will honor her memory every day for the rest of my life. When I get home to North Carolina, I'm going to establish an annual prize, in EmJ's name, for one gifted student graduating from the music performance program at the University of North Carolina to record in my studio. Her name will live on, as should the names of all fallen warriors." Marianne's bottom lip trembled. "When we met, EmJ said, 'I just want it to go away for a while.' Wherever you are, sweetheart, may you be at peace. And I hope you're laughing as hard as you are on this recording that we're about to play.

"I made this when we were practicing—in our bedroom at the rectory—with a mic, an audio interface, and my laptop. In other words, it's bargain-basement recording. Or it was until my husband got his hands on it. He's a sound wizard who can mix anything. He did this as a gift for me, because he knew how desperately I wanted the last word to belong to EmJ."

Wiping her eyes, Marianne walked down the pulpit steps, and EmJ's voice drifted through the PA system. Her words and her singing filled the church, and as the music faded out, another sound faded in over the top: EmJ's sweet laugh. There was a moment of silence and then Matt stood and clapped. Followed by Tom, Charlotte, and Jack. One by one, his congregation followed suit.

Gabriel, however, sat. Lost in the promise of Marianne, he could hear her teenage voice: "Together we're going to change the world, or die trying."

He had always admired her strength, her determination, her fearlessness, and her courage. And there it all was, laid out on display. And it would never be his. It hadn't been from the second Simon barged into their secret world. Yes, Gabriel had loved her with a passion he could never replicate, a passion that ruined every chance of happiness he glimpsed with another woman. Marianne talked about failed friendships; he collected failed relationships, and with each failure, he retreated further.

The day she magically appeared in this very building and he invited her into his home, he mistook it for a test from God, when he was merely testing himself. Seeing if he still had the capacity for a love of that depth. Not duty, not loyalty, not friendship, not the need to do the right thing, but the unquestionable devotion of a husband like Darius. And now he had his answer. He'd been telling anyone who would listen he wasn't in love with Marianne. Finally he believed it. Marianne talked about an endgame on that first day. Had this been his all along, to find out the answer to that thirty-year-old question: Did he still love Marianne? And hadn't his greatest fear been not that he did, but that he didn't?

The church fell silent as the congregation, seated once more, waited for him to act. Marianne beamed at him, her arm linked through Darius's. And Gabriel looked away from everything that had been his, everything that had ended in a deafening crunch of metal. With a cough he stood.

"I think it only fitting that we should now hear from EmJ's band, Shadowbox."

Gabriel sat down heavily. He needed to get through the service and retreat to the rectory. Plead exhaustion and make a hasty exit. He didn't approve of vicars who swanned out of a service, leaving the laity to clear up. But being falsely polite to everyone gathered in his church seemed more than he was capable of today. It demanded the courage Marianne had mentioned and he had never possessed.

When the band finished playing, everyone cheered. People blew their noses and dabbed at their eyes with tissues. It was an oddly evangelical moment created by rock 'n' roll. Gabriel almost expected his normally reserved parishioners to start waving their arms around and singing, "Praise be to God." What he didn't expect was to see Marianne slip out of her pew when the song had finished and stand on the chancel steps, her back to him, and sing the Lord's Prayer unaccompanied, with the voice of an angel. Darius showed no surprise.

The world seemed to spin away from him. His world. The one he had built with fortified walls. In his church, surrounded by his faith, he was in control. And that too Marianne had stolen from him. More memories of the crash bled out as if from a fresh wound. He tipped back his head, giving the semblance of rapture as he drowned out Marianne's voice with his own prayer.

Please Lord, give me the strength to get through this.

If he couldn't find that strength, he should go back to the vestry, crack open the communion wine, and make the bishop's day by resigning.

FORTY-SEVEN
MARIANNE

"Babe, we need to get you into the studio," Darius said as soon as they stood up. "To record some religious music."

Gathering her belongings, she willed her heartbeat to return to normal. She'd done it, but she still needed to make it through the obstacle course of people moving toward them instead of the door. "Not happening. That was a one-off, a gift for EmJ if she's listening. Gabriel says religion brings people peace. I'm hoping he's right."

Darius leaned in close. "All this talk of God is giving me the heebie-jeebies. Let's get out of here. Besides—" His hand slid down her back to her thigh. "For the last hour I've been fantasizing about tearing that dress off you."

He reached past her to shake hands like a political candidate fresh off a stump speech. People introduced themselves; voices congratulated her. One woman told Marianne they'd been in playgroup together and made a joke about her ripping down the curtain during a nativity play. Marianne had no memory of the woman or the incident. She glanced around to find Gabriel, but he was standing by the font, shaking hands in a weird receiving line. As the crowd pressing in on her and Darius thickened, panic rose; her heart raced. She snatched at Darius's sleeve.

"If you'll excuse us," he said loudly, "I think my wife needs some fresh air."

People moved away, and she and Darius had a clear run down the aisle. Her heartbeat slowed. "Thank you," she whispered. "I thought I was going under."

"Think of me as your seizure-response dog, like epileptics have."

Marianne laughed until she spotted the church ladies serving tea and chocolate digestive biscuits in front of the choir vestry. Standing by the end of the table, clutching a chipped white mug, not unlike the ones her mother used to schlep around when she organized the monthly coffee mornings, and staring directly at her, was Bill Collins.

It didn't take a PhD to figure out who had placed that call to the archdeacon. Darius stopped to shake someone's hand, and she set her sights on Bill. The bastard was going down. Hopefully with an audience.

Behind her Darius said, "Yes, I'm incredibly proud of my wife. She's a total rock star."

"You owe Gabriel an apology." She pointed her index finger at Bill. Up close his teeth were gray and crooked, and as for those nose hairs . . . "Tattling to the archdeacon because of some petty grudge you've harbored against us since we were kids was mean and unchristian." Did she say *unchristian* loud enough? She should repeat it in case not everyone heard.

He put down his mug, reached for his stick, and limped closer.

"No," he said. "I owe you an apology."

Despite his coffee breath, Marianne didn't move.

"The wife had her ups and downs," Bill said quietly. "All her family did. They had a name for it, called it the bad bile. Don't know where that came from. Guess her family'd been using it for generations."

"I—I'm sorry, I don't remember your wife."

"She wouldn't talk to the GP or nothing. She didn't leave the house much. That's why she got upset about them pranks you two played."

Oh God. Stupid, mean pranks when they thought the house was empty: splattering mud on the windows, throwing rotten apples onto the perfectly mown lawn, opening the paper and throwing pages up into the cherry tree. Except the house hadn't been empty.

"You and Gabriel scared her half to death. Made her convinced the house were under attack. She started seeing aliens. I tried to look after her, best I could, but weren't nothing I could do." He grabbed Marianne's hand with his moist, bony one. "The wife wouldn't get no treatment, you see. And I blamed you two for everything."

"You should have blamed me, and me alone. Gabriel worked hard to talk me out of some of that stuff."

"But he always followed you, didn't he?"

"Not exactly. He knew I was an unstoppable force when I got an idea for a prank. He came along as quality control." She gave a tired smile. "To make sure I didn't go completely bananas. Without his influence, trust me, it would have been a thousand times worse. I take full responsibility, and I'm so sorry." She closed both her hands around his.

"Different time," he mumbled, lowering his gaze. "I wanted to get her help, but we didn't talk about such things. No one did. And there weren't the Internet like there is now. I wish I'd known more."

"Can I ask what happened to Mrs. Collins?"

"She died." He looked back up. She'd never noticed before, but his eyes were deep blue. "By her own hand. That's why I called the archdeacon. I thought you two was carrying on again. Not caring who you hurt."

Marianne swallowed hard. "I'm so sorry for the hell I put you both through."

"I'm sorry too, about that girl. Awful business."

Marianne nodded. Darius joined them, and Bill Collins released her.

"I can see you're a good man," Bill said. "You keep on doing your duty as a husband."

"I intend to, sir." Darius sounded oddly formal. "She's a keeper."

"If you'll excuse me"—Bill picked up his mug—"I need to put this in the sink and then go talk to the reverend. Want to compliment him on the service." And he shuffled off.

"Did I miss something?" Darius frowned.

"A miracle," Marianne said.

FORTY-EIGHT
GABRIEL

Staring at a balled-up crisp packet rolling around in the corner of the bus shelter, Gabriel leaned back against the mural Marianne had referenced in her address. A light drizzle began to fall as he replayed the conversation with Bill Collins. After complimenting him on the service, Bill had declared his intention to call the bishop and set things right, even if that meant abusing his relationship with the archbishop of Canterbury. Apparently there was some tenuous family connection. Not that Gabriel was listening closely to that part of Bill's monologue. And it was a monologue, because Gabriel found himself unable to register a single response.

For years he refused to give up hope for a good outcome with Bill, despite believing that the man was a lost cause. But without warning, Bill flashed his Christian heart and offered forgiveness and charity. And Gabriel had barely managed a smile, let alone the euphoric happy vicar dance. He really should resign, because if he cared so little about one repentant sinner returning to the fold, he was no longer fit to be a priest. He could volunteer for the British Red Cross. Or he could contact the woman he'd met today from the teens in crisis group and see if she knew of any job openings. Or he could ask Marianne and Darius to leave.

He pulled out his mobile to read the text from Jade.

```
I gather Marianne was a big hit. Don't
forget their makeup sex gets loud. Might
want to put off going home.
```

Another text came through.

```
You holding up OK?
```

He slipped the phone back into his pocket, the messages unanswered. On the A428, traffic crawled by in little spurts. One of those big French lorries followed by a line of cars. A gap and then a moped. How many of those drivers had crossed the site of the crash, oblivious? He avoided that stretch of road in the same way he was avoiding returning to his house. Avoidance, he was brilliant at that. But he was, quite simply, done. Tonight, over supper, he would ask Marianne and Darius to fly home.

Her memories of the accident were missing; his were not. Normally he kept them locked away, but today they had broken free. Every word spoken in anger; every ripple those words caused. A ripple effect leading to a maelstrom of remorse.

The present had caught up with the past, a place he couldn't revisit, and it was time for decisive action. Darius was a good man; Jade an amazing woman. Marianne needed to go home and love them. Be grateful that they were part of her life, and leave the past where it belonged— buried in Newton Rushford cemetery.

A shadow fell over him. "You left without me," Hugh said.

Gabriel glanced up and then back at the empty crisp packet. One puff of wind from a speeding lorry, and that piece of rubbish would tumble out onto the High Street. Possibly end up littering someone's garden. "Lots to think about."

"You did a fine job." Hugh sat next to him. "Lots of healing. Hard for you, though, I imagine."

"And why would that be?"

"Unfinished business between you and Marianne, my friend. Love's a tough old bird."

"Hugh, I thought we'd moved beyond this assumption. I have feelings for Marianne, but I'm not in love with her. I find myself no longer capable of real passion. And I think that's worse."

The Saturday afternoon traffic became a constant stream, destroying the quiet of the village. The crisp packet stayed put, caught behind the wall. Hugh reached into his pocket, pulled out a roll of Polo mints, and peeled back the wrapping. He offered it to Gabriel, who shook his head.

Hugh popped a mint into his mouth. "I suppose we'll be two old, crusty bachelors together, then. Think we can share a caregiver in our declining years?"

Gabriel gave a weak laugh. "I'm putting off going home. Jade reminded me they have loud makeup sex. I'm not sure my spare room has ever seen that kind of action."

Hugh slapped his knees and stood. "Then you and I will turn around and walk to the Swan. I feel the need for a pint, a game of darts, and a bit of flirtation with that buxom barmaid."

"She's recently engaged."

"Blast. There goes my fantasy. Might need two pints to drown my sorrows. Come on, we'll discuss our new, exclusive club, Bachelors R Us. It's going to come with a splendid rewards program and a cruise around the Greek islands—if we start saving now."

Gabriel's phone bleeped with another text. He pulled it out and opened the message, knowing that Jade's phone would mark it as read.

Don't ignore me, she'd typed.

He did.

FORTY-NINE
MARIANNE

Marianne's body rose and fell as Darius continued to pant. She tucked her hand into the secret nook where his thigh disappeared into his groin, and stroked back and forth. Why couldn't joy always be this simple?

Still holding her to his chest, Darius threw his right arm behind his head and gave a low, satisfied groan. "I orbited the moon. At least twice."

"Me too." She ran her hand up to his chest and sensed his heartbeat pumping through her fingertips, through her bloodstream, and into the chambers of her own heart.

He sucked in the smallest of breaths. "Now will you come home with me?"

She propped herself up on an elbow and stared into his eyes. "No."

Wriggling free of her, he grabbed his briefs from the floor and tugged them back on. Then he sat on the edge of the bed, his back toward her, and rested his arms across his thighs. "Why?" he half laughed, his voice as feeble as if she'd beaten him to a pulp.

She pulled herself up and hugged her knees. "Darius, baby, you rock my world. You're my soul mate. I know this the same way I know it's day outside and not night. Why you have such faith in me is a constant wonder. But my psycho behavior this summer threatened to smash apart everything we've built. And I still haven't figured out what the consequences will be. My mood might have stabilized for now, but coming back here has ripped open a can of vipers. I can't duct-tape the lid back on and say, 'Stay inside and hide your fangs, guys.' Whatever I've disturbed has spilled over into all our lives: yours, mine, Jade's, Gabriel's. The day EmJ ran off, Dr. White told me he thought I have PTSD from the first crash."

"Jade could have told you that." With a glance over his naked shoulder, he stood. "Come home, Marianne. We'll tackle this as a team, with Dr. White's help. I've downloaded all kinds of shit about mindfulness and psychotherapy, CBT, and DBT. I'm not afraid to do the work, but please, can we figure this out together? I want our life back. I want you back. And it's not fair to keep relying on Jade to hold our business together while we sort out our marriage."

Why did he have to bite down on the word *marriage* as if it were something hard and ugly he no longer wanted? A cool breeze came through the open window and tickled her cheek. She shivered.

"I need to make sense of everything that happened thirty years ago. And so does Gabriel. I know I'm asking a lot, but I need you to trust me for a while longer."

"Terrific. You're telling me this *is* all about you and Gabriel? So you guys are, what, still in love, and I'm a dumbass for choosing to believe both of you when you tell me there's nothing going on?"

"Yes to the first part and no to that last bit, although I got totally lost in the question because I'm sick of this petty jealousy over Gabriel." She punched a pillow.

"You're sick of it?" His voice rose. "How do you think I feel? We're having this argument in your ex-boyfriend's guest bedroom. Enough, Marianne. Enough."

"Exactly. Look at what he's done for us—yes, for you as well as me. And did you see how he avoided me after the service? He's started running, too."

"And you think I care about Gabriel's angst, why?"

"Because you're a decent person, and he's in pain. Everything for Gabriel and me traces back to Simon's death. But I can only remember disjointed images, and the one person who knows the truth about what happened isn't sharing. He hasn't dealt with events of that night any more than I have, and once I leave, he's back to square one."

"How altruistic of you."

"I don't like your tone. Are you accusing me of being selfish?"

"I'm warning you to be careful about mislabeling your obsession as someone else's need. If he's chosen to keep things hidden, that's his prerogative. And I've been more than patient, but I'm done, Marianne." He raked his hands through his hair. "Shit happens and it doesn't always make sense. That's life."

"Oh, don't you dare." She leaped up. "You don't get to say, 'Get over it.' You don't know how hard this is. You don't know the truth."

"Then tell me. Isn't supporting each other through the rough shit the whole point of marriage and not this?" He swung his arm out to gesture at the disheveled, now-empty twin beds shoved together, and she grabbed a T-shirt from the tumble of dirty laundry in the corner of the room. Arguing buck naked was plain wrong.

"I can only repeat myself so many times, Marianne: What don't I know? Tell me." He put his hands on his hips. "Because right now I'm considering packing up and heading to Heathrow. Yes, the sex is fantastic, always has been, but that's not enough. I want more, I want the whole package. I want the truth about you and the Bonham brothers."

In the plum tree a thrush warbled, and she remembered the weight of a dead mockingbird in her hand, its body still warm.

She took a deep breath. "The CliffsNotes?"

"Stop stalling and tell me."

"Stop yelling and sit down."

"I'm not fucking yelling," he yelled.

"Darius"—she swung around, turning her back to him—"I can't do this if you don't calm down."

His arms wrapped around her and gentle kisses rained on the back of her neck. Then he lowered the T-shirt and kissed her tattoo. "I'm sorry," he said. "I'm listening."

"Please, sit down."

He did. Kneeling in front of him, she inched between his legs and rested her cheek on his thigh. "It's not a happy bedtime story, Darius. And I don't know how you'll feel about me when you've heard it."

As he ran his fingers through her hair, she closed her eyes and began.

"When we were kids Gabriel and I were best buds till death do us part. I was tougher than most of the boys. Always getting into fights. A tomboy through and through with no interest in anything girly. But then I got boobs, Gabriel kissed me, and we decided we were in love. I guess it was fine for a year or so, but it got messy real fast. We'd always been heading in different directions, but neither of us could figure out how to leave the other one behind. One of us would retreat, then the other. Our friendship with limited benefits became an exhausting tug-of-war. Sex was the battleground: I wanted now, now, now; Gabriel wanted to wait for the picket fence. Simon tuned in to all that uncertainty. He asked for nothing, he offered nothing; he let me set the pace. The first time we slept together, it just sort of happened. Gabriel had gone off for the week, and I was mad at him. Simon was gorgeous and available. But then it kept happening. And it was secretive and exciting. Like mania, I guess. He was two years older, head boy, devilishly charming, and totally messed up. All the girls were in love with him. And I didn't have to think about the future or where it was heading, because he didn't care any more than I did. I was having fun. We both were, and then—" She sat up, and he cupped her face. She took a deep breath.

"Simon discovered I was pregnant, and he freaked out. The fun was gone." She tried to turn her head away, but Darius wouldn't let her.

"The next night Gabriel and I went to a party, and he kissed me while we were waiting for his mom to pick us up. Only she got sick and sent Simon. He saw the whole thing. That's where the timeline gets fuzzy and my mind goes blank."

"And the baby?" he said quietly.

"I fractured my pelvis in the crash, had a miscarriage, got an infection. Gabriel never really talked to me again, we lost contact, and boom. Here I am. Sterile as an old crone, which seems more than enough retribution for destroying a family. That second crash forced me to relive the worst of my past—with half the memories ripped away. So." She watched his face. "There you have it."

"I'm sorry. I know how much you've always wanted kids. But why the fuck didn't you tell me?" There was no anger in his voice, just tired resignation. "Did you really think I'd stop loving you because of a teen pregnancy?"

"We made a deal to not rehash the past." She sank back on her heels.

"Yeah, that was my mistake, and I'm ready to put it aside. Are you?"

"My past is a horror show. It's not something I'm eager to share."

He stood up. "You're great at talking about trust when it suits your purpose."

"What's that supposed to mean?" She stood too.

"You can trust Gabriel with all this and not me?"

"That's different. We lived it together." She backed away from him and hit the bedroom wall, knocking the angel picture to the floor.

"I would too . . . if you would let me."

"But you never wanted kids. You don't understand that need."

"And the vicar does? What, did you guys plan a family together?" His eyes darkened to black. "You did. Didn't you?"

"Stop. You're missing the point. I grew up wanting to be a mother, dreaming about being a mother. And not any old mother, but the best. I was going to have a huge family. So many kids, Darius. Happy and loved. And then I torpedoed my own dream."

"No, you didn't." He sighed. "Think about Jade and Sasha, and all the girls you've helped through Girls In Motion. You still figured out how to be a mom. Let me guess?" His voice softened. "Your baby was a girl?"

She nodded. But she wouldn't tell him the last grain of truth. That her baby was buried with Simon. That it had all been a terrible mistake. "I hate the word *closure*, but I need to untangle this huge knot that has Simon's death at the center. Walking away is no longer an option."

"And what if the knot can't be unpicked?"

"Honestly? I don't know."

"Christ, Marianne, I—" He slapped a hand over his mouth.

"I love you," she said quickly. "I don't want to fight, and I'm sorry. Sorry for all of it—for ruining the perfect moment, for messing up our lives, for not being able to tell you what you want to hear. If you want out, I get it. I have a chronic disease, and it's not going away, and . . . you didn't sign up for this."

"Unfortunately I did. You never lied to me about being crazy. I've just never seen you in action before."

"And now that you have?"

"I worship you, Marianne, with an intensity I can't handle most of the time. There is no one else for me, and I'm sorry about the baby. I get what that means to you, I do. But I'm cold out of patience. Jade tried to tell me, when all this started, that our mental health matters, and she was right. I need to get back to music, to the studio, to real life. I'm losing myself in all this. If I said, 'Come home or our marriage is over,' how would you answer?"

"I'm hoping you won't do that. But if you did, I'd start packing. To lose you is my unimaginable."

"And if I weren't to give you an ultimatum?"

"I'd ask for one more week—to try to make sense of everything."

He stood in front of her and spread his hands on the wall, on either side of her head. With a wicked little grin, he ground into her. She closed her eyes and fell back through time, to her forty-first birthday and this cute guy from AA who was asking her to have coffee.

"I have one question for you, the only one that matters." He dipped forward and, brushing her hair aside, nuzzled behind her ear. "Are you done, for now, with going crazy?"

"Yes. I think this particular round of crazy is over. But no promises for the future. One more car crash, and I'll probably be in a straitjacket."

"Stay off the roads, then, because I have to go home and save our business. Jade's turning away clients." He nipped at her neck, and then his mouth moved lower.

"Does this mean I can stay?" she murmured.

"Take off the T-shirt."

She tugged it over her head.

"Yes. On two conditions."

"Uh-huh." She was finding it hard to breathe and talk simultaneously. His right hand had found her breast.

"I'm going to start coming to your appointments with Dr. White."

"Okay," she whispered, even though a few months ago she'd thrown a shoe at him for asking, very nicely, if he could sit in on a psych session. "And?"

"And you promise that if I book the ticket"—he tweaked her nipple, and she gasped—"you'll use it."

She grabbed his head and forced it down to her breast. He sucked hard. "Yes," she said. "Yes. Cross my heart and hope to die together after a long and turbulent marriage."

He stood up and clamped his hands on her ass. "In that case I'll need a going-away gift. Something I can live off until you come home. You have one week."

And she forced him backward onto the bed.

FIFTY

JADE

Sunday brunch at the Honeysuckle Tea House, an apothecary café, didn't classify as a date. Right? The place was a bit new agey, but it was out in the country and constructed like a tree house with open sides that let in a cross breeze. Everything was holistic and packaged with a full dose of om. Right now Jade would sell her soul for one-tenth of a dose.

She clambered out of Ernie, and an oak leaf spiraled down to her feet. In the trees behind the parking area, leaves were beginning to turn in small patches of brilliance glowing against the Carolina-blue sky. Back in town the dogwoods were already warming up for their annual crimson display.

While she'd been barricaded in her cave with lava lamps and strings of red holiday lights, summer slipped away and the gradual descent into the dreaded family season had begun. Marianne and Darius weren't big on Christmas. Thanksgiving was their thing, with a huge spread for the studio family. Except for Zeke, none of them had anywhere else to go. The last two Christmases, Marianne and Darius went back to see his mom—going strong at ninety—and despite an open invitation, Jade spent the day in her apartment watching holiday movies and stuffing her face with chocolate-covered cherries from A Southern Season. What a difference nine months could make, because right now the thought of being alone at Christmas made her want to howl like the neighborhood coyote.

Swallowing a yawn, Jade walked up the wooden ramp into the café. Yesterday's session had ended at two a.m., and she slept badly. Gabriel had done a disappearing act, and her texts remained unanswered. Darius, however, was nauseatingly happy, bugging her way more than necessary about his flight home the next day.

Looking past the glass containers filled with loose tea, she studied the chalkboard of specials and contemplated her order. An order for one, as usual. She settled on a smoothie and a muffin, not that she was hungry, but she had to eat something before heading to the studio for another late session. After Darius got home and settled, she'd catch up on sleep, clean the apartment, and check out the thrift stores and new releases at the library. By this time next week, life would have returned to normal. And it sucked.

Her phone buzzed with another text from Darius: How's the date going? If it doesn't work out, I can fix you up with this really cute guitarist.

Stay out of my personal life, boss.

Can't. I'm worried about you.

I'm fine.

You're not.

Am so. He's here. Gotta go. 'Bye! Jade turned her phone off and picked a table overlooking the crowded play area down below. One of the tots waddled away from the sand toward the pond, but his mom sprang into action and scooped him up with a laugh. Jesse had been that way—always wandering off if she didn't keep eyes on him. As he got older he followed her everywhere, clinging to her like a security blanket when he was way too old for such things. These days he probably didn't trust anyone enough to even offer a hug.

She turned and smiled at six feet five of Ricky Tanner. Most southerners were slow talkers but not Ricky, a guy who'd told her that while he talked fast, he listened slow. An ex-cop, he was now a private eye. When they met he'd been painting over a racial slur on Winnie's café door. He stopped, paintbrush dripping, to reassure Jade that he was doing some off-the-books detecting to make sure the little punk responsible knew that to mess with Winnie meant to take on Ricky Tanner. Jade had liked him straight off, despite the knit shirts that screamed *frat boy*.

He'd picked up a tan since then. She couldn't remember where he'd been—Ocean Isle? Topsail? The tan accentuated the testosterone image created by the Incredible Hulk biceps. Her mind bounced back to Gabriel in his worn U2 T-shirt and baggy jeans.

Ricky grinned at her muffin. "Darn, this was going to be my treat. Get you anything else?" He flashed perfect molars, and she tried not to think about Gabriel's sexy gap between his front teeth. Longing tiptoed down the length of her. Missing him was getting worse.

Before she could think of a witty reply, Ricky jetted off to the counter. He fiddled endlessly with his phone, occasionally bobbing his head up to talk to the young woman filling his order.

"You look pretty," he said as he settled across from her with his herbal tea. "Did you change your hair? How's work going? Your boss back yet?"

Ricky could cram several thoughts into one sentence. It took a while to unpack them.

"Like it—" he said. "The new hairdo."

Jade held up a handful of hair. "It's called neglect."

Ricky examined his watch. "Guess I need a new battery. Sorry I'm late." He raised his head. "Lucinda Williams is coming to Saxapahaw next week. Should be quite a show. I have an extra ticket. Wanna join me?"

That was definitely a date. "I'm a little music'd out these days."

"No problem." He checked his phone. "Another time?"

A red cardinal, the male of the species, landed on the ledge next to her and preened himself—the feathered version of a beefcake, all bright and well pressed, not unlike Ricky. She looked down at her half-eaten muffin, wishing she could call Gabriel. Who was she kidding? She couldn't do this. Jade wrapped up what was left of her muffin in a napkin. "How do you know I don't have a hulking boyfriend tucked away?"

"I'm a detective, remember. I did my job."

"If you weren't an ex-cop, I'd tell you that's creepy."

"Didn't want to make a fool of myself." He nodded at her muffin. "Don't leave, I just got here."

It was cute, that touch of vulnerability. And one drink with Ricky Tanner might not be so bad. She needed a life, and he wasn't a total dud. Likely as not he talked slower when he was drunk. And he was way closer to her age than Gabriel, which had to be good, right?

"How about a drink one night next week." She unwrapped her muffin. "After I've figured out my work schedule."

And then he talked at warp speed while she listened.

But how many drinks would it take before she could see Ricky and not Gabriel? Figuring out the standard recovery period for falling head-over-ass in love was so far out of her experience it belonged in another galaxy, in another dimension, in another time zone. Five hours away.

FIFTY-ONE
MARIANNE

The cold predawn air slapped her awake as she stood in Gabriel's minuscule front yard, waving to Darius's retreating taxi. Summer wasn't attempting to hold on for an encore. It had given up the stage.

She'd begun missing Darius the moment he booked the plane ticket. A wacko thought even for a wacko. It was her choice to stay; her choice that he leave. Everything was always her choice, but new Ultimatum Darius was pretty damn sexy. Who knew he had the superpower to pin her against a wall and within seconds have her panting, "Yes, honey; no, honey; three bags full, honey." And the sex? Newlywed orgasmic, despite being in a vicarage with a framed picture of a crying angel passing judgment.

The taxi reached the end of the lane and she ran to the metal gate, gripping it to stop herself from running out into Nell's Lane, screeching, *Don't leave me.* Which would be super embarrassing for Gabriel. Yes, Bill Collins had closed down his gossip mill, but he wasn't the only one who'd been eyeing her up as a hybrid of Nell Gwyn and a she-devil.

The taxi's brake lights lit up, and the rear door flew open.

"Love you, my goddess," Darius called out. Then he slammed the door and was gone.

"Love you too," she said into the fading night. A few houses down, a cat mewed, and then? Silence. A smell of bonfire lingered in the lane; the only light came from Gabriel's front door, left ajar.

Marianne pulled her cardigan around her and went back inside. She had one week to do this thing, to confront the man who rose early to make Darius breakfast and then disappeared back into his bedroom without tossing her a bread crumb of a greeting.

After Darius announced at Saturday night dinner that he was leaving on Monday morning and Marianne was staying for one more week, Gabriel retreated to his study pleading more work than a CEO sitting on multiple nonprofit boards. Highly unlikely scenario. Something in her eulogy had scared him off, and he wanted her gone.

Tough shit, because she was staying and throwing down the gauntlet. They were going to relive that night. Even if she had to drug him, strap him to a chair, and hold him hostage. She hadn't figured out the drug part of the scenario, but how hard could it be in a country that sold codeine over the counter?

She tiptoed up the stairs and cast a glance at Gabriel's closed—probably bolted—door. If he could have planted a minefield outside his bedroom, he probably would have. Did he not remember how stubborn she could be?

"Game on, Gabriel," she muttered, half hoping he was awake and listening.

But the moment she closed her door, the absence of Darius returned for another swing. She stared at her Queen Bee bag, waiting to be packed. As was the sparkly new suitcase Darius had bought for all her purchases, the ones they hadn't been able to return. A stay in the mental hospital wasn't, apparently, a viable excuse for extending the thirty-day refund policy.

In one week she and those bags would be home. Back to her life. And Gabriel would be alone in his secondhand house.

Suppose Darius was right—again, unlikely scenario, but Bill Collins's recent behavior confirmed the existence of miracles—and her crazy-ass stunt to put the past to rest meant she was on a collision course with Gabriel's peace of mind for a second time? Or was that a third time? When you were a human wrecking ball, it was hard to keep things straight.

And underneath, that egocentric thought burned: What if he still loved her? EmJ had died believing it, and Hugh seemed to believe it—from what Marianne had overheard. Surely love was the most logical explanation for Gabriel's sudden strategy of retreat. Not that her penchant for men on the Dark Side gave her much experience of normal guy behavior: Simon. Exhibit A. Looking back—*got to love hindsight*—Simon was dancing with depression when he stumbled into her secret world with Gabriel. Wandering around the village by himself late at night with a stolen bottle of vodka? Very suspect. And he fell into their sexual games with less care than she did. Maybe the only thing Simon wanted from her was escape. Maybe that was the reason he'd agreed, so easily, to keeping their liaison hidden.

Thoughts to consider as she began erasing her presence from Gabriel's house. First job? Return this room to the way it had been. Next up, she would do a walk through the rectory. Reclaim the possessions she'd strewn all over and return the borrowed items—his iron, his laundry basket, his T-shirts.

The beds were easy to push apart, the nightstand a bit trickier to wrestle into its space. She made noise, but Gabriel didn't appear, not even to tell her off for disturbing Phyllis. Marianne picked up the old nursing chair—so light—and something rattled. Setting it down, she pushed aside the ruffle of the slipcover and eased open the drawer. It was empty but for a small velvet box. Sinking to her knees, Marianne flipped it open, and a memory tumbled out: Gabriel hoarding his allowance for a year; Gabriel asking for money for his birthday and not spending it; Gabriel working two jobs the Easter before the crash and still always broke. When she'd asked what he was doing with all that money, he'd grinned and said, "You'll see."

"Goddammit, Gabriel," she said. "Why did you have to buy me a ring?"

And not any ring. A diamond solitaire. A ring that symbolized endurance, perseverance. Love that was meant to last a lifetime. A ring so different from the one on her left hand that sparkled a declaration: *I have married into the Montgomery clan, a family famous for raising racehorses in Kentucky.* Darius was the black sheep from the day he learned to walk. He hated horses. Worse, he was scared of them. His passion had always been music. Apparently he was a genetic throwback to a disowned great-uncle who'd spent his life touring speakeasies with a bluegrass band. The ache for him returned.

The small diamond glinted at her like a novelty from a fairground, a toy that was never meant to be more than an understudy. Another memory played: being at the party with Gabriel on the night of the crash. They were outside waiting for his mom to pick them up and they were laughing. Gabriel leaned in to whisper: "Meet me later at the cemetery. I've got an early birthday present for you." When he pulled back, Simon was watching. Events had been set in motion.

She snapped the lid shut. Obviously the ring wasn't meant to be found; obviously the right thing would be to put it back and walk away. But she had a long history of doing the wrong thing.

Marianne placed the box on the nightstand in front of the digital alarm clock. The ring would stay there until she figured how to crack Gabriel. There was one memory he didn't have, and it was hers to give. If he still loved her, it was a game changer, and so was that ring. Which meant they were visiting hell together one last time, because she owed him her life, and it was time to return his.

*

Marianne stayed in her room until late morning. When she emerged, her heart thumping a Latin dance beat, she found a note pinned by the french press to the middle of the kitchen table. Gabriel had left her half the pot, long cold.

"'Gone all day. Home late. Feel free to forage,'" she read aloud, her voice steady in the empty house.

Right. Plan A out the window. She grabbed a mug to nuke some coffee and exhaled. She didn't have to do this. Day one was a washout, but she still had six to go.

Then the next day went down the tubes, too. Gabriel was an absentee homeowner, and Marianne spent the morning at the cemetery. She sat on the spiky grass by her baby's grave, damp with dew, and tried to remember the moment that had forever changed the history of two families. But the crash kept its secrets. Then she returned to the rectory, fixed simple meals, did a load of laundry, and made herself useful by answering the phone and taking messages for Gabriel. That night she called Darius, who suggested phone sex, and Skyped with Jade. Jade had lost weight and needed a haircut.

Marianne was beginning—in baby steps that didn't scream *I'm manic*—to take an interest in the studio again. Interest was good; interest came back to desire, to living. Lying in bed that night, she almost conned herself into believing the past didn't matter. But the ring, still on her nightstand, told a different story.

The following morning Marianne decided to come clean about finding the ring. It was hardly her fault she'd discovered it. But Gabriel continued to be a no-show.

Post-supper-for-one she was on her way upstairs to Skype Jade when the phone rang. Something to do! Another message to take. Hell's bells, she could have been a church secretary. She shot into Gabriel's bedroom and, launching herself across the unmade bed with the duvet tossed to the floor, grabbed the receiver.

"Good evening. Newton Rushford rectory."

It was a young woman, wanting to talk with Gabriel about a christening. Marianne couldn't help herself; she asked for details. How old was the baby? What was her name? The mom chatted away: only six months old, and little Sarah was trying to crawl.

Marianne said, "Cherish every moment."

The baby started fussing and the mother's voice switched from friendly to harried. "Look, can you have him call me?"

"Sure. Let me get your name and number." Marianne opened Gabriel's nightstand and felt around for a pen and a piece of paper. The baby started bawling. Marianne tugged the drawer free and dumped its contents on the bed. "Hang on a sec . . ."

Nightstands were intimate places. She stashed all her memorabilia in hers: the last birthday card from her mom, a short story Jade had written at eighteen, a paper napkin from the Looking Glass Café with Darius's cell phone number scribbled on it, their wedding invitation. Gabriel's stash was oddly impersonal: a battered Book of Common Prayer, a broken watch with a worn leather strap, a nearly full prescription bottle of sleeping pills that had expired a year ago.

The mom lost patience, said she had to go. Marianne was still apologizing when the phone line went dead. A rogue wave of grief rolled in from nowhere. Marianne covered her face with her hands and cried.

The next thing she knew, Gabriel was standing over her. "Marianne. What are you doing in my bed?"

She shot up and jumped to the floor. "I know this looks bad, but a young mom wanted to talk about a christening for a six-month-old called Sarah, and I was trying to take down her number but you don't even keep a pen in that drawer." *Way to go, Marianne, blame him.* "I didn't mean to fall asleep, but all these drugs make me . . ."

He backed away from her as if she were contagious.

"I'm sorry. I just wanted to help." She grabbed the drawer and shoved it back into his nightstand. He didn't offer to help.

"I'd like you to leave my bedroom," he said quietly.

And she ran to the guest room and slammed the door.

She slept late the next day, and when she came down, Gabriel was shut in his study with multiple voices. Another meeting. She wrote a note and left it on the kitchen table, and because it was time to vary the note pinning, secured it with the pepper grinder.

"Please come to Café Stokes for dinner tonight. 7:30 p.m. in the kitchen."

Then she went for a ramble across Dead Woman. When she came back, her note had been replaced with a new one, secured by the fruit bowl.

"Most generous offer, but I must decline. I have a PCC meeting. Back late."

It was the sort of note that you might leave out for a B-and-B guest, not for someone you'd once bought an engagement ring for. She balled up the note and tossed it in the recycling. Enough. He could play ostrich all he liked, but she was done pussyfooting around him. They could talk when he was finished with the business of the parish. But Gabriel walked in around ten thirty p.m. with his lay band, and they retreated into the study, leaving behind a smell of beer and muffled laughter.

Marianne went upstairs and began preparing for her eleven p.m. lights-out. But as she waited for the sleep meds to kick in, she plotted. Time was running out, and tomorrow was do or die.

FIFTY-TWO

MARIANNE

Marianne towel-dried her hair. *Rub, rub, rub.* Mornings were normally a bitch on this level of her meds, but she'd sprung awake with her alarm and rushed straight into that tepid shower. *Rub, rub, rub.* Such a sensible choice to turn the heat way down and not drain the hot-water tank that was smaller than a bucket. *Rub, rub, rub.* Such a sensible choice to keep the shower short when Gabriel was so big on all things green. *Rub, rub, rub.* So many logical, selfless decisions right now she could spit.

She threw the damp towel on the floor and twizzled her index fingers around each other. All these jitters over talking to Gabriel. The honest kid who'd turned into a thief for her. Plain ol' Gabriel. Okay, so never plain, not even in the gawky pubescent stage.

Stop, Marianne. Nothing matters except the present moment. Time to remember some radical acceptance coping statements. Why was therapy always such a mouthful?

"This moment is as it should be," she recited, "given all that's happened before."

She spread her fingers, held them still, and then brushed her arms through the air, as if parting a red sea of adrenaline.

I've got this. I'm making breakfast for an old friend. Just. Making. Breakfast.

She tiptoed down the stairs, brewed the coffee, and started grating cheese for cheesy scrambled eggs. No—she put down the grater and chopped up an onion and green pepper—omelets were a better choice. Wholesome and substantial, more formal. Business-meeting-type food. Besides, handling a huge knife without a little voice saying, "Go on, stick that blade into your arm and give it a twist," was strangely gratifying.

Gabriel padded in, feet bare, hair sticking up, a few minutes before seven forty-five a.m. He touched the side of the french press.

"Fresh!" she said.

He yanked back his hand as if the cheer in her voice had scalded him. So much cheer. Enough to give them both third-degree burns. Crap, he might translate that as abnormal cheer. Manic cheer.

"I'm making omelets for breakfast," she said without cheer. All cheer edited out.

"Lovely," he said, and grabbed a crumpled *Church Times* that looked thoroughly read. He turned as if to disappear into his study.

"No, sit!" she snapped, and he froze. "I mean . . . Take a load off." She pulled out a chair and smiled a muted smile. *Nothing manic here, Gabriel.*

He did as ordered. It was not a good feeling, the knowledge that she could yell, "Roll over and die for England," and he would. When she was younger, she had abused that power shamelessly. Now it might be the only way to get him to listen.

"Sleep well?"

"The usual," he said.

"So that's a no?"

"Correct." He opened the paper, even though he wasn't wearing his reading glasses.

She dropped a dollop of margarine into the skillet.

"Listen, I know that invading your bedroom like Goldilocks was a monumental screwup. And I'm truly sorry." She kept her back to him. When he didn't answer, she glanced over her shoulder.

"The woman on the phone"—she'd already forgotten her name—"was talking about the baby, and I had some horrible flashback. The grief came roaring in and knocked me for six."

He screwed up his eyes to squint at the newsprint. "It was a long time ago, Marianne."

The margarine sizzled. She tossed in the onions and peppers, stirred and watched, stirred and watched. Thought about the physical pain that came only from a burn; the emotional pain that came only from losing a child. She turned with the wooden spoon in her hand. His look was almost a dare: *Go on, hit me.*

"Please don't tell me I was a kid and it was for the best. I've heard that far too often."

Slowly, he closed up the paper and put it aside. Then, stretching across the table, he claimed everything she'd left out for him: the coffee mug, the french press, and the small pitcher of milk. Milk in a china jug was a habit picked up from his mother. Funny the details she could remember, ridiculous the life-altering facts she could not.

She turned back to the skillet. "And another thing—you can't keep avoiding me." Her voice was a sea of flatness, a whole friggin' ocean without waves. Emotions could be such traitors, and for once she would be their master. She imagined a halo of light moving down her body, bringing calm. A slight pressure rang in her ears; her bottom teeth tapped gently against her top teeth; the muscles in her right arm tightened as she stirred.

"I'm not avoiding you, Marianne. It's been intensely disruptive having you and Darius to stay. I'm merely trying to get my life back on track. I appreciate Bill Collins offering to talk with the bishop on my behalf, but eyes are still on me and how I perform my job."

"Lucky for you that I'm leaving on Monday morning, then. By the way, Monday's also Jade's thirtieth birthday, in case you want to send a card back with me. Save the postage."

"If you give me your flight details, I'll ask one of the parishioners to give you a lift to the airport. I'm sure Ian would do it. He likes odd jobs."

"I've become an odd job?"

He didn't answer; she kept stirring. The kitchen filled with the smell of fried onions, and in her jeans pocket the ring box nudged her left leg.

"What I'm about to say comes from a place of good intentions." How did you ask someone if he still loved you without sounding like a raving narcissist? But the question needed to be asked, because he needed to be free of her, and on some level, she needed to be free of him.

"Then you should keep it to yourself. You know what they say about good intentions."

Out in the hall the grandfather clock struck the hour, as the church clock had done on the day she'd stumbled out of his past and into his church. They were always competing against time.

She turned and opened her mouth. "How about we just enjoy breakfast together?"

He glanced up as if waiting for the *but* to drop. She half expected it, too. That was not the question she'd intended to ask.

"What do you have planned for the day?" she said.

"Endless meetings after my morning prayer." He reached for his coffee.

"Of course. And I appreciate you letting me stay this extra week." She moved back to the counter by the oven and cracked six eggs into a glass bowl. *A three-egg omelet, Gabriel. That's how serious I am.* "I'm in a much better place than when I arrived, even though everything that pulled me back here is still tugging at me, still forcing me to question what happened thirty years ago." Was that subtle enough?

"It's quite simple, Marianne. Two brothers, who didn't understand each other, fell for the same girl. The outcome was tragedy."

The phone rang; they both ignored it.

"I'm sure Simon treated you like a queen, but from my perspective, he was a tormentor. Would that have changed if he'd lived? Undoubtedly. Jade said something when she was here that reminded me Simon and I were close when we were little, a stage I'm sure we would have returned to after the horror of the teen years. But denied the chance to rebond, our relationship is frozen in brotherly rivalry."

"What if you could change that?" She cranked the pepper mill. "What if I knew something about the accident that might help you?"

"If you're going to ask me to relive the events of that night, my answer is no."

"Understood." Even professional soldiers knew when to retreat, and withdrawal wasn't surrender. She was merely regrouping to consider strategies, armed with the understanding that a battle of wills lay ahead. Gabriel could be extraordinarily pliable, but once he'd dug in his heels, there was no U-turn.

Wasn't that the real reason she'd strayed to Simon? Gabriel blocked her from his bed with no hope of changing his mind. But whatever his game plan back then, right now he needed to believe he'd been victorious.

"I'll try to stay out of your way as much as possible in the next few days," she said. "I'd also like to help out more. Can I cook supper tonight?"

He smiled, and she saw a flash of the old Gabriel. "You're asking for my opinion, not telling me what you're doing and expecting me to fall into line? That's twice now."

"You mean there's hope for me?"

"Thank you. Supper tonight would be much appreciated."

His words, oddly formal, sliced like a paper cut.

FIFTY-THREE

MARIANNE

A bat swooped low under the wooden pergola covered in the rambling rector rose that had all but strangled a clematis. Legs hugged to her chest, Marianne rocked back and forth. The chair—old, graying—wobbled and squeaked. Probably a hand-me-down like everything else Gabriel owned. Forty-seven and he'd never outgrown the younger-brother mentality.

If she stopped moving she could easily morph into the one-eyed feral cat that strayed into her yard to piss and hiss. One mean little bastard. And if she couldn't stay calm, all would be lost. Gabriel handled chaos well, but he never engaged with it. And she needed one thing from him: engagement. She glanced sideways at the small velvet box on the table next to her. Okay, poor choice of words.

Dammit. This was like waiting in the departure lounge for a delayed flight and listening to stupid announcements spread to con restless passengers into believing they'd soon be on their way. Delays had always "ticked her off something rotten," to quote Mrs. Tandy. Where the hell was Gabriel?

Dinner was not destined to be a cordon bleu affair—lasagna, garlic bread, and salad—but she hadn't gone to all that trouble so Gabriel could bail on her. She could eat the salad, dump the garlic bread, and freeze the lasagna in individual portions. Easy meals for one when he was living alone and she was back with her family. She stopped moving and tugged his cashmere sweater down low to cover as much of her body as she could.

"Oh, Gabriel," she said into the night. "We messed it all up so badly."

The concrete birdbath that appeared to be his pride and joy loomed out of the darkness. He scrubbed it every Sunday night with an old scrubbing brush he kept in the garden shed, often muttering about pigeon shit. A little routine she'd clocked because it reminded her of cleaning out the hummingbird feeders. They lived an ocean apart, had never known each other as adults, and yet they shared a Sunday night domestic ritual.

A car honked on the A428; the front door opened and closed; she sat up straight.

"I'm in the garden," she called out, and waited. She would not rush him, she would breathe in the nighttime floral scent she couldn't identify and repeat an endless refrain in her head: *I am calm.*

When he appeared, he was holding a heavy glass tumbler with way more than one shot of whisky. The smell hit her nostrils like nectar. *I am calm.*

He shrugged off his black jacket, tossed it onto the table, and seemed to collapse into the rickety chair next to her. That was not his first drink of the evening.

"I should've called," he said.

She looked at the whisky. An odd choice for Gabriel.

"I'm sorry, but I needed a drink. I'll get rid of it fast."

"Don't worry about it. People drink around me all the time. Except for the musicians in AA. What's going on?"

"A family in one of the barn conversions," he said. "They lost a child."

"Oh no." Marianne flattened her hand over her heart. Another dead baby. When did it end? "What happened?"

"Drowned in a swimming pool full of children and in front of two lifeguards." Gabriel took a slug of whisky. "It doesn't matter how many funeral services you've conducted, how many burials, you never make peace with the death of a child."

"No, you don't."

In the house next door, Phyllis turned on the television too loudly. Stars twinkled above them like tiny diamonds.

Gabriel's phone buzzed in his jacket pocket, and as he tried to find it, something fell from the table onto the concrete patio. When she looked up, he was holding the ring box.

"Where did you find this?" he said, his voice sharp.

"Inside the drawer of the old nursing chair, and no"—she sighed, her mind stuck on the image of a kid floating facedown—"I wasn't snooping. I moved the chair and it rattled."

Gabriel stood, put the box back on the table, and turned toward the open patio doors.

"Wait! You're not walking away." She shot up. "We're still talking."

"No, Marianne. We're done. We were done a long time ago."

Snatching up the ring box, she followed. In the kitchen he grabbed a bottle of whisky off the table and filled his now-empty glass. Drunk Gabriel was foreign territory—like being lost on a county road at night surrounded by black forest, in the fog, with a broken headlight and no GPS. Frightening for most people, thrilling for her. She never could resist the lure of the unknown.

"I think I'll skip supper," he said.

"No, you won't. We're both eating. I'm trying to make better decisions about my health, and you're a grumpy bastard when you're hungry."

"I am not." He scowled.

Gabriel behaving badly. They were definitely off the map, which gave her the upper hand. Off the map she could do with bells on. Plus, he was drunk, she was sober. Finally being an alcoholic on the wagon was working in her favor.

Holding her breath, she grabbed the bottle from the table, screwed the cap on and, carrying it at arm's length, put it in the pantry and slammed the door. Then she scrubbed her hands with the vegetable scrubbing brush by the sink. When they were beet red and smelled of nothing but his lavender pump soap, her breathing returned to normal.

Gabriel stared out the kitchen window while she made a dressing and tossed the salad. Then he turned abruptly and said, "Here, let me." He attempted to set the table and dropped the forks. Neither of them commented.

She gave him a large serving of lukewarm lasagna and decided to forgo the garlic bread. "All I'm asking right now is that you eat, Gabriel. If you have a hangover tomorrow, news will travel faster than the *Titanic* sank."

"She took three hours to sink," he said.

"How the hell do know that?"

"How the hell do you not?" He pulled out a chair and slumped onto it. With hooded eyes, he squinted up at her; the wrinkles that curved down around his mouth—his first signs of age—were more pronounced than they had been when she'd arrived. His skin was almost gray. He closed his eyes and spoke through a drawn-out sigh. "I'm sorry, Marianne. The crash, it was my fault."

A thousand questions thudded in her brain: *What, when, why?* But Dr. White, the grand inquisitor, had taught her the art of interrogation restraint. Warm up your patient before going in for the kill.

"How much have you had to drink?" she said.

"Not enough." He pushed his plate away; she pushed it back. Then she filled him a glass of water.

"Trust me, as someone who used to drink two bottles of cheap wine every night, you'll feel better with food and water in you. Did you eat lunch today?"

Gabriel shook his head. "I had a meeting about the organ fundraiser." He scooped a forkful of lasagna into his mouth, swallowed, ate more. "This is good, Marianne. Thank you."

"You're welcome. Hot enough?"

"Yes."

They were talking without saying anything.

Gabriel wiped his mouth on his napkin and sat back. "Zachary, the little boy who died, was with his big brother. Victor was meant to be watching over him. That's going to haunt him for the rest of his life."

"Encourage his family to get counseling. You must, Gabriel, you must."

"His mother doesn't believe in therapy."

"That's ridiculous. I would be dead without therapy. Convince her she's wrong. A kid shouldn't have to shoulder that kind of guilt without professional help."

His fork clattered to his plate. "Don't you think I know that better than anyone?"

"Gabriel—" She opened the ring box and put it on the table. "It's time to talk. I'm going to tell you what I remember about the crash, and you're going to do the same. We're going to deal with this, together, once and for all. And then you're going to tell me why you never gave me that ring."

"Are you joking, after the evening I've had?"

"No. I've never been more serious." She walked to the door, closed it, and turned with her arms crossed. "You're not leaving this room until we've bashed this out."

"Really? You don't think I could pick you up and move you aside?"

"You could, but I have two factors working in my favor. One, you're drunk, and two, you would never manhandle a woman. I know you,

Gabriel. I know everything about you, except what matters—how you feel about me, about us, about all of it."

He picked up the whisky glass, emptied it in one gulp, then went back to the pantry, took out the bottle, poured a respectable shot, downed it, and refilled his glass.

Go for it, Gabriel. If he needed to do this drunk, she'd let him.

"You want to know why I bought that ring? It was going to be your seventeenth-birthday present. I was going to ask you to marry me." His voice had turned slurry. "And while I was planning our future, you were sleeping with my brother. Who announced, in the car, that you were carrying his child. And I responded by informing him that I wished he were dead. And then he was."

"What else?" she said.

"Marianne, what's the point? The past is over. We've both moved on."

"No. We haven't. For all your ministering and good works, there's something dark eating away at you. Something you're not showing me. Something I doubt you've shown anyone."

"I see your time in the mental hospital has made you philosophical." He threw himself back down on his chair.

"For three decades we've carried around this guilt, and we can't both be responsible. Together we can pool our memories. Make sense of it all."

"And I can only repeat, why?"

"Gabriel, that night has haunted me for thirty years. Why did you tell me to turn off the music?"

"That's what's been bothering you for three decades? Fine," he said. "I'll play along. When we kissed at the party, I thought you were letting me back in. I thought whatever had forced us apart was over. But what followed were the worst twenty minutes of my life. Why the hell do you think I asked you to turn off the music? You thought what—I'd be happy for you? It wasn't enough that I had to find out from him that you two were sleeping together, you had to be irresponsible enough to get pregnant?"

She flinched.

"The noise and anger in the car were palpable. I couldn't think. You were bouncing off the walls in the front seat, singing your heart out; the music was blaring; Simon was clearly drunk—God only knows why the two of us got in the car with him—and then he made that snide comment about whether you were happy because you'd been snogging me, and I can still remember his face when he looked up in the rearview mirror to see my reaction. That's how I knew you two were sleeping together. And then I started yelling at both of you." He wrapped his hands around his glass. "I called you a whore. Then Simon was yelling that he loved you and you were having a baby together, and I had no right to talk to you that way. You don't remember any of this?"

"Simon never told me he loved me."

"He screamed it that night." Gabriel took a sip of whisky. "What do you remember?"

"You asking me to kill the music, and I've always assumed I distracted Simon as I fiddled with the radio."

"No, you didn't turn off the music. Simon did. He leaned down to see what he was doing and lost control of the car. He missed the curve and we went straight into that tree. It took a year for the inquest to make a ruling, and by then you were gone. The lack of skid marks had suggested suicide, but—"

"Oh my God." She slid down the door and sat on the cold tile. "You didn't let everyone believe he'd committed suicide?"

"Of course not. But in the aftermath of the accident there were a lot of questions, and neither of us gave satisfactory answers. You didn't make sense when the police interviewed you, and given all that followed, they decided you were an unreliable witness. And I kept quiet about the fight in the car because I'd assumed the crash would go down as an alcohol-related accident. Bad enough I was the jilted one—did I have to share all the details?" In the lane a dog barked. "After I came clean, the crash was ruled an accident. My mother was too tangled up in her own guilt to blame me, but Dad kept clear of me for years. Why do you think I went to Sandhurst? I was trying to make amends."

"How did Simon die?"

"His heart tore free of his aorta with the impact of the crash. He bled to death internally. It was quick; he didn't suffer." Gabriel folded his arms and collapsed onto the table with a soft thump. "Why, Marianne?" he mumbled into his arms. "Why did you sleep with my brother?"

A cobweb Mrs. Tandy had missed with her long feather duster dangled in the corner of the ceiling.

"Because you wouldn't touch me," she said.

Gabriel sat up straight. "I asked you to wait until I was ready. I thought you'd agreed."

"You never suspected anything, in all those months?"

He shook his head slowly. "I knew things were off between us, and Simon went after me more than usual, but I was working round the clock to pay for the ring, and when I wasn't, I was revising for my exams like everybody else—including you, I assumed. Was it so hard to wait for me?"

"It wasn't hard, it was impossible. We'd been fooling around for years, and my sex drive suddenly ramped up. I wanted to do it. Like a rabbit—all the time. And Simon was the guy every sixth former at my school fantasized about and yet he was interested in me." She tapped her chest. "Me, a kid in the fifth form. But the first time, it sort of happened because you weren't around, and—"

"You're blaming me?" He wobbled up to standing.

"No, no. That came out wrong. I wanted someone to hang out with—to party with. And Simon had no plans and tons of alcohol. Then we did it again. And again."

He kicked back his chair. "I get the picture, Marianne." His blue eyes bored into her with contempt.

Maybe pushing Gabriel's buttons had been a really, really bad idea. "It was mindless fun." She kept her voice as level as if she were humming a single note. "A game. That was all. We were never a couple."

"And how did you think it was going to turn out, this game?" Gabriel finished his drink in one gulp. "You knew I loved you."

"I loved you too."

"You had a bloody strange way of showing it. And as for Simon? He wrecked my life and then he died."

"Time-out, Gabriel. I threw myself at your brother. What eighteen-year-old guy is going to say no to that?"

"You don't believe in free choice? You want to say, 'Any bloke who commits rape isn't at fault if the woman is wearing a short skirt and flashes her eyes at him'?" His voice gained volume like a hurricane sucking up strength out over the ocean. "Simon had a conscience. He knew you were mine."

"Whoa, double time-out. I'm no one's."

He slammed his hands down on the table, and she jumped.

"You and I were inseparable. He used to torment us, for goodness' sake."

"Gabriel, Simon was in a bad place when we hooked up. I know what depression looks like. I don't think he cared about anything at that point."

"So depression stripped away his morality? As Jade would say, bullshit." He threw his glass at the fridge, and it shattered. She stayed quiet. Would he hurt her? Had she pushed him to the point of no return?

"He knew I loved you and he slept with you anyway. He didn't care. He took it from me, Marianne. All of it. You, my future, he took it for no other reason than he could." In one swift movement, he swept the clutter of phone directories, papers, and cookbooks off the pine dresser. Gabriel collapsed onto his knees. "And I hated him. I hated him for what he did. I hate him still. I may preach forgiveness, but I will never forgive my own brother. I hate him." His voice cracked. "And I hate you."

Fists clenched, he pounded at his temples. Gabriel, the most solid person she'd ever known, finally got it—the pull of emotions too powerful to ignore.

Watching for shards of glass, she crawled across the kitchen floor toward him. He tried to push her away, but his movements were sloppy, uncoordinated. Intoxicated. When he fell against her, she massaged his back. Had she ever been this person—the one who remained in control while the world around her flipped inside out?

"*Shhh,*" she said, as he juddered. He'd never cried in front of her before. Not even when Simon pushed him through a glass door.

The freezer made a spitting noise, and somewhere a window closed. If Phyllis had heard Gabriel yelling, he would be so embarrassed. They huddled, surrounded by broken glass and chaos. And yet it wasn't over. She had ruined his life, but she could give him a gift. Although chances were high he would tell her to pack up and leave.

She waited until he grew still and then sat back. "Simon took nothing from you," she said. "I'm the one who did that. And hating me is a perfectly logical response. To be honest, I'm relieved. I thought you still loved me."

He wiped his eyes with the heels of his hands. "What do you mean?"

She took his hands, slightly damp, and placed them in her lap. "I hadn't planned to tell you this ever, but finding the ring changed everything. So, here it is. My really big secret." She blew out a shallow breath. "Wow. Harder than I thought it would be."

His red eyes stared.

"You never asked my baby's name. My parents did, but you didn't. Why?"

"I didn't want to know."

"Gabriela. Her name was Gabriela."

"I—I don't understand."

"She was yours. Our baby." Everything blurred at the edge of her sight. "Ours."

"But we only . . . once . . ."

"February fourteenth, 1984. It only takes once, and we didn't use protection. You wouldn't touch me again, and I didn't know what to do, how to be a single mom at sixteen like my birth mom. I suspected I was pregnant when I slept with Simon. I'd already skipped a period, and my hormones were jumping all over the place. I needed sex, and you wouldn't come near me. And then everything blew up, including my only shot at motherhood."

"You let him believe the baby was—"

"Yes. I lied to both of you. Didn't you ever wonder why Simon kept our relationship secret? Because I made him promise. I was buying time until I figured out what to do. I was simply buying time, Gabriel. And the sex had no consequences in my mind, because I was already pregnant. Which means it's not Simon you need to forgive. It's me."

His chest heaved and he continued to stare. What was he thinking? The blind was back down, the storm had passed. Once again, he was shutting her out.

"The ring, Gabriel, you bought it after we slept together, didn't you?"

"I was so disappointed in myself," he said quietly. "At my lack of control. I'd wanted to wait until we were married."

"That's why you went on the Easter pilgrimage. I thought you were embarrassed about what had happened, that you wanted to forget."

"I needed to think. I could never do that when you were near me." He pushed her hair behind her ear.

"I was going to tell you about the baby, but then Simon figured out I was pregnant. I was lucky that I didn't have any morning sickness, and I disguised my bulge pretty easily. Mom and Dad knew nothing until I ended up in the hospital. But there's only so much you can hide from the person you're sleeping with. Simon thought I was merely putting on weight until my breasts started getting larger." She sighed. "He was drunk that night because he was pissed at me. When he guessed about the baby, he went apeshit. All the usual stuff—I'd trapped him, he was too young to be a dad, blah, blah, blah. The irony is that he was looking for a way out, and I was about to hand it to him. When you suggested going to the cemetery after the party, like old times, I was finally happy. I figured whatever had gone on between us was over, and I'd tell you about the baby, and it would all work out. That's why I was singing in the car. Suddenly my life made sense, and then it didn't. It never made sense again until I met Jade. But Simon was gunning for me that night, trying to figure out his own feelings, and you got caught in the crossfire."

Gabriel put his hand in his pocket and pulled out a white hanky. He blew his nose, put the hanky back. Said nothing.

"He was locked in his own battle," she said. "Should he do the right thing or run away? I think he transferred all that to you when he saw us kiss, and I guess the alcohol turned him possessive."

"I was almost a father. And our baby is buried—"

"Where she was conceived. I didn't want her alone for all eternity. And then I decided to join her. Everyone thinks I tried to off myself because of Simon's death. No one knew the truth but Mom and Dad. And now you." She tried to smile.

"Does Darius know—about any of this?"

"Before he flew home I told him about the baby. He made the same assumption as you and your parents, that Simon was the dad. Telling him would have achieved nothing. Although he might not have let me stay. Gabriel." She paused. "Do you forgive me?"

He took her hand and held it against his cheek. "Yes. It's a lot to take in, but thank you. For the truth." Gabriel looked around his kitchen. "It appears I temporarily lost my mind."

"Take it from an expert: you're never truly lost if someone cares enough to come find you. Lost is waiting to be found."

She got up and went to the tiny pantry to retrieve the broom. While he picked up phone books and papers and piled them back on the dresser, she swept up the glass. They worked to the distant hum of evening traffic.

"I can't believe I used the word *hate*. I'm so sorry, Marianne. I had no idea I was capable of saying such heinous things."

"You buried it because you had to. It's no different than me refusing to come back here for thirty years."

"So why did you come back, really?"

"For you."

"I'm not in love with you. I thought we'd established that."

"I know, and I'm not in love with you, but I never forgot the feeling of us. I think that's what I ran back to. Subconsciously I knew there was something here that only you could give me. And now I understand what it is. I thought you could save me. Turns out I had it backward. You were the one who needed saving. Yours was the life I destroyed."

Gabriel sat down, a little unsteadily. "You didn't destroy anything. I'm content, and I'm good at my job because I have a detachment that eluded me when I was in love with you. Let's be honest, I couldn't see straight when you were within spitting distance."

"Charming. You just compared me to spit." She smiled. "But I pretty much ruined your chance of love, marriage, and a baby carriage. I know how much you always wanted kids. That was the one part of the future we agreed on."

"Loving you never felt like a choice, Marianne. It was too much. A kind of lunacy. I never wanted those extremes again."

"I can share my lithium anytime you want emotional flatness," she said. "But you have to give yourself permission to love again. You have so much to offer."

"Much as I appreciate the vote of confidence, I'm settled in my bachelorhood with Hugh. We've started planning our retirement cruise." He paused. "And you, Marianne. Are you happy? Do you love your husband?"

"With all my heart." She glanced up at the kitchen clock. They still had time. "Come to the cemetery with me, now. Tonight. I want to visit our baby together. Do you still have that old blanket?"

"Sadly, I do. I kept everything that linked me to you."

"We conceived a baby on that blanket. That's more than I've ever given anyone else. We're going to face every ghost we can find and then get back to the business of living. But I have to warn you, I need to be tucked up in bed by eleven p.m. That's my bipolar witching hour."

Gabriel picked up his now-cold plate from the kitchen table and put it in the microwave. Then he spooned out more lasagna onto a second plate.

"But first," he said, "we both need to eat. Because if I'm a grumpy bastard when I'm hungry, you're a snappy little dog." And then he hiccupped.

FIFTY-FOUR
GABRIEL

Gabriel attempted to push down on the latch of the cemetery gate and missed. *Good grief, still blottoed.* One fuzzy thought did a slid-sidey thing around his brain: God did not demand perfection. True, but he'd tossed the word *hate*—and a fair chunk of change about lack of forgiveness—around the rectory as if it were a badminton shuttlecock. He tried to remember another thought, but his mind went blank. Not a sausage in there. Just as well since he'd missed evening prayer. Well, he and God would have plenty to talk about in tomorrow's chitchat.

Away from the lights of the village, the yew trees and headstones disappeared into a never-ending black hole. Gabriel grappled with the latch a second time.

"Come on, you drunkard."

The latch clicked up and Marianne brushed past. He attempted to follow but tripped and nearly belly-flopped into the trough of stagnant rainwater used for watering the flowers.

She flicked on the torch she must have grabbed on the way out of the rectory. Following the thin beam, they sidestepped through the maze of closely packed, sunken graves to the end of the second row.

Gabriel leaned on his brother's headstone for support while Marianne shook out the blanket and sat, cross-legged. He dumped himself down next to her. Off to their right, a creature, probably a badger, snuffled through the undergrowth. The weeds were back. Time to get another volunteer work crew out here.

"What's going through your mind?" She rested her head on his shoulder.

"Drunken disconnect, almighty embarrassment, and a pounding headache."

"Aspirin and water before bed." She paused. "Are you angry at me?"

A car crawled by on the road, its headlights briefly illuminating the black gates. Gabriel waited until the cemetery was shrouded, once more, in darkness. Their best conversations had always been here, in the night, when they couldn't quite see each other. "No. I'm angry at myself. Simon had such charm, but I saw everything he snuck by Mum. Growing up, I believed I had the stronger moral compass."

"Except for that brief foray into stealing."

"Fair enough. Apart from a short-lived career as a thief, I was the good son, the one who always washed up the supper things, pegged out the laundry, walked the dog. I always thought I was better than Simon, but I was as weak as he was."

"You were a teenage boy with a girlfriend who thought she was hot stuff *and* knew how to get what she wanted. Do you have any idea why I encouraged you to steal candy?"

"To see if I was corruptible?"

"Pretty much. I mean, you took the blame for stuff you hadn't done, brought home wounded pigeons in your book bag, tried to talk me out of vandalizing Bill's daffodils. I wanted you to be as wild and crazy as I was, but you always held back. Except for that one night in the cemetery, when we conceived Gabriela. And it was amazing."

He frowned. "I hurt you. I distinctly remember you telling me it hurt."

"It did, and it was exquisite. I thought my heart was going to burst. You took over and did something wonderfully irresponsible and impulsive without even asking about birth control. It was as if you were missing in the madness of passion."

"Let's not get too romantic. I was a horny teenager." *And then I spent years afterward wrestling with angels . . .*

"If I could go back and undo that night we made a baby here, on this blanket, I wouldn't. Losing my virginity to you is the one part of all this I got right." She sat up and took his hand. "I'm glad we were each other's first. That worked out exactly as it should have. I'm just sorry we botched everything that followed. And I think I'd like to say a prayer."

In one of the yew trees at the back of the cemetery, an owl hooted.

"You don't believe in God." He swallowed another hiccup.

"My opinions change with my moods. Honestly, I don't know what I believe, but right now I'm at peace. And peace is not a destination I visit for long. I want to acknowledge this moment; I want to be thankful and grateful. If that means saying a prayer, then yes, I guess I'm talking to God."

"It's going to take me a while to get used to the idea that we had a baby together."

"You, me, and Gabriela. The family that wasn't . . . but lives in my heart."

He tried to imagine Christmases and birthdays, summer Saturdays eating ice cream cones and winter Saturdays building snowmen, but he couldn't get traction in the memories. They weren't real; they weren't meant to exist. His world picture could never have stretched to accommodate a family. Even when he'd bought the ring for Marianne, he never questioned that she would want to live the life he'd chosen. That was the real reason people like him ended up alone: they couldn't adapt. Whoa, not a great realization to have while blind drunk.

Gabriel stared at the rosebushes growing over the earthly remains of his baby and his brother. In a few weeks the plants would start dropping leaves and prepare to go dormant until spring. Marianne had talked about peace, but how long before he found it? How long before he could sit here and say, "Simon, I'm sorry. Gabriela, I'm sorry." Gabriel closed his eyes but opened them when a wave of seasickness hit. He tried to focus on what little of the world he could see that wasn't spinning, and laughed.

"What's funny?"

"Jade. You probably don't remember, but she was drunk when they arrived. She told me the rectory was spinning."

"Gabriel, why not leave the village for a while and visit us in North Carolina? You wouldn't have any expenses once you arrived, and the four of us would have fun together."

"A generous offer, but I can't afford international travel. The train to Cornwall is expensive enough."

"Cornwall?"

"Last time I took a holiday I went back to revisit some of our old family haunts. Mum used to love the Frenchman's Creek walk. Why?"

"Nothing. I . . . Look!" Marianne pointed up. "A shooting star. Oh, you have to make a wish."

Gabriel craned his neck until it hurt. Above them stars twinkled in a rare display. Light pollution from Milton Keynes normally dulled their night skies. He couldn't make out what she was talking about, but then again, he'd never seen a shooting star. Or maybe he'd never looked hard enough.

They talked, they prayed, they reminisced, and when the church clock struck eleven, Marianne stood. "Thank you. For the first time in months, I feel like me again. Still a loon but ready to do the work it takes to stay healthy."

Gabriel stood, awkwardly, stiffly, and watched Marianne pick up the blanket. She bundled it under her arm, whereas he would have shaken it out and asked her to help him fold it. But then again, they'd always done things differently.

"I'd like you to keep the ring," he said as they walked back to the gate. "Will it be a problem, with Darius?"

"As if. He doesn't notice when I've had a haircut."

Gabriel couldn't see in the darkness, but instinct told him she was smiling.

"If he asks, I'll tell him the truth: that it was mine when I was a teenager, I lost it after the crash, and you've been keeping it for me."

"Do you have it with you?" Gabriel said.

She pulled it out of her pocket.

"Hold out your right hand." He slipped it on and then, folding her fingers over, kissed her knuckle. "If you ever need me, I'm here."

"Ditto. You know, we loved a whole lifetime before we reached adulthood."

He sighed. "Indeed. And it never left the cemetery."

FIFTY-FIVE

MARIANNE

Outside the immigration hall, the Carolina-blue sky beat down on a stationary plane sitting on the tarmac. Air-conditioning blasted, and an exhausted toddler whimpered. Darius was in the same building, waiting for her on the other side of customs, and Jade was only a forty-minute drive away. Thirty today and she was going to flip when she unwrapped the white knee-high Dr. Martens—very retro, very Jade. So much to anticipate—Jade's squeals of delight, the warmth of Darius's lips, the softness of her own bed—and yet the tightness in her chest suggested that she was being buried alive. Slowly. Two and a half months since she'd run away from her family, her home, her business. Were they enough to keep her from fleeing again? What if the moment she stepped into the bright Carolina sunshine, the darkness returned to swallow her whole?

Marianne reached inside the pocket of her leather jacket and felt around for Gabriel's hanky. He'd driven her to the airport, as she knew he would, and after he kissed both her cheeks in a formal, European good-bye, she clung to him. No simple adieu like a normal person.

Nope, instead she bawled through a tsunami of grief—for her mother, EmJ, Gabriela, Simon, her old life. All her losses tossed together into a tumble dryer. And Gabriel pulled out that ridiculous white handkerchief that smelled of him, and she shoved it into the pocket of her leather jacket, hoping he wouldn't ask for it back. He hadn't.

Marianne glanced at the stationary line of non-nationals, clutching their passports and plastic bags of duty-free. The moment she stepped through the automatic doors into the terminal, she would leave the other Brits behind and revert to being an American. Few people knew she was English by birth, and she'd never figured out whether she was a southerner by choice or by circumstance. All she knew, right now, was that an ocean separated her from Newton Rushford, from the cemetery, from the church, from Mrs. Tandy, from Phyllis the neighbor, from Bill Collins and his silly little dog. From Gabriel. From her childhood home near the river, which she didn't visit once in two and a half months. Why? Because she'd known the house had nothing left to offer. The memories of her mother she carried with her, always.

"Ma'am?" a slow, southern voice said.

"Sorry! Sorry!" Marianne glanced back down the line. Then she grabbed her Queen Bee bag and the heavy carrier of Cadbury chocolate purchased at Heathrow for Darius, and walked toward the immigration booth. She collected her suitcase, cleared customs, and the moment the opaque glass doors whooshed open, she spotted Darius. He was standing next to a bunch of kids, eyes fixed on the doors.

"Babe!" he yelled, and ducked under the barrier.

She launched herself at him, throwing her arms around his neck. The leather jacket fell to the floor, and—to hell with the audience—she kissed him as if nothing had ever mattered more.

Now she was home.

Before long they were hurtling down I-40 in his old Jeep, his hair blowing all over the place. He drove with one hand on the wheel and one on her thigh, chatting away: he'd bought fresh shrimp and picked up Jade's birthday cake from Winnie—yes, carrot cake, as Marianne had instructed—and Jade was going to join them for dinner and then get smashed with Sasha and Zeke and the crew from Girls In Motion. Did she know Sasha and Zeke were now doing the deed? They were ridiculously cute together. True *luuuv*, Zeke kept telling him. Oh, and Dr. White wanted to see them the next day. Darius had made an appointment for two p.m.

He stopped talking and flashed his wolfish grin. "Sorry. I don't mean to bombard you with crap, but I'm ridiculously excited to see you."

"I can tell." She wove her fingers through his and closed her eyes.

When she woke up, the car was pulling into the driveway and Jade was waving a banner that said, "Welcome home, Mama Bird."

Marianne opened the door before they stopped moving.

"Dammit, woman. No more crazy stunts."

She grinned at Darius and held the door almost closed. The second the engine stopped, she was out, one arm pushing aside the bamboo that needed taming as the other reached for Jade. Rocking slowly, they clung to each other. Jade said nothing; she said nothing, but she couldn't let go. She would never let go. And God only knew which one of them started crying first.

"I thought you weren't coming back." Jade sniffed.

"For you," Marianne said, "I would have swum home."

"Hey, it's okay, you two," Darius said as he hugged them both from behind.

✳

After she saw Dr. White, Marianne stopped leaving the house. She told Darius she'd go to the store, get their lives back up and running, but she crawled into bed exhausted from their first joint therapy session and slept as if she were hibernating. On Friday morning, she stretched, got out of bed, and opened the gauzy linen curtains. In the garden her yellow Maryland aster was blooming, and fallen leaves had begun to create drifts of copper, brown, and gold. Crisp, rich colors that warned her to watch over her shoulder for October. To honor EmJ, she would be extra vigilant.

There was a knock on the bedroom door.

"I heard you moving around." Jade stuck her head inside. "Brought you coffee."

"Thank you, sweetheart."

Jade turned to leave.

"Hey, stay a while." Marianne walked back to her bed, sat down, and scooted into the middle. "I've seen so little of you since I got back. I haven't had the chance to thank you properly for holding down the fort while I went full-blown mental patient."

"Nada. It's what family does." Jade examined her unpainted fingernails. "I should get back to work."

"Your boss is giving you an excused absence." Marianne patted the duvet. "Stop avoiding me and sit."

"I'm not avoiding you. All you've done in the last four days is sleep. You going for the new world record?"

Drunk Gabriel and now prickly Jade. The only person who didn't need handling with care was Darius. Although his demands in other areas were quite spectacular. Seemed they were going for their own record. Maybe that was why she was sleeping so much. Physical, not emotional, exhaustion. Jade sat next to her, leaned back against the bedroom wall, and closed her eyes.

"It's bizarre seeing your natural hair color." Marianne brushed a stray hair from Jade's face. "A conscious decision to let it grow out or lack of time for a hair appointment?"

"Bit of both. I'm going in tomorrow to chop out what's left of the red."

"Back to purple?" Marianne sipped her coffee.

"Nah. Now that I'm a staid woman of thirty, I'm done making statements with my hair." Jade stretched out her legs and wiggled her toes. "This is the new, boring me."

"And what's this other new thing you have for bare feet?"

Jade shrugged. "Dunno." Like hell she didn't.

"You look tired. Sleeping okay?"

Another shrug.

"Want to tell me what's really going on? I have time to listen."

Outside in the black walnut tree by the deck, a Carolina wren whistled.

Jade sat up. "It's been tough with you and Darius gone."

"And now we're both back."

Jade crossed her legs and concentrated on pulling a loose thread from the hem of her cutoffs. She didn't normally look quite so casual on a workday. "I didn't believe you would. You know, come back."

"Why, because you would have stayed in England?" Marianne dipped down to look up into Jade's eyes. "But then, I'm not you. And I'm not in love with Gabriel."

"Yeah? Good to know. I bet Darius is thrilled." Jade turned away to stare out the window at the beautiful Carolina day.

A robin landed on the windowsill and sang his little heart out. A whole flock answered, and then he flew away and the others followed. An entire community of robins on the move.

"The new ring isn't Darius's usual taste," Jade said without turning.

Marianne splayed her fingers. "No, it isn't. It's something from the past, from life before Darius." She touched Jade's knee. "Honey, Gabriel's not in love with me. He told me."

"And you're passing this on because . . . ?"

"Oh please, give me some credit. I wasn't sure at first. I've never seen you in love before."

"Who said anything about—"

"You look like your cat and your dog and half your neighborhood died. Plus you've lost weight, Ms. Skinny Minny. Truth or dare. Are you in love with Gabriel Bonham?"

"I can't have this conversation with you, Marianne." Jade stood up. "I know we do everything in our own deeply weird way, but you're not like my mom, you are my mom. Which makes Gabriel—"

"Nothing, sweetheart. It makes him nothing." Marianne frowned. "Wow, that came out wrong. Gabriel's way more than nothing. We were best friends in another lifetime, and it should have ended there. I slept with Simon because I was looking for the next best thing, and part of me knew Gabriel wasn't it. So let me ask you a second time. Are you in love with Gabriel?"

"Why does it matter?"

"Because I have a surprise gift for you. Your real thirtieth birthday present. The Dr. Martens were the opening act. But first, I need your answer." Today she would get up, get dressed, and clean out the hummingbird feeders. It was time to store them for another year.

"Yes, I'm in love with Gabriel. Happy? Good, because I'm not," Jade said. "It sucks balls. And if you guys aren't in love with each other, go ahead and tell me why you came home wearing his ring. Stab me through the heart with a wooden stake, why don't you."

"Great, I go crazy for two months and you take over as Ms. Nightjar Drama Queen."

"Blame the vicar."

Marianne laughed. "Okay, sweetheart. Straight to the plain truth. We lost our virginity together. It was the only time we had sex." Marianne glanced at her open bedroom door. "And I got pregnant."

"But you and Simon—"

"Yup. I was pregnant with Gabriel's baby when I slept with his brother. How's that for screwed up? Oh God. Terrible pun." In the office above, Darius's footsteps suggested he was on the move. Marianne leaned in and whispered, "I told Darius about the baby, but he thinks it was Simon's. No one knows the truth except for Gabriel, me, and now you. Well, Dad knew but he's forgotten. And Gabriel didn't know until last week. Anyway, I'd like to keep it between the three of us."

"Why tell me?"

"To help you unlock the mystery that is Gabriel Bonham, because God knows I failed, and Gabriel's way too special to be a grumpy old bachelor going on cruises with Hugh." Marianne smiled. "He bought the ring for my seventeenth birthday but never gave it to me because of everything that happened the night of the crash. I found it by mistake and figured he deserved to know who the baby's real father was. We put everything to rest, and he told me to keep the ring. But Gabriel and me, we never wanted the same things. He wanted a quiet life in the English countryside. I had my heart set on the rest of the world. Hard to compete with that."

"And what do you think he wants now?" Jade said.

"That's for someone else to find out." Marianne fiddled with her ring. "But I should warn you, when Gabriel loves, it's all or nothing. And I'm not sure you'll ever pull up his roots. What did you think about Newton Rushford? It's a bit quiet for a Bronx girl."

"It felt—"

"Familiar? Somewhere that could become home?"

Jade nodded. "Was that meant to be an engagement ring?"

"Yes."

"So why're you wearing it now?"

"To never forget that I want to be a better person in the future than I was in the past. And that I want to make better decisions as"— Marianne twitched her mouth back and forth—"a mother. I thought the Media Rage gig was your future, but I'm having a rethink, which means it's time you stretched your wings."

"Are you kicking me out?"

"Never, missy. I'm giving you a little push toward the horizon, that's all. Because I think you and Gabriel need to explore your feelings for each other, and he's never going to make the first move, and I'm guessing you aren't, either. That fight you guys had. Smacked of a lovers' spat."

"That's when I lost weight," Jade said. "I couldn't eat. Do you really think he's interested, or are you telling me what I want to hear?"

"Stop being so cynical."

"Yeah, and who did I learn that from?"

Jade slumped back onto the bed and leaned against her.

"I have another question for you." Marianne wrapped her free arm around Jade. "One that's equally important. If you had a chance with Gabriel, would you take it? Would you risk everything knowing that breaking his heart was not an option?"

"Yes."

"Then it's time to tell you about your present. I was talking to Darius last night, and . . ."

Darius bounded in. "Heard my name. How are my two favorite girls this morning?" He hurled himself onto the other side of the bed, and it seemed to vibrate under his energy.

"Baby—" Marianne held up her coffee mug. "Be careful!"

He took it from her, put it down on the nightstand, and kissed her softly. Marianne couldn't help it, she giggled.

"Don't mind me, guys," Jade said.

Darius grinned like a little boy about to tear open every present in his Christmas stocking. "Still can't believe you're back in my bed."

"Seriously, boss. Too much information."

"Have you told her the plan yet?"

"What plan?" Jade said.

"Darius and I have agreed that you've earned an all-expenses-paid vacation. You're going at the end of next week—a thirtieth-birthday present meets the trip of a lifetime. At least that's what we're hoping it'll be."

"Earth to Marianne and Darius—Media Rage coming back, a band we can't screw over a second time. And we're taking most of next week for repairs. The snake channels and the signal paths need checking; we're resoldering the cables, and on it goes. Or did you forget, Darius?"

Snippy Jade was definitely not getting enough sleep.

"Sasha and Zeke have it covered," Darius said. "You, doll, are leaving on a jet plane."

"No offense, but what if I don't feel like going away?"

"Well"—Marianne smiled—"we didn't tell you the catch."

"You'll like the catch," Darius said. "Go on, tell her."

The doorbell rang. "UPS!" Darius leaped up. "Tell her. Tell her now. I can't take any more moping in the studio." And then he gave Marianne a quick kiss and disappeared.

"I'm not moping," Jade yelled after him. "I'm heartbroken," she said quietly. "And I don't want a vacation. Thank you very much. Plus I have a second date with an ex-cop, a hunk who knows how to handle a gun. That alone is a total turn-on."

"Utter crap. And you'll want to cancel when I've told you the catch." Marianne smacked a kiss on the top of Jade's head. "There's only so much manipulating even I can do. Which means that I've picked the destination, but the rest, daughter of my heart, is up to you."

FIFTY-SIX
GABRIEL

"Reverend, Reverend!" With remarkable dexterity, Moyra Savage swung round the huge, black pram that she'd used for all four of her babies and set Gabriel in her sights. Silently he acknowledged his guilt over not confirming a christening date with her and crossed to the other side of the High Street.

Today he'd chosen to be off duty, which was why he'd dressed in mufti: jeans and a T-shirt. Wearing a dog collar was like hanging an "Open for Business" sign around his neck. That had never been a problem for someone who rarely shut up shop, but in the twelve days since Marianne's departure, retreat and contemplation had become as vital as oxygen.

Before she'd turned up in his church, her mind worn ragged, he'd been comfortable by himself. But once again she spun his world upside down, and left. Although this time he wasn't caught between the extremes of anger and love. He was suspended in the loneliness that hung from every nook and cranny of his house. Never before had his life echoed with emptiness; never before had the silence in the rectory said, *There's no one here except you.*

Newton Rushford was crawling with ramblers on this glorious October Saturday. No sign as yet of the Indian summer retreating. A couple sat outside Puddings Galore, fanning themselves with the new pamphlets Ian had designed on the history of the church. Hopefully they had given the suggested donation of one pound. And the village children were out in full force. A gaggle of them raced past, clutching iced lollies, and one bashed into his leg.

"Jimmy, come back here and apologize to the reverend." Annie Green's voice screeched behind him.

Gabriel turned, ignoring the huge splatter of pink and orange slush on his jeans. Sweat tickled his chest, and his facial muscles strained into a smile. "No harm done, Annie."

He gave a wave that said *Conversation terminated,* and picked up his pace. With each step, an imaginary scenario unfolded: a little girl with a ponytail giving him a good-bye kiss before running inside the village school. Gabriel batted the thought away. Fantasies were for dreamers and creative people, and he was woefully behind on harvest festival. Silently he recited John Keats's "To Autumn" but failed to find comfort in the familiar words. He failed to find comfort in anything these days.

Hugh had suggested talking with a professional, but Gabriel had resisted. Prayer and contemplation had always been enough, but that only worked if you were willing to turn inward to face your darkest corners—the sin you had hidden from yourself and God. He had traveled full circle and met his true self, a man who used the word *hate.* A man who, unlike Bill Collins, was unable to forgive.

Before supper he would sit on his patio with a pink gin and contemplate human weakness—his. And he would keep struggling toward peace with actions that had cost him his daughter, his love, his brother. Marianne was right. In that one tempestuous encounter, he let go and then retreated into shame. Which was a perfectly logical response to making love in a cemetery, but the repercussions had led to his brother's death.

As he headed away from the sounds of people, his gait settled into a steady rhythm that contradicted the turbulence of his thoughts. He walked past the Newton Rushford sign to the outskirts of the village. To the grave of his baby. Pigeons cooed and sheep bleated as he pushed open the cemetery gates. A sparrow hawk flew by in a flap-flap-glide motion.

Even Jade's texts had dried up. Although he was probably to blame. He hadn't given her much to hold on to while he retreated into his inner world. He missed those texts more than he cared to admit. She didn't demand anything from him, and he'd grown used to their communication. He took a deep breath. See? He was still lying to himself. He didn't miss their *communication*; he missed her. What did that mean? If God knew, he wasn't answering.

Gabriel wove around the graves and stopped by Gabriela's. How many times had he been here and never once sensed a whisper of a connection? He sat on the grass, crossed his legs, and glanced at the headstone that mentioned only his brother. Simon had been under the influence of one thing that night: raging desire. The same force that led to Gabriela's conception. It seemed he and Simon hadn't been so different.

"Hello, Gabriela." He paused. "Hello, Simon." Staring at the headstone, he mined his memories for a happy one: Simon sharing his copy of *The Beano* on a camping trip to the Lake District. Simon had loved camping. This was a new habit: finding one happy memory of Simon every day. It was an easier task than he would have imagined. Again he thought of Jade, asking if they'd ever been close. She showed him the path forward, and he'd been too wrapped up in himself to realize it.

A jackdaw landed on Ursula Finch's grave, and a car drove past with music blaring. His phone pinged with a text. He ignored it; it pinged again. Sighing, he tugged it out of his back jeans pocket. Much as he tried, he could never disconnect.

He smiled.

How's life without the crazies? Jade had typed.

Quiet. He paused, looked at the jackdaw, kept typing. Are you sure you're not psychic? I was just thinking about you.

Yeah?

I've missed you.

How much?

Some trapped emotion he couldn't name scrabbled around inside his chest.

More than I'd like to admit. He hit "Send" before he could change his mind.

Have you ever been to Cornwall, to Daphne du Maurier country?

What did that mean?

Yes. Many times.

Want to go again?

His heart began pounding so fast he could hear the blood pumping, could imagine his heart valves struggling to keep up.

With you? He typed quickly.

Yes, Einstein. With me.

The pulsing gray bubble suggested she was still typing. It was taking so long, too long. The bubble disappeared and a fully formed message popped up.

I'm asking you to go away with me. It's a yes or no question, and you're taking too long to answer, because I'd like to leave tonight.

The back of his neck prickled. He stood up and turned. Leaning against the old rainwater trough was Jade. With a large suitcase and without scarlet hair. Jade with strangely normal hair—very Audrey Hepburn or very Halle Berry or very . . . His brain conked out. Simply ground to a halt. Texting with someone in another time zone was one thing, but this . . . He stared at her, she stared back, and neither of them moved.

Scratching through his hair, he started laughing, and her face transformed into the most wondrous smile he'd ever seen. He stepped cautiously around sunken graves, making his way through the row of dead people until he reached her.

"How did you get here?" he said.

"A plane." She took a step toward him. "They're an amazing invention, planes."

"But you hate flying."

"Yeah, how about that? I guess I really wanted to see you."

"Are you always this impulsive?" He was standing so close he could feel her. Was she wearing that red bra again?

"Au contraire. I think of myself as calculating." She swallowed, and the bravado slipped. "I took a chance, a huge one."

Did she mean what he thought she meant? "Forgive me for being dense, but can we establish the reason you got on the plane?"

"For you."

"For me," he said.

"Yeah. Want me to draw a diagram?"

"What would that look like?"

"A big heart with an arrow through it. Possibly two initials on either side, a *J* and a *G*."

She held out her hand, and he took it, weaving his fingers between hers. Her thumb stroked his palm and he shivered. Or was he shaking?

"Will this cause some horrible scandal if you walk through the village holding hands with a tattooed, mixed-race foreigner with multiple piercings?"

"Absolutely," he said. "Although not as much as if anyone sees me do this."

And he brushed her lips with a kiss—hesitant, warm, and gentle. He rested his forehead against hers and hoped his knees—the bad one and the good one—wouldn't give way. "I can't believe you're here." He pulled back. "It is just you, right?"

"Only me. I left the family at home."

He swallowed. "There's so much to say, but I don't know where to start. That conversation we had when I flew off the handle about Darius being in London. I was jealous. I wanted you to put me first."

"I think I just did." She was breathing rapidly. "I think I'm about to walk away from an album that could make my career."

"For me?"

"Haven't we established that?"

"I'm a slow learner." His mobile rang and he ignored it. "I'm not sure I can get away to Cornwall tonight, but—" His phone stopped and started again. Why was the cemetery the only place at this end of the village with reception?

"Sorry, I've got to take this. It's my mother." Instinctively he turned away from Jade. "Mum. Yes, I did get your message, but I'm a little busy. I can't talk." He turned back to make sure Jade was still there. He watched her watching him.

"You're always busy, Gabriel. You need to work on your priorities. And I can't get up on the stepladder to change the lightbulb in the downstairs loo. Do you have any idea of the risk your father is taking every time he spends a penny? His balance is awful, and I can't have him taking a tinkle in the dark."

"I'm sorry, Mum. I will sort it out, but I'll have to call you back."

"No, Gabriel, I want—"

He hung up and turned his phone off. God help him, he didn't care what his aging mother wanted.

Jade took a step back. "You're busy, and I shouldn't have turned up like this. I was worried that if I asked you'd say no. And I couldn't have dealt with that. The rejection. And maybe it's all too weird with our connection through Marianne. I mean you and she once—"

"Only once and before you were born."

"Not helping, Gabriel."

Heat rose up his chest. "Please don't walk away. I know it's not Cornwall, but will you come with me to my parents' in Milton Keynes?"

"Do you do that often," she said, "invite women to meet your parents?"

Gabriel hid his phone in his back pocket. "No, hardly ever." He took a deep breath. "I have a strange life, a very public life, and I make no money, and I have two aging parents who need more attention than I can give. And when you're my age, I'll probably have a disabled parking badge."

Had he said too much? What was he thinking, asking her to meet his parents? What was he thinking, talking about his salary and disabled parking? And now she would run, as any sensible woman would. He was doing exactly what he'd done with Marianne when they were teenagers. He was saying, *This is my life, live it with me.*

"I didn't mean to corner you. Come on so strong." He tried to smile. "Can we forget I said any of that and start over? Hello, Jade. How was your flight?"

"I don't know how to do this," she said. "How to love someone. I'm good at looking after me. Other people not so much."

"From what I've seen that's all you do. Put other people first."

"Bull. I hold back. I have a shit track record with relationships. I've dumped more guys than—"

"Me too. Obviously not the dumping-men part. Actually, not much dumping at all. And not many relationships. But I don't know how to do this, either. What if you stay for a while and we . . . I don't know . . . talk about starting an English arm of Girls In Motion? Or I bet you could get a job in London. Doesn't Darius have contacts in the city?"

"What are you saying?"

"I don't know." He laughed, because it was that or cry. "I have no idea what I'm talking about. I know nothing except that I don't want you to leave, and I'm prepared to beg." What he wanted was to kiss her again. She had tasted of coffee and peppermint. "Please stay."

"I need to tell you something. Something I've never told anyone, not even Marianne."

He took her hands.

"I left them behind. My siblings, when I ran. I left them behind." She paused, but he wasn't going to interrupt. She could take all the time she needed. "My brother tried to stop me. He asked me to take him, and I refused. Our stepdad was abusive, and I left my baby brother behind—abandoned him to evil. I had one thought when I ran away that day: that my brother would slow me down. He clung to me and begged me to reconsider. He was crying, and I pushed him off. I physically pushed him off. Pushed him so hard he fell to the ground. I knew he couldn't cope without me. He was dependent on me, and I left him anyway." Jade glanced at one of the leaning historic gravestones. "So you see, underneath, I'm a lousy person. And I worry that I'm more broken than Marianne."

She turned back to stare at him with those big brown eyes and long lashes. No makeup. He'd never understood why women used makeup, certainly not a woman as beautiful as Jade. And he knew, with absolute certainty, that he loved her. His life had been dragged through the muck, and in the middle of it, he'd fallen in love. It was impossible, it was ridiculous, it was the sort of behavior he would expect from Marianne. And it was true.

"Have you considered that we're both as broken as each other?" he said. "I preach forgiveness and I can't forgive my own brother. I'm trying, but the truth is, I'm still angry."

"Marianne told me, about the baby. I'm sorry."

"I think you and I need to forgive ourselves. Guilt should come with an expiration date, and what we did as teenagers was a long time ago"—he gave a wobbly smile—"especially for me." He eased her into an embrace, tucking her against his chest. She fit perfectly, and his breath turned into sparks of pure energy. "And I think we should start over, together. Because I want to look after you and I want you to look after me, and I want us to build a home, a real home, together, my darling."

"Did you just call me *darling*?" She raised her head.

"Yes." He cleared his throat. "Because I think something else, too . . ."

Her big eyes stared up at him.

"I think I love you, and—"

"You think or you know?"

"Are you going to make me say it? Because I'm scared shitless right now."

"Shitless?" She gave a small laugh. "I've been trying to stop swearing, and you've started?"

"Jade, I'm shaking, but nothing terrifies me more than you walking out of my life and not coming back. I don't know what that means, but I need to find out."

"I kind of love you, too. Like an insane amount."

"I knew the moment you took off your jacket to protect Marianne, but it took my brain a while to catch up, given how broken I am." He grinned. "You were like an angel—a drunken, spectacularly nonconformist angel with truly horrific hair." He dipped toward her. "And I have a weakness for angels"—his breathing slowed; his voice became a whisper—"but not the perfect kind."

And then he kissed her, really kissed her. And he wasn't a priest, he was a man lost in love, and he didn't care where he was or who was watching.

CARRBORO, NORTH CAROLINA
OCTOBER

In the dusky light on the other side of the open kitchen window, a raccoon failed to navigate her new bird feeder defenses.

"Ha, ha, ha," Marianne said in the dastardly-villain voice she reserved for the local varmints.

Then she picked up her phone and typed a joint text: If you two haven't kissed yet, I'm going to be pissed as hell, which will not make Darius happy. And then he'll drag it up in our next session with Dr. White, and accountability is exhausting. So do it already. Then figure out the sex thing before year's end, because we call dibs on the rectory guest bedroom for ringing in the New Year. Love you both. P.S. Coffee machine arriving on Monday morning. It's a gift from Darius. Xox

She added a manic smiley face emoticon. And a Union Jack. And a couple of hearts, a shooting star, a microphone, a guitar, and a row of musical notes.

The security light came on, and Darius walked toward the deck, whistling as he jangled his keys to Nightjar. For a guy who worked in a soundproof environment, he certainly liked to make noise. But both of them had always preferred to record with a touch of sound reflection. And now that the echoes of her past had mixed with the sounds of her present, a new song was about to begin. She grinned, the thought quietly exhilarating.

ACKNOWLEDGMENTS

Yet again I have a long list of people to thank, especially those who shared stories of a bipolar life. You inspired me with your courage and your humor, and reminded me of the most important lesson of all: a person, or a character, is not his or her disorder.

As always I am beyond grateful to my agent, Nalini Akolekar. She continues to get the quirky BCW characters despite the synopses that never make sense. By extension, thanks to everyone at Spencerhill Associates. Carol Guerin, your emails brighten my days.

Endless gratitude to Gabe Dumpit and the team at Lake Union Publishing for their enthusiasm and dedication—even though I'm making up my author life as I go. Special thanks to Jodi Warshaw and Clete Barrett Smith, whose edits not only deepened and tightened the manuscript but fired up my enthusiasm for Darius. (I was in the zone, man.)

Many thanks to my local indie booksellers for their continued support: Jamie Fiocco at Flyleaf Books, Sharon Wheeler at Purple Crow Books, Kimberly Daniels Taws at the Country Bookshop, and Keebe Fitch at McIntyre's Books. I'm thrilled to add Suzanne Lucey at Page 158 Books to the list, and I'm looking forward to my first event at Scuppernong Books.

Deepest thanks to web designer Adam Rottinghaus and author assistant extraordinaire Carolyn Ring for their endless patience. Yes, I am as techno-challenged as you both suspect.

Thank you to book clubs and loyal readers who cheered me on when I was flagging, especially Carol Boyer and Susan Walters Peterson. Big hugs to transatlantic Facebook friends who answered every crazy plea for research help. To my writer friends at Book Pregnant, Fiction Writers Co-Op, Girlfriends Book Club, and WFWA, thank you for sharing my foxhole. Extra warm fuzzies for the WFWA retreat where I finished my second draft, although I'm still miffed about missing the margarita fountain. And humble thanks to Catherine McKenzie, Diane Chamberlain, and Barbara Davis, who are always so generous with their time, support, and friendship. Other writers are the best.

For miscellaneous brainstorming and fact-finding missions, hugs to Kim Allman, Cullen Cornett, Danlee Gildersleeve, Fiona Heath, Heather and Kimberly Montgomery, Julie Randles, Melanie Satterthwaite, Laura Spinella, Jessica Topper, Christine Westrom, Carolyn Wilson, and my nephew, Harry Rose—an officer and a gentleman in the Light Dragoons.

Thank you to Collier Reeves for explaining Girls Rock and Appalachian music to me, and kicking off the idea for Girls In Motion. And thank you to the amazing people who attempted to educate me about the life of a sound engineer (apologies for any erroneous facts about mixing): Mark Simonsen, John Plymale at Overdub Lane Recording, and Meghan Puryear and Chris Wimberley at Nightsound Studios in Carrboro. (I wear my Nightsound T-shirt with pride.) And a wave to Kathleen Basi for explaining the fiddle to someone whose musical talent started and ended with second trumpet in the school band.

Special thanks to my American psychiatrists "on call," Dr. Charles Michael Gammon and Dr. Michael Larson. For all things related to the English medical world, gratitude to my brother-in-law Dr. Charles

Rose, and a shout-out to Sue Hampson at the Priory Group for helping me visualize five-star residential care.

Thank you, John Pharo, for introducing me to the world of emancipated minors, and thank you to Ryan Hill and Jan M. Bazemore in the North Carolina Department of Health and Human Services for explaining what that term means.

I could not have worked out the details of the first car crash without Karen Lee-Roberts, and I'm extraordinarily grateful to Deputy Chief Constable Andrew Cooke and DCI Christopher Sephton of the Merseyside Police for taking the time to explain English police procedure to an author desperately seeking facts that reinforced fiction.

Much love to family on both sides of the pond, including the Grossberg clan; the Rose family; my mother, Anne Claypole White, who named the village and provided super important details about cream teas and bin collection in rural Bedfordshire (am I forgiven for moving bin collection day to Friday to fit my timeline?); and never forgotten, the best vicar in the world, Rev. Douglas Eric Claypole White (Daddy to me).

Writing about the Church of England with my outdated memories was a toughie. I could neither have mapped Gabriel's daily life nor found the man behind the collar without Rev. Jo Spray and Rev. Peter N. Jeffery. And my multitalented sister, Susan Rose—queen of English bone china, churchwarden, and a lay band member.

Hugs to early readers Priscille Sibley, Laura Drake, and Sheryl Cornett, all of whom convinced me I had a story worth telling, and to WFWA sistas who asked tough questions about Marianne in our Donald Maass workshop. Endless thanks to Elizabeth Brown of Swift Edits, who poked holes in my second draft with such graceful precision and continues to provide commas.

What can I say to beta reader Leslie Gildersleeve, other than, "I owe you a trip to the beach"? Once again Leslie read, critiqued, brainstormed, and bolstered. My favorite Leslie question during this process: "Is this a night for the good gin?" Then she told me to add a prologue, and because she's always right, I listened.

I'm running out of new ways to thank Zachariah Claypole White and Larry Grossberg, but I cannot do this without their emotional support and brilliance as wordsmiths. My creative writing major, Zachariah, answered every text that screamed for help, continued to allow me to steal from his life, left a list of title ideas pinned to the kitchen table, and gave outstanding feedback that included, "You can do better, Mom." I did.

My beloved husband, Larry Grossberg, is a professor of international acclaim and has far more important things to do than help me make up stuff. And yet he never says no when I ask if we can brainstorm, and he never sighs when I interrupt his work with, "Please read this—again." Plus he cooks dinner every night, deals with my technology, and guards my door when I'm on deadline. If I ever write anything worth reading, it's because he always believed I could.

Finally transatlantic kisses to the two places that inspired this story: All Saints Turvey and Turvey cemetery. You can take the girl out of the English village and dump her in the North Carolina forest, but you can't take the village out of the girl.

The following books were immensely helpful:

- *The Bedfordshire Village Book* by the Bedfordshire Federation of Women's Institutes
- *How to Read a Church: A Guide to Images, Symbols and Meanings in Churches and Cathedrals* by Richard Taylor
- *Haldol and Hyacinths: A Bipolar Life* by Melody Moezzi
- *Touched with Fire: Manic-Depressive Illness and the Artistic Temperament* by Kay Redfield Jamison

- *An Unquiet Mind: A Memoir of Moods and Madness* by Kay Redfield Jamison
- *Perfect Chaos: A Daughter's Journey to Survive Bipolar, a Mother's Struggle to Save Her* by Linea Johnson and Cinda Johnson
- *Scattershot: A Memoir* by David Lovelace
- *Girl in a Band: A Memoir* by Kim Gordon
- *The Daily Adventures of Mixerman* by Mixerman

BOOK CLUB DISCUSSION QUESTIONS

1. This is a novel about an unconventional family. What do you think makes a family?

2. Darius believes he should be able to solve Marianne's problems through love, and Marianne is determined to beat her devils alone, and they both fail. What do you think the role of family should be in helping a loved one with mental illness? Do you have any experience with this, and if so, how has your family responded? Has it found balance?

3. There is still shame and stigma attached to a diagnosis of mental illness, which spills over into treatments such as ECT and residential care. What did you make of Marianne's experiences with both? Were you surprised that she had never talked openly about her manic-depressive illness?

4. How much did you know about mania, depression, hallucinations, or psychotic episodes before reading this novel? Did you learn anything about schizoaffective disorder or the bipolar disorders?

5. Did you make assumptions about Gabriel based on the fact that he's a priest? What did you think of his responses to the personal tests he's forced to navigate?

6. Guilt plays an important role in the novel. Has this story made you rethink anything in your own life?

7. The three female characters are each damaged, and yet they've responded to the challenges facing them in different ways. Why do you think this is? Do you believe that what happens in life is not always as important as how we handle it?

8. EmJ feels that she's invisible. Might she have felt differently if she'd had the support of family and friends? Does Marianne make things better or worse for her? Had you been Marianne, what would you have done?

9. Different characters exhibit different kinds of heroism in the story. Who do you think the real hero is and why?

10. Marianne is a woman of extreme mood swings, whereas Gabriel has learned the art of emotional detachment. Lack of emotional control creates problems for both of them and drives the plot. How much in our lives is steered by emotion? How have you learned to balance and manage strong emotions? Or do you feel that you haven't?

11. On the flip side, what is the role of reason? From the beginning, Marianne is determined to find sense where there appears to be none. Do you agree with her epiphany that there is reason in everything, even if we can find it only with hindsight?

12. Marianne has worked hard to manage and control her bipolar illness, and yet still the monster returns. How does she change and grow in the story? What do you see in her future?

13. What did you think about Darius? Were you rooting for him or not? How does he change and grow in the story?

14. What do you think the future holds for Gabriel and Jade? (Invite me to your book club and I'll share my thoughts!)

A CONVERSATION WITH THE AUTHOR

What was the inspiration for this novel?

My first three novels grew out of dark *what-if* moments related to my life, but this novel came to me through a scene. One summer my family and I were visiting my childhood village in England when the opening of a story—set in the church—began playing in my mind. I saw the church ladies twittering over wedding flowers up by the altar while an elegant American woman watched from the back pew, eyes hidden by sunglasses. I felt their rising concern for the stranger and witnessed one of them dash off to fetch the vicar, who was attacking stinging nettles with a weed whacker. When he crouched down to say, "What's brought you back after all this time, Marianne?" she replied, "I've come home to die." That was all I knew.

I put the scene aside, but I was curious about this woman who talked of death although she wasn't dying. Understanding Marianne's thought process, however, was a challenge, and the only thing that made sense was her homing instinct. Like Marianne, I have a strong connection to my childhood village, and I've never reclaimed the part of my heart that lives there. I love walking into the butcher's and hearing the owner say, "Hello, Barbara, how are you?" as if I've been buying his chipolatas every week. On some level this novel is about the pull of my childhood village and the sense of community that I still miss.

I was also drawn to the idea of a character who had done everything right to manage her mental illness and still everything had gone wrong. My experience from living in the trenches with mental illness is that the challenges never end. The triggers are out there, waiting. And there are always new levels of acceptance to attain.

The last piece of the story puzzle came from my fascination with music as therapy. When my son was younger, I worked hard to find something that would bring peace to his battles with obsessive-compulsive disorder (OCD). We tried meditation, yoga, all the usual suspects, but once he got his first electric guitar, he discovered that creating music was a natural tonic for his anxiety. By the time he'd become an intern at Nightsound Studios in Carrboro, I'd already abandoned a story about a bipolar teen and her dad, a musician who ran a small local recording studio. One evening my son came home talking about his work, and the next morning I woke up with Jade front and center in my mind. Jade was the missing piece of Marianne's story.

What drew you to these characters?

Originally I was drawn to the strong female characters. Marianne and Jade are both survivors, and I have deep admiration for the way they've fought back to take control of their lives. I knew from the beginning that Gabriel and Marianne would try to help a child no one wanted, and I fleshed out EmJ through watching interviews with Kurt Cobain. He was such a gifted, yet tragic figure, and something about him has always haunted me.

I was intrigued too by the stress Marianne's crisis would place on Jade and Darius, because loving someone with mental illness is a never-ending learning curve. Both of them were running away from their pasts when they found Marianne, and suddenly they become care-givers. Jade is used to that role; Darius not so much.

Gabriel was a different kind of hero for me. When I first saw him, he was barefoot and writing a sermon to U2. He seemed to have his coping mechanisms in place, and yet I kept glimpsing dark corners. Watching him slowly unravel was pretty satisfying.

What were the particular challenges of writing this novel?

In a word: Marianne. Being inside her head was exhausting and didn't always make sense. I have legal pads filled with endless notes during which I tried to pick apart her actions like huge math problems. (I flunked math.) And early on I committed the sin of trying to write a bipolar heroine as opposed to creating a complex woman who happens to be manic-depressive. I didn't want her to be a victim, but I wanted her struggles with the illness to be authentic. And somewhere in there I allowed the disease to take over. But once I'd found her dry cynicism, I was off and running.

Gabriel was equally tough for similar reasons. As he says, people make assumptions about priests. I really didn't want to write a man of faith (even though my father was a vicar). I'm married to a Jew and far removed from my old life in the Church of England, but Gabriel was Gabriel. He knew his heart even if I didn't. Again, I had to find the person behind the label. Or in his case, the collar.

The pace of this story was also different for me. Every novel has its own rhythm, and this one evolved with short, quick-moving chapters, snappy dialogue, and fewer descriptions of the natural world than I'm used to. Part of that came from the chaos that is Marianne, but all the characters chattered at me nonstop. New scenes kept popping up, and I had to wrestle them back down. It was hard to find the balance between one story and four strong characters, all of whom wanted their say. I think that's the reason we never hear directly from Mrs. Tandy or Sasha. It got to the point where I was saying, "Enough voices, Barbara!"

Did anything surprise you while researching and writing this novel?
I never know where I'm heading with a story, and it changes with my research and each rewrite. Jade's heritage, however, was my biggest surprise. She was the one character who popped out fully formed, and yet I never realized that her mother was black. I heard her voice from the beginning, and the line about Sasha being a skinny white chick intrigued me. Then I was in the Carrboro post office and saw this beautiful African American woman with a funky sense of style. She turned around and I nearly said, "Oh, you're Jade."

The protagonists in your last two novels have been men. Why did you switch to a woman this time?
It wasn't a conscious decision. Typically I'm more drawn to male characters because I love figuring out emotionally detached men. (I'll be honest, I want to make men cry.) But that opening scene in the church wouldn't go away, and the idea of fleshing out the emotional life of a woman with a mood disorder was a challenge I couldn't resist. Marianne is emotion amplified, which makes her unlike any character I've written before. Even on her meds, she's the opposite of emotionally detached.

Do you have a favorite scene?
So many scenes were fun to write, especially when Jade opened her mouth. I love the first scene between her and Gabriel, but my favorite scene is probably their last one. I've always been drawn to the idea that people who need each other find each other, and the last chapter made me sing. (Literally, since I wrote and rewrote it with "Summertime" by My Chemical Romance playing on my iPod.)

You write about families coping with the demands of invisible disabilities, but in this story you don't have a traditional family. Why is that?

These characters are not just a social group. They are four broken people who choose to support each other. I see them as an unconventional family—yes, even Gabriel becomes part of it. The world is changing, and the definition of family isn't quite as simple as it used to be. I also wanted to flip *The Perfect Son*, which is a story driven by the notion that you can't escape genetics, to write about a family with no blood ties.

Can you tell us a little about your writing process?

It's a messy disaster until the end, because I have a few problems with that big thing called plot. I'm an organic writer who likes to meander and take her time. That's not an option when you're under contract, so I've learned to speed up. Once I get an idea I simultaneously write and research, reaching out to interview anyone who can potentially help me find my story. If my deadline allows it, my preference is always to write a crappy first draft before I do anything, and then to pull back and create a storyboard—see what works, what doesn't. Since I'm a visual person, books on screenwriting have always made more sense than books about how to outline. My storyboard, which at some point gets broken down into a chapter-by-chapter timeline highlighting point of view, setting, turning point, and emotional change, is the closest I get to an outline. (Although it's really about me keeping track of details.) And then I rewrite endlessly, which means throwing out half of the storyboard. The magic doesn't happen for me until the third draft, and often it's not until the fourth or fifth draft that I get a sense of the emotional layers. The gardener in me loves to keep digging.

ABOUT THE AUTHOR

A Brit living in North Carolina, Barbara Claypole White writes hopeful family drama with a healthy dose of mental illness. Her debut novel, *The Unfinished Garden*, won the 2013 Golden Quill Contest for Best First Book, and *The In-Between Hour* was chosen by the Southern Independent Booksellers Alliance as a Winter 2014 Okra Pick. Her third novel, *The Perfect Son*, was a semifinalist in the 2015 Goodreads Choice Awards for Best Fiction. For more information, or to connect with Barbara, visit www.barbaraclaypolewhite.com.